非裔美国文学名篇选读

（1730—1950）

主　编　陈后亮

副主编　王辰晨

编　者　段丽丽　王亚萍　宁艺阳　马　可

WUHAN UNIVERSITY PRESS

武汉大学出版社

图书在版编目(CIP)数据

非裔美国文学名篇选读:1730-1950/陈后亮主编.—武汉:武汉大学出版社,2021.12
　ISBN 978-7-307-22443-8

　Ⅰ.非… Ⅱ.陈… Ⅲ.美国黑人—文学研究—美国—1730-1950
Ⅳ.I712.06

中国版本图书馆 CIP 数据核字(2021)第 137596 号

责任编辑:李 琼　　责任校对:汪欣怡　　版式设计:马 佳

出版发行:**武汉大学出版社**　　(430072　武昌　珞珈山)
　　(电子邮箱:cbs22@whu.edu.cn　网址:www.wdp.com.cn)
印刷:湖北恒泰印务有限公司
开本:787×1092　1/16　印张:16　字数:389 千字　插页:1
版次:2021 年 12 月第 1 版　　2021 年 12 月第 1 次印刷
ISBN 978-7-307-22443-8　　定价:48.00 元

前　言

　　自 20 世纪 90 年代以来，尤其是在托尼·莫里森(Tony Morrison)于 1993 年成为第一位黑人诺贝尔文学奖得主之后，黑人文学在整个美国文学版图中的地位越来越重要。非裔作家已成为一个非常壮大的创作群体，他们的名字经常出现在包括普利策奖和国家图书奖在内的一些重要文学奖项的获奖名单之上。与之相对应，黑人文学研究也已不再是学术边缘，而是顺利进入很多美国大学人文学科，甚至日益成为显学。也正是为了满足不断增长的教学和研究需要，各种版本的非裔美国文学史和文学选集纷纷出现，其中最具代表性的包括玛丽恩玛·格雷厄姆和杰瑞·沃德(Maryemma Graham & Jerry Ward)合著的《剑桥非裔美国文学史》(*The Cambridge History of African American Literature*, Cambridge University Press, 2011)、史蒂芬·卡瑞(Stephen Currie)编著的《非裔美国文学》(*African American Literature*, Greenhaven Publishing, 2011)、弗雷德里克·米勒(Frederic Miller)等人编写的《非裔美国文学》(*African American Literature*, Alphascript Publishing, 2009)、奥玛·道森(Alma Dawson)等人合编的《非裔美国文学：阅读兴趣指南》(*African American Literature：A Guide to Reading Interests*, Libraries Unlimited, 2004)、威廉·安德鲁斯(William Andrews)等人的《牛津非裔美国文学导读》(*The Oxford Companion to African American Literature*, Oxford University Press, 1997)，以及 D. 昆汀·米勒(D. Quentin Miller)所著的《劳特里奇非裔美国文学导读》(*The Routledge Introduction to African American Literature*, Routledge, 2016)等。

　　虽然这些非裔美国文学教材都已成为经典，但由于内容过于全面且在国内不容易获取等原因，并不完全适合国内课堂教学实践。出于这些考虑，我们编写了这本《非裔美国文学名篇选读(1730—1950)》，选取非裔美国文学史上较有代表性的 15 位作家，又在每位作家最有代表性的作品中选择适当的篇幅，附上适度的作家简介、选读篇章评析以及重要文献推荐，以辅助学习和进一步研究。本教材编写的初衷是选材的体量和难易度适中，适合在一个学期内完成教学，既能帮助学生在短时间内对非裔美国文学的整体面貌有一个大致认识，又有助于引导学生深化对个别重点作家的了解和研究。因此，本教材希望既可以给首次接触非裔美国文学的初学者提供一份导览图，又能为从事非裔文学研究的专业人员提供信息丰富的精确概述。为此，我们在对重要作家和作品进行分析介绍的同时，也把重点放在介绍对象与其所处的社会条件之间的关系上。因此，本书既适合对非裔美国文学感兴趣的普通读者，也适合英语专业本科生和外国文学方向的研究生课堂教学使用。

　　需要指出，由于受作品版权问题以及编者能力所限，本书选取内容主要都是非裔美国文学中早期阶段(1730—1950)的经典散文和小说作品，并未涉及诗歌和戏剧文学，也没有把 20 世纪 50 年代之后的作品收入进来，这是本书的一个遗憾。非裔美国文学在诗歌和戏剧创作领域同样成就非凡，20 世纪 50 年代之后的当代经典作品更是数不胜数。我们希望以后如果有机会对本教材进行修订，将增加这些方面的内容。

本书是集体智慧的结晶。特别感谢我的同事王辰晨博士。她对美国非裔文学有非常好的研究基础，在得到我的提议后，欣然应允与我共同编写这本教材，并付出巨大努力。也感谢我的博士生段丽丽、王亚萍、宁艺阳和马可，他们都参与了本书的编写。本书各章节具体分工如下：陈后亮负责撰写导论、第三章、第十三章，以及全书统筹、设计和校订工作；王辰晨负责第二章、第四章、第八章、第九章、第十章；王亚萍负责第六章、第七章；宁艺阳负责第十四章、第十五章；段丽丽负责第一章、第五章；马可负责第十一章、第十二章。

本教材为华中科技大学研究生高水平课程建设"美国黑人文学"结项成果，并获得华中科技大学研究生教材建设立项资助，在此表示感谢！

由于编者水平有限，本书必有很多不足和疏漏之处，恳请读者和同行专家批评指正。

编者

目　　录

导论 …………………………………………………………………………………… 1

蓄奴制时期(17 世纪初至 19 世纪 60 年代)

第一章　布里顿·哈蒙(Briton Hammon，约 1730—约 1780) ………………… 11
　A Narrative of the Uncommon Sufferings, *and Surprizing*
　Deliverance of Briton Hammon, *A Negro Man* …………………………………… 11

第二章　戴维·沃克(David Walker，1785—1830) ………………………………… 18
　(1) Our Wretchedness in Consequence of Slavery ………………………… 19
　(2) Our Wretchedness in Consequence of Ignorance ……………………… 27

第三章　弗雷德里克·道格拉斯(Frederick Douglass，1818—1895) …………… 39
　Narrative of the Life of Frederick Douglass, *an American Slave* ……………… 40

第四章　马丁·罗宾逊·德拉尼(Martin Robison Delany，1812—1885) ………… 52
　The Condition, *Elevation*, *Emigration and Destiny of the Colored People of the*
　United States Politically Considered ……………………………………………… 53

种族重构时期(约 19 世纪 70 年代至 20 世纪 10 年代)

第五章　布克·T. 华盛顿(Booker T. Washington，1856—1915) ……………… 71
　The Atlanta Exposition Address …………………………………………………… 72

第六章　杜波依斯(W. E. B. Du Bois，1868—1963) ……………………………… 85
　The Souls of Black Folk …………………………………………………………… 87

第七章　查尔斯·切斯纳特(Charles Chesnutt，1858—1932) ………………… 96
　The Marrow of Tradition ………………………………………………………… 97

What Is a White Man? ··· 106

第八章 安娜·茉莉亚·库珀(Anna Julia Cooper, 1858—1964) ········ 114
Womanhood：A Vital Element in the Regeneration and Progress of a Race ········ 115

哈莱姆文艺复兴时期(约 20 世纪 20 年代至 20 世纪 30 年代)

第九章 詹姆斯·韦尔登·约翰逊(James Weldon Johnson, 1871—1938) ········ 135
Preface to The Book of American Negro Poetry ····················· 136

第十章 阿兰·洛克(Alain Locke, 1886—1954) ····················· 162
The New Negro ··· 163

第十一章 基恩·图默(Jean Toomer, 1894—1967) ····················· 175
Karintha ·· 176
Blood-Burning Moon ·· 178

第十二章 兰斯顿·休斯(Langston Hughes, 1901—1967) ·············· 188
The Negro Artist and the Racial Mountain ·························· 190

第十三章 佐拉·尼尔·赫斯顿(Zora Neale Hurston, 1891—1960) ········ 196
Their Eyes Were Watching God ···································· 197
How It Feels to Be Colored Me ···································· 209

第十四章 乔治·塞缪尔·斯凯勒(George Samuel Schuyler, 1895—1977) ······ 215
The Negro Art Hokum ·· 216

20 世纪中期(约 20 世纪 40 年代至 20 世纪 50 年代)

第十五章 理查德·赖特(Richard Wright, 1908—1960) ·············· 225
Native Son ·· 226
Blueprint for Negro Writing ······································ 239

主要参考文献 ··· 251

导　论

参照 D. 昆汀·米勒在《劳特里奇非裔美国文学导读》中的观点，非裔美国文学可以划分为七个阶段。① 第一个阶段是蓄奴制时期，从 1619 年第一批非洲黑奴被贩卖至北美殖民地开始到 1865 年南北战争结束。奴隶叙事无疑是这段时期最主要的黑人文学类型。用今天的眼光来看，绝大多数奴隶叙事都枯燥乏味，不但形式单一，而且在内容上充满基督教式的道德说教和政治宣传。它们假定的读者都是白人中的开明人士，目的是让他们了解奴隶制度的邪恶，唤起道德良知，帮助黑人解除奴隶制枷锁。米勒告诫人们，虽然奴隶叙事的文学性不高，但它们都是在极度贫瘠的文学土壤上产生的。考虑到黑奴的生存条件之恶劣，他们能够完成这样的作品已经是奇迹。在这一时期的非裔作家中，本书主要选择了四位代表性人物，分别是布里顿·哈蒙（Briton Hammon）、大卫·沃克（David Walker）、弗雷德里克·道格拉斯（Frederick Douglass）和马丁·德拉尼（Martin Delany）。哈蒙于 1760 年完成的自传体记述《关于黑奴布里顿·哈蒙非同一般的苦难和出乎意料的获救经历的自述》(*A Narrative of the Uncommon Sufferings，and Surprising Deliverance of Briton Hammon，A Negro Man*) 通常被视为美国最早的奴隶叙事。沃克的废奴宣传手册《呼吁四章，同序言一道献给全世界的有色公民，尤其致美利坚合众国的有色公民》(*Appeal in Four Articles；Together with a Preamble，to the Coloured Citizens of the World，but in Particular and Very Expressly，to Those of the United States of America*) 是激进废奴主义的代表性声音。德拉尼的《关于美国有色人种的生存条件、种族提升、移民和命运的政治思考》(*The Condition，Elevation，Emigration and Destiny of the Colored People of the United States Politically Considered*) 是黑人民族主义和种族分离主义的代表性文献。道格拉斯的《黑奴弗雷德里克·道格拉斯的生平自述》(*Narrative of the Life of Frederick Douglass，an American Slave*) 则标志着奴隶叙事已经发展成为最具原创性的美国本土文学类型，为后来真正的黑人虚构文学的出现铺平道路。

从 19 世纪末南北战争结束直到 20 世纪初，美国进入所谓的种族重构时期（racial

---

① 虽然非裔美国文学(African American literature) 与美国黑人文学(Black American literature) 并非完全相同的两个概念，但其外延和内涵都基本重合。非裔美国人(African American) 和美国黑人(Black American) 也是情况类似的两个概念。本书中对它们不做严格区分，而是按照上下文表述的需要灵活运用。

reconstruction），这也是非裔美国文学发展的第二阶段。在这一时期，虽然废除南方蓄奴制极大地促进了美国社会经济发展，迎来表面繁荣的"镀金时代"，但种族剥削依然十分严重。所谓的种族重构没能有效改善黑人的生存条件，摆脱奴隶身份的黑人并未获得真正意义上的自由。因此这一时期仍然不能为黑人文学的发展提供好的土壤。虽然第一位黑人职业作家查尔斯·切斯纳特（Charles Chesnutt）的出现常被视为黑人文学发展的一道分水岭，但是他在当时的影响远没有后来人们想象的那样大。这段时期最重要的黑人写作类型仍不是虚构文学，而是以布克·华盛顿（Booker T. Washington）和杜波依斯（W. E. B. Du Bois）为代表的非虚构散文写作。两者同为影响巨大的黑人精神领袖，却提出完全不同的民族发展路径。前者号召黑人向前看，从苦难的奴隶经历中汲取前进力量，用努力地付出赢得民族进步和尊严，但由于其过于幼稚的乐观主义精神而遭人批评；后者用"双重意识"精确剖析了奴隶制给黑人留下的看不见的心理创伤，同时又号召黑人积极肯定自我价值，在文化和教育方面积极进取，敢于追求高尚的奋斗目标。相比之下杜波依斯对后世黑人文学的发展产生的影响难以估量，他上承道格拉斯，下启鲍德温、艾里森、胡克斯和巴拉克等人，构成黑人民族主义的隐性脉络。安娜·库珀（Anna Julia Cooper）是美国历史上第一位重要的黑人女性知识分子，也是一名杰出的黑人自由运动活动者、女性主义者、教育家、社会活动家和作家。她的《来自南方的声音》（*A Voice from the South*）是对黑人女性处境进行分析的最早长篇著作之一。本书对这四位作家的代表性作品都作了较为细致的导读介绍。

20 世纪 20—30 年代是非裔美国文学发展的第三个阶段，通常被称为"哈莱姆文艺复兴时期"。这是黑人文学发展的第一座高峰，大量黑人文学作品被白人主导的文化体制所认可，成为"一个井喷式的艺术景观"[①]，极大地提升了黑人民族自豪感，有力回击了此前有关黑人缺乏艺术创造力的种族偏见。黑人作家获得了前所未有的创作自由，敢于尝试不同的文学题材和艺术形式，但与此同时也引发诸多争议。这些争议主要集中在三个问题上。首先，黑人作家应该为谁代言，是整个黑人民族还是作家个体，是受过良好教育的黑人民族精英还是仍然挣扎在种族主义泥潭中的底层黑人？其次，黑人文学应该写给谁看，是给那些有良知的白人，还是"为艺术而艺术"？再次，哈莱姆文艺复兴究竟是创新突破，还是对以往传统的发展延续？这些问题代表了当时黑人作家的主要分歧，也预示了此后黑人文学发展的不同取向。在这一时期的黑人作家中，本书主要选取了基恩·图默（Jean Toomer）、佐拉·尼尔·赫斯顿（Zora Neale Hurston）、詹姆斯·约翰逊（James Weldon Johnson）、阿兰·洛克（Alain Locke）、乔治·S. 斯凯勒（George S. Schuyler）和兰斯顿·休斯（Langston Hughes）等六位代表。图默是黑人作家中比较罕见的一位，他非常善于运用现代主义实验手法。他的代表作《甘蔗》（*Cane*）受到理查德·赖特（Richard Wright）和兰斯顿·休斯等许多著名非裔美国评论家和作家的大加赞誉，被视为美国黑人文学史上艺术成就最高的作品之一，图默也被视为黑人知识分子型的作家代表。赫斯顿则被公认为哈莱姆文艺复兴时期最重要的黑人女作家，也是当代美国文学史上最有争议的人物之一。她的代

[①]　D. Quentin Miller. *The Routledge Introduction to African American Literature*. New York：Routledge，2016：61.

表作《他们眼望上苍》(*Their Eyes Were Watching God*)是黑人文学中第一部充分展示黑人女子内心女性意识觉醒的作品,它不仅打破了传统美国文学禁区,而且为后来黑人文学整体振兴铺平了道路,在黑人女性形象的创造上具有里程碑式的意义,被公认是哈莱姆文艺复兴时期最伟大的作品之一。约翰逊对哈莱姆文艺复兴的影响可与杜波依斯比肩。他的代表作《一个前有色人种的自传》(*The Autobiography of an Ex-Colored Man*)被认为是从美国内战到哈莱姆文艺复兴期间对黑人影响最为深远的作品,他谱写的歌曲《歌唱每个声音》("Lift Every Voice and Sing")被誉为"黑人民族之歌"。洛克是新黑人运动的领军人物,被誉为哈莱姆文艺复兴之父。他的代表作《新黑人》被视为哈莱姆文艺复兴宣言。休斯是美国黑人文坛堪称最久负盛名的诗人。作为爵士诗的首创者之一,他将爵士乐、蓝调乐的节奏和音调融入自由诗的创作,形成了以既似吟咏又似书写般深沉别致的诗风和开阔深远的意境为特点的新艺术形式。他通过文学实验不断探索黑人民间素材与种族情感之间的契合,奠定了他在哈莱姆文艺复兴运动中的领袖地位,也成为他终其一生都在为激发种族共鸣而发声的缩影。斯凯勒是这一时期的一个另类声音,常被视为哈莱姆文艺复兴的批评者,但无论他的声音是怎样另类的存在,它彰显出的充满激情的思辨都是哈莱姆文艺复兴以及整个美国黑人文学界的重要组成部分。

20世纪40—50年代是非裔美国文学的第四个阶段,这是黑人文学发展的第二个高峰,也是真正巨星云集、佳作迭出的时代。1950年布鲁克斯(G. Brooks)为黑人赢得首个普利策奖,1952年艾里森(R. Ellison)成为首个国家图书奖黑人得主,1959年汉斯波利(G. Hansberry)的戏剧作品获得纽约剧评家年度最佳剧作奖。黑人文学在这段时期取得如此巨大成功的原因有很多,主要包括美国文学场域的变化、黑人文学传统日渐成熟、作家个人天赋和后天努力,以及全社会对黑人权利的关注等。伴随越来越高的社会知名度以及更加容易得到的出版机会和销售利润,黑人作家变得愈加自信,敢于向文学传统和读者的阅读期待发出挑战。于是各种频繁的文学论战就成为这一时期的一大景观。赖特、艾里森和鲍德温等人都曾卷入其中。他们时而抨击黑人文学传统缺乏自信,时而批评白人文化霸权,时而又相互指责彼此的文学主张。巨大的社会声望和长期的辩论对他们的文学创作造成消极影响。怀特和艾里森在写出各自的成名作之后再也没能拿出同样震撼人心的佳作。只有鲍德温一生坚持探索,在各种风格和主题之间做尝试,拒绝臣服于任何既有范式。从另一个角度看,这些论战也表明黑人作家获得了空前的发言权。一方面是个体创作自由,另一方面是仍被寄予厚望的种族责任,对这两者关系的不同理解正是导致他们互相争辩的关键所在。本书从这一阶段的作家中主要选择了最具代表性的赖特。赖特被誉为"现代美国黑人小说之父",他的代表作《土生子》一改"汤姆叔叔式"的传统黑人形象,成功塑造了别格这一具有反叛精神的新黑人形象,开创了种族抗议小说的先河,被誉为"黑人文学中的里程碑",对后来的黑人文学创作影响深远。艾里森是第一个获得美国国家图书奖的黑人作家,他在代表作《看不见的人》中展现了美国黑人文化的丰富性和多样性,并借个人的身份困境反映黑人种族的身份问题。《看不见的人》自问世以来始终畅销不衰,被公认为美国文学中的经典之作。鲍德温则堪称种族抗议小说的集大成者。他的代表作《向苍天呼吁》(*Go Tell It on the Mountain*)是一部半自传体小说,主要讲述了黑人家庭生活中的复杂情感关系,表现出宗教在黑人生活中所扮演的角色。这部小说与赖特的《土生子》和艾里森的《看不见的人》被并列为20世纪四五十年代美国黑人文学的典范之作。

发生于20世纪60年代的黑人艺术运动是黑人文学的第五个阶段。无论从文学、文化还是社会政治方面来看，这都是一个纷乱多变的年代。垮掉的一代、后现代主义、性解放、民权运动、各种街头冲突和政治暗杀等，都给这个时代带来巨大冲击。在这样一种剧烈动荡的社会氛围下，美国黑人文学也迎来一个革命性的时代，开始重新认识和界定自我，于是黑人艺术运动应运而生。在麦尔考姆·X.（Malcolm X.）的影响下，以阿米里·巴拉卡（Amiri Baraka）和拉里·尼尔（Larry Neal）为代表的黑人艺术运动倡导者认为，黑人文学不只是为了教育感化那些有良知的白人，而应成为底层人民斗争的有力武器。文学必须能够激发政治行动，作家个性表达要让位于民族集体诉求。种族压迫仍是黑人面临的主要问题，文学必须配合黑人民族主义运动，成为政治宣传和斗争的武器。它不仅要求黑人文学在内容上偏向种族政治题材，而且在形式上同样要有革命性效果，比如多采用黑人方言，使用粗俗的攻击性语言，在文字书写和印刷排版上也要大胆实验等。受黑人艺术运动的影响，这一时期的黑人文学总体而言艺术性要弱于政治性。尼尔对20世纪60年代和70年代的黑人艺术运动作出了巨大贡献，在界定和描述艺术在黑人权利运动时代的作用方面具有极大影响力。他在1968年与巴拉卡合编的《黑火：美国非裔文学全集》（*Black Fire：An Anthology of Afro-American Writing*）对整个70年代的美国黑人文学和艺术产生了决定性影响，至今仍被公认为黑人艺术运动最权威的作品选集。巴拉卡则代表着黑人文化、社会和经济革命的激进政治声音，他提出"我们想要杀人的诗"这样的口号，将文学视为行动的武器，号召黑人艺术家开创一种新的、具有文化战斗力的黑人艺术运动。

20世纪70年代至20世纪末是非裔美国文学的第六个阶段。随着民权运动结束，社会种族矛盾趋于缓和。种族政治色彩浓厚的黑人美学原则逐渐退出，黑人文学又迎来新的发展机遇，并迅速攀上前所未有的新高度。受黑人艺术运动影响，20世纪60年代的黑人文学更关注黑人在当下急需解决的种族生活困境。而从20世纪70年代开始，随着新历史主义思潮的兴起，转向历史寻找创作题材成为新潮流。如果说20世纪60年代的关键词是反叛和革命的话，那么这一时期的关键词就是反思和重建。以查尔斯·约翰逊（Charles Johnson）和托尼·莫里森（Tony Morrison）为代表的新一批作家既不回避种族主义持续至今的消极影响，又以更传统和细腻的手法去反省它，重新审视过去，把注意力从当下的贫民窟生存困境转向更广阔的历史图景。以托尼·凯德·班巴拉（Toni Cade Bambara）、格洛丽亚·内勒（Gloria Naylor）、莫里森和爱丽丝·沃克（Alice Walker）为代表的女性黑人作家的兴起是这一时期又一个显著特征。与男性作家相比，她们不太关注种族之间的直接矛盾冲突，而是更擅长描写"种族主义给人与人之间的亲密关系造成的痛苦后果，包括亲情、友情和爱情等"①。班巴拉是黑人女性主义的重要代表作家，也是一位黑人民族主义者。她在1970年编纂的论文集《黑人女性文学选集》（*The Black Woman：An Anthology*）是非裔美国文学史上第一部全部汇集女性作家作品的文选，吹响了美国黑人女性主义运动的号角，具

---

① D. Quentin Miller. *The Routledge Introduction to African American Literature*. New York：Routledge，2016：135.

有划时代的意义，为黑人美学的发展作出卓越贡献。内勒则擅长使用非裔方言写作，是非裔流散文学的代表性作家之一。内勒认为黑人女性的经历是宏大历史书写中被隐藏的那部分，也是美国历史和女性历史都遗漏掉的角落，因此写作正是发掘黑人女性历史、书写个体、边缘历史的实践。她的代表作《布鲁斯特街的女人们》（*The Women of Brewster Place*）获得 1983 年美国国家图书奖最佳处女作奖，使底层非裔女性的日常生活受到社会各界的关注。沃克则因为最先把"妇女主义"置于学界视野之中而为人熟知，她的长篇代表作《紫色》（*Purple*）是书信体小说的典范，获国家图书奖和普利策小说奖。《紫色》一经出版便引起轰动，并被改编成了电影、音乐剧等多种艺术形式，被译成多国语言，在全世界广为传播。莫里森更是美国当代最杰出的学者型非裔女作家之一。她的作品多次获得美国国家图书奖，并在 1993 年凭借《宠儿》（*Beloved*）获得诺贝尔文学奖，使美国非裔文学赢得世界级声誉。查尔斯·约翰逊是当代最杰出的非裔作家之一，他的代表作《中间航道》于 1990 年荣获国家图书奖，成为继艾里森之后第二位获此殊荣的黑人男作家。在众多美国非裔作家中，约翰逊的小说创作最突出的特点就是他深受东方文化，尤其是禅宗佛教和道家思想的影响。这些东方传统思想之所以对约翰逊有如此大的吸引力，主要由于它们传达了一种完全不同于西方的价值观和伦理观，为人类实现对现实生活的超越指出了不一样的途径，并对以白人种族主义意识形态为主导、坚持二元对立思维的西方思想构成质疑。

21 世纪以来的黑人文学通常被划分为第七个阶段。21 世纪以来，很多人乐观地认为美国社会已经进入所谓后种族时代。以奥巴马当选首任黑人美国总统并成功连任为标志，一大批杰出的黑人代表在文化、政治、体育、经济等领域涌现，跨种族婚姻也不再是禁忌，似乎种族身份已经不再是问题。但这实际上遮蔽了占更大多数的黑人底层民众仍深受种族主义遗留问题困扰的现实。近年来出现的"黑命贵"运动以及越来越猖獗的白人右翼势力表明，种族分界线依然存在，只是更加隐而不见。处在这样一个后种族主义幻觉时代，黑人文学无论在主题还是类型上都展示出空前的多样性。除了"非洲裔"这个具有本质主义意味的身份标签以外，人们已经很难在黑人作家身上找到多少共性。事实上有很多黑人作家公开表示不希望被特别关注其族裔身份，他们更愿意被视为作家而不是非裔作家。科幻小说、侦探文学、酷儿写作、奇幻故事、罗曼司……几乎所有的文学类型中都可以找到黑人作家身影。实际上，随着时代的变迁，种族在今天不是不重要了，而是它的意蕴已经大不同于从前。黑人文学也变得不再像以前那样有明显的种族政治属性。这些变化要求我们必须修正此前已有的观念预设。正如米勒所说："与之前任意一个阶段相比，黑人文学已经变了，变得难以预料，越来越不像一个统一连贯的整体，只是不知道我们对此是应该庆祝还是惋惜。"[①]虽然 21 世纪以来的美国黑人文学依然保持了繁荣的发展态势，佳作迭出，但由于大部分作品问世的时间仍不久远，究竟哪些作品能够称得上是"经典"仍需经受时间的检验，故而在本书中并未涉及这些作家。

其实，任何有关非裔美国文学史的讲述都必须首先面对一个问题，即什么是非裔美国文学？这个问题的答案看似不言自喻，实际上却值得深究。《新世界百科全书》和《不列颠

---

① D. Quentin Miller. *The Routledge Introduction to African American Literature*. New York：Routledge，2016：154.

百科全书》给出的定义几乎完全一样，即"非裔美国文学就是美国非裔作家创作的文学"①。但另一个问题接踵而至，那就是：谁是非裔美国人或者美国黑人？是否我们还要沿用奴隶制时期流行的"一滴血原则"？在有关种族、性别等身份建构性的秘密早已被后结构和后殖民主义破解后的今天，如果我们还用这种带有本质主义色彩的身份标准来界定黑人文学，是否合适？由白人作家创作的小说，比如斯托夫人的《汤姆叔叔的小屋》，尽管它在内容上完全与黑人相关，却被排除在黑人文学研究对象之外。但反过来，由黑人作家创作的"纯白"作品又该如何归类？比如鲍德温的《乔凡尼的房间》(*Giovanni's Room*)，书中不但没有种族政治的内容，甚至连一个黑人身影也难看到。在拉尔夫·艾里森创作《看不见的人》时的 20 世纪 50 年代，他还清楚意识到"我是绝对不能写科幻小说的"②，但自进入 21 世纪以来，黑人作家创作的包括科幻小说在内的各种通俗类型小说已经蔚为壮观。难道仅仅因为它们的作者有黑人血统，就要把它们归入黑人文学之列吗？事实上在伯克维奇(Sacvan Bercovitch)主编的八卷本《剑桥美国文学史》中，从第七卷开始，对 20 世纪 50 年代以后的黑人文学已不再专门开辟章节论述，而是把它融入美国文学整体中讨论。这就像最终汇入大海的河流，它的边界已经很难看清了。

正如米勒所发现的，在反种族主义斗争异常尖锐的时刻，黑人文学总是被要求参与种族政治。也总有一些文学或文化领袖站出来，以不容置疑的语气做出有关黑人文学应当如何而为的纲领性要求。再加上黑人作家在文学市场上的生存能力有限，很多人不得不放弃个性艺术追求，服从于黑人民族主义的指令，或者屈服于白人"金主"对他们的文化期待，甘愿做白人文学的"养子"。否则便极有可能被压制，沉寂在历史角落。其中只有极少数人能像赫斯顿那样幸运地被艾丽斯·沃克重新发掘。但随着种族矛盾趋于缓和，尤其是黑人作家的市场生存能力得到显著提升，他们的生存空间和创作自由均得到极大改善。他们不必再屈服于任何传统或权威的声音也照样能够获得成功。正是由于这些原因，当代著名黑人作家怀特海(Colson Whitehead)才会在 2013 年的一次访谈中做出如下这段颇有争议的表示：

> 　　当我二十年前开始写作的时候，我并不把自己界定为非裔美国作家。我只是在写作，并专注于写作内容。那种术语一般来说不过是外在的，为批评界所用。……它对我的写作没什么用处，我坐在桌前写的不是一部有关非裔美国僵尸的故事，也不是有关电梯的非裔美国故事。我写的不过是一部与电梯有关的故事，它碰巧以不同的方式涉及种族而已。或者我写一部僵尸小说，它与美国黑人生活没多少关系。它只是与生存有关。③

---

　　①　参见 http://www. newworldencyclopedia. org/entry/African_American_literature；https://www.britannica./art/African-American-literature.

　　②　拉尔夫·艾里森：《看不见的人·自序》，任绍曾等译，上海：上海文艺出版社 2014 年版，第 7 页。

　　③　Whitehead, Colson. "Each Book An Antidote." ［April 24, 2013］. https://www.guernicamag.com/colson-whitehead-each-book-an-antidote/.

虽然为了研究的方便或者出于对事物进行归类的认知习惯，我们仍在使用美国黑人文学这一术语，但是我们必须认识到它的内涵和外延都在发生变化。另外我们也要看到，一个人的身份建构总是多元杂糅的。一位作家可以既是非裔作家又是女性作家、后现代作家或酷儿小说家。我们不能只看到他的族裔身份而遮蔽了其余属性。

"黑人文学传统既不稳定也不完整"①，这是米勒在他的《劳特里奇非裔美国文学导读》导论部分所强调的一点。越往前看，黑人文学无论在类型还是题材上都呈现出越鲜明的统一性；越往后看，则越是种类驳杂，越难找到共性。在对历经近 300 年的美国黑人文学进行梳理介绍后，米勒发现几乎不可能清楚、准确地回答"什么是非裔美国文学"的问题。他说："虽然我们承认存在一个传统，并试图去界定它，我们还是必须意识到，它的形态总是在成长和变化。换句话说，我们所讲述的关于非裔美国文学的故事会随时间而变化，现在和将来都是如此。"②这也是我们在学习和研究非裔美国文学时必须注意的一点。

---

① D. Quentin Miller. *The Routledge Introduction to African American Literature*. New York：Routledge，2016：2.

② D. Quentin Miller. *The Routledge Introduction to African American Literature*. New York：Routledge，2016：8.

蓄奴制时期

（17世纪初至19世纪60年代）

第一章　布里顿·哈蒙
（Briton Hammon，约 1730—约 1780）

布里顿·哈蒙是 18 世纪中期生活在英属北美殖民地的一名黑奴，具体生卒年月不详。根据他在自述中记载，大约在 1747 年，由于主人家中变故，他从马萨诸塞州的一个庄园离开，登上一艘驶往牙买加的帆船工作。大约在 1748 年，由于船只失事，他和船员被驱逐出佛罗里达海岸，开始了一系列的艰难历程。他先是被印第安人俘虏，在古巴的西班牙监狱里被关押了 4 年，后被一名英国中尉营救，加入英国海军服役数年，之后在与法国军舰的冲突中受伤。最后哈蒙从皇家海军光荣退伍，并在伦敦与他的老主人团聚后，跟随主人返回新英格兰。这些经历都被他写在大约于 1760 年完成的自传体记述《关于黑奴布里顿·哈蒙非同一般的苦难和出乎意料的获救经历的自述》（*A Narrative of the Uncommon Sufferings*，*and Surprising Deliverance of Briton Hammon*，*A Negro Man*）中。

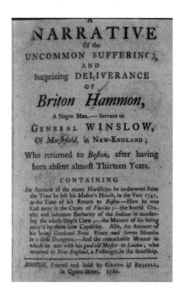

哈蒙的这部自述通常被视为美国最早的奴隶叙述，要比菲利丝·惠特莉（Phillis Wheatley）的《诗歌杂咏》（*Poems on Various Subjects*）在伦敦出版早约 13 年。不过和早期几乎所有其他奴隶叙述一样，它在不少地方也明显带有被他人加工修改过的痕迹。这主要是因为早期的奴隶大多文化水平有限，难以完全独立完成写作。即便有这些外来的编辑干预，学者们还是普遍承认它是哈蒙的作品，视其为第一部由非裔美国人完成的散文写作。

📖 作品选读：

A Narrative of the Uncommon Sufferings，*and Surprizing Deliverance of Briton Hammon*，*A Negro Man*

A NARRATIVE of the UNCOMMON SUFFERINGS AND Surprising DELIVERANCE OF

BRITON HAMMON, A Negro Man — Servant to GENERAL WINSLOW, of Marshfield, in NEW-ENGLAND; Who returned to Boston, after having been absent almost Thirteen Years. CONTAINING An Account of the many Hardships he underwent from the Time he left his Master's House, in the Year 1747, to the Time of his Return to Boston. How he was Castaway in the Capes of Florida — the horrid Cruelty and inhuman Barbarity of the Indians in murdering the whole Ship's Crew — the Manner of his being carry'd by them into Captivity. Also, An Account of his being Confined Four Years and Seven Months in a close Dungeon — And the remarkable Manner in which he met with his good old Master in London; who returned to New England, a Passenger, in the same Ship. BOSTON, Printed and Sold by [John] GREEN & [Joseph] RUSSELL, in Queen-Street, 1760.

TO THE READER,

AS my Capacities and Condition of Life are very low, it cannot be expected that I should make those Remarks on the Sufferings I have met with, or the kind Providence of a good GOD for my Preservation, as one in a higher Station; but shall leave that to the Reader as he goes along, and so I shall only relate Matters of Fact as they occur to my Mind — On Monday, 25th Day of December, 1747, with the leave of my Master, I went from Marshfield, with an Intention to go a Voyage to Sea, and the next Day, the 26th, got to Plymouth, where I immediately ship'd myself on board of a Sloop, Capt. John Howland, Master, bound to Jamaica and the Bay — We sailed from Plymouth in a short Time, and after a pleasant Passage of about 30 Days, arrived at Jamaica; we were detain'd at Jamaica only 5 Days, from whence we sailed for the Bay, where we arrived safe in 10 Days. We loaded our Vessel with Logwood, and sailed from the Bay the 25th Day of May following, and the 15th Day of June, we were cast away on Cape Florida, about 5 Leagues from the Shore; being now destitute of every Help, we knew not what to do or what Course to take in this our sad Condition — The Captain was advised, intreated, and beg'd on, by every Person on board, to heave over but only 20 Ton of the Wood, and we should get clear, which if he had done, might have sav'd his Vessel and Cargo, and not only so, but his own Life, as well as the Lives of the Mate and Nine Hands, as I shall presently relate.

After being upon this Reef two Days, the Captain order'd the Boat to be hoisted out, and then ask'd who were willing to tarry on board? The whole Crew was for going on Shore at this Time, but as the Boat would not carry 12 persons at once, and to prevent any Uneasiness, the Captain, a Passenger, and one Hand tarry'd on board, while the Mate, with Seven Hands besides myself, were order'd to go on Shore in the Boat, which as soon as we had reached, one half were to be Landed, and the other four to return to the Sloop, to fetch the Captain and the others on Shore. The Captain order'd us to take with us our Arms, Ammunition, Provisions and Necessaries for Cooking, as also a Sail to make a Tent of, to shelter us from the Weather; after having left the Sloop we stood towards the Shore, and being within Two Leagues of the same, we espy'd a Number of Canoes, which we at first took to be Rocks, but soon found our Mistake, for we perceiv'd they moved towards us; we presently saw an English Colour① hoisted in one of the Canoes, at the Sight of which we were not a little rejoiced, but on our advancing yet nearer, we found them, to our very great Surprise, to be Indians of which there were Sixty; being now so near them we could not possibly make our Escape; they soon came up with and boarded us, took away all our Arms, Ammunition, and Provision. The whole Number of Canoes (being about Twenty) then made for the Sloop, except Two which they left to guard us, who order'd us to follow on with them; the Eighteen which made for the Sloop, went so much faster than we that they got on board above Three Hours before we came along side, and had kill'd Captain Howland, the Passenger and the other hand; we came to the Larboard side of the Sloop, and they order'd us round to the Starboard, and as we were passing round the Bow, we saw the whole Number of Indians, advancing forward and loading their Guns, upon which the Mate said, "my Lads we are all dead Men" and before we had got round, they discharged their Small Arms upon us, and kill'd Three of our hands, viz. Reuben Young of Cape-Cod, Mate; Joseph Little and Lemuel Doty of Plymouth, upon which I immediately jump'd overboard, choosing rather to be drowned, than to be kill'd by those barbarous and inhuman Savages. In three or four Minutes after, I heard another Volley② which dispatched the other five, viz. John Nowland, and Nathaniel Rich, both belonging to Plymouth, and Elkanah Collymore, and James Webb, Strangers, and Moses Newmock, Molatto. As soon as they had kill'd the whole of the People, one of the Canoes paddled after me, and soon came up with me, hauled me into the Canoe, and beat me most terribly with a Cutlass, after that they tied me down, then this Canoe stood for the Sloop again and as soon as she came along side, the Indians on board the Sloop betook themselves to their Canoes, then set the Vessel on Fire, making a prodigious shouting and hallowing like so many Devils. As soon as the Vessel was burnt down to the Water's edge, the Indians stood for the Shore, together with our Boat, on board of which they put 5 hands. After we came to the Shore, they led me to their Huts, where I expected nothing but immediate Death, and as they spoke broken English, were often telling me, while coming from the Sloop to the Shore, that they intended to roast me alive.

But the Providence of God order'd it other ways, for He appeared for my Help, in this Mount of Difficulty, and they were better to me than my Fears, and soon unbound me, but set a Guard over me every Night. They kept me with them about five Weeks, during which Time they us'd me pretty well, and gave me boil'd Corn, which was what they often eat themselves. The Way I made my Escape from these Villains was this; A Spanish Schooner arriving there from St. Augustine, the Master of which, whose Name was Romond, asked the Indians to let me go on board his Vessel, which they granted, and the Captain, knowing me very well, weigh'd Anchor and carry'd me off to the Havanna, and after being there four Days the Indians came after me, and insisted on having me again, as I was their Prisoner — They made Application to the Governor, and

---

① English Colour：指悬挂在船上表示效忠于英国的旗帜。

② Volley：指连发枪声。

demanded me again from him; in answer to which the Governor told them, that as they had put the whole Crew to Death, they should not have me again, and so paid them Ten Dollars for me, adding, that he would not have them kill any Person hereafter, but take as many of them as they could, of those that should be cast away, and bring them to him for which he would pay them Ten Dollars a-head.

At the Havanna I lived with the Governor in the Castle about a Twelve-month, where I was walking thro' the Street, I met with a Press-Gang who immediately prest me, and put me into Gaol, and with a Number of others I was confin'd till next Morning, when we were all brought out, and ask'd who would go on board the King's Ships, four of which having been lately built, were bound to Old Spain, and on my refusing to serve on board, they put me in a close Dungeon, where I was confin'd Four Years and seven months; during which time I often made application to the Governor, by Persons who came to see the Prisoners, but they never acquainted him with it, nor did he know all this Time what became of me, which was the means of my being confin'd there so long. But kind Providence so order'd it, that after I had been in this Place so long as the Time mention'd above the Captain of a Merchantman, belonging to Boston, having sprung a Leak was obliged to put into the Havanna to rest, and while he was at Dinner at Mrs. Betty Howard's, she told the Captain of my deplorable Condition, and said she would be glad, if he could by some means or other relieve me; The Captain told Mrs. Howard he would use his best Endeavours for my Relief and Enlargement.

Accordingly, after Dinner, the Captain came to the Prison, and ask'd the Keeper if he might see me; upon his Request I was brought out of the Dungeon, and after the Captain had Interrogated me, told me, he would intercede with the Governor for my Relief out of that miserable Place, which he did, and the next Day the Governor sent an order to release me; I lived with the Governor about a Year after I was delivered from the Dungeon, in which Time I endeavour'd three Times to make my Escape, the last of which proved effectual; the first Time I got on board of Captain Marsh, an English Twenty Gun Ship, with a Number of others, and lay on board conceal'd that Night; and the next Day the Ship being under sail, I thought myself safe, and so made my Appearance upon Deck, but as soon as we were discovered the Captain ordered the Boat out, and sent us all on Shore — I intreated the Captain to let me, in particular, tarry on board, begging, and crying to him, to commiserate my unhappy Condition, and added, that I had been confin'd almost five Years in a close Dungeon, but the Captain would not hearken to any Intreaties, for fear of having the Governor's Displeasure, and so I was obliged to go on Shore.

After being on Shore another Twelvemonth, I endeavour'd to make my Escape the second Time, by trying to get on board of a Sloop bound to Jamaica, and as I was going from the City to the Sloop, was unhappily taken by the Guard, and ordered back to the Castle, and there confined. However, in a short Time I was set at Liberty, and order'd with a Number of others to carry the Bishop from the Castle, thro' the Country, to confirm the old People, baptize Children, & c. for which he receives large Sums of Money. I was employ'd in this Service about Seven

Months, during which Time I lived very well, and then returned to the Castle again, where I had my Liberty to walk about the City, and do Work for myself — The Beaver, an English Man of War then lay in the Harbour, and having been informed by some of the Ship's Crew that she was to sail in a few Days, I had nothing now to do, but to seek an Opportunity how I should make my Escape.

Accordingly, one Sunday Night the Lieutenant of the Ship with a Number of the Barge Crew were in a Tavern, and Mrs. Howard who had before been a Friend to me, interceded with the Lieutenant to carry me on board: the Lieutenant said he would with all his Heart, and immediately I went on board in the Barge. The next Day the Spaniards came alongside the Beaver, and demanded me again, with a Number of others who had made their Escape from them, and got on board the Ship, but just before I did; but the Captain, who was a true Englishman, refus'd them, and said he could not answer it, to deliver up any Englishman under English Colours. In a few Days we set Sail for Jamaica, where we arrived safe, after a short and pleasant Passage.

After being at Jamaica a short Time we sail'd for London, as convoy to a Fleet of Merchantmen, who all arrived safe in the Downs, I was turned over to another Ship, the Arcenceil, and there remained about a Month. From this Ship I went on board the Sandwich of 90 Guns; on board the Sandwich, I tarry'd 6 Weeks, and then was order'd on board the Hercules, Capt. John Porter, a 74 Gun Ship, we sail'd on a Cruize, and met with a French 84 Gun Ship, and had a very smart Engagement[1], in which about 70 of our Hands were Kill'd and Wounded, the Captain lost his Leg in the Engagement, and I was Wounded in the Head by a small Shot. We should have taken this Ship, if they had not cut away the most of our Rigging; however, in about three Hours after, a 64 Gun Ship, came up with and took her — I was discharged from the Hercules the 12th Day of May 1759 (having been on board of that Ship 3 Months) on account of my being disabled in the Arm, and render'd incapable of Service, after being honourably paid the Wages due to me. I was put into the Greenwich Hospital where I stay'd and soon recovered.

I then ship'd myself a Cook on board Captain Martyn, an arm'd Ship in the King's Service. I was on board this Ship almost Two Months, and after being paid my Wages, was discharg'd in the Month of October. After my discharge from Captain Martyn, I was taken sick in London of a Fever, and was confin'd about 6 Weeks, where I expended all my Money, and left in very poor Circumstances; and unhappy for me I knew nothing of my good Master's being in London at this my very difficult Time. After I got well of my sickness, I ship'd myself on board of a large Ship bound to Guinea, and being in a public House[2] one Evening, I overheard a Number of Persons talking about Rigging a Vessel bound to New England, I ask'd them to what Part of New England this Vessel was bound? They told me, to Boston; and having ask'd them who was Commander? they told me, Capt. Watt; in a few Minutes after this the Mate of the Ship came in, and I ask'd him if Captain Watt did not want a Cook, who told me he did, and that the Captain would be in,

---

① 此处"engagement"指战斗。

② 指酒吧。

in a few Minutes; and in about half an Hour the Captain came in, and then I ship'd myself at once, after begging off from the Ship bound to Guinea; I work'd on board Captain Watt's Ship almost Three Months, before she sail'd, and one Day being at Work in the Hold, I overheard some Persons on board mention the Name of Winslow, at the Name of which I was very inquisitive, and having ask'd what Winslow they were talking about? They told me it was General Winslow; and that he was one of the Passengers, I ask'd them what General Winslow? For I never knew my good Master, by that Title before; but after enquiring more particularly I found it must be Master, and in a few Days' Time the Truth was joyfully verify'd by a happy Sight of his Person, which so overcome me, that I could not speak to him for some Time — My good Master was exceeding glad to see me, telling me that I was like one arose from the Dead; for he thought I had been Dead a great many Years, having heard nothing of me for almost Thirteen Years.

I think I have not deviated from Truth, in any particular of this my Narrative, and tho' I have omitted a great many Things, yet what is wrote may suffice to convince the Reader, that I have been most grievously afflicted, and yet thro' the **Divine Goodness**, as miraculously preserved, and delivered out of many Dangers; of which I desire to retain **a grateful Remembrance**, as long as I live in the World.

And now, that in the Providence of that GOD, who delivered his Servant David out of the Paw of the Lion and out of the Paw of the Bear, 38 I am freed from a long and dreadful Captivity, among worse Savages than they; And am return'd to my own Native Land, to Shew how Great Things the Lord hath done for Me; I would call upon all Men, and Say, O Magnify the Lord with Me, and let us Exalt his Name together! — O that Men would Praise the Lord for His Goodness, and for his Wonderful Works to the Children of Men!

📝 选文评析：

虽然哈蒙的这篇奴隶自述篇幅并不长，在写作上也有很多缺陷，谈不上有多少艺术成就，但作为历史上保存下来的最早的一部奴隶叙述，在美国非裔文学史上还是有其不可替代的重要地位。在这篇作品中，最值得关注的一点就是叙述人对自我身份以及与主人关系的认识，其实也就是对蓄奴制度的认识。自始至终，哈蒙从未明确定义他与主人温斯洛(Winslow)之间的关系，或者说他并不了解这种关系的本质，他甚至连主人是干什么的都不太清楚。哈蒙一直称温斯洛为"我的好主人"，但他对自己的称呼却始终是"仆人"而非"奴隶"。如果不是小说标题将哈蒙确定为"a negro man"，那么读者很难认出他是一名奴隶，甚至连他是不是黑人都不好确定。

事实上，与其说哈蒙开创了奴隶叙述传统，不如说他是在效仿那些曾被印第安部落囚禁的白人俘虏叙述的惯例，比如他在叙述中和白人殖民者一样，也称呼那些印第安土著是"坏蛋"(villain)，描述了他们在屠杀船员俘虏时表现得"非常残忍、野蛮和不人道"，"像一群魔鬼般嗷嗷直叫"，"他们狠狠地打我"，甚至打算"把我活活烤了吃"，以至于"我""宁肯跳海淹死也不愿意被这些毫无人性的凶残野蛮人杀掉"。反观白人殖民者在他心目中的形象，则大多是仁慈、友善的，至少比那些印第安人更人道一些。特别是当他被英国人解救出来后，印第安人追来索要人，想再把他抓回去，英国人在他眼中表现得都是"真正的英国汉子"，严词拒绝印第安人的要求。总之，在他眼中，白人通常都是保护者的形象，他们做事相对仁慈和公正，能够让他感到有安全感甚至尊严。他并没有认识到自己终究不过是白人的一份财产，是他们和印第安人之间交易的一件价值 10 美元的商品而已。事实上，搭救他的白人殖民总督甚至鼓励印第安人从事黑奴交易，"尽可能多抓一些……送到他那里去，他将按照 10 美元一个人的价格付钱"。后来他在白人船上当厨师、到英国海军服役，都没有感到是被剥削，反倒有通过雇佣劳动获得报酬的自豪感。"我被雇佣了大约 7 个月，在此期间我过得非常好。后来我回到了城堡，在那里我可以在城中自由走动并工作。""我得到了薪酬。"在战争中受伤后，他被宣布从英国海军退役，同时"拿到了自己应得的那份值得荣耀的报酬"。总之，只要能够让他获得生命安全保障和最基本的行动自由，他就心甘情愿地与白人主人们合作，做他们的仆人和侍从。

另外值得注意的一点是，和 18 世纪之前的大部分写作一样，哈蒙也需要为自己的叙述理由做出合法性解释。不过与后来的奴隶叙述大多是为了控诉蓄奴制度的惨无人道，进而唤起部分有良知的白人帮助黑奴获得解放的目的不同，哈蒙在这里主要是强调自己真实叙说了自己的经历，同时又要把一切归功于上帝的保佑，进而劝导世人信奉上帝。他在叙述中多次强调，每次遇险之所以能够化险为夷，是因为"上帝的旨意另有安排，每到危难关头，祂总会前来搭救"。他在文末尤为强调："我想我并没有偏离真理，尤其是我的叙述，虽然我遗漏了许多东西，但我所写的足以使读者相信我曾遭受过最严重的痛苦，但我仍通过神的仁慈，奇迹般地活了下来，并脱离了许多危险；只要我活在这个世界上，我就想保留一份感恩的回忆。……我从长期可怕的掳掠中……获得了自由；我要回到我的故地，向世人展示耶和华在我身上做出的神迹；我要呼求众人说，愿你与我一同尊崇耶和华，使我们一同尊崇他的名！愿人称颂耶和华的慈爱，和他向世人所行的奇事！"这些表明了哈蒙的作品作为第一部奴隶叙述的特殊性。

推荐阅读文献：

Carretta, Vincent and Gould, Philip. *Genius in Bondage*：*Literature of the Early Black Atlantic*. UP of Kentucky, 2001.

Foster, Frances and Haywood, Chanta. Christian Recordings：Afro-Protestantism, Its Press, and the Production of African-American Literature. *Religion & Literature*, 1995, 27(1)：15-33.

Green, Keith M. *Bound to Respect*：*Antebellum Narratives of Black Imprisonment*, *Servitude*, *and Bondage*, 1816-1861. U Alabama P, 2015.

Morgan, Philip D. Origins of American Slavery. *OAH Magazine of History*, 2005, 19(4)：51-56.

Nelson, Emmanuel S. *African American Authors* 1745-1945：*A Bio-Bibliographical Critical Sourcebook*. Greenwood Publishing Group, 2000.

Sekora, John. Black Message/White Envelope：Genre, Authenticity, and Authority in the Antebellum Slave Narrative. *Callaloo*, 1987(32)：482-515.

第二章　戴维·沃克
（David Walker，1785—1830）

戴维·沃克是著名的激进派废奴主义者，对美国的废奴运动产生过重要影响。沃克于 1785 年出生在北卡罗来纳州，父亲是奴隶，母亲是自由民。按照子女身份随母的法律规定，沃克得以自由成长并接受教育。他敏锐地意识到奴隶制度的残酷，在青年时期参与了废奴主义者但马可·维赛（Denmark Vesey）于 1817 年组织的以南方黑人奴隶为主要参与者、具有宗教性质的暴力反抗运动，这次反抗以遭到叛徒泄密告终，维赛等领导人被捕并被处以绞刑。运动失败后，沃克周游全国，于 1825 年在马萨诸塞州波士顿定居。沃克积极宣传废奴主张，多次在公开场合发表废奴演说，成为当地黑人抗议团体的领袖，是全美第一家黑人报纸《自由杂志》（Freedom's Journal）的代理人，还是波士顿非洲卫理公会锡安圣公会成员以及马萨诸塞有色人种协进会的创立者之一。与维赛领导的奴隶革命组织不同，马萨诸塞有色人种协进会是北方自由黑人领导的种族平等改革组织，但相似的是后者的主导思想也是激进的。基于参加废奴运动的丰富经验，沃克在 1829 年出版了废奴宣传手册《呼吁四章，同序言一道献给全世界的有色公民，尤其致美利坚合众国的有色公民》（Appeal in Four Articles；Together with a Preamble, to the Coloured Citizens of the World, but in Particular and Very Expressly, to Those of the United States of America）（下文简称《呼吁》），系统阐述了他的废奴主义思想。

沃克在波士顿以贩卖二手衣物为业，他借向水手收购和售卖布料之机悄悄将《呼吁》混入货物中带到各港口，在整个美国传播开来。《呼吁》在美国社会获得强烈反响，其激进的革命主张引起南方奴隶主的恐惧和仇恨，一些州颁布法令禁止传播废奴宣传资料，并规定任何人不得教授奴隶阅读和写作，佐治亚州甚至出现了缉杀沃克的悬赏令。沃克死于《呼吁》出版后的第二年，死因莫测，可能因肺结核病逝，但有人认为他死于暗杀。

《呼吁》是废奴运动中最激进的文献之一，沃克在文中引用《圣经》和《独立宣言》的内容，揭露了开国元勋杰斐逊总统粉饰奴隶制度的花言巧语，并预见了内战前夕的南北对峙和黑人民族主义的高涨。同很多知识分子阶层的废奴主义者不同，沃克认为奴隶制是一种灾难，需要立即废除，他不支持逐步废除奴隶制的温和改革主张，并认为每一个美国非裔有权成为享有同白人一样权利的美国公民，反对把黑人送回非洲。他的激进思想对废奴运动产生了深刻影响，几乎改变了当时废奴运动的基调和目标，在他死后的第二年，纳特·特纳(Nat Turner)领导黑奴起义，暴力反抗奴隶制度。当然，沃克的暴力主张也受到了当时一些废奴主义者的谴责，但沃克坚持自己的立场，他声称自己对暴力的支持是黑奴重获人权的必要手段而非报复策略，他乐观地设想"随着美国奴隶制的结束，黑人和白人将一起生活在和平和幸福中"。下文选自《呼吁》中的前两篇文章，他呼吁黑人识破白人的欺骗言论，暴力反抗白人奴隶主的奴役，正确认识自己的才能，为自己的自由而战，并指出文化知识的重要性，强调黑人应当利用一切机会让年轻人读书明理学习基督教义，而不是无知愚昧任由白人差遣。

📖 作品选读：

(1) Our Wretchedness in Consequence of Slavery

My beloved brethren: The Indians of North and of South America — the Greeks — the Irish, subjected under the king of Great Britain — the Jews, that ancient people of the Lord — the inhabitants of the islands of the sea — in fine, all the inhabitants of the earth (except, however, the sons of Africa) are called men, and of course are, and ought to be free. But we, (coloured people) and our children are brutes!! and of course are, and ought to be Slaves to the American people and their children forever!! to dig their mines and work their farms; and thus go on enriching them, from one generation to another with our blood and our tears!!!!

I promised in a preceding page to demonstrate to the satisfaction of the most incredulous, that we (coloured people of these United States of America) are the most wretched, degraded and abject set of beings that ever lived since the world began, and that the white Americans having reduced us to the wretched state of slavery, treat us in that condition more cruel (they being an enlightened and Christian people) than any heathen nation did any people whom it had reduced to our condition. These affirmations are so well confirmed in the minds of all unprejudiced men, who have taken the trouble to read histories, that they need no elucidation from me. But to put them beyond all doubt, I refer you in the first place to the children of Jacob, or of Israel in Egypt, under Pharaoh and his people. Some of my brethren do not know who Pharaoh and the Egyptians were — I know it to be a fact, that some of them take the Egyptians to have been a gang of devils, not knowing any better, and that they (Egyptians) having got possession of the Lord's people, treated them nearly as cruel as Christian Americans do us, at the present day. For the information of such, I would only mention that the Egyptians, were Africans or coloured people, such as we are — some of them yellow and others dark — a mixture of Ethiopians and the natives of Egypt — about the same as you see the coloured people of the United States at the present day — I say, I call your attention then, to the children of Jacob, while I point out particularly to you his son Joseph, among the rest, in Egypt.

"And Pharaoh, said unto Joseph... thou shalt be over my house, and according unto thy word shall all my people be ruled: only in the throne will I be greater than thou.

"And Pharaoh said unto Joseph, see, I have set thee over all the land of Egypt."

"And Pharaoh said unto Joseph, I am Pharaoh, and without thee shall no man lift up his hand or foot in all the land of Egypt."

Now I appeal to heaven and to earth, and particularly to the American people themselves, who cease not to declare that our condition is not hard, and that we are comparatively satisfied to rest in wretchedness and misery, under them and their children. Not, indeed, to show me a coloured President, a Governor, a Legislator, a Senator, a Mayor, or an Attorney at the Bar. But to show me a man of colour, who holds the low office of Constable, or one who sits in a Juror Box, even on a case of one of his wretched brethren, throughout this great Republic!! — But let us pass Joseph the son of Israel a little farther in review, as he existed with that heathen nation.

"And Pharaoh called Joseph's name Zaphnathpaaneah; and he gave him to wife Asenath the daughter of Potipherah priest of On. And Joseph went out over all the land of Egypt."

Compare the above, with the American institutions. Do they not institute laws to prohibit us from marrying the whites? I would wish, candidly, however, before the Lord, to be understood, that I would not give a pinch of snuff to be married to any white person I ever saw in all the days of my life. And I do say it, that the black man, or man of colour, who will leave his own colour (provided he can get one, who is good for anything) and marry a white woman, to be a double slave to her, just because she is white, ought to be treated by her as he surely will be, viz: as a nigger!!!! It is not, indeed, what I care about inter-marriages with the whites, which induced me to pass this subject in review; for the Lord knows, that there is a day coming when they will be glad enough to get into the company of the blacks, notwithstanding, we are, in this generation, levelled by them, almost on a level with the brute creation: and some of us they treat even worse than they do the brutes that perish. I only made this extract to show how much lower we are held, and how much more cruel we are treated by the Americans, than were the children of Jacob, by the Egyptians — We will notice the sufferings of Israel some further, under heathen Pharaoh, compared with ours under the enlightened Christians of America.

"And Pharaoh spoke unto Joseph, saying, thy father and thy brethren are come unto thee:

The land of Egypt is before thee: in the best of the land make thy father and brethren to dwell; in the land of Goshen let them dwell: and if thou knowest any men of activity among them, then make them rulers over my cattle.

I ask those people who treat us so well, Oh! I ask them, where is the most barren spot of land which they have given unto us? Israel had the most fertile land in all Egypt. Need I mention the very notorious fact, that I have known a poor man of colour, who laboured night and day, to acquire a little money, and having acquired it, he vested it in a small piece of land, and got him a house erected thereon, and having paid for the whole, he moved his family into it, where he was suffered to remain but nine months, when he was cheated out of his property by a white man, and driven out of door! And is not this the case generally? Can a man of colour buy a piece of land and keep it peaceably? Will not some white man try to get it from him, even if it is in a mud hole? I need not comment any further on a subject, which all, both black and white, will readily admit. But I must, really, observe that in this very city, when a man of colour dies, if he owned any real estate it most generally falls into the hands of some white person. The wife and children of the deceased may weep and lament if they please, but the estate will be kept snug enough by its white possessor.

But to prove farther that the condition of the Israelites was better under the Egyptians than ours is under the whites. I call upon the professing Christians, I call upon the philanthropist, I call upon the very tyrant himself, to show me a page of history, either sacred or profane, on which a verse can be found, which maintains that the Egyptians heaped the insupportable insult upon the children of Israel, by telling them that they were not of the human family. Can the whites deny this charge? Have they not, after having reduced us to the deplorable condition of slaves under their feet, held us up as descending originally from the tribes of Monkeys or Orang-Outangs? O! my God! I appeal to every man of feeling — is not this insupportable? Is it not heaping the most gross insult upon our miseries, because they have got us under their feet and we cannot help ourselves? Oh! pity us we pray thee, Lord Jesus, Master. Has Mr. Jefferson declared to the world, that we are inferior to the whites both in the endowments of our bodies and our minds?[①] It is indeed surprising, that a man of such great learning, combined with such excellent natural parts, should speak so of a set of men in chains. I do not know what to compare it to, unless, like putting one wild deer in an iron cage, where it will be secured, and hold another by the side of the same, then let it go, and expect the one in the cage to run as fast as the one at liberty. So far, my brethren, were the Egyptians from heaping these insults upon their slaves, that Pharaoh's daughter took Moses, a son of Israel for her own, as will appear by the following.

"And Pharaoh's daughter said unto her [Moses' mother], take this child away, and nurse it for me, and I will pay thee thy wages. And the woman took the child [Moses] and nursed it.

"And the child grew, and she brought him unto Pharaoh's daughter and he became her son. And she called his name Moses: and she said because I drew him out of the water." In all probability, Moses would have become Prince Regent to the throne, and no doubt, in process of time but he would have been seated on the throne of Egypt. But he had rather suffer shame, with

①　"Has Mr. Jefferson... our bodies and our minds?"：沃克在此处回应托马斯·杰斐逊总统的《弗吉尼亚笔记》(1785)，在这本书中杰斐逊认为黑人从智力和体力上都逊于白人。

the people of God, than to enjoy pleasures with that wicked people for a season. O! that the coloured people were long since of Moses' excellent disposition, instead of courting favour with and telling news and lies to our natural enemies, against each other — aiding them to keep their hellish chains of slavery upon us. Would we not long before this time, have been respectable men, instead of such wretched victims of oppression as we are? Would they be able to drag our mothers, our fathers, our wives, our children and ourselves, around the world in chains and handcuffs as they do, to dig up gold and silver for them and theirs? This question, my brethren, I leave for you to digest; and may God Almighty force it home to your hearts. Remember that unless you are united, keeping your tongues within your teeth, you will be afraid to trust your secrets to each other, and thus perpetuate our miseries under the Christians!!!!

Addition — Remember, also to lay humble at the feet of our Lord and Master Jesus Christ, with prayers and fastings. Let our enemies go on with their butcheries, and at once fill up their cup. Never make an attempt to gain our freedom or natural right, from under our cruel oppressors and murderers, until you see your way clear①— when that hour arrives and you move, be not afraid or dismayed; for be you assured that Jesus Christ the King of heaven and of earth who is the God of justice and of armies will surely go before you. And those enemies who have for hundreds of years stolen our rights, and kept us ignorant of Him and His divine worship, He will remove. Millions of whom, are this day, so ignorant and avaricious, that they cannot conceive how God can have an attribute of justice, and show mercy to us because it pleased Him to make us black — which colour, Mr. Jefferson calls unfortunate!!!!!! As though we are not as thankful to our God, for having made us as it pleased himself, as they, (the whites,) are for having made them white. They think because they hold us in their infernal chains of slavery, that we wish to be white, or of their color — but they are dreadfully deceived — we wish to be just as it pleased our Creator to have made us, and no avaricious and unmerciful wretches, have any business to make slaves of, or hold us in slavery. How would they like for us to make slaves of, and hold them in cruel slavery, and murder them as they do us? — But are Mr. Jefferson's assertions true? viz. "that it is unfortunate for us that our Creator has been pleased to make us black." We will not take his say so, for the fact. The world will have an opportunity to see whether it is unfortunate for us, that our Creator has made us darker than the whites.

Fear not the number and education of our enemies, against whom we shall have to contend

---

① It is not to be understood here, that I mean for us to wait until God shall take us by the hair of our heads and drag us out of abject wretchedness and slavery, nor do I mean to convey the idea for us to wait until our enemies shall make preparations, and call us to seize those preparations, take it away from them, and put everything before us to death, in order to gain our freedom which God has given us. For you must remember that we are men as well as they. God has been pleased to give us two eyes, two hands, two feet, and some sense in our heads as well as they. They have no more right to hold us in slavery than we have to hold them; we have just as much right, in the sight of God, to hold them and their children in slavery and wretchedness, as they have to hold us, and no more. (此处为原文注释)

for our lawful right; guaranteed to us by our Maker; for why should we be afraid, when God is, and will continue (if we continue humble) to be, on our side?

The man who would not fight under our Lord and Master Jesus Christ, in the glorious and heavenly cause of freedom and of God — to be delivered from the most wretched, abject and servile slavery, that ever a people was afflicted with since the foundation of the world, to the present day — ought to be kept with all of his children or family, in slavery, or in chains, to be butchered by his cruel enemies.

I saw a paragraph, a few years since, in a South Carolina paper, which, speaking of the barbarity of the Turks, it said: "The Turks are the most barbarous people in the world — they treat the Greeks more like brutes than human beings." And in the same paper was an advertisement, which said: "Eight well-built Virginia and Maryland Negro fellows and four wenches will positively be sold this day, to the highest bidder!" And what astonished me still more was to see in this same humane paper!! the cuts of three men, with clubs and budgets on their backs, and an advertisement offering a considerable sum of money for their apprehension and delivery. I declare, it is really so amusing to hear the Southerners and Westerners of this country talk about barbarity, that it is positively enough to make a man smile.

The sufferings of the Helots among the Spartans were somewhat severe, it is true, but to say that theirs were as severe as ours among the Americans I do most strenuously deny — for instance, can any man show me an article on a page of ancient history which specifies that the Spartans chained and handcuffed the Helots, and dragged them from their wives and children, children from their parents, mothers from their suckling babes, wives from their husbands, driving them from one end of the country to the other? Notice the Spartans were heathens, who lived long before our Divine Master made his appearance in the flesh. Can Christian Americans deny these barbarous cruel-ties? Have you not, Americans, having subjected us under you, added to these miseries, by insulting us in telling us to our face, because we are helpless, that we are not of the human family? I ask you, O! Americans, I ask you, in the name of the Lord, can you deny these charges? Some perhaps may deny, by saying that they never thought or said that we were not men. But do not actions speak louder than words? Have they not made provisions for the Greeks, and Irish? Nations who have never done the least thing for them, while we, who have enriched their country with our blood and tears — have dug up gold and silver for them and their children, from generation to generation, and are in more miseries than any other people under heaven, are not seen but by comparatively a handful of the American people? There are, indeed, more ways to kill a dog, besides choking it to death with butter. Further — The Spartans or Lacedaemonians, had some frivolous pretext for enslaving the Helots, for they (Helots), while being free inhabitants of Sparta, stirred up an intestine commotion, and were, by the Spartans subdued, and made prisoners of war. Consequently, they and their children were condemned to perpetual slavery.

I have been for years troubling the pages of historians, to find out what our fathers have done to the white Christians of America, to merit such condign punishment as they have inflicted on them, and do continue to inflict on us their children. But I must aver that my researches have hitherto been to no effect. I have, therefore, come to the immoveable conclusion that they (Americans) have and do continue to punish us for nothing else, but for enriching them and their country. For I cannot conceive of anything else. Nor will I ever believe otherwise, until the Lord shall convince me.

The world knows that slavery as it existed among the Romans (which was the primary cause of their destruction) was, comparatively speaking, no more than a cypher, when compared with ours under the Americans. Indeed, I should not have noticed the Roman slaves, had not the very learned and penetrating Mr. Jefferson said, "when a master was murdered, all his slaves in the same house, or within hearing, were condemned to death." — Here let me ask Mr. Jefferson (but he is gone to answer at the bar of God, for the deeds done in his body while living), I therefore ask the whole American people, had I not rather die, or be put to death, than to be a slave to any tyrant, who takes not only my own, but my wife and children's lives by the inches? Yea, would I meet death with avidity far! far!! in preference to such servile submission to the murderous hands of tyrants. Mr. Jefferson's very severe remarks on us have been so extensively argued upon by men whose attainments in literature I shall never be able to reach, that I would not have meddled with it, were it not to solicit each of my brethren, who has the spirit of a man, to buy a copy of Mr. Jefferson's "Notes on Virginia," and put it in the hand of his son. For let no one of us suppose that the refutations which have been written by our white friends are enough — they are whites — we are blacks. We, and the world wish to see the charges of Mr. Jefferson refuted by the blacks themselves, according to their chance; for we must remember that what the whites have written respecting this subject is other men's labours, and did not emanate from the blacks. I know well, that there are some talents and learning among the coloured people of this country, which we have not a chance to develop, in consequence of oppression; but our oppression ought not to hinder us from acquiring all we can. For we will have a chance to develop them by and by. God will not suffer us, always to be oppressed. Our sufferings will come to an end, in spite of all the Americans this side of eternity. Then we will want all the learning and talents among ourselves, and perhaps more, to govern ourselves. "Every dog must have its day," the American's is coming to an end.

But let us review Mr. Jefferson's remarks respecting us some further. Comparing our miserable fathers, with the learned philosophers of Greece, he says: "Yet notwithstanding these and other discouraging circumstances among the Romans, their slaves were often their rarest artists. They excelled too, in science, insomuch as to be usually employed as tutors to their master's children; Epictetus, Terence and Phaedrus,① were slaves — but they were of the race of whites. It is not

---

① Epictetus, Terence, and Phaedrus: 分别是古希腊斯多葛派哲学家伊壁鸠鲁(前 55—前 135)、古罗马剧作家特伦斯(前 195—前 159)以及古罗马寓言家斐德鲁斯(前 15—50)。

their condition then, but nature, which has produced the distinction." See this, my brethren!! Do you believe that this assertion is swallowed by millions of the whites? Do you know that Mr. Jefferson was one of as great characters as ever lived among the whites? See his writings for the world, and public labours for the United States of America. Do you believe that the assertions of such a man will pass away into oblivion unobserved by this people and the world?

If you do you are much mistaken — See how the American people treat us — have we souls in our bodies? Are we men who have any spirits at all? I know that there are many swell-bellied fellows among us, whose greatest object is to fill their stomachs. Such I do not mean — I am after those who know and feel, that we are MEN, as well as other people; to them, I say, that unless we try to refute Mr. Jefferson's arguments respecting us, we will only establish them.

But the slaves among the Romans. Everybody who has read history knows that as soon as a slave among the Romans obtained his freedom, he could rise to the greatest eminence in the State, and there was no law instituted to hinder a slave from buying his freedom. Have not the Americans instituted laws to hinder us from obtaining our freedom? Do any deny this charge? Read the laws of Virginia, North Carolina, &c. Further: have not the Americans instituted laws to prohibit a man of colour from obtaining and holding any office whatever, under the government of the United States of America? Now, Mr. Jefferson tells us, that our condition is not so hard, as the slaves were under the Romans!!!!!!

It is time for me to bring this article to a close. But before I close it, I must observe to my brethren that at the close of the first Revolution in this country with Great Britain, there were but thirteen States in the Union, now there are twenty-four, most of which are slave-holding States, and the whites are dragging us around in chains and in handcuffs, to their new States and Territories to work their mines and farms, to enrich them and their children — and millions of them believing firmly that we being a little darker than they, were made by our Creator to be an inheritance to them and their children for ever — the same as a parcel of brutes.

Are we men!! — I ask you, O my brethren! are we MEN? Did our Creator make us to be slaves to dust and ashes like ourselves? Are they not dying worms as well as we? Have they not to make their appearance before the tribunal of Heaven, to answer for the deeds done in the body, as well as we? Have we any other Master but Jesus Christ alone? Is he not their Master as well as ours? What right then, have we to obey and call any other Master, but Himself? How we could be so submissive to a gang of men, whom we cannot tell whether they are as good as ourselves or not, I never could conceive. However, this is shut up with the Lord, and we cannot precisely tell — but I declare, we judge men by their works.

The whites have always been an unjust, jealous, unmerciful, avaricious and blood-thirsty set of beings, always seeking after power and authority. We view them all over the confederacy of Greece, where they were first known to be anything (in consequence of education) we see them there, cutting each other's throats — trying to subject each other to wretchedness and misery — to effect which they used all kinds of deceitful, unfair, and unmerciful means. We view them next in Rome, where the spirit of tyranny and deceit raged still higher. We view them in Gaul,① Spain, and in Britain. In fine, we view them all over Europe, together with what were scattered about in Asia and Africa, as heathens, and we see them acting more like devils than accountable men. But some may ask, did not the blacks of Africa, and the mulattoes of Asia, go on in the same way as did the whites of Europe. I answer, no — they never were half so avaricious, deceitful and unmerciful as the whites, according to their knowledge.

But we will leave the whites or Europeans as heathens, and take a view of them as Christians, in which capacity we see them as cruel, if not more so than ever. In fact, take them as a body, they are ten times more cruel, avaricious and unmerciful than ever they were; for while they were heathens, they were bad enough it is true, but it is positively a fact that they were not quite so audacious as to go and take vessel loads of men, women and children, and in cold blood, and through devilishness, throw them into the sea, and murder them in all kind of ways. While they were heathens, they were too ignorant for such barbarity. But being Christians, enlightened and sensible, they are completely prepared for such hellish cruelties. Now suppose God were to give them more sense, what would they do? If it were possible, would they not dethrone Jehovah and seat themselves upon His throne? I therefore, in the name and fear of the Lord God of Heaven and of earth, divested of prejudice either on the side of my col-our or that of the whites, advance my suspicion of them, whether they are as good by nature as we are or not. Their actions, since they were known as a people, have been the reverse, I do indeed suspect them, but this, as I before observed, is shut up with the Lord, we cannot exactly tell, it will be proved in succeeding generations. The whites have had the essence of the gospel as it was preached by my master and his apostles — the Ethiopians have not, who are to have it in its meridian splendor — the Lord will give it to them to their satisfaction. I hope and pray my God, that they will make good use of it, that it may be well with them.②

---

① Gaul：高卢，今法国。

② It is my solemn belief, that if ever the world becomes Christianized (which must certainly take place before long), it will be through the means, under God of the *Blacks*, who are now held in wretchedness, and degradation, by the white *Christians* of the world, who before they learn to do justice to us before our Maker — and be reconciled to us, and reconcile us to them, and by that means have clear consciences before God and man — send out Missionaries to convert the Heathens, many of whom after they cease to worship gods, which neither see nor hear, become ten times more the children of Hell, then ever they were. Why, what is the reason? Why, the reason is obvious, they must learn to do justice at home, before they go into distant lands, to display their charity, Christianity, and benevolence; when they learn to do jus-tice, God will accept their offering (no man may think that I am against Missionaries for I am not, my object is to see justice done at home, before we go to convert the Heathens.) 此处为原文注释。

(2) Our Wretchedness in Consequence of Ignorance

Ignorance, my brethren, is a mist, low down into the very dark and almost impenetrable abyss in which our fathers for many centuries have been plunged. The Christians, and enlightened of Europe, and some of Asia, seeing the ignorance and consequent degradation of our fathers, instead of trying to enlighten them by teaching them that religion and light with which God had blessed them, they have plunged them into wretchedness ten thousand times more intolerable than if they had left them entirely to the Lord, and to add to their miseries, deep down into which they have plunged them tell them, that they are an inferior and distinct race of beings, which they will be glad enough to recall and swallow by and by. Fortune and misfortune, two inseparable companions, lay rolled up in the wheel of events, which have from the creation of the world, and will continue to take place among men until God shall dash worlds together.

When we take a retrospective view of the arts and sciences — the wise legislators — the Pyramids, and other magnificent buildings — the turning of the channel of the river Nile, by the sons of Africa or of Ham,① among whom learning originated, and was carried thence into Greece, where it was improved upon and refined. Thence among the Romans, and all over the then enlightened parts of the world, and it has been enlightening the dark and benighted minds of men from then, down to this day. I say, when I view retrospectively, the renown of that once mighty people, the children of our great progenitor I am indeed cheered. Yea further, when I view that mighty son of Africa, Hannibal,② one of the greatest generals of antiquity, who defeated and cut off so many thousands of the white Romans or murderers, and who carried his victorious arms to the very gate of Rome, and I give it as my candid opinion, that had Carthage been well united and had given him good support, he would have carried that cruel and barbarous city by storm. But they were dis-united, as the coloured people are now, in the United States of America, the reason our natural enemies are enabled to keep their feet on our throats.

Beloved brethren — here let me tell you, and believe it, that the Lord our God, as true as He sits on His throne in heaven, and as true as our Saviour died to redeem the world, will give you a Hannibal, and when the Lord shall have raised him up, and given him to you for your possession, O my suffering brethren! remember the divisions and consequent sufferings of

---

① sons of... Ham：源自《圣经》，含(Ham)是诺亚之子，非洲和中东地区居民的先祖。

② 汉尼拔(Hannibal：前247—前182)：传说中古代迦太基将军和军事战略家，在第二次布匿战争中入侵意大利并几乎征服罗马。

Carthage and of Hayti①. Read the history particularly of Hayti, and see how they were butchered by the whites, and do you take warning. The person whom God shall give you, give him your support and let him go his length, and behold in him the salvation of your God. God will, indeed, deliver you through him from your deplorable and wretched condition under the Christians of America. I charge you this day before my God to lay no obstacle in his way, but let him go.

The whites want slaves, and want us for their slaves, but some of them will curse the day they ever saw us. As true as the sun ever shone in its meridian splendor, my colour will root some of them out of the very face of the earth. They shall have enough of making slaves of, and butchering, and murdering us in the manner which they have.

No doubt some may say that I write with a bad spirit, and that I being a black, wish these things to occur. Whether I write with a bad or a good spirit, I say if these things do not occur in their proper time, it is because the world in which we live does not exist, and we are deceived with regard to its existence — It is immaterial however to me, who believe, or who refuse — though I should like to see the whites repent peradventure God may have mercy on them. Some, however, have gone so far that their cup must be filled.

But what need have I to refer to antiquity, when Hayti, the glory of the blacks and terror of tyrants, is enough to convince the most avaricious and stupid of wretches — which is at this time, and I am sorry to say it, plagued with that scourge of nations, the Catholic religion; but I hope and pray God that she may yet rid herself of it, and adopt in its stead the Protestant faith; also, I hope that she may keep peace within her borders and be united, keeping a strict look out for tyrants, for if they get the least chance to injure her, they will avail themselves of it, as true as the Lord lives in heaven. But one thing which gives me joy is, that they are men who would be cut off to a man, before they would yield to the combined forces of the whole world — in fact, if the whole world was combined against them, it could not do anything with them, unless the Lord delivers them up.

Ignorance and treachery one against the other — a grovelling servile and abject submission to the lash of tyrants, we see plainly, my brethren, are not the natural elements of the blacks, as the Americans try to make us believe; but these are misfortunes which God has suffered our fathers to be enveloped in for many ages, no doubt in consequence of their disobedience to their Maker, and which do, indeed, reign at this time among us, almost to the destruction of all other principles: for I must truly say, that ignorance, the mother of treachery and deceit, gnaws into our very vitals. Ignorance, as it now exists among us, produces a state of things, Oh my Lord! too horrible to present to the world. Any man who is curious to see the full force of ignorance developed among the coloured people of the United States of America has only to go into the southern and western states of this confederacy, where, if he is not a tyrant, but has the feelings

---

① Hayti：海地革命(1791—1804)，唯一一次以建立国家政权结束的奴隶起义，然而在革命后海地充斥着分裂和内讧。

of a human being, who can feel for a fellow creature, he may see enough to make his very heart bleed! He may see there, a son take his mother, who bore almost the pains of death to give him birth, and by the command of a tyrant, strip her as naked as she came into the world, and apply the cow-hide to her, until she falls a victim to death in the road! He may see a husband take his dear wife, not unfrequently in a pregnant state, and perhaps far advanced, and beat her for an unmerciful wretch, until his infant falls a lifeless lump at her feet! Can the Americans escape God Almighty? If they do, can He be to us a God of Justice? God is just, and I know it — for He has convinced me to my satisfaction — I cannot doubt Him. My observer may see fathers beating their sons, mothers their daughters, and children their parents, all to pacify the passions of unrelenting tyrants. He may also, see them telling news and lies, making mischief one upon another. These are some of the productions of ignorance, which he will see practised among my dear brethren, who are held in unjust slavery and wretchedness, by avaricious and unmerciful tyrants, to whom, and their hellish deeds, I would suffer my life to be taken before I would submit. And when my curious observer comes to take notice of those who are said to be free (which assertion I deny), and who are making some frivolous pretentions to common sense, he will see that branch of ignorance among the slaves assuming a more cunning and deceitful course of procedure. He may see some of my brethren in league with tyrants, selling their own brethren into hell upon earth, not dissimilar to the exhibitions in Africa, but in a more secret, servile and abject manner. Oh Heaven! I am full!!! I can hardly move my pen!!!! and as I expect some will try to put me to death, to strike terror into others, and to obliterate from their minds the notion of freedom, so as to keep my brethren the more secure in wretchedness, where they will be permitted to stay but a short time (whether tyrants believe it or not) — I shall give the world a development of facts, which are already witnessed in the courts of heaven. My observer may see some of those ignorant and treacherous creatures (coloured people) sneaking about in the large cities, endeavouring to find out all strange coloured people, where they work and where they reside, asking them questions, and trying to ascertain whether they are runaways or not, telling them, at the same time, that they always have been, are, and always will be, friends to their brethren; and, perhaps, that they themselves are absconders, and a thousand such treacherous lies to get the better information of the more ignorant!!! There have been and are at this day in Boston, New-York, Philadelphia, and Baltimore, coloured men, who are in league with tyrants, and who receive a great portion of their daily bread, of the moneys which they acquire from the blood and tears of their more miserable brethren, whom they scandalously delivered into the hands of our natural enemies!!!!!!

To show the force of degraded ignorance and deceit among us some farther, I will give here an extract from a paragraph, which may be found in the *Columbian Centinel*① of this city, for September 9, 1829, on the first page of which, the curious may find an article, headed

---

① *Columbian Centinel*:《波士顿新闻》,在波士顿地区发行于 1790 年至 1840 年的报纸。

"AFFRAY AND MURDER." "Portsmouth, (Ohio) Aug. 22, 1829.

"A most shocking outrage was committed in Kentucky, about eight miles from this place, on 14th inst. A negro driver, by the name of Gordon, who had purchased in Maryland about sixty negroes, was taking them, assisted by an associate named Allen, and the wagoner who conveyed the baggage, to the Mississippi. The men were hand-cuffed and chained together, in the usual manner for driving those poor wretches, while the women and children were suffered to proceed without incumbrance. It appears that, by means of a file the negroes, unobserved, had succeeded in separating the iron which bound their hands, in such a way as to be able to throw them off at any moment. About 8 o'clock in the morning, while proceeding on the state road leading from Greenup to Vanceburg, two of them dropped their shackles and commenced a fight, when the wagoner (Petit) rushed in with his whip to compel them to desist. At this moment, every negro was found to be perfectly at liberty; and one of them seizing a club, gave Petit a violent blow on the head, and laid him dead at his feet; and Allen, who came to his assistance, met a similar fate, from the contents of a pistol fired by another of the gang. Gordon was then attacked, seized and held by one of the negroes, whilst another fired twice at him with a pistol, the ball of which each time grazed his head, but not proving effectual, he was beaten with clubs, and left for dead. They then commenced pillaging the wagon, and with an axe split open the trunk of Gordon, and rifled it of the money, about $2,400. Sixteen of the negroes then took to the woods; Gordon, in the meantime, not being materially injured, was enabled, by the assistance of one of the women, to mount his horse and flee; pursued, however, by one of the gang on another horse, with a drawn pistol; fortunately, he escaped with his life barely, arriving at a plantation, as the negro came in sight; who then turned about and retreated.

"The neighbourhood was immediately rallied, and a hot pursuit given — which, we understand, has resulted in the capture of the whole gang and the recovery of the greatest part of the money. Seven of the negro men and one woman, it is said were engaged in the murders, and will be brought to trial at the next court in Greenupsburg."

Here my brethren, I want you to notice particularly in the above article, the ignorant and deceitful actions of this coloured woman. I beg you to view it candidly, as for eternity!!!! Here a notorious wretch, with two other confederates had sixty of them in a gang, driving them like brutes — the men all in chains and hand-cuffs, and by the help of God they got their chains and hand-cuffs thrown off, and caught two of the wretches and put them to death, and beat the other until they thought he was dead, and left him for dead; however, he deceived them, and rising from the ground, this servile woman helped him upon his horse, and he made his escape. Brethren, what do you think of this? Was it the natural fine feelings of this woman, to save such a wretch alive? I know that the blacks, take them half enlightened and ignorant, are more humane and merciful than the most enlightened and refined European that can be found in all the earth. Let no one say that I assert this because I am prejudiced on the side of my colour, and against the whites or Europeans. For what I write, I do it candidly, for my God and the good of both parties:

Natural observations have taught me these things; there is a solemn awe in the hearts of the blacks, as it respects murdering men: whereas the whites, (though they are great cowards) where they have the advantage, or think that there are any prospects of getting it, they murder all before them, in order to subject men to wretchedness and degradation under them. This is the natural result of pride and avarice. But I declare, the actions of this black woman are really insupportable. For my own part, I cannot think it was anything but servile deceit, combined with the most gross ignorance: for we must remember that humanity, kindness and the fear of the Lord, does not consist in protecting devils. Here is a set of wretches, who had sixty of them in a gang, driving them around the country like brutes, to dig up gold and silver for them (which they will get enough of yet). Should the lives of such creatures be spared? Are God and Mammon in league? What has the Lord to do with a gang of desperate wretches, who go sneaking about the country like robbers — light upon his people wherever they can get a chance, binding them with chains and hand-cuffs, beat and murder them as they would rattlesnakes? Are they not the Lord's enemies? Ought they not to be destroyed? Any person who will save such wretches from destruction is fighting against the Lord, and will receive his just recompense. The black men acted like block-heads. Why did they not make sure of the wretch? He would have made sure of them, if he could. It is just the way with black men — eight white men can frighten fifty of them; whereas, if you can only get courage into the blacks, I do declare it, that one good black man can put to death six white men; and I give it as a fact, let twelve black men get well armed for battle, and they will kill and put to flight fifty whites. The rea-son is, the blacks, once you get them started, they glory in death. The whites have had us under them for more than three centuries, murdering, and treating us like brutes; and, as Mr. Jefferson wisely said, they have never found us out — they do not know, indeed, that there is an unconquerable disposition in the breasts of the blacks, which, when it is fully awakened and put in motion, will be subdued, only with the destruction of the animal existence. Get the blacks started, and if you do not have a gang of tigers and lions to deal with, I am a deceiver of the blacks and of the whites. How sixty of them could let that wretch escape unkilled, I cannot conceive — they will have to suffer as much for the two whom, they secured, as if they had put one hundred to death: if you commence, make sure work — do not trifle, for they will not trifle with you — they want us for their slaves, and think nothing of murdering us in order to subject us to that wretched condition — therefore, if there is an attempt made by us, kill or be killed. Now, I ask you, had you not rather be killed than to be a slave to a tyrant, who takes the life of your mother, wife, and dear little children? Look upon your mother, wife and children, and answer God Almighty; and believe this, that it is no more harm for you to kill a man who is trying to kill you, than it is for you to take a drink of water when thirsty; in fact, the man who will stand still and let another murder him, is worse than an infidel, and, if he has common sense, ought not to be pitied. The actions of this deceitful and ignorant coloured woman, in saving the life of a desperate wretch, whose avaricious and cruel object was to drive her, and her companions in miseries through the country like cattle, to make his fortune on their carcasses, are but too much like that of thousands of our brethren in these states: if anything is whispered by one which has any allusion to the melioration of their dreadful condition, they run and tell tyrants, that they may be enabled to keep them the longer in wretchedness and miseries. Oh! coloured people of these United States, I ask you, in the name of that God who made us, have we, in consequence of oppression, nearly lost the spirit of man, and, in no very trifling degree, adopted that of brutes? Do you answer, no? I ask you, then, what set of men can you point me to, in all the world, who are so abjectly employed by their oppressors as we are by our natural enemies? How can, Oh! how can those enemies but say that we and our children are not of the HUMAN FAMILY, but were made by our Creator to be an inheritance to them and theirs for ever? How can the slaveholders but say that they can bribe the best coloured person in the country, to sell his brethren for a trifling sum of money, and take that atrocity to confirm them in their avaricious opinion, that we were made to be slaves to them and their children? How could Mr. Jefferson but say, "I advance it therefore as a suspicion only, that the blacks, whether originally a distinct race, or made distinct by time and circumstances, are inferior to the whites in the endowments both of body and mind?" — "It," says he, "is not against experience to suppose, that different species of the same genius, or varieties of the same species, may possess different qualifications." [Here, my brethren, listen to him.]

"Will not a lover of natural history, then, one who views the gradations in all the races of animals with the eye of philosophy, excuse an effort to keep those in the department of man as distinct as nature has formed them?" — I hope you will try to find out the meaning of this verse — its widest sense and all its bearings: whether you do or not, remember the whites do. This very verse, brethren, having emanated from Mr. Jefferson, a much greater philosopher the world never afforded, has in truth injured us more, and has been as great a barrier to our emancipation as anything that has ever been advanced against us. I hope you will not let it pass unnoticed. He goes on further, and says: "This unfortunate difference of colour, and perhaps of faculty, is a powerful obstacle to the emancipation of these people. Many of their advocates, while they wish to vindicate the liberty of human nature are anxious also to preserve its dignity and beauty. Some of these, embarrassed by the question, 'What further is to be done with them?' join them-selves in opposition with those who are actuated by sordid avarice only." Now I ask you candidly, my suffering brethren in time, who are candidates for the eternal worlds, how could Mr. Jefferson but have given the world these remarks respecting us, when we are so submissive to them, and so much servile deceit prevail among ourselves — when we so meanly submit to their murderous lashes, to which neither the Indians nor any other people under Heaven would submit? No, they would die to a man, before they would suffer such things from men who are no better than themselves, and perhaps not so good. Yes, how can our friends but be embarrassed, as Mr. Jefferson says, by the question, "What further is to be done with these people?" For while they are working for our emancipation, we are, by our treachery, wickedness and deceit, working against our-selves and our children — helping ours, and the enemies of God, to keep us and our dear little children in their infernal chains of slavery!!! Indeed, our friends cannot but relapse and join themselves "with those who are actuated by sordid avarice only!!!!" For my own part, I am glad Mr. Jefferson has advanced his positions for your sake; for you will either have to contradict or confirm him by your own actions, and not by what our friends have said or done for us; for those things are other men's labours, and do not satisfy the Americans, who are waiting for us to prove to them ourselves, that we are men, before they will be willing to admit the fact; for I pledge you my sacred word of honour that Mr. Jefferson's remarks respecting us, have sunk deep into the hearts of millions of the whites, and never will be removed this side of eternity. For how can they, when we are confirming him every day, by our groveling submissions and treachery? I aver, that when I look over these United States of America, and the world, and see the ignorant deceptions and consequent wretchedness of my brethren, I am brought off-times solemnly to a stand, and in the midst of my reflections I exclaim to my God, "Lord didst thou make us to be slaves to our brethren, the whites?" But when I reflect that God is just, and that millions of my wretched brethren would meet death with glory — yea, more, would plunge into the very mouths of cannons and be torn into particles as minute as the atoms which compose the elements of the earth, in preference to a mean submission to the lash of tyrants, I am with streaming eyes compelled to shrink back into nothingness before my Maker, and exclaim again, thy will be done, O Lord God Almighty.

Men of colour, who are also of sense, for you particularly is my appeal designed. Our more ignorant brethren are not able to penetrate its value. I call upon you therefore to cast your eyes upon the wretchedness of your brethren, and to do your utmost to enlighten them — go to work and enlighten your brethren! — Let the Lord see you doing what you can to rescue them and yourselves from degradation. Do any of you say that you and your family are free and happy, and what have you to do with the wretched slaves and other people? So can I say, for I enjoy as much freedom as any of you, if I am not quite as well off as the best of you. Look into our freedom and happiness, and see of what kind they are composed!! They are of the very lowest kind — they are the very dregs! — they are the most servile and abject kind, that ever a people was in possession of! If any of you wish to know how free you are, let one of you start and go through the southern and western States of this country, and unless you travel as a slave to a white man (a servant is a slave to the man whom he serves) or have your free papers (which if you are not careful they will get from you), if they do not take you up and put you in jail, and if you cannot give good evidence of your freedom, sell you into eternal slavery, I am not a living man: or any man of colour, immaterial who he is, or where he came from, if he is not the fourth from the negro race!! (as we are called) the white Christians of America will serve him the same, they will sink him into wretchedness and degradation for ever while he lives. And yet some of you have the hardihood to say that you are free and happy! May God have mercy on your freedom and happiness!! I met a coloured man in the street a short time since, with a string of boots on his shoulders; we fell into conversation, and in course of which, I said to him, what a miserable set of people we are! He asked, why? Said I, we are so subjected under the whites, that we cannot obtain the comforts of life, but by cleaning their boots and shoes, old clothes, waiting on them, shaving them &c. Said he, (with the boots on his shoulders) "I am completely happy!!! I never want to live any better or happier than when I can get a plenty of boots and shoes to clean!!!" Oh! how can those who are actuated by avarice only, but think, that our Creator made us to be an inheritance to them for ever, when they see that our greatest glory is centered in such mean and low objects? Understand me, brethren, I do not mean to speak against the occupations by which we acquire enough and sometimes scarcely that, to render our-selves and families comfortable through life. I am subjected to the same inconvenience, as you all. My objections are, to our glorying and being happy in such low employments; for if we are men, we ought to be thankful to the Lord for the past, and for the future. Be looking forward with thankful hearts to higher attainments than wielding the razor and cleaning boots and shoes. The man whose aspirations are not above, and even below these, is, indeed, ignorant and wretched enough. I advanced it therefore to you, not as a problematical, but as an unshaken and forever immovable fact, that your full glory and happiness, as well as all other coloured people under Heaven, shall never be fully consummated, but with the entire emancipation of your enslaved brethren all over the world. You may there-fore, go to work and do what you can to rescue, or join in with tyrants to oppress them and yourselves, until the Lord shall come upon you all like a thief in the night. For I believe it is the will of the Lord that our greatest happiness shall consist in working for the salvation of our whole body. When this is accomplished a burst of glory will shine upon you, which will indeed astonish you and the world. Do any of you say this never will be done? I assure you that God will accomplish it — if nothing else will answer, he will hurl tyrants and devils into atoms and make way for his people. But O my brethren! I say unto you again, you must go to work and prepare the way of the Lord.

There is a great work for you to do, as trifling as some of you may think of it. You have to prove to the Americans and the world, that we are men, and not brutes, as we have been represented, and by millions treated. Remember, to let the aim of your labours among your brethren, and particularly the youths, be the dissemination of education and religion.[①] It is lamentable, that many of our children go to school, from four until they are eight or ten, and sometimes fifteen years of age, and leave school knowing but a little more about the grammar of their language than a horse does about handling a musket — and not a few of them are really so

---

① Never mind what the ignorant ones among us may say, many of whom when you speak to them for their good, and try to enlighten their minds, laugh at you, and perhaps tell you plump to your face, that they want no instruction from you or any other Niger, and all such aggravating language. Now if you are a man of understanding and sound sense, I conjure you in the name of the Lord, and of all that is good, to impute their actions to ignorance, and wink at their follies, and do your very best to get around them some way or other, for remember they are your brethren; and I declare to you that it is for your interests to teach and enlighten them. (此处为原文注释)

ignorant, that they are unable to answer a person correctly, general questions in geography, and to hear them read, would only be to disgust a man who has a taste for reading; which, to do well, as trifling as it may appear to some (to the ignorant in particular), is a great part of learning. Some few of them may make out to scribble tolerably well, over a half sheet of paper, which I believe has hitherto been a powerful obstacle in our way, to keep us from acquiring knowledge. An ignorant father, who knows no more than what nature has taught him, together with what little he acquires by the senses of hearing and seeing, finding his son able to write a neat hand, sets it down for granted that he has as good learning as anybody; the young, ignorant gump, hearing his father or mother, who perhaps may be ten times more ignorant, in point of literature, than himself, extolling his learning, struts about, in the full assurance, that his attainments in literature are sufficient to take him through the world, when, in fact, he has scarcely any learning at all!!!!

I promiscuously fell in conversation once, with an elderly coloured man on the topics of education, and of the great prevalency of ignorance among us: Said he, "I know that our people are very ignorant but my son has a good education: I spent a great deal of money on his education: he can write as well as any white man, and I assure you that no one can fool him," &c. Said I, what else can your son do, besides writing a good hand? Can he post a set of books in a mercantile manner? Can he write a neat piece of composition in prose or in verse? To these interrogations he answered in the negative. Said I, did your son learn, while he was at school, the width and depth of English Grammar? To which he also replied in the negative, telling me his son did not learn those things. Your son, said I, then, has hardly any learning at all — he is almost as ignorant, and more so, than many of those who never went to school one day in all their lives. My friend got a little put out, and so walking off, said that his son could write as well as any white man. Most of the coloured people, when they speak of the education of one among us who can write a neat hand, and who perhaps knows nothing but to scribble and puff pretty fair on a small scrap of paper, immaterial whether his words are grammatical, or spelt correctly, or not; if it only looks beautiful, they say he has as good an education as any white man — he can write as well as any white man, & c. The poor, ignorant creature, hearing this, he is ashamed, forever after to let any person see him humbling himself to another for knowledge but going about trying to deceive those who are more ignorant than himself, he at last falls an ignorant victim to death in wretchedness. I pray that the Lord may undeceive my ignorant brethren, and permit them to throw away pretensions, and seek after the substance of learning. I would crawl on my hands and knees through mud and mire, to the feet of a learned man, where I would sit and humbly supplicate him to instill into me, that which neither devils nor tyrants could remove, only with my life — for coloured people to acquire learning in this country, makes tyrants quake and tremble on their sandy foundation. Why, what is the matter? Why, they know that their infernal deeds of cruelty will be made known to the world. Do you suppose one man of good sense and learning would submit himself, his father, mother, wife and children, to be slaves to a wretched man like himself, who, instead of compensating him for his labours, chains, hand-cuffs and beats him and family almost to death, leaving life enough in them, however, to work for, and call him master? No! no! he would cut his devilish throat from ear to ear and well do slave-holders know it. The bare name of educating the coloured people, scares our cruel oppressors almost to death. But if they do not have enough to be frightened for yet, it will be, because they can always keep us ignorant, and because God approbates their cruelties, with which they have been for centuries murdering us. The whites shall have enough of the blacks, yet as true as God sits on his throne in Heaven.

Some of our brethren are so very full of learning, that you cannot mention anything to them which they do not know better than yourself!! — nothing is strange to them!! — they knew everything years ago! — if anything should be mentioned in company where they are, immaterial how important it is respecting us or the world, if they had not divulged it; they make light of it, and affect to have known it long before it was mentioned and try to make all in the room, or wherever you may be, believe that your conversation is nothing!! — not worth hearing! All this is the result of ignorance and ill-breeding; for a man of good-breeding, sense and penetration, if he had heard a subject told twenty times over, and should happen to be in company where one should commence telling it again, he would wait with patience on its narrator, and see if he would tell it as it was told in his presence before — paying the most strict attention to what is said, to see if any more light will be thrown on the subject: for all men are not gifted alike in telling, or even hearing the most simple narration. These ignorant, vicious, and wretched men contribute almost as much injury to our body as tyrants themselves, by doing so much for the promotion of ignorance amongst us; for they, making such pretensions to knowledge, such of our youth as are seeking after knowledge, and can get access to them, take them as criterions to go by, who will lead them into a channel, where, unless the Lord blesses them with the privilege of seeing their folly, they will be irretrievably lost forever, while in time!!!

I must close this article by relating the very heart-rending fact, that I have examined school-boys and young men of colour in different parts of the country, in the most simple parts of Murray's *English Grammar*,[①] and not more than one in thirty was able to give a correct answer to my interrogations. If anyone contradicts me, let him step out of his door into the streets of Boston, New-York, Philadelphia, or Baltimore (no use to mention any other, for the Christians are too charitable further south or west!) — I say, let him who disputes me, step out of his door into the streets of either of those four cities, and promiscuously collect one hundred school-boys, or young men of colour, who have been to school, and who are considered by the coloured people to have received an excellent education, because, perhaps, some of them can write a good hand, but who, notwithstanding their neat writing, may be almost as ignorant, in comparison, as a horse —

---

① Murray's *English Grammar*：林德利·穆里(Lindley Murray, 1745—1826)的《英语语法》(*English Grammar*)是 19 世纪美国和英国使用最为广泛的语法教科书之一。

And, I say it, he will hardly find (in this enlightened day, and in the midst of this charitable people) five in one hundred, who are able to correct the false grammar of their language — The cause of this almost universal ignorance among us, I appeal to our schoolmasters to declare. Here is a fact, which I this very minute take from the mouth of a young coloured man, who has been to school in this state (Massachusetts) nearly nine years, and who knows grammar this day, nearly as well as he did the day he first entered the school-house under a white master. This young man says："My master would never allow me to study grammar." I asked him, why? "The school committee," said he "forbid the coloured children learning grammar — they would not allow any but the white children to study grammar." It is a notorious fact, that the major part of the white Americans have, ever since we have been among them, tried to keep us ignorant, and make us believe that God made us and our children to be slaves to them and theirs. Oh! my God, have mercy on Christian Americans!!!

✍ 选文评析：

　　《呼吁》作为面向广大黑人民众的政治宣传手册，以黑人社区熟悉的宗教故事为例证，引用《圣经》和卫理公会教义为政治立场提供依据，植根于黑人社区根深蒂固的宗教传统，其宗教色彩与政治性话语相结合共同作用于激进的废奴意识形态宣传，通俗易懂且极具感染力，具备广泛传播和造成影响的可能性。选文为《呼吁》的前两篇文章，沃克分别从奴隶制和黑人不通文墨两方面的社会现状出发探讨其后果，以鼓励黑人奋起改变现状。

　　在第一篇文章《奴隶制给我们带来的不幸》中，沃克以《圣经》中埃及人和以色列人的故事为参照，以极具煽动性的话语控诉美国奴隶制度的野蛮和残酷，指出同其他时代和其他国家的奴隶制度相比，美国的奴隶制度惨绝人寰。他以卫理公会教义"上帝子民具有继承财产的权利"为依据，谴责白人对黑人从婚姻到财产等一切生活资料的剥夺，揭露白人基督徒的虚伪，并指出奴隶制度的实质是把非裔视为非人类的财产随意买卖处置的制度。他在文中以激烈的言辞驳斥了美国开国元勋杰斐逊总统的种族主义论调，借用基督教教义质疑了美国奴隶制度官方话语的合法性，从而为废奴主义和黑白平等的政治思想提供了有力依据。因此，他主张立即废除奴隶制，并要求美国依照基督教教义给予黑人平等的工作机会、正常的婚姻及土地等基本人权。当时主流的废奴主张是缓和、渐进地废除奴隶制，很多废奴主义者倡导把黑人送回非洲或黑白分治，"立即废除奴隶制"和"黑白平等"是革命性的激进主张。沃克恳请同胞们采取行动，敦促"受苦和沉睡的兄弟"从束缚自己思想和身体的枷锁中解放出来，呼吁黑人同胞不论何种身份都要勇于反抗美国人（白人）的统治，挣脱套在自己脖颈上的枷锁，用包括暴力手段在内的一切反抗压迫者。

　　在第二篇文章《无知给我们带来不幸》中，沃克以历史上骁勇的迦太基将军汉尼拔为例，指出种族团结的重要性，鼓励黑人团结一致获得种族抗争的胜利。他肯定黑人不输于白人的天赋和勇气，向黑人传达暴力抗争的必要性和赢得胜利的可能性。同时，他告诉同胞"背信弃义和卑躬屈膝"并非黑人的本性，而是白人为了奴役黑人编造出的神话，白人利用黑人的无知把一切恶劣的品质强加于黑人，妄图使黑人臣服于自己的统治。沃克以报纸上的一则无知黑人妇女帮助白人抓捕黑奴反抗者的消息为例，指责一些黑人助纣为虐残害同胞，并揭示其根本原因在于一些黑人民智未开，由此他指出愚昧无知给黑人斗争带来的消极影响。沃克强调文化知识的重要性，指出黑人年轻一代文化知识的不足和专业能力的缺失是种族发展的不利因素。他呼吁黑人应当视自己为与白人一样的人，以白人的工作技能水准和知识水平要求自己，并在年轻人中传播宗教教义和文化知识，打破白人的知识垄断，从而得以识破白人的诡计，粉碎种族主义话语桎梏。

推荐阅读文献：

Crockett, Hasan. The Incendiary Pamphlet: David Walker's Appeal in *Georgia. The Journal of Negro History*, 2001, 86(3): 305-318.

Dinius, Marcy J. 'Look!! Look!!! at This!!!!': The Radical Typography of David Walker's 'Appeal'. *PMLA*, 2011, 126(1): 55-72.

Jarrett, Gene. 'To Refute Mr. Jefferson's Arguments Respecting Us': Thomas Jefferson, David Walker, and the Politics of Early African American Literature. *Early American Literature*, 2011, 46(2): 291-318.

Pelletier, Kevin. David Walker, Harriet Beecher Stowe, and the Logic of Sentimental Terror. *African American Review*, 2013, 46(2/3): 255-269.

Rachleff, Marshall. David Walker's Southern Agent. *The Journal of Negro History*, 1977, 62(1): 100-103.

Rogers, Melvin L. David Walker and the Political Power of the Appeal. *Political Theory*, 2015, 43(2): 208-233.

Smith, Ted J. Mastering Farm and Family: David Walker as Slaveholder. *The Arkansas Historical Quarterly*, 1999, 58(1): 61-79.

Worley, Ted R. Letters to David Walker Relating to Reconstruction in Arkansas, 1866-1874. *The Arkansas Historical Quarterly*, 1957, 16(3): 319-326.

第三章 弗雷德里克·道格拉斯
（Frederick Douglass，1818—1895）

弗雷德里克·道格拉斯（1818—1895）是一位著名的美国非裔社会改革家、废奴主义者、演说家、作家和政治家，被誉为"19世纪最有影响力的非裔美国人"（Roy Finkenbine）。他是一个混血儿，母亲有印第安和黑人血统，父亲则是白人。和许多奴隶一样，他对自己的出生日期和父母背景并不太了解。从马里兰州的奴隶庄园逃脱后，他成为马萨诸塞州和纽约废奴运动的领导人，因擅长演说并发表尖锐的反蓄奴制著作而影响极大。当时有很多支持蓄奴制的人认为，黑人智力低下，不具有成为独立的美国公民的智力能力，因此继续实行蓄奴制对黑人进行"监督和保护"是合理的。而道格拉斯因其非凡的演讲和领导才能而被废奴主义者树立为黑人中的典范，以此反驳贬低黑人的观点。当时的北方人很难相信这样一位伟大的演说家曾经是奴隶。

道格拉斯一生写了好几部自传。其中，他在1845年完成的第一部自传《美国奴隶弗雷德里克·道格拉斯生平记述》（*Narrative of the Life of Frederick Douglass，an American Slave*）记述了自己作为奴隶的经历，该书多年来畅销不衰，对推动废奴事业产生了影响，也被公认为一部最有代表性的奴隶叙述。该书无论在艺术成就还是思想水平上，都堪称这类作品中的巅峰之作。他的第二部自传《我的奴役与自由》（*My Bondage and My Freedom*，1855）和最后一部自传《弗雷德里克·道格拉斯的生活与时代》（*Life and Times of Frederick Douglass*，1881）也产生了很大影响。

与许多废奴主义者一样，道格拉斯相信教育对改善黑人生活至关重要。这使得他成为学校废除种族隔离的早期倡导者。早在19世纪50年代，道格拉斯就注意到，黑人儿童的受教育水平和条件远远不如白人。他呼吁推行教育改革，向所有儿童开放所有学校，认为教育改革甚至要比争取平等选举权等政治问题更为迫切。道格拉斯后来曾给他以前的奴隶主写了一封信，谴责他故意不让道格拉斯接受教育："你在这方面对你的同胞所犯下的恶行和残暴，比你在我背上或他们背上所加的一切罪还要大。这是对灵魂的施暴，是对不朽精神的战争，你将来必须在我们共同的父和造物主那里做出交代。"

虽然他是一个基督徒，但是他强烈批评基督教的虚伪，并指责奴隶主邪恶、道德沦丧和不遵守上帝教诲。从这个意义上说，道格拉斯区分了"基督的基督教"和"美国的基督教"，并认为那些捍卫蓄奴制的基督教奴隶主信徒和牧师们是最残忍、最罪恶、最虚伪的"披着羊皮的狼"。他同时也尖锐地批评了那些对蓄奴制保持沉默的宗教人士的态度，并认为他们也因为和蓄奴制共谋而犯下了亵渎上帝之罪。他认为支持蓄奴制就是"对基督教自由最严重的侵犯之一"。

以下篇章分别节选自道格拉斯的第一部自传《美国奴隶弗雷德里克·道格拉斯生平记述》中的第1章、第6章、第7章和第10章，分别主要讲述了道格拉斯的成长背景，以及他离开主人安东尼船长的种植园后，先后被转给休·奥尔德、托马斯·奥尔德和爱德华·科维等不同类型奴隶主的遭遇。

📖 作品选读：

Narrative of the Life of Frederick Douglass, an American Slave

Chapter 1

I was born in Tuckahoe, near Hillsborough, and about twelve miles from Easton, in Talbot county, Maryland. I have no accurate knowledge of my age, never having seen any authentic record containing it. By far the larger part of the slaves know as little of their ages as horses know of theirs, and it is the wish of most masters within my knowledge to keep their slaves thus ignorant. I do not remember to have ever met a slave who could tell of his birthday. They seldom come nearer to it than planting-time, harvest time, cherry-time, springtime, or fall-time. A want of information concerning my own was a source of unhappiness to me even during childhood. The white children could tell their ages. I could not tell why I ought to be deprived of the same privilege. I was not allowed to make any inquiries of my master concerning it. He deemed all such inquiries on the part of a slave improper and impertinent, and evidence of a restless spirit. The nearest estimate I can give makes me now between twenty-seven and twenty-eight years of age. I come to this, from hearing my master say, sometime during 1835, I was about seventeen years old.

My mother was named Harriet Bailey. She was the daughter of Isaac and Betsey Bailey, both colored, and quite dark. My mother was of a darker complexion than either my grandmother or grandfather.

My father was a white man. He was admitted to be such by all I ever heard speak of my parentage. The opinion was also whispered that my master was my father; but of the correctness of this opinion, I know nothing; the means of knowing was withheld from me. My mother and I were separated when I was but an infant — before I knew her as my mother. It is a common custom, in the part of Maryland from which I ran away, to part children from their mothers at a very early age. Frequently, before the child has reached its twelfth month, its mother is taken from it, and hired out on some farm a considerable distance off, and the child is placed under the care of an old woman, too old for field labor. For what this separation is done, I do not know, unless it be to hinder the development of the child's affection toward its mother, and to blunt and destroy the natural affection of the mother for the child. This is the inevitable result.

I never saw my mother, to know her as such, more than four or five times in my life; and each of these times was very short in duration, and at night. She was hired by a Mr. Stewart, who lived about twelve miles from my home. She made her journeys to see me in the night, travelling the whole distance on foot, after the performance of her day's work. She was a field hand, and a whipping is the penalty of not being in the field at sunrise, unless a slave has special permission from his or her master to the contrary — a permission which they seldom get, and one that gives to him that gives it the proud name of being a kind master. I do not recollect of ever seeing my mother by the light of day. She was with me in the night. She would lie down with me, and get me to sleep, but long before I waked she was gone. Very little communication ever took place between us. Death soon ended what little we could have while she lived, and with it her hardships and suffering. She died when I was about seven years old, on one of my master's farms, near Lee's Mill. I was not allowed to be present during her illness, at her death, or burial. She was gone long before I knew anything about it. Never having enjoyed, to any considerable extent, her soothing presence, her tender and watchful care, I received the tidings of her death with much the same emotions I should have probably felt at the death of a stranger.

Called thus suddenly away, she left me without the slightest intimation of who my father was. The whisper that my master was my father, may or may not be true; and, true or false, it is of but little consequence to my purpose whilst the fact remains, in all its glaring odiousness, that slaveholders have ordained, and by law established, that the children of slave women shall in all cases follow the condition of their mothers; and this is done too obviously to administer to their own lusts, and make a gratification of their wicked desires profitable as well as pleasurable; for by this cunning arrangement, the slaveholder, in cases not a few, sustains to his slaves the double relation of master and father.

Chapter 6

My new mistress proved to be all she appeared when I first met her at the door, — a woman of the kindest heart and finest feelings. She had never had a slave under her control previously to myself, and prior to her marriage she had been dependent upon her own industry for a living. She was by trade a weaver; and by constant application to her business, she had been in a good degree preserved from the blighting and dehumanizing effects of slavery. I was utterly astonished at her goodness. I scarcely knew how to behave towards her. She was entirely unlike any other white woman I had ever seen. I could not approach her as I was accustomed to approach other white ladies. My early instruction was all out of place. The crouching servility, usually so acceptable a quality in a slave, did not answer when manifested toward her. Her favor was not gained by it; she seemed to be disturbed by it. She did not deem it impudent or unmannerly for a slave to look her in the face. The meanest slave was put fully at ease in her presence, and none left without feeling better for having seen her. Her face was made of heavenly smiles, and her voice of tranquil music.

But, alas! this kind heart had but a short time to remain such. The fatal poison of irresponsible power was already in her hands, and soon commenced its infernal work. That cheerful eye, under the influence of slavery, soon became red with rage; that voice, made all of sweet accord, changed to one of harsh and horrid discord; and that angelic face gave place to that of a demon. Very soon after I went to live with Mr. and Mrs. Auld, she very kindly commenced to teach me the A, B, C. After I had learned this, she assisted me in learning to spell words of three or four letters. Just at this point of my progress, Mr. Auld found out what was going on, and at once forbade Mrs. Auld to instruct me further, telling her, among other things, that it was unlawful, as well as unsafe, to teach a slave to read. To use his own words, further, he said, "If you give a nigger an inch, he will take an ell. A nigger should know nothing but to obey his master — to do as he is told to do. Learning would spoil the best nigger in the world. Now," said he, "if you teach that nigger (speaking of myself) how to read, there would be no keeping him. It would forever unfit him to be a slave. He would at once become unmanageable, and of no value to his master. As to himself, it could do him no good, but a great deal of harm. It would make him discontented and unhappy." These words sank deep into my heart, stirred up sentiments within that lay slumbering, and called into existence an entirely new train of thought. It was a new and special revelation, explaining dark and mysterious things, with which my youthful understanding had struggled, but struggled in vain. I now understood what had been to me a most perplexing difficulty — to wit, the white man's power to enslave the black man. It was a grand achievement, and I prized it highly. From that moment, I understood the pathway from slavery to freedom. It was just what I wanted, and I got it at a time when I the least expected it. Whilst I was saddened by the thought of losing the aid of my kind mistress, I was gladdened by the invaluable instruction which, by the merest accident, I had gained from my master. Though conscious of the difficulty of learning without a teacher, I set out with high hope, and a fixed purpose, at whatever cost of trouble, to learn how to read. The very decided manner with which he spoke, and strove to impress his wife with the evil consequences of giving me instruction, served to convince me that he was deeply sensible of the truths he was uttering. It gave me the best assurance that I might rely with the utmost confidence on the results which, he said, would flow from teaching me to read. What he most dreaded, that I most desired. What he most loved, that I most hated. That which to him was a great evil, to be carefully shunned, was to me a great good, to be diligently sought; and the argument which he so warmly urged, against my learning to read, only served to inspire me with a desire and determination to learn. In learning to read, I owe almost as much to the bitter opposition of my master, as to the kindly aid of my mistress. I acknowledge the benefit of both.

I had resided but a short time in Baltimore before I observed a marked difference, in the treatment of slaves, from that which I had witnessed in the country. A city slave is almost a freeman, compared with a slave on the plantation. He is much better fed and clothed, and enjoys privileges altogether unknown to the slave on the plantation. There is a vestige of decency, a sense of shame, that does much to curb and check those outbreaks of atrocious cruelty so commonly enacted upon the plantation. He is a desperate slaveholder, who will shock the humanity of his non-slaveholding neighbors with the cries of his lacerated slave. Few are willing to incur the odium attaching to the reputation of being a cruel master; and above all things, they would not be known as not giving a slave enough to eat. Every city slaveholder is anxious to have it known of him, that he feeds his slaves well; and it is due to them to say, that most of them do give their slaves enough to eat. There are, however, some painful exceptions to this rule. Directly opposite to us, on Philpot Street, lived Mr. Thomas Hamilton. He owned two slaves. Their names were Henrietta and Mary. Henrietta was about twenty-two years of age, Mary was about fourteen; and of all the mangled and emaciated creatures I ever looked upon, these two were the most so. His heart must be harder than stone, that could look upon these unmoved. The head, neck, and shoulders of Mary were literally cut to pieces. I have frequently felt her head, and found it nearly covered with festering sores, caused by the lash of her cruel mistress. I do not know that her master ever whipped her, but I have been an eye-witness to the cruelty of Mrs. Hamilton. I used to be in Mr. Hamilton's house nearly every day. Mrs. Hamilton used to sit in a large chair in the middle of the room, with a heavy cowskin always by her side, and scarce an hour passed during the day but was marked by the blood of one of these slaves. The girls seldom passed her without her saying, "Move faster, you black gip!" at the same time giving them a blow with the cowskin over the head or shoulders, often drawing the blood. She would then say, "Take that, you black gip!" continuing, "If you don't move faster, I'll move you!" Added to the cruel lashings to which these slaves were subjected, they were kept nearly half-starved. They seldom knew what it was to eat a full meal. I have seen Mary contending with the pigs for the offal thrown into the street. So much was Mary kicked and cut to pieces, that she was oftener called "pecked" than by her name.

Chapter 7

I lived in Master Hugh's family about seven years. During this time, I succeeded in learning to read and write. In accomplishing this, I was compelled to resort to various stratagems. I had no regular teacher. My mistress, who had kindly commenced to instruct me, had, in compliance with the advice and direction of her husband, not only ceased to instruct, but had set her face against my being instructed by anyone else. It is due, however, to my mistress to say of her, that she did not adopt this course of treatment immediately. She at first lacked the depravity indispensable to shutting me up in mental darkness. It was at least necessary for her to have some training in the exercise of irresponsible power, to make her equal to the task of treating me as though I were a brute.

My mistress was, as I have said, a kind and tenderhearted woman; and in the simplicity of her soul she commenced, when I first went to live with her, to treat me as she supposed one human being ought to treat another. In entering upon the duties of a slaveholder, she did not seem to perceive that I sustained to her the relation of a mere chattel, and that for her to treat me as a human being was not only wrong, but dangerously so. Slavery proved as injurious to her as it did to me. When I went there, she was a pious, warm, and tenderhearted woman. There was no sorrow or suffering for which she had not a tear. She had bread for the hungry, clothes for the naked, and comfort for every mourner that came within her reach. Slavery soon proved its ability to divest her of these heavenly qualities. Under its influence, the tender heart became stone, and the lamblike disposition gave way to one of tiger-like fierceness. The first step in her downward course was in her ceasing to instruct me. She now commenced to practise her husband's precepts. She finally became even more violent in her opposition than her husband himself. She was not satisfied with simply doing as well as he had commanded; she seemed anxious to do better. Nothing seemed to make her more angry than to see me with a newspaper. She seemed to think that here lay the danger. I have had her rush at me with a face made all up of fury, and snatch from me a newspaper, in a manner that fully revealed her apprehension. She was an apt woman; and a little experience soon demonstrated, to her satisfaction, that education and slavery were incompatible with each other.

From this time I was most narrowly watched. If I was in a separate room any considerable length of time, I was sure to be suspected of having a book, and was at once called to give an account of myself. All this, however, was too late. The first step had been taken. Mistress, in teaching me the alphabet, had given me the inch, and no precaution could prevent me from taking the hell. The plan which I adopted, and the one by which I was most successful, was that of making friends of all the little white boys whom I met in the street. As many of these as I could, I converted into teachers. With their kindly aid, obtained at different times and in different places, I finally succeeded in learning to read. When I was sent of errands, I always took my book with me, and by going one part of my errand quickly, I found time to get a lesson before my return. I used also to carry bread with me, enough of which was always in the house, and to which I was always welcome; for I was much better off in this regard than many of the poor white children in our neighborhood. This bread I used to bestow upon the hungry little urchins, who, in return, would give me that more valuable bread of knowledge. I am strongly tempted to give the names of two or three of those little boys, as a testimonial of the gratitude and affection I bear them; but prudence forbids；— not that it would injure me，but it might embarrass them；for it is almost an unpardonable of fence to teach slaves to read in this Christian country. It is enough to say of the dear little fellows，that they lived on Philpot Street，very near Durgin and Bailey's ship-yard. I used to talk this matter of slavery over with them. I would sometimes say to them，I wished I could be as free as they would be when they got to be men. "You will be free as soon as you are twenty-one，but I am a slave for life！ Have not I as good a right to be free as you have？" These words used to trouble them；they would express for me the liveliest sympathy，and console me with the hope that something would occur by which I might be free.

I was now about twelve years old，and the thought of being a slave for life began to bear heavily upon my heart. Just about this time，I got hold of a book entitled "The Columbian Orator." Every opportunity I got，I used to read this book. Among much of other interesting matter，I found in it a dialogue between a master and his slave. The slave was represented as having run away from his master three times. The dialogue represented the conversation which took place between them，when the slave was retaken the third time. In this dialogue，the whole argument in behalf of slavery was brought forward by the master，all of which was disposed of by the slave. The slave was made to say some very smart as well as impressive things in reply to his master — things which had the desired though unexpected effect；for the conversation resulted in the voluntary emancipation of the slave on the part of the master.

In the same book，I met with one of Sheridan's mighty speeches on and in behalf of Catholic emancipation. These were choice documents to me. I read them over and over again with unabated interest. They gave tongue to interesting thoughts of my own soul，which had frequently flashed through my mind，and died away for want of utterance. The moral which I gained from the dialogue was the power of truth over the conscience of even a slaveholder. What I got from Sheridan was a bold denunciation of slavery，and a powerful vindication of human rights. The reading of these documents enabled me to utter my thoughts，and to meet the arguments brought forward to sustain slavery；but while they relieved me of one difficulty，they brought on another even more painful than the one of which I was relieved. The more I read，the more I was led to abhor and detest my enslavers. I could regard them in no other light than a band of successful robbers，who had left their homes，and gone to Africa，and stolen us from our homes，and in a strange land reduced us to slavery. I loathed them as being the meanest as well as the most wicked of men. As I read and contemplated the subject，behold！ that very discontentment which Master Hugh had predicted would follow my learning to read had already come，to torment and sting my soul to unutterable anguish. As I writhed under it，I would at times feel that learning to read had been a curse rather than a blessing. It had given me a view of my wretched condition，without the remedy. It opened my eyes to the horrible pit，but to no ladder upon which to get out. In moments of agony，I envied my fellow-slaves for their stupidity. I have often wished myself a beast. I preferred the condition of the meanest reptile to my own. Anything，no matter what，to get rid of thinking！ It was this everlasting thinking of my condition that tormented me. There was no getting rid of it. It was pressed upon me by every object within sight or hearing, animate or inanimate. The silver trump of freedom had roused my soul to eternal wakefulness. Freedom now appeared, to disappear no more forever. It was heard in every sound, and seen in everything. It was ever present to torment me with a sense of my wretched condition. I saw nothing without seeing it, I heard nothing without hearing it, and felt nothing without feeling it. It looked from every star, it smiled in every calm, breathed in every wind, and moved in every storm.

Chapter 10

I had left Master Thomas's house, and went to live with Mr. Covey, on the 1st of January, 1833. I was now, for the first time in my life, a field hand. In my new employment, I found myself even more awkward than a country boy appeared to be in a large city. I had been at my new home but one week before Mr. Covey gave me a very severe whipping, cutting my back, causing the blood to run, and raising ridges on my flesh as large as my little finger. The details of this affair are as follows: Mr. Covey sent me, very early in the morning of one of our coldest days in the month of January, to the woods, to get a load of wood. He gave me a team of unbroken oxen. He told me which was the in-hand ox, and which the off-hand one. He then tied the end of a large rope around the horns of the in-hand ox, and gave me the other end of it, and told me, if the oxen started to run, that I must hold on upon the rope. I had never driven oxen before, and of course I was very awkward. I, however, succeeded in getting to the edge of the woods with little difficulty; but I had got a very few rods into the woods, when the oxen took fright, and started full tilt, carrying the cart against trees, and over stumps, in the most frightful manner. I expected every moment that my brains would be dashed out against the trees. After running thus for a considerable distance, they finally upset the cart, dashing it with great force against a tree, and threw themselves into a dense thicket. How I escaped death, I do not know. There I was, entirely alone, in a thick wood, in a place new to me. My cart was upset and shattered, my oxen were entangled among the young trees, and there was none to help me. After a long spell of effort, I succeeded in getting my cart righted, my oxen disentangled, and again yoked to the cart. I now proceeded with my team to the place where I had, the day before, been chopping wood, and loaded my cart pretty heavily, thinking in this way to tame my oxen. I then proceeded on my way home. I had now consumed one half of the day. I got out of the woods safely, and now felt out of danger. I stopped my oxen to open the woods gate; and just as I did so, before I could get hold of my ox-rope, the oxen again started, rushed through the gate, catching it between the wheel and the body of the cart, tearing it to pieces, and coming within a few inches of crushing me against the gate-post. Thus twice, in one short day, I escaped death by the merest chance. On my return, I told Mr. Covey what had happened, and how it happened. He ordered me to return to the woods again immediately. I did so, and he followed on after me. Just as I got into the woods, he came up and told me to stop my cart, and that he would teach me how to trifle away my time, and break gates. He then went to a large gum-tree, and with his axe cut three large switches, and, after trimming them up neatly with his pocketknife, he ordered me to take off my clothes. I made him no answer, but stood with my clothes on. He repeated his order. I still made him no answer, nor did I move to strip myself. Upon this he rushed at me with the fierceness of a tiger, tore off my clothes, and lashed me till he had worn out his switches, cutting me so savagely as to leave the marks visible for a long time after. This whipping was the first of a number just like it, and for similar offences.

I lived with Mr. Covey one year. During the first six months, of that year, scarce a week passed without his whipping me. I was seldom free from a sore back. My awkwardness was almost always his excuse for whipping me. We were worked fully up to the point of endurance. Long before day we were up, our horses fed, and by the first approach of day we were off to the field with our hoes and ploughing teams. Mr. Covey gave us enough to eat, but scarce time to eat it. We were often less than five minutes taking our meals. We were often in the field from the first approach of day till its last lingering ray had left us; and at saving-fodder time, midnight often caught us in the field binding blades.

Covey would be out with us. The way he used to stand it, was this. He would spend the most of his afternoons in bed. He would then come out fresh in the evening, ready to urge us on with his words, example, and frequently with the whip. Mr. Covey was one of the few slaveholders who could and did work with his hands. He was a hard-working man. He knew by himself just what a man or a boy could do. There was no deceiving him. His work went on in his absence almost as well as in his presence; and he had the faculty of making us feel that he was ever present with us. This he did by surprising us. He seldom approached the spot where we were at work openly, if he could do it secretly. He always aimed at taking us by surprise. Such was his cunning, that we used to call him, among ourselves, "the snake." When we were at work in the cornfield, he would sometimes crawl on his hands and knees to avoid detection, and all at once he would rise nearly in our midst, and scream out, "Ha, ha! Come, come! Dash on, dash on!" This being his mode of attack, it was never safe to stop a single minute. His comings were like a thief in the night. He appeared to us as being ever at hand. He was under every tree, behind every stump, in every bush, and at every window, on the plantation. He would sometimes mount his horse, as if bound to St. Michael's, a distance of seven miles, and in half an hour afterwards you would see him coiled up in the corner of the wood-fence, watching every motion of the slaves. He would, for this purpose, leave his horse tied up in the woods. Again, he would sometimes walk up to us, and give us orders as though he was upon the point of starting on a long journey, turn his back upon us, and make as though he was going to the house to get ready; and, before he would get half way thither, he would turn short and crawl into a fencecorner, or behind some tree, and there watch us till the going down of the sun.

Mr. Covey's FORTE consisted in his power to deceive. His life was devoted to planning and perpetrating the grossest deceptions. Everything he possessed in the shape of learning or religion, he made conform to his disposition to deceive. He seemed to think himself equal to deceiving the Almighty. He would make a short prayer in the morning, and a long prayer at night; and, strange as it may seem, few men would at times appear more devotional than he. The exercises of his family devotions were always commenced with singing; and, as he was a very poor singer himself, the duty of raising the hymn generally came upon me. He would read his hymn, and nod at me to commence. I would at times do so; at others, I would not. My non-compliance would almost always produce much confusion. To show himself independent of me, he would start and stagger through with his hymn in the most discordant manner. In this state of mind, he prayed with more than ordinary spirit. Poor man! such was his disposition, and success at deceiving, I do verily believe that he sometimes deceived himself into the solemn belief, that he was a sincere worshipper of the most high God; and this, too, at a time when he may be said to have been guilty of compelling his woman slave to commit the sin of adultery. The facts in the case are these: Mr. Covey was a poor man; he was just commencing in life; he was only able to buy one slave; and, shocking as is the fact, he bought her, as he said, for A BREEDER. This woman was named Caroline. Mr. Covey bought her from Mr. Thomas Lowe, about six miles from St. Michael's. She was a large, able-bodied woman, about twenty years old. She had already given birth to one child, which proved her to be just what he wanted. After buying her, he hired a married man of Mr. Samuel Harrison, to live with him one year; and him he used to fasten up with her every night! The result was, that, at the end of the year, the miserable woman gave birth to twins. At this result Mr. Covey seemed to be highly pleased, both with the man and the wretched woman. Such was his joy, and that of his wife, that nothing they could do for Caroline during her confinement was too good, or too hard, to be done. The children were regarded as being quite an addition to his wealth.

选文评析:

从道格拉斯的自述来看，他最初在主人安东尼船长的种植园里的生活并不像其他大多数奴隶那样艰难。作为一个孩子，他在主人家里而不是在地里服务，属于家庭侍仆而不是田间苦力。7 岁时，他被安东尼船长转给其女婿的弟弟休·奥尔德，后者住在巴尔的摩。在巴尔的摩，道格拉斯也过着比较自由的生活，因为相对来说，城市奴隶主更注意自己在他人面前的形象，尽可能避免被认为是残忍之徒。休的妻子索菲亚最初"是一个心地最善良、感情最美好的女人"，"没有什么悲伤和痛苦不会让她流下眼泪。她为饥饿的人准备面包，为赤身露体的人准备衣服，为她所能及的每一个哀悼者提供慰藉"。在结婚之前，她并不依赖剥削奴隶生活，而是一直靠自己的双手，以织布为业，由此她的善良天性得以"免受蓄奴制度的摧残和非人化的影响"。道格拉斯声称"她和我见过的其他白人女人完全不同"，"最卑鄙的奴隶在她面前也能感到十分自在，没有人离开时不为见到她而感到高兴"，"她的脸上洋溢着天使般的微笑。我的女主人是一个善良而温柔的女人"。道格拉斯刚到的时候，她从不会把他当奴隶虐待，而是"像她认为一个人应该对待另一个人一样对待我"。然而就像道格拉斯逐渐认识到的那样，蓄奴制度的邪恶之处就在于，它不但会让奴隶生活在严酷的受剥削环境下，也会让奴隶主丧失人性，从富有同情心的正常人变成残忍无情的剥削者。在蓄奴制度的影响下，善良美丽的索菲亚很快也变得性格扭曲，"那愉快的眼睛很快就因愤怒而变红了；那悦耳和谐的声音变成了刺耳可怕的不和谐音；那天使般的脸变成了魔鬼的脸"。"蓄奴制度很快证明了它有能力剥夺她这些神圣的品质。在它的影响下，温柔的心变成了石头，羔羊般的性情让位于老虎般的凶猛。"起初，道格拉斯刚到的时候，她还很友好地开始教他识字。但后来在丈夫奥尔德的警告和阻止下，她也很快像丈夫一样明白了，"教奴隶读书是违法的，也是不安全的……一个黑鬼应该什么都不知道，只要按照主人的命令去做。学习会毁掉世界上最好的黑奴"。于是她立即停止对道格拉斯的文化教育，甚至变得比丈夫更加暴力。"她不满足于仅仅按照他吩咐的去做；她似乎急于做得更好。没什么比看到我拿着报纸更让她生气了。"

道格拉斯通过这些叙述揭示出，让黑奴保持蒙昧无知和麻木无情恰恰是白人奴隶主延续对奴隶进行控制的有效策略。在19世纪之前，许多支持蓄奴制的种族主义分子认为奴隶制是一种自古以来就自然存在的状态。他们认为，黑人天生就没有能力参与公民社会，他们麻木无知，缺少正常社会公民应该具有的智力和情感，因此应该作为白人的工人和仆人来服务。为了保持这种长久的控制，奴隶主从一开始就有意让奴隶不知道自己的基本情况，如出生日期或父子关系。就像道格拉斯在第一章开头部分所叙述的：

> 我对自己的年龄一无所知，从未看过任何真实的记录。到目前为止，大部分奴隶对他们的年龄所知甚少，正如马匹对它们自己的年龄一无所知一样，我所知的大多数主人都希望让他们的奴隶如此无知……即使在我的童年，对我自己的信息缺乏也是一个不快乐的来源。白人孩子们能说出他们的年龄。我不知道为什么我应该被剥夺同样的特权。

家庭成长环境的缺失还导致他们被剥夺了正常的情感发育能力，"我和妈妈在我还是个婴儿的时候就分开了……在我离家出走的马里兰州，在很小的时候就把孩子和母亲分开是一种普遍的习俗。……我不知道这种分离是怎么回事，除非它会妨碍孩子对母亲感情的发展，削弱和破坏母亲对孩子的自然感情。这是必然的结果"。这种强迫的无知和无情剥夺了黑奴从小对个人身份的自然感觉，以及与他人的共情能力。随着黑奴儿童年龄的增长，奴隶主又会拒绝给他们提供文化教育，因为识字会让他们逐渐开悟，他们会越来越不满足于仅仅获得基本的衣着和食物，还会渴望获得自由和尊严，进而会对蓄奴制的合理性产生怀疑。这无疑会对白人地位造成严重威胁。

道格拉斯正是通过学习文化，逐渐对自己的处境有了更清醒、深刻的认识。"我读得越多，我就越憎恶那些奴役我的人……我厌恶他们，认为他们是最卑鄙和最邪恶的人。"他不再像早期奴隶叙述的作者布里顿·哈蒙那样，仅满足于找一位相对仁慈的白人主人，从那里获得一些吃穿保障，而是对摆脱奴隶制、获得自由身份产生了巨大的渴望。"我现在明白了……从那一刻起，我明白了从蓄奴制到自由的道路。"而知识也正是通往真正解放的唯一道路，因为它可以让黑奴获得真正的力量。所以道格拉斯才决心"不惜一切代价，去学习如何阅读"。奥尔德夫妇越是拒绝让他读书识字，越是说明学习文化的重要性，也就越激励了他学习的欲望和决心，因为越是让他们感到害怕的东西必定越蕴含巨大力量。

不过，尽管索菲亚和奥尔德夫妇对他日渐残酷，道格拉斯仍然想尽一切办法通过自学学会了读书写字，他越来越意识到蓄奴制的罪恶，并下决心逃往北方。当道格拉斯的主人安东尼船长和他剩下的继承人都先后去世后，道格拉斯的命运发生了重大转折。他先是被带回去，为安东尼船长的女婿、卑鄙虚伪的托马斯·奥尔德服务，后又被转租给了爱德华·科维，后者因为经常残酷虐待奴隶而臭名昭著。因不堪忍受科维的折磨，道格拉斯最终奋起反抗，使得科维再也不敢轻易招惹道格拉斯，也为自己赢来相对自主的工作时间和活动自由。他通过不断积蓄力量和秘密筹划，最后逃到了纽约，并最终成为一名废奴主义作家和演说家。

本书节选的第十章有关白人监工爱德华·科维的叙述片段也十分精彩。作为道格拉斯的死敌，科维堪称道格拉斯的整部叙述中最坏的人物。他是一个典型的恶棍，似乎天生邪恶，对待奴隶手段残忍且十分狡诈。他不但经常对黑奴进行各种残酷体罚，还更擅长对他们进行心理虐待。当其他种植园的黑奴们通常可以耍一些花招来蒙混他们的奴隶主和监工时，科维却用非常奸诈的伎俩让黑奴对他胆战心惊。道格拉斯生动叙述了科维用来对付黑奴的狡猾手段：

> 谁也骗不了他。无论他在不在场，他都有办法把工作做得很好。他有办法使我们觉得他始终没离开我们身边。他通过吓唬我们来做到这一点。如果他能神不知鬼不觉地来到我们工作场合的话，他就很少会大模大样地过来。他总是想让我们猝不及防。他就是这样狡诈，故而我们常常背地里称他是一条蛇。当我们在玉米地里干活的时候，他会用手和膝盖爬行，以免被我们察觉，然后他就会突然之间出现在我们中间，并且伴着一声大喊："哈，哈！来吧，来吧！快跑，快跑！"他总是这样突然袭击，让我们片刻也不敢停下来偷懒。他就像夜间的小偷，来去无踪。在我们看来，他一直就在我们身边。他在每一棵树下，在每一个树桩后面，在每一个灌木丛里，在每一个窗口，在种植园里。他有时会骑上他的马，好像是要前往圣迈克尔家一样，距离七英里，半小时后你会看到他蜷缩在木栅栏的角落里，注视着奴隶们的一举一动。为此，他会把马拴在树林里。他有时也会走到我们跟前，命令我们，好像他要开始一段漫长的旅程似的，背对着我们，假装他要到房子里去准备；在他走到半路之前，他会变矮，爬到篱笆角，或是某棵树后面，看着我们直到太阳下山。

杰克·泰勒曾指出，白人凝视就是福柯所说的那种"带有生命政治内涵的规训技术"，其目的就是建构起一种"种植园模式的政治服从"①。而道格拉斯在此所描写的这段场景堪称种植园模式的监视的原型场景，也是福柯所谓"全景敞视监狱"的另一种表现。它就

---

① Jack Taylor, "The Political Subjection of Bigger Thomas：The Gaze, Biopolitics, and The Court of Law in Richard Right's *Native Son*". *CR：The New Centennial Review*，2016，16(2)：198.

是要让黑奴彻底没有安全感，每时每刻都感受到无处不在但又不确定如何发生的威胁，进而把白人监工的眼光内化到心里，似乎他们永远处于白人的视觉包围下，身边有无数双眼睛在盯着他们，提醒他们要规规矩矩行事。

推荐阅读文献：

Barnes, L. Diane. *Frederick Douglass：Reformer and Statesman*. Taylor & Francis Group, 2012.

Boxill, Bernard R. Frederick Douglass's Patriotism. *The Journal of Ethics*, 2009, 13(4)：301-317.

Dilbeck, D. H. *Frederick Douglass：America's Prophet*. The U of North Carolina P, 2018.

Douglass, Frederick and McKivigan, John R. *The Speeches of Frederick Douglass：A Critical Edition*. Yale UP, 2018.

Lampe, Gregory P. *Frederick Douglass：Freedom's Voice*, 1818-1845. Michigan State UP, 1998.

Levine, Robert S. Frederick Douglass, War, Haiti. *PMLA*, 2009, 124(5)：1864-1868.

Martin Jr., Waldo E. *Mind of Frederick Douglass*. The U of North Carolina P, 1985.

McKivigan, John R. Introduction：Rediscovering the Life and Times of Frederic Douglass. *The Journal of African American History*, 2014, 99(1-2)：4-11.

Ramsey, William M. Frederick Douglass, Southerner. *The Southern Literary Journal*, 2007, 40(1)：19-38.

Roberts, Neil and Myers, Peter C. *A Political Companion to Frederick Douglass*. UP of Kentucky, 2018.

第四章　马丁·罗宾逊·德拉尼
（Martin Robison Delany，1812—1885）

马丁·罗宾逊·德拉尼是美国 19
世纪极具影响力的一位废奴主义者。
他出生在西弗吉尼亚州，其父亲是奴
隶，母亲是自由黑人，祖父母均是奴
隶贸易的受害者，从非洲故土被贩卖
到美国为奴。据其家族历史记录，德
拉尼的外祖父是西非曼丁果部落的王
子，母亲正是由于这一缘故得以赎回
自由，因此德拉尼也是自由黑人。由
于德拉尼的母亲雇佣一名北方商贩教
孩子们读书识字，在被邻居发现并举

报之后，德拉尼一家逃到宾夕法尼亚州的匹兹堡，德拉尼在这里进入非洲圣公会夜校学
习，并跟从一名医生学医，同时还在匹兹堡废奴组织工作。1843 年，德拉尼开始发行周
报《秘密》(*The Mystery*)，并很快得到弗雷德里克·道格拉斯的邀约，成为刊物《北极星》
(*The North Star*)的联合编辑。1850 年，德拉尼被哈佛大学医学院录取，成为该校第一批
非裔学生之一。然而，白人学生的抗议和校方的压力迫使他在一个学期之后退学。德拉尼
在这一打击之后重返匹兹堡，他在愤怒之余，重新思考了种族融合的意义和价值，并决定
投身非裔移民事业。

此后，德拉尼陆续发表了《关于美国有色人种的生存条件、种族提升、移民和命运的
政治思考》(*The Condition，Elevation，Emigration and Destiny of the Colored People of the United
States Politically Considered*)和《古代共济会的起源和目标：在美国的引入以及在有色人种
中的合法性》(*The Origin and Objects of Ancient Freemasonry：Its Introduction into the United
States and Legitimacy Among Colored Men*)等著作，之后举家搬迁到加拿大安大略省。他的
核心主张是建立黑人的"国中国"，主要包括黑人自决、黑人移民、全球黑人联盟等内容。
1859 年，德拉尼到非洲调查实现黑人移民的可能性，并到尼日利亚去谈判，但并未获得
成功。在美国内战期间，德拉尼站在北方联邦政府一方，他对种族融合重拾信心，亲自前
往新英格兰和中西部地区招募黑人军队支持北军，并在战争结束后参与南方重建，在南卡
罗来纳州多个政府岗位任职。1877 年，德拉尼成立了利比里亚联合股份轮船公司，试图

为美国黑人移民非洲提供帮助。1879 年，他出版了《民族学原理：种族和肤色的起源——基于考古纲要、埃及文明以及多年的调查》（*Principia of Ethnology：The Origin of Races and Color*，*with an Archeological Compendium and Egyptian Civilization*，*from Years of Careful Examination and Enquiry*），详细阐明了非裔的文化成就，体现了强烈的种族自豪感。1880 年，德拉尼回到俄亥俄州度过晚年。在南方重建、种族融合的幻想破灭之后，他依然对黑人移民事业抱有期待。

德拉尼一生中多次改变自己的政治主张，从支持种族融合到黑人自治，再到南北战争时期支持北方军队、支持种族融合，晚年倾向于黑人移民非洲的社会运动。以下选文出自《关于美国有色人种的生存条件、种族提升、移民和命运的政治思考》，这是德拉尼最有影响力，也是最有争议的一部著作。这部专著发表于 1892 年，当时正是废奴主义者和奴隶制支持者两股力量激烈争锋的时期。这部作品被认为是黑人民族主义的早期文献之一，阐述了黑人自治思想，是种族分离主义的代表作品。

📖 作品选读：

The Condition, Elevation, Emigration and Destiny of the Colored People of the United States Politically Considered

Chapter 3　American Colonization

When we speak of colonization, we wish distinctly to be understood as speaking of the "American Colonization Society" — or that which is under its influence — commenced in Richmond, Virginia, in 1817, under the influence of Mr. Henry Clay of Ky., Judge Bushrod Washington of Va.,[①] and other Southern slaveholders, having for their express object, as their speeches and doings all justify us in asserting in good faith, the removal of the free colored people from the land of their birth, for the security of the slaves, as property to the slave propagandists.

This scheme had no sooner been propagated than the old and leading colored men of Philadelphia, Pa., with Richard Allen, James Forten, and others at their head, true to their trust and the cause of their brethren, summoned the colored people together, and then and there, in language and with voices pointed and loud, protested against the scheme as an outrage, having no

---

① 亨利·克雷（Henry Clay，1777—1852）：美国政治家，曾任国会议员、参议院议长和国务卿；布什罗德·华盛顿法官（Judge Bushrod Washington，1762—1829）：曾任美国最高法院助理法官，是乔治·华盛顿的侄子。

other object in view than the benefit of the slave-holding interests of the country, and that as freemen, they would never prove recreant to the cause of their brethren in bondage by leaving them without hope of redemption from their chains. This determination of the colored patriots of Philadelphia was published in full, authentically, and circulated throughout the length and breadth of the country by the papers of the day. The colored people everywhere received the news, and at once endorsed with heart and soul the doings of the Anti-Colonization Meeting of colored freemen. From that time forth, the colored people generally have had no sympathy with the colonization scheme, nor confidence in its leaders, looking upon them all as arrant hypocrites seeking every opportunity to deceive them. In a word, the monster was crippled in its infancy, and has never as yet recovered from the stroke. It is true that, like its ancient sire, which was "more subtle than all the beasts of the field," it has inherited a large portion of his most prominent characteristic — an idiosyncrasy of the animal that enables him to entwine himself into the greater part of the Church and other institutions of the country, and, having once entered there, leave his venom, which puts such a spell on the conductors of those institutions, that is only on condition that a colored person consents to go to the neighborhood of his kindred brother monster the boa, that he may find admission in the one or the other. We look upon the American Colonization Society as one of the most arrant enemies of the colored man, ever seeking to discomfit him, and envying him of every privilege that he may enjoy. We believe it to be anti-Christian in its character, and misanthropic in its pretended sympathies. Because if this were not the case, men could not be found professing morality and Christianity — as to our astonishment we have found them — who unhesitatingly say, "I know it is right" — that is, in itself — "to do" so and so, "and I am willing and ready to do it, but only on condition that you go to Africa." Indeed, a highly talented clergyman informed us in November last (three months ago), in the city of Philadelphia, that he was present when the Rev. Doctor J. P. Durbin, late President of Dickinson College, called on Rev. Mr. P. or B. to consult him about going to Liberia to take charge of the literary department of a University in contemplation, when the following conversation ensued: Mr. P. — "Doctor, I have as much and more than I can do here in educating the youth of our own country and preparing them for usefulness here at home." Dr. D. — "Yes, but do as you may, you can never be elevated here." Mr. P. — "Doctor, do you not believe that the religion of our blessed Redeemer Jesus Christ has morality, humanity, philanthropy, and justice enough in it to elevate us and enable us to obtain our rights in this our own country?" Dr. D. — "No, indeed, sir, I do not, and if you depend upon that, your hopes are vain!" Mr. P. — Turning to Doctor Durbin, looking him solemnly, though affectionately, in the face, remarked — "Well, Doctor Durbin, we both profess to be ministers of Christ; but dearly as I love the cause of my Redeemer, if for a moment I could entertain the opinion you do about Christianity, I would not serve him another hour!" We do not know, as we were not advised, that the Rev. Doctor added, in fine, "Well, you may quit now, for all your serving him will not avail against the power of the god (hydra) of Colonization." Will anyone doubt for a single moment the justice of our strictures on colonization, after reading the conversation between the Rev. Dr. Durbin and the colored clergyman? Surely not. We can therefore make no account of it, but that of setting it down as being the worst enemy of the colored people.

Recently, there has been a strained effort in the city of New York on the part of the Rev. J. B. Pinney and others of the leading white Colonizationists, to get up a movement among some poor pitiable colored men — we say pitiable, for certainly the colored persons who are at this period capable of loaning themselves to the enemies of their race, against the best interest of all that we hold sacred to that race, are pitiable in the lowest extreme, far beneath the dignity of an enemy, and therefore, we pass them by with the simple remark that this is the hobby that colonization is riding all over the country, as the "tremendous" access of colored people to their cause within the last twelve months. We should make another remark here perhaps, in justification of governor Pinney's New York allies — that is, report says that in the short space of some three or five months, one of his confidants benefited himself to the "reckoning" of from eleven to fifteen hundred dollars, or "such a matter," while others were benefited in sums "pretty considerable" but of a less "reckoning." Well, we do not know, after all, that they may not have quite as good a right to pocket part of the spoils of this "grab game" as anybody else. However, they are of little consequence, as the ever watchful eye of those excellent gentlemen and faithful guardians of their people's rights — the Committee of Thirteen, consisting of Messrs. John J. Zuille, Chairman, T. Joiner White, Philip A. Bell, Secretaries, Robert Hamilton, George T. Downing, Jeremiah Powers, John T. Raymond, Wm. Burnett, James McCune Smith, Ezekiel Dias, Junius C. Morel, Thomas Downing, and Wm. J. Wilson, — have properly chastised this pet-slave of Mr. Pinney, and made it "know its place" by keeping within the bounds of its master's enclosure.

In expressing our honest conviction of the designedly injurious character of the Colonization Society, we should do violence to our own sense of individual justice if we did not express the belief that there are some honest-hearted men, who not having seen things in the proper light, favor that scheme, simply as a means of elevating the colored people. Such persons, so soon as they become convinced of their error, immediately change their policy, and advocate the elevation of the colored people, any-where and everywhere, in common with other men. Of such were the early abolitionists as before stated; and the great and good Dr. F. J. Lemoyne,[①] Gerrit Smith,[②] and Rev. Charles Avery,[③] and a host of others, who were Colonizationists before espousing the cause of our elevation here at home, and nothing but an honorable sense of justice induces us to make these exceptions, as there are many good persons within our knowledge, whom we believe to

---

① 弗朗西斯·朱利叶斯·勒莫因（Francis Julius LeMoyne，1798—1879）：宾夕法尼亚州慈善家、医生和地下铁路售票员。

② 盖瑞特·史密斯（Gerrit Smith，1797—1874）：美国政治家、激进废奴主义者。

③ 查尔斯·艾弗里牧师（Rev. Charles Avery，1784—1858）：匹兹堡商人、废奴主义者、卫理公会牧师。

be well-wishers of the colored people, who may favor colonization. But the animal itself is the same "hydra-headed monster," let whomsoever may fancy to pet it. A serpent is a serpent, and none the less a viper because nestled in the bosom of an honest-hearted man. This the colored people must bear in mind, and keep clear of the hideous thing, lest its venom may be tested upon them. But why deem any argument necessary to show the unrighteousness of colonization? Its very origin, as before shown — the source from whence it sprung being the offspring of slavery — is in itself sufficient to blast it in the estimation of every colored person in the United States who has sufficient intelligence to comprehend it.

We dismiss this part of the subject, and proceed to consider the mode and means of our elevation in the United States.

Chapter 4　Our Elevation in the United States

That very little comparatively as yet has been done to attain a respectable position as a class in this country will not be denied, and that the successful accomplishments of this end is also possible must also be admitted; but in what manner, and by what means has long been, and is even now, by the best thinking mind among the colored people themselves, a matter of difference of opinion.

We believe in the universal equality of man, and believe in that declaration of God's word in which it is there positively said that "God has made of one blood all the nations that dwell on the face of the earth." Now of "the nations that dwell on the face of the earth," that is, all the people, there are one thousand millions of souls, and of this vast number of human beings, two thirds are colored, from black tending in complexion to the olive, or that of the Chinese with all the intermediate and admixtures of black and white, with the various "crosses" as they are physiologically, but erroneously termed, to white. We are thus explicit in stating these points because we are determined to be understood by all. We have then: two colored to one white person throughout the earth, and yet, singular as it may appear, according to the present geographical and political history of the world, the white race predominates over the colored; or in other words, wherever there is one white person, that one rules and governs two colored persons.

This is a living undeniable truth to which we call the especial attention of the colored reader in particular. Now there is cause for this, as there is no effect without a cause, a comprehensible remediable cause. We all believe in the justice of God, that he is impartial, "looking upon his children with an eye of care," dealing out to them all the measure of his goodness; yet, how can we reconcile ourselves to the difference that exists between the colored and the white races, as they truthfully present themselves before our eyes? To solve this problem is to know the remedy; and to know it is but necessary, in order successfully to apply it. And we shall but take the colored people of the United States, as a fair sample of the colored races everywhere of the present age, as the arguments that apply to the one will apply to the other, whether Christians,

Mahomedans or pagans.

The colored races are highly susceptible of religion, it is a constituent principle of their nature, and an excellent trait in their character. But unfortunately for them they carry it too far. Their hope is largely developed and consequently they usually stand still, hope in God, and really expect Him to do that for them which it is necessary they should do themselves. This is their great mistake, and arises from a misconception of the character and ways of Deity. We must know God, that is understand His Nature and purposes, in order to serve Him; and to serve Him well is but to know Him rightly. To depend for assistance upon God, is a duty and right, but to know when, how, and in what manner to obtain it, is the key to this great Bulwark of Strength, and Depository of Aid.

God himself is perfect; perfect in all his works and ways. He had means for every end; and every means used must be adequate to the end to be gained. God's means are laws, fixed laws of nature, a part of His own being, and as immutable, as unchangeable as Himself. Nothing can be accomplished but through the medium of, and conformable to these laws.

They are three, and like God himself, represented in the three persons in the Godhead, the Spiritual, Moral, and Physical Laws.

That which is Spiritual can only be accomplished through the medium of the Spiritual law; that which is Moral, through the medium of the Moral law; and that which is Physical, through the medium of Physical law. Otherwise than this, it is useless to expect anything. Should a person want a spiritual blessing, he must apply through the medium of the spiritual law: pray for it in order to obtain it. If they desire to do a moral good, they must apply through the medium of the moral law: exercise their sense and feeling of right and justice, in order to effect it. Do they want to attain a physical end, they can only do so through the medium of the physical law: go to work with muscles, hands, limbs, might, and strength and this, and nothing else will attain it.

The argument that man must pray for what he receives is a mistake, and one that is doing the colored people, especially, incalculable injury. That man must pray in order to get to Heaven every Christian will admit, but a great truth we have yet got to learn is that he can live on earth whether he is religious or not, so that he conforms to the great law of God, regulating the things of earth; the great physical laws. It is only necessary, in order to convince our people of their error and palpable mistake in this matter to call their attention to the fact that there are no people more religious in the Country, than the colored people, and none so poor and miserable as they. That prosperity and wealth smile upon the efforts of wicked white men, whom we know to utter the name of God with curses, instead of praises; that among the slaves, there are thousands of them religious, continually raising their voices, sending up their prayers to God, invoking His aid in their behalf, asking for a speedy deliverance; but they are still in chains, although they have thrice suffered out their three score years and ten. That "God send the rain upon the just and unjust," should be sufficient to convince us that our success in life does not depend upon our religious character, but that the physical laws governing all earthly and temporary affairs benefit equally the just and the unjust. Any other doctrine than this is downright delusion unworthy of a free people, and only intended for slaves. That all men and women should be moral, upright, good, and religious, (we mean Christians), we would not utter a word against, and could only wish that it were so; but, what we here desire to do is to correct the long standing error among a large body of the colored people in this country that the cause of our oppression and degradation is the displeasure of God towards us; because if God is just, and He is, there could be no justice in prospering white men with his fostering care, for more than two thousand years, in all their wickedness while dealing out to the colored people, the measure of his displeasure, for not half the wickedness as that of the whites. Here then is our mistake, and let it forever henceforth be corrected. We are no longer slaves, believing any interpretation that our oppressors may give the word of God, for the purpose of deluding us to the more easy subjugation; but freemen, comprising some of the first minds of intelligence and rudimental qualifications in the country. What then is the remedy for our degradation and oppression? This appears now to be the only remaining question, the means of successful elevation in this our own native land? This depends entirely upon the application of the means of Elevation.

Chapter 5   Means of Elevation

Moral theories have long been resorted to by us, as a means of effecting the redemption of our brethren in bonds, and the elevation of the free colored people in this country. Experience has taught us, that speculations are not enough; that the practical application of principles are not enough; that the thing carried out, is the only true and proper course to pursue.

We have speculated and moralized much about equality, claiming to be as good as our neighbors and everybody else, all of which, may do very well in ethics, but not in politics. We live in society among men, conducted by men, governed by rules and regulations. However arbitrary, there are certain policies that regulate all well-organized institutions and corporate bodies. We do not intend here to speak of the legal political relations of society, for those are treated on elsewhere. The business and social, or voluntary and mutual policies are those that now claim our attention. Society regulates itself, being governed by mind, which like water, finds its own level. "Like seeks like," is a principle in the laws of matter, as well as of mind. There is such a thing as inferiority of things, and positions; at least society has made them so, and while we continue to live among men, we must agree to all just measures, all those we mean that do not necessarily infringe on the rights of others. By the regulations of society, there is no equality of persons, where there is not an equality of attainments. By this, we do not wish to be understood as advocating the actual equal attainments of every individual; but we mean to say that, if these attainments be necessary for the elevation of the white man, they are necessary for the elevation of the colored man. That some colored men and women, in a like proportion to the whites, should be qualified in all the attainments possessed by them. It is one of the regulations of society the world over, and we shall have to conform to it, or be discarded as unworthy of the association of our fellows.

Cast our eyes about us and reflect for a moment, and what do we behold! Everything that presents to view gives evidence of the skill of the white man. Should we purchase a pound of groceries, a yard of linens, a vessel of crockery ware, a piece of furniture, the very provisions that we eat, all, all are the products of the white man, purchased by us from the white man. Consequently, our earnings and means are all given to the white man.

Pass along the avenues of any city or town in which you live, behold the trading shops, the manufactories, see the operations of the various machinery, see the stage coaches coming in, bringing the mails of intelligence, look at the railroads interlining every section, bearing upon them their mighty trains, flying with the velocity of the swallow, ushering in the hundreds of industrious, enterprising travelers. Cast again your eyes, widespread over the ocean, see the vessels in every direction, with their white sheets spread to the winds of heaven, freighted with the commerce, merchandise and wealth of many nations. Look as you pass along through the cities at the great and massive buildings, the beautiful and extensive structures of architecture, behold the ten thousand cupolas with their spires all reared up towards heaven, intersecting the territory of the clouds, all standing as mighty living monuments, of the industry, enterprise, and intelligence of the white man. And yet, with all these living truths, rebuking us with scorn, we strut about, place our hands akimbo, straighten up ourselves to our greatest height, and talk loudly about being "as good as anybody." How do we compare with them? Our fathers are their coachmen, our brothers their cookmen, and ourselves their waiting men. Our mothers their nurse women, our sisters their scrub women, our daughters their maid women, and our wives their washer women. Until colored men attain to a position above permitting their mothers, sisters, and wives and daughters, to do the drudgery and menial offices of other men's wives and daughters, it is useless, it is nonsense, it is pitiable mockery to talk about equality and elevation in society. The world is looking upon us with feelings of commiseration, sorrow, and contempt. We scarcely deserve sympathy, if we peremptorily refuse advice, bearing upon our elevation.

We will suppose a case for argument: In this city resides two colored families of three sons and three daughters each. At the head of each family, there is an old father and mother. The opportunities of these families, may or may not be the same for educational advantages, be that as it may, the children of the one go to school, and become qualified for the duties of life. One daughter becomes a school teacher, another a mantua-maker[①], and a third a fancy shop keeper; while one son becomes a farmer, another a merchant, and a third a mechanic. All enter into business with fine prospects, marry respectably, and settle in domestic comfort, while the six sons and daughters of the other family grow up without educational business qualifications and the highest aim they have is to apply to the sons and daughters of the first named family to hire for

---

① mantua-maker: "mantua"是一种宽松长袍。

domestics! Would there be an equality here between the children of these two families? Certainly not. This, then is precisely the position of the colored people generally in the United States, compared with the whites. What is necessary to be done in order to attain an equality, is to change the condition, and the person is at once changed. If, as before stated, a knowledge of all the various business enterprises, trades, professions, and sciences, is necessary for the elevation of the white, a knowledge of them also is necessary for the elevation of the colored man; and he cannot be elevated without them.

White men are producers; we are consumers. They build houses and we rent them. They raise produce, and we consume it. They manufacture clothes and wares, and we garnish ourselves with them. They build coaches, vessels, cars, hotels, saloons, and other vehicles and places of accommodation, and we deliberately wait until they have got them in readiness, then walk in, and contend with as much assurance for a "right," as though the whole thing was bought by, paid for, and belonged to us. By their literary attainments, they are the contributors to, authors of, and teachers of literature, science, religion, law, medicine, and all other useful attainments that the world now makes use of. We have no reference to ancient times, we speak of modern things.

These are the means by which God intended man to succeed: and this discloses the secret of the white man's success with all of his wickedness, over the head of the colored man with all of his religion. We have been pointed and plain on this part of the subject, because we desire our readers to see persons and things in their true position. Until we are determined to change the condition of things, and raise ourselves above the position in which we are now prostrated, we must hang our heads in sorrow, and hide our faces in shame. It is enough to know that these things are so; the causes we care little about and moralizing over all our life time. This we are weary of. What we desire to learn now is, how to effect a remedy; this we have endeavored to point out. Our elevation must be the results of self efforts, and work of our own hands. No other human power can accomplish it. If we but determine it shall be so, it will be so. Let each one make the case his own and endeavor to rival his neighbor in honorable competition.

These are the proper and only means of elevating ourselves and attaining equality in this country or any other, and it is useless, utterly futile, to think about going anywhere, except we are determined to use these as the necessary means of developing our manhood. The means are at hand, within our reach. Are we willing to try them? Are we willing to raise ourselves superior to the condition of slaves, or continue the meanest underlings, subject to the beck and call of every creature, bearing a pale complexion? If we are, we had as well remained in the South, as to have to come to the North in search of more freedom. What was the object of our parents in leaving the South, if it were not for the purpose of attaining equality in common with others of their fellow citizens by giving their children access to all the advantages enjoyed by others? Surely this was their object. They heard of liberty and equality here, and they hastened on to enjoy it, and no people are more astonished and disappointed than they who for the first time on beholding the position we occupy here in the free North, what is called, and what they expect to find, the free

States. They at once tell us that they have as much liberty in the South as we have in the North, that there as free people, they are protected in their rights, that we have nothing more than, in other respects, they have the same opportunity, indeed, the preferred opportunity of being their maids, servants, cooks, waiters and menials in general there, as we have here, that had they known for a moment before leaving that such was to be the only position they occupied here, they would have remained where they were and never left. Indeed, such is the disappointment in many cases that they immediately return back again, completely insulted at the idea, of having superiors. Indeed, if our superior advantages of the free States, do not induce and stimulate us to the higher attainments in life, what in the name of degraded humanity will do it? Nothing, surely nothing. If, in fine, the advantages of free schools in Massachusetts, New York, Pennsylvania, Ohio, Michigan, and wherever else we may have them, do not give us advantages and pursuits superior to our slave brethren, then are the unjust assertions of Mssrs. Henry Clay, John C. Calhoun, Theodore Frelinghuysen, late governor Poindexter of Mississippi, George McDuffy, Governor Hammond of South Carolina, Extra Billy (present Governor) Smith of Virginia and the host of our oppressors, slave holders and others true that we are insusceptible and incapable of elevation to the more respectable, honorable, and higher attainments among white men. But this we do not believe. Neither do you, although our whole life and course of policy in this country are such that it would seem to prove otherwise. The degradation of the slave parent has been entailed upon the child, induced by the subtle policy of the oppressor, in regular succession handed down from father to son, a system of regular submission and servitude, menialism and dependence, until it has become almost a physiological function of our system, an actual condition of our nature. Let this no longer be so, but let us determine to equal the whites among whom we live, not by declarations and unexpressed self opinion, for we have always had enough of that, but by actual prof in acting, doing and carrying out practically the measures of equality. Here is our nativity and here have we the natural right to abide and be elevated through the measures of our own efforts.

Chapter 6 The United States Our Country

Our common country is the United States. Here were we born, here raised and educated; here are the scenes of childhood; the pleasant associations of our school-going days; the loved enjoyments of our domestic and fireside relations, and the sacred graves of our departed fathers and mothers, and from here will we not be driven by any policy that may be schemed against us.

We are Americans, having a birthright citizenship — natural claims upon the country — claims common to all others of our fellow citizens — natural rights, which may, by virtue of unjust laws, be obstructed, but never can be annulled. Upon these do we place ourselves, as immovably fixed as the decrees of the living God. But according to the economy that regulates the policy of nations, upon which rests the basis of justifiable claims to all freeman's rights, it may be necessary to take another view of, and enquire into the political claims of, colored men.

Chapter 23　A Glance at Ourselves — Conclusion

With broken hopes — sad, devastation;

A race resigned to DEGREDATION!

We have said much to our young men and women, about their vocation and calling; we have dwelt much upon the menial position of our people in this county. Upon this point we cannot say too much, because there is a seeming satisfaction and seeking after such positions manifested on their part, unknown to any other people. There appears to be, a want of a sense of propriety or self-respect, altogether inexplicable because young men and women among us, many of whom have good trades and homes, adequate to their support, voluntarily leave them, and seek positions, such as servants, waiting maids, coachmen, nurses, cooks in gentlemen's kitchen, or such like occupations, when they can gain a livelihood at something more respectable, or elevating in character. And the worst part of the whole matter is that they have become so accustomed to it, it has become so "fashionable" that it seems to have become second nature, and they really become offended, when it is spoken against.

Among the German, Irish, and other European peasantry who came to this country, it matters not what they were employed at before and after they come; just so soon as they can better their condition by keeping shops, cultivating the soil, the young men and women going to night schools, qualifying themselves for usefulness, and learning trades, they do so. Their first and last care, object and aim is to better their condition by raising themselves above the condition that necessity places them in. We do not say too much, when we say, as an evidence of the deep degradation of our race in the United States, that there are those among us, the wives and daughters, some of the first ladies, (and who dare say they are not the "first," because they belong to the "first class" and associate where anybody among us can?) whose husbands are industrious, able and willing to support them, who voluntarily leave home, and become chambermaids, and stewardesses, upon vessels and steamboats, in all probability, to enable them to obtain some more fine or costly article of dress or furniture. We have nothing to say against those whom necessity compels to do these things, those who can do no better; we have only to do with those who can, and will not, or do not do better. The whites are always in the advance, and we either standing still or retrograding; as that which does not go forward, must either stand in one place or go back. The father in all probability is a farmer, mechanic, or man of some independent business; and the wife, sons and daughters are chamber maids, on vessels, nurses and waiting maids, or coachmen and cooks in families. This is retrogradation. The wife, sons, and daughters should be elevated above this condition as a necessary consequence.

If we did not love our race superior to others, we would not concern ourselves about their degradation; for the greatest desire of our heart is to see them stand on a level with the most elevated of mankind. No people are ever elevated above the condition of their females; hence the condition of the mother determines the condition of the child. To know the position of a people, it is only necessary to know the condition of their females; and despite themselves, they cannot rise above their level. Then what is our condition? Our best ladies being washerwomen, chamber maids, children's traveling nurses, and common house servants, and menials, we are all a degraded miserable people, inferior to any other people as a whole, on the face of the globe.

These great truths, however unpleasant, must be brought before the minds of our people in its true and proper light, as we have been too delicate about them, and too long concealed them for fear of giving offence. It would have been infinitely better for our race if these facts had been presented before us half a century ago, we would have been now proportionably benefitted by it.

As an evidence of the degradation to which we have been reduced, we dare premise, that this chapter will give offence to many, very many, and why? Because they may say, "He dared to say that the occupation of a servant is a degradation." It is not necessarily degrading; it would not be, to one or a few people of a kind; but a whole race of servants are a degradation to that people.

Efforts made by men of qualifications for the toiling and degraded millions among the whites, neither gives offence to that class, nor is it taken unkindly by them; but received with manifestations of gratitude; to know that they are thought to be equally worthy of, and entitled to stand on a level with the elevated classes; and they have only got to be informed of the way to raise themselves to make the effort and do so as far as they can. But how different with us. Speak of our position in society, and it at once gives insult, though we are servants; among ourselves we claim to be ladies and gentlemen, equal in standing, and as the popular expression goes, "Just as good as anybody" and so believing, we make no efforts to raise above the common level of menials, because the best being in that capacity, all are content with the position. We cannot at the same time, be domestic and lady; servant and gentleman. We must be the one of the other. Sad, sad indeed, is the thought, that hangs drooping in our mind, when contemplating the picture drawn before us. Young men and women, "We write these things unto you, because ye are strong," because the writer, a few years ago, gave unpardonable offence to many of the young people of Philadelphia and other places, because he dared tell them, that he thought too much of them to be content with seeing them the servants of other people. Surely, she that could be the mistress would not be the maid; neither would he that could be the master, be content with being the servant; then why be offended, when we point out to you, the way that leads from the menial to the mistress or the master. All this we seem to reject with fixed determination, repelling with anger, every effort on the part of our intelligent men and women to elevate us, with true Israelitish degradation, in reply to any suggestion or proposition that may be offered, "Who made thee a ruler and judge?"

The writer is no "Public Man," in the sense in which this is understood among our people, but simply a humble individual endeavoring to seek a livelihood by a profession obtained entirely by his own efforts, without relatives as he gained by the merit of his course and conduct, which he here gratefully acknowledges; and whatever he has accomplished, other young men may, by making corresponding efforts, also accomplish.

We have advised an emigration to Central and South America, and even to Mexico and the West Indies to those who prefer to either of the last named places, all of which are free countries, Brazil being the only real slave holding State in South America, there being nominal slavery in Dutch Guiana, Peru, Buenos Ayres, Paraguay, and Uruguay, in all of which places colored people have equality in social, civil, political, and religious privileges; Brazil making it punishable with death to import slaves into the empire.

Our oppressors, when urging us to go to Africa, tell us that we are better adapted to the climate than they, that the physical condition of the constitution of colored people better endures the heart of warm climates than that of the whites; this we are willing to admit, without argument, without adducing the physiological reason why, that colored people can and do stand warm climates better than whites; and find an answer fully to the point in the fact that they also stand modified that white people can stand; therefore, according to our oppressors' own showing, we are a superior race, being endowed with properties fitting us for all parts of the earth, while they are only adapted to certain parts. Of course, this proves our right and duty to live wherever we may choose; while the white race may only live where they can. We are content with the fact, and have ever claimed it. Upon this rock, they and we shall ever agree.

Of the West India Islands, Santa Cruz, belonging to Denmark; Porto Rico and Cuba with its little adjuncts, belonging to Spain, are the only slaveholding Islands among them, three fifths of the whole population of Cuba being colored people who cannot and will not much longer endure the burden and the yoke. They only want intelligent leaders of their own color, when they are ready at any moment to charge to the conflict to liberty or death. The remembrance of the noble mulatto, Placido, the gentleman, scholar, poet and intended Chief Engineer of the Army of Liberty and Freedom in Cuba; and the equally noble black, Charles Blair, who was to have been Commander in Chief, who were shamefully put to death in 1844, by that living monster, Captain General O'donnell is still fresh and indelible to the mind of every bondsman of Cuba.

In our own country, the United States, there are three millions five hundred thousand slaves; and we, the nominally free colored people, are six hundred thousand in number; estimating one sixth to be men, we have one hundred thousand able bodied freeman, which will make a powerful auxiliary in any country to which we may become adopted, an ally not to be despised by any power on earth. We love our country, dearly love her, but she doesn't love us, she despises us and bids us begone, driving us from her embraces; but we do go, whatever love we have for her, we shall love the country none the less that receives us as her adopted children.

For the want of business habits and training, our energies have become paralyzed; our young men never think of business, any more than if they were so many bondsmen, without the right to pursue any calling they may think most advisable. With our people in this country, dress and good appearances have been made the only test of gentleman and ladyship and that vocation which offers the best opportunity to dress and appear well has generally been preferred, however, menial and degrading by our young people, without even, in the majority of cases, an effort to do better; indeed, in many instances, refusing situations equally lucrative, and superior in position, but which would not allow as much display of dress and personal appearance. This, if we ever expect to rise, must be discarded from among us, and a high and respectable position assumed.

One of our great temporal curses is our consummate poverty. We are the poorest people as a class in the world of civilized mankind, abjectly, miserably poor, no one scarcely being able to assist the other. To this, of course, there are noble exceptions; but that which is common to, and the very process by which white men exist and succeed in life, is unknown to colored men in genera l. In any and every considerable community may be found, some one of our white fellow citizens, who is worth more than all the colored people in that community put together. We consequently have little or no efficiency. We must have men to be practically efficient in all the undertakings of life; and to obtain them, it is necessary that we should be engaged in lucrative pursuits, trade and general business transactions. In order to be thus engaged, it is necessary that we should occupy positions that afford the facilities for such pursuits. To compete now with the mighty odds of wealth, social and religious preferences, and political influences of this country, at this advanced state of its national existence, we never may expect. A new country and new beginning is the only true rational, politic remedy for our disadvantageous position; and that country we have already pointed out, with triple golden advantages all things considered, to that of any country to which it has been the province of man to embark.

Every other than we have at various periods of necessity been a migratory people; and all when oppressed, shown a greater abhorrence of oppression, if not a greater love of liberty than we. We cling to our oppressors as the objects of our love. It is true that our enslaved brethren are here, and we have been led to believe that it is necessary for us to remain, on that account. Is it true, that all should remain in degradation, because a part are degraded? We believe no such thing. We believe it to be the duty of the Free to elevate themselves in the most speedy and effective manner possible; as the redemption of the bondman depends entirely upon the elevation of the freeman; therefore, to elevate the free colored people of America, anywhere upon this continent forebodes the speedy redemption of the slaves. We shall hope to hear no more of so fallacious a doctrine, the necessity of the free remaining in degradation for the sake of the oppressed. Let us apply, first, the lever to ourselves; and the force that elevates us to the position of manhood's considerations and honors will cleft the manacle of every slave in the land.

When such great worth and talents, for want of a better sphere, of men like Rev. Jonathan Robinson,[1] Robert Douglass, Frederick A. Hinton,[2] and a hundred others that might be named, were permitted to expire in a barber shop; and such living men as may be found in

---

① 罗伯特・道格拉斯（Robert Douglass，1809—1887）：美国黑人艺术家。

② 弗雷德里克・亨顿（Frederick A. Hinton，1804—1849）：美国道德改革协会主席。

Boston, New York Philadelphia, Baltimore, Richmond, Washington City, Charleston, (S. C.), New Orleans, Cincinnati, Lousiville, St. Louis, Pittsburg, Buffalo, Rochester, Albany, Utica, Cleveland, Detroit, Milwaukee, Chicago, Columbus, Zanesville, Wheeling, and a hundred other places, confining themselves to Barber shops and waiter-ships in Hotels; certainly the necessity of such a course as we have pointed out must be cordially acknowledged; appreciated by every brother and sister of oppression; and not rejected as heretofore, as though they preferred inferiority to equality. These minds must become "unfettered" and have "space to rise." This cannot be in their present positions. A continuance in any position becomes what is termed. "Second Nature;" it begins an adaptation, and reconciliation of mind to such condition. It changes the whole physiological condition of the system, and adapts man and woman to a higher or lower sphere in the pursuits of life. The offspring of slaves and peasantry have the general characteristics of their parents; and nothing but a different course of training and education will change this character.

The slave may become a lover of his master, and learn to forgive him for continual deeds of maltreatment and abuse; just as the Spaniel would couch and fondle at the feet that kick him; because he has been taught to reverence them; and consequently becomes adapted in body and mind to his condition. Even the shrubbery loving Canary, and lofty soaring Eagle may be tamed to the cage, and learn to love it from habit of confinement. It has been so with us in our position among our oppressors; we have learned to love them. When reflecting upon this all important, and to us, all absorbing subject; we feel in the agony and anxiety of the moment, as though we could cry out in the language of a Prophet of old: "Oh that my head were waters, and mine eyes a fountain of tears that I might weep day and night for the" degradation "of my people! Oh that I had in the wilderness a lodging place of wayfaring men; that I might leave my people and go from them"!

The Irishman and German in the United States are very different persons to what they were when in Ireland and Germany, the countries of their nativity. Their spirits were depressed and downcast; but the instant they set their foot upon unrestricted soil; free to act and untrammeled to move; their physical condition undergoes a change, which in time becomes physiological, which is transmitted to the offspring, who when born under the circumstances is a decidedly different being to what it would have been, had it been born under different circumstances.

A child born under oppression has all the elements of servility in its constitution; who when born under favorable circumstances, has to the contrary, all the elements of freedom and independence of feeling. Our children then may not be expected, to maintain that position and manly bearing; born under the unfavorable circumstances with which we are surrounded in this country; that we so much desire. To use the language of the talented Mr. Whipper, "they cannot be raised in this country without being stoop shouldered," Heaven's pathway stands unobstructed which will lead us into a Paradise of bliss. Let us go on and possess the land, and the God of Israel will be our God.

The lessons of every school book, the pages of every history, and columns of every newspaper are so replete with stimuli to nerve us on to manly aspirations that those of our young people, who will now refuse to enter upon this great theatre of Polynesian adventure, and take their position on the stage of Central and South America, where a brilliant engagement of certain and most triumphant success, in the drama of human equality awaits them; then with the blood of slaves, write upon the lintel of every door in sterling Capitals, to be gazed and hissed at by every passerby:

> Doomed by the Creator,
> To servility and degradation;
> The SERVANT of the white man,
> And despised of every nation!

选文评析：

节选部分主要涵盖了德拉尼对殖民主张的评价以及美国黑人提高社会地位、改善处境的方法。德拉尼特别指出了美国黑人的国族身份，并从经济商业等种族之外的领域阐述了美国黑人所处阶层及其贫困与肤色的关系。他将美国殖民与黑人移民的概念区分开来，阐明黑人的种族和国家身份认同，将黑人的困境根源从种族问题拓宽到阶层、经济等社会问题上去，初步揭示了黑人在美国社会中遭受的多重剥削。同时，德拉尼卓有见地地提出黑人的教育问题，指出黑人改变目前现状的根本办法是提高文化水平和职业技能。

德拉尼列举欧洲诸国的少数族裔社区现状，指出美国黑人的处境比这些欧洲少数族裔更为糟糕，他们面对的社会环境更加恶劣。在这种处境之下，黑人移民、黑人殖民的种族政治策略是废奴主义者和奴隶制度支持者们关注的焦点，德拉尼从倡导者主体、目的和效果等方面分析了美国的非洲殖民计划和黑人移民的区别。他强烈反对美国殖民协会（American Colonization Society）所倡导的组织黑人到利比里亚等地的殖民计划。美国殖民协会由白人主导，其成员大多是白人奴隶主，他们鼓吹将黑人自由民送至非洲并帮助他们获得独立生活的能力以实现解放黑人、扩大美国影响力的双赢局面。德拉尼认为"我们要把美国殖民协会视作黑人最歹毒的敌人"，他指出这一策略是反基督精神的、伪善的，其殖民目的并非为了有效提高黑人的社会地位和生活条件，而是实现扩张并继续实施对非洲黑人同胞的奴役，本质是维护奴隶制度，保护白人奴隶主利益。德拉尼倡导美国黑人向中美洲和南美洲移民，并强调移民行动必须由黑人来主导，坚决主张黑人自治和自力更生。

德拉尼在移民问题上谈及美国黑人的国家身份认同，他肯定美国黑人作为"美国人"和"黑人"的双重身份，"美国是美国黑人的祖国，美国黑人是美国人且热爱自己的祖国"。他把种族身份认同放在第一位，认为"美国并不爱自己的黑人子民，黑人不能移民到美国希望他们去的地方"，这也是德拉尼反对移民非洲的原因之一。

在《关于美国有色人种的生存条件、种族提升、移民和命运的政治思考》的撰写阶段，德拉尼并不反对黑人离开美国，在国内黑人抗争运动效果并不乐观的情况下，他提倡黑人离开美国，实现自治，成立属于黑人自己的国度。他在亲身经历被哈佛大学医学院取消入学资格等一系列种族歧视事件后，对自己曾经笃信的种族融合策略失去信任，转向黑人移民的事业中去。他对黑人移民的目的地的构想几经变化，但总体来看，德拉尼强调"黑人自治"，肯定黑人的智慧，捍卫黑人人权，具有黑人民族主义的雏形。

同杜波依斯等知识分子一样，德拉尼卓有先见地指出教育、职业对提高黑人社会地位的重要性。在德拉尼看来，黑人目前处境之困不仅在于种族歧视，而且生活贫困更是其燃眉之急，多数黑人满足于不需要专业技能、薪资微薄的底层工作，目光短浅。德拉尼在黑人教育问题的看法上倾向于功用主义，把教育同技能和职业挂钩，他认为黑人若想改变贫困现状，提高社会地位，必须从接受教育、提高知识水平和职业技能开始，通过学习获得技能，从事商业等盈利活动或从事较高社会地位和经济收益的工作，而不是像目前这样满足于女佣、洗衣工等低层次工作及卑微地位。他再三强调黑人的唯一出路是自力更生、自我提升，不能寄希望于白人机构的扶助和同情。不过，德拉尼多少有些轻视种族主义对黑人的伤害程度，黑人受种族主义制度之困不能享有平等的教育机会和工作机会，这构成贫困的恶性循环。

推荐阅读文献：

Adeleke, Tunde. *Without Regard to Race：The Other Martin Robison Delany*. UP of Mississippi, 2004.

Adeleke, Tunde. *UnAfrican Americans：Nineteenth-Century Black Nationalists and the Civilizing Mission*. UP of Kentucky, 1998.

Adeleke, Tunde. *Martin R. Delany's Civil War and Reconstruction：A Primary Source Reader*. UP of Mississippi, 2019.

Levine, Robert S. *Martin R. Delany：A Documentary Reader*. The U of North Carolina P, 2003.

Stone, Andrea. *Black Well-Being：Health and Selfhood in Antebellum Black Literature*. UP of Florida, 2016.

Kytle, Ethan J. *Romantic Reformers and the Antislavery Struggle in the Civil War Era*. Cambridge UP, 2014.

Zamalin, Alex. *Black Utopia：The History of an Idea from Black Nationalism to Afrofuturism*. Columbia UP, 2019.

Islam, Pierre. *Perplexing Patriarchies：Fatherhood Among Black Opponents and White Defenders of Slavery*. Vernon Press, 2019.

Ogunleye, Tolagbe. Dr. Martin Robison Delany, 19th-Century Africana Womanists：Reflections on His Avant-Garde Politics Concerning Gender, Colorism, and Nation Building. *Journal of Black Studies*, 1998, 28(5)：628-649.

种族重构时期

（约 19 世纪 70 年代至 20 世纪 10 年代）

第五章　布克·T. 华盛顿
（Booker T. Washington，1856—1915）

布克·T. 华盛顿是美国著名黑人教育家、作家、演说家，并曾担任多位美国总统顾问，也是第一个在白宫与美国总统共进晚餐的非裔美国人，被誉为那个时代最具创新精神的美国非裔教育家和成功的政治家。他在南北战争爆发前五年出生于弗吉尼亚州西南部，曾是一名奴隶，在盐炉和煤矿里度过童年，对蓄奴制被废除之前黑人的残酷生活境遇深有体会，在黑人获得解放之后逐渐成为奴隶及其后代的代言人。在 1890 年至
1915 年，他是美国非裔群体的主要领导人和精神领袖。华盛顿也是美国全国黑人商业联盟的创始人之一，曾在亚拉巴马州塔斯基吉市创建著名的黑人教育机构塔斯基吉学院（Tuskegee Institute）。1895 年美国南方种族矛盾非常尖锐，白人种族分子针对黑人的私刑迫害十分猖獗。在危急关头，华盛顿发表了一次被称为"亚特兰大妥协"（Atlanta compromise）的著名演讲，为他赢得了全国声誉。他呼吁通过教育和创业推动黑人种族进步，而不是试图直接挑战南方种族隔离法案或者争取选举权。

华盛顿曾发起一个由黑人精英群体和白人慈善家、政治家组成的全国性联盟，其长期目标是通过注重自助和教育来提高黑人经济实力和种族自豪感，进而逐步改善整个黑人种族群体状况。他具有杰出的政治智慧和领导才能，能够非常巧妙地利用媒体，广泛筹集资金，建立合作网络，同时打击那些反对他的路线的人，这些使他能够在黑人中间长期拥有极高威望和号召力。以杜波依斯为首的北方黑人激进分子起初支持华盛顿的种族妥协立场以及发展路线，但后来又出现分歧，分道扬镳。杜波依斯等人选择成立全美有色人种促进会（NAACP），试图以政治变革促进黑人社会地位的改善，但并没能挑战华盛顿在黑人群体中的政治领导地位。但在华盛顿去世后，他的遗产却越来越受到黑人民权运动者的质疑。他所倡导的温和、妥协路线也逐渐被抛弃，特别是 20 世纪 50 年代的民权运动越来越倾向于更加积极和激进的政治斗争方式。

《超越奴役》（*Up from Slavery*）是华盛顿在 1901 年出版的自传。他在书中主要讲述了他在 40 年生涯内，如何从南北战争时期的一个奴隶的孩子经历重重困难，终于进入新汉普顿学院接受教育，以及后来如何克服各种障碍创建职业学校的过程。其中最主要的就是创建塔斯基吉学院，该学院的主要宗旨是帮助黑人和其他弱势少数民族学习有用的职业技能，以便能够靠自己努力改善生存状况。他还反思了教师和慈善家在教育黑人和美洲原住民方面的慷慨，讲述了他如何努力对学生进行道德教育，注重培养学生的品德修养，唤醒他们的自我尊严感。他的教育哲学主要强调将书本知识与职业技能结合起来，重视黑人教育的实用性，并认为黑人教育是缓和南方种族关系的合理且有效的策略。在他看来，对非裔美国人来说，节俭、努力工作和社会效益比政治鼓动种族平等更重要。虽然华盛顿在这部自传中的很多观点遭到杜波依斯等人批评，认为华盛顿的立场过于软弱，说明他缺乏对黑人同胞的真正同情，并没有真正关心黑人民族的进步，不过它仍旧十分畅销，且一直是最受欢迎的美国黑人自传之一，曾被美国现代图书馆（Modern Library）列为 20 世纪 100 部最佳非小说类图书排行榜第三位，并在 1999 年被《校际评论》（*Intercollegiate Review*）列为 20 世纪 50 部最佳图书之一。

在 19 世纪 80—90 年代，南北战争结束后虽然废除蓄奴制，让黑人普遍获得解放，但美国社会的种族矛盾却异常尖锐，白人普遍对黑人怀有较深敌意和种族偏见，认为黑人天生容易犯罪和道德沦丧，黑人离开奴隶制度和白人监管将无法生存下去。《吉姆·克劳法案》也正是在这样的背景下出现的。甚至在当时，私刑在南方也仍旧很普遍。白人暴徒将法律掌握在自己手中，经常会找一些借口滥用私刑惩罚黑人。甚至同情或保护黑人的少数白人也会被贴上同谋者的标签而受到报复。华盛顿进行演讲的一个重要目的也就是反对那些认为美国黑人天生愚昧、无法进步的观念。在种族关系不断恶化、种族冲突随时有可能爆发的背景下，他希望尽可能多地谈论进步话题，他希望通过演讲让白人和黑人听众都相信，黑人民族的进步完全可以实现，进而缓和种族关系，避免激化矛盾，使局势恶化。

下文选自《超越奴役》第 14 章，内容主要是华盛顿于 1895 年 9 月 18 日亚特兰大市举行的棉花州和国际博览会（Cotton States and International Exposition）上发表的一次著名演讲，以及后来围绕这次演讲，华盛顿与其他人的书信来往。

📖 作品选读：

The Atlanta Exposition Address

The Atlanta Exposition, at which I had been asked to make an address as a representative of the Negro race, as stated in the last chapter, was opened with a short address from Governor Bullock. After other interesting exercises, including an invocation from Bishop Nelson, of Georgia, a dedicatory ode by Albert Howell, Jr., and addresses by the President of the Exposition and Mrs. Joseph Thompson, the President of the Woman's Board, Governor Bullock introduced me with the words, "We have with us to-day a representative of Negro enterprise and Negro civilization."

When I arose to speak, there was considerable cheering, especially from the coloured people. As I remember it now, the thing that was uppermost in my mind was the desire to say something that would cement the friendship of the races and bring about hearty cooperation between them. So far as my outward surroundings were concerned, the only thing that I recall distinctly now is that when I got up, I saw thousands of eyes looking intently into my face. The following is the address which I delivered: —

Mr. President and Gentlemen of the Board of Directors and Citizens,

One-third of the population of the South is of the Negro race. No enterprise seeking the material, civil, or moral welfare of this section can disregard this element of our population and reach the highest success. I but convey to you, Mr. President and Directors, the sentiment of the masses of my race when I say that in no way have the value and manhood of the American Negro been more fittingly and generously recognized than by the managers of this magnificent Exposition at every stage of its progress. It is a recognition that will do more to cement the friendship of the two races than any occurrence since the dawn of our freedom.

Not only this, but the opportunity here afforded will awaken among us a new era of industrial progress. Ignorant and inexperienced, it is not strange that in the first years of our new life we began at the top instead of at the bottom; that a seat in Congress or the state legislature was more sought than real estate or industrial skill; that the political convention or stump speaking had more attractions than starting a dairy farm or truck garden.

A ship lost at sea for many days suddenly sighted a friendly vessel. From the mast of the unfortunate vessel was seen a signal, "Water, water; we die of thirst!" The answer from the friendly vessel at once came back, "Cast down your bucket where you are." A second time the signal, "Water, water; send us water!" ran up from the distressed vessel, and was answered, "Cast down your bucket where you are." And a third and fourth signal for water was answered, "Cast down your bucket where you are." The captain of the distressed vessel, at last heeding the injunction, cast down his bucket, and it came up full of fresh, sparkling water from the mouth of the Amazon River. To those of my race who depend on bettering their condition in a foreign land or who underestimate the importance of cultivating friendly relations with the Southern white man, who is their next-door neighbour, I would say: "Cast down your bucket where you are" — cast it down in making friends in every manly way of the people of all races by whom we are surrounded.

Cast it down in agriculture, mechanics, in commerce, in domestic service, and in the professions. And in this connection it is well to bear in mind that whatever other sins the South may be called to bear, when it comes to business, pure and simple, it is in the South that the Negro is given a man's chance in the commercial world, and in nothing is this Exposition more eloquent than in emphasizing this chance. Our greatest danger is that in the great leap from slavery to freedom we may overlook the fact that the masses of us are to live by the productions of our hands, and fail to keep in mind that we shall prosper in proportion as we learn to dignify and glorify common labour and put brains and skill into the common occupations of life; shall prosper in proportion as we learn to draw the line between the superficial and the substantial, the ornamental gewgaws of life and the useful. No race can prosper till it learns that there is as much dignity in tilling a field as in writing a poem. It is at the bottom of life we must begin, and not at the top. Nor should we permit our grievances to overshadow our opportunities.

To those of the white race who look to the incoming of those of foreign birth and strange tongue and habits for the prosperity of the South, were I permitted I would repeat what I say to my own race, "Cast down your bucket where you are." Cast it down among the eight millions of Negroes whose habits you know, whose fidelity and love you have tested in days when to have proved treacherous meant the ruin of your firesides. Cast down your bucket among these people who have, without strikes and labour wars, tilled your fields, cleared your forests, builded your railroads and cities, and brought forth treasures from the bowels of the earth, and helped make possible this magnificent representation of the progress of the South. Casting down your bucket among my people, helping and encouraging them as you are doing on these grounds, and to education of head, hand, and heart, you will find that they will buy your surplus land, make blossom the waste places in your fields, and run your factories. While doing this, you can be sure in the future, as in the past, that you and your families will be surrounded by the most patient, faithful, law-abiding, and unresentful people that the world has seen. As we have proved our loyalty to you in the past, in nursing your children, watching by the sick-bed of your mothers and fathers, and often following them with tear-dimmed eyes to their graves, so in the future, in our humble way, we shall stand by you with a devotion that no foreigner can approach, ready to lay down our lives, if need be, in defence of yours, interlacing our industrial, commercial, civil, and religious life with yours in a way that shall make the interests of both races one. In all things that are purely social we can be as separate as the fingers, yet one as the hand in all things essential to mutual progress.

There is no defence or security for any of us except in the highest intelligence and development of all. If anywhere there are efforts tending to curtail the fullest growth of the Negro, let these efforts be turned into stimulating, encouraging, and making him the most useful and intelligent citizen. Effort or means so invested will pay a thousand per cent interest. These efforts will be twice blessed — "blessing him that gives and him that takes.

There is no escape through law of man or God from the inevitable: —

The laws of changeless justice bind
Oppressor with oppressed;
And close as sin and suffering joined

We march to fate abreast. ①

Nearly sixteen millions of hands will aid you in pulling the load upward, or they will pull against you the load downward. We shall constitute one-third and more of the ignorance and crime of the South, or one-third its intelligence and progress; we shall contribute one-third to the business and industrial prosperity of the South, or we shall prove a veritable body of death, stagnating, depressing, retarding every effort to advance the body politic.

Gentlemen of the Exposition, as we present to you our humble effort at an exhibition of our progress, you must not expect overmuch. Starting thirty years ago with ownership here and there in a few quilts and pumpkins and chickens (gathered from miscellaneous sources), remember the path that has led from these to the inventions and production of agricultural implements, buggies, steam-engines, newspapers, books, statuary, carving, paintings, the management of drug-stores and banks, has not been trodden without contact with thorns and thistles. While we take pride in what we exhibit as a result of our independent efforts, we do not for a moment forget that our part in this exhibition would fall far short of your expectations but for the constant help that has come to our educational life, not only from the Southern states, but especially from Northern philanthropists, who have made their gifts a constant stream of blessing and encouragement.

The wisest among my race understand that the agitation of questions of social equality is the extremest folly, and that progress in the enjoyment of all the privileges that will come to us must be the result of severe and constant struggle rather than of artificial forcing. No race that has anything to contribute to the markets of the world is long in any degree ostracized. It is important and right that all privileges of the law be ours, but it is vastly more important that we be prepared for the exercises of these privileges. The opportunity to earn a dollar in a factory just now is worth infinitely more than the opportunity to spend a dollar in an opera-house. In conclusion, may I repeat that nothing in thirty years has given us more hope and encouragement, and drawn us so near to you of the white race, as this opportunity offered by the Exposition; and here bending, as it were, over the altar that represents the results of the struggles of your race and mine, both starting practically empty-handed three decades ago, I pledge that in your effort to work out the great and intricate problem which God has laid at the doors of the South, you shall have at all times the patient, sympathetic help of my race; only let this be constantly in mind, that, while from representations in these buildings of the product of field, of forest, of mine, of factory, letters, an art, much good will come, yet far above and beyond material benefits will be that higher good, that, let us pray God, will come, in a blotting out of sectional differences and racial animosities and suspicions, in a determination to administer absolute justice, in a willing obedience among all classes to the mandates of law. This, this, coupled with our material

---

① 这首诗出自美国新英格兰诗人约翰·格林里夫·惠蒂埃(John Greenleaf Whittier, 1807—1893)的诗歌《黑人船夫之歌》(*Song of the Negro Boatmen*, 1862)。

prosperity, will bring into our beloved South a new heaven and a new earth.

The first thing that I remember, after I had finished speaking, was that Governor Bullock rushed across the platform and took me by the hand, and that others did the same. I received so many and such hearty congratulations that I found it difficult to get out of the building. I did not appreciate to any degree, however, the impression which my address seemed to have made, until the next morning, when I went into the business part of the city. As soon as I was recognized, I was surprised to find myself pointed out and surrounded by a crowd of men who wished to shake hands with me. This was kept up on every street on to which I went, to an extent which embarrassed me so much that I went back to my boarding-place. The next morning I returned to Tuskegee. At the station in Atlanta, and at almost all of the stations at which the train stopped between that city and Tuskegee, I found a crowd of people anxious to shake hands with me.

The papers in all parts of the United States published the address in full, and for months afterward there were complimentary editorial references to it. Mr. Clark Howell, the editor of the *Atlanta Constitution*, telegraphed to a New York paper, among other words, the following, "I do not exaggerate when I say that Professor Booker T. Washington's address yesterday was one of the most notable speeches, both as to character and as to the warmth of its reception, ever delivered to a Southern audience. The address was a revelation. The whole speech is a platform upon which blacks and whites can stand with full justice to each other."

The Boston Transcript said editorially: "The speech of Booker T. Washington at the Atlanta Exposition, this week, seems to have dwarfed all the other proceedings and the Exposition itself. The sensation that it has caused in the press has never been equalled."

I very soon began receiving all kinds of propositions from lecture bureaus, and editors of magazines and papers, to take the lecture platform, and to write articles. One lecture bureau offered me fifty thousand dollars, or two hundred dollars a night and expenses, if I would place my services at its disposal for a given period. To all these communications I replied that my life-work was at Tuskegee; and that whenever I spoke it must be in the interests of the Tuskegee school and my race, and that I would enter into no arrangements that seemed to place a mere commercial value upon my services.

Some days after its delivery I sent a copy of my address to the President of the United States, the Hon. Grover Cleveland.① I received from him the following autograph reply: —

　　Gray Gables, Buzzard's Bay, Mass.,

---

　　① 格罗弗·克利夫兰(Grover Cleveland, 1837—1908),曾先后担任美国第 22 任(1885—1889)和第 24 任(1893—1897)总统,是唯一一分开任两届的总统,也是内战后第一个当选总统的民主党人。他为人正直、诚实,但政绩平平,被后世视为美国最好的无名总统。

October 6, 1895.

Booker T. Washington, Esq.:

My Dear Sir: I thank you for sending me a copy of your address delivered at the Atlanta Exposition.

I thank you with much enthusiasm for making the address. I have read it with intense interest, and I think the Exposition would be fully justified if it did not do more than furnish the opportunity for its delivery. Your words cannot fail to delight and encourage all who wish well for your race; and if our coloured fellow-citizens do not from your utterances gather new hope and form new determinations to gain every valuable advantage offered them by their citizenship, it will be strange indeed.

Yours very truly,

Grover Cleveland

Later I met Mr. Cleveland, for the first time, when, as President, he visited the Atlanta Exposition. At the request of myself and others he consented to spend an hour in the Negro Building, for the purpose of inspecting the Negro exhibit and of giving the coloured people in attendance an opportunity to shake hands with him. As soon as I met Mr. Cleveland I became impressed with his simplicity, greatness, and rugged honesty. I have met him many times since then, both at public functions and at his private residence in Princeton, and the more I see of him the more I admire him. When he visited the Negro Building in Atlanta he seemed to give himself up wholly, for that hour, to the coloured people. He seemed to be as careful to shake hands with some old coloured "auntie" clad partially in rags, and to take as much pleasure in doing so, as if he were greeting some millionaire. Many of the coloured people took advantage of the occasion to get him to write his name in a book or on a slip of paper. He was as careful and patient in doing this as if he were putting his signature to some great state document.

Mr. Cleveland has not only shown his friendship for me in many personal ways, but has always consented to do anything I have asked of him for our school. This he has done, whether it was to make a personal donation or to use his influence in securing the donations of others. Judging from my personal acquaintance with Mr. Cleveland, I do not believe that he is conscious of possessing any colour prejudice. He is too great for that. In my contact with people I find that, as a rule, it is only the little, narrow people who live for themselves, who never read good books, who do not travel, who never open up their souls in a way to permit them to come into contact with other souls — with the great outside world. No man whose vision is bounded by colour can come into contact with what is highest and best in the world. In meeting men, in many places, I have found that the happiest people are those who do the most for others; the most miserable are those who do the least. I have also found that few things, if any, are capable of making one so blind and narrow as race prejudice. I often say to our students, in the course of my talks to them on Sunday evenings in the chapel, that the longer I live and the more experience I have of the world, the more I am convinced that, after all, the one thing that is most worth living for — and dying for, if need be — is the opportunity of making someone else more happy and more useful.

The coloured people and the coloured newspapers at first seemed to be greatly pleased with the character of my Atlanta address, as well as with its reception. But after the first burst of enthusiasm began to die away, and the coloured people began reading the speech in cold type, some of them seemed to feel that they had been hypnotized. They seemed to feel that I had been too liberal in my remarks toward the Southern whites, and that I had not spoken out strongly enough for what they termed the "rights" of the race. For a while there was a reaction, so far as a certain element of my own race was concerned, but later these reactionary ones seemed to have been won over to my way of believing and acting.

While speaking of changes in public sentiment, I recall that about ten years after the school at Tuskegee was established, I had an experience that I shall never forget.

Dr. Lyman Abbott, then the pastor of Plymouth Church, and also editor of the *Outlook* (then the Christian Union), asked me to write a letter for his paper giving my opinion of the exact condition, mental and moral, of the coloured ministers in the South, as based upon my observations. I wrote the letter, giving the exact facts as I conceived them to be. The picture painted was a rather black one — or, since I am black, shall I say "white"? It could not be otherwise with a race but a few years out of slavery, a race which had not had time or opportunity to produce a competent ministry.

What I said soon reached every Negro minister in the country, I think, and the letters of condemnation which I received from them were not few. I think that for a year after the publication of this article every association and every conference or religious body of any kind, of my race, that met, did not fail before adjourning to pass a resolution condemning me, or calling upon me to retract or modify what I had said. Many of these organizations went so far in their resolutions as to advise parents to cease sending their children to Tuskegee. One association even appointed a "missionary" whose duty it was to warn the people against sending their children to Tuskegee. This missionary had a son in the school, and I noticed that, whatever the "missionary" might have said or done with regard to others, he was careful not to take his son away from the institution. Many of the coloured papers, especially those that were the organs of religious bodies, joined in the general chorus of condemnation or demands for retraction.

During the whole time of the excitement, and through all the criticism, I did not utter a word of explanation or retraction. I knew that I was right, and that time and the sober second thought of the people would vindicate me. It was not long before the bishops and other church leaders began to make a careful investigation of the conditions of the ministry, and they found out that I was right. In fact, the oldest and most influential bishop in one branch of the Methodist Church said that my words were far too mild. Very soon public sentiment began making itself felt, in demanding a purifying of the ministry. While this is not yet complete by any means, I think I may say, without egotism, and I have been told by many of our most influential ministers, that my words had much to do with starting a demand for the placing of a higher type of men in the pulpit. I have had the satisfaction of having many who once condemned me thank me heartily for my frank words.

The change of the attitude of the Negro ministry, so far as regards myself, is so complete that at the present time I have no warmer friends among any class than I have among the clergymen. The improvement in the character and life of the Negro ministers is one of the most gratifying evidences of the progress of the race. My experience with them, as well as other events in my life, convinces me that the thing to do, when one feels sure that he has said or done the right thing, and is condemned, is to stand still and keep quiet. If he is right, time will show it.

In the midst of the discussion which was going on concerning my Atlanta speech, I received the letter which I give below, from Dr. Gilman, the President of Johns Hopkins University, who had been made chairman of the judges of award in connection with the Atlanta Exposition: —

Johns Hopkins University, Baltimore, President's Office,
September 30, 1895.
Dear Mr. Washington:

Would it be agreeable to you to be one of the Judges of Award in the Department of Education at Atlanta? If so, I shall be glad to place your name upon the list. A line by telegraph will be welcomed.

Yours very truly,
D. C. Gilman.

I think I was even more surprised to receive this invitation than I had been to receive the invitation to speak at the opening of the Exposition. It was to be a part of my duty, as one of the jurors, to pass not only upon the exhibits of the coloured schools, but also upon those of the white schools. I accepted the position, and spent a month in Atlanta in performance of the duties which it entailed. The board of jurors was a large one, consisting in all of sixty members. It was about equally divided between Southern white people and Northern white people. Among them were college presidents, leading scientists and men of letters, and specialists in many subjects. When the group of jurors to which I was assigned met for organization, Mr. Thomas Nelson Page, who was one of the number, moved that I be made secretary of that division, and the motion was unanimously adopted. Nearly half of our division were Southern people. In performing my duties in the inspection of the exhibits of white schools I was in every case treated with respect, and at the close of our labours I parted from my associates with regret.

I am often asked to express myself more freely than I do upon the political condition and the political future of my race. These recollections of my experience in Atlanta give me the opportunity to do so briefly. My own belief is, although I have never before said so in so many words, that the time will come when the Negro in the South will be accorded all the political rights which his ability, character, and material possessions entitle him to. I think, though, that the opportunity to freely exercise such political rights will not come in any large degree through outside or artificial forcing, but will be accorded to the Negro by the Southern white people themselves, and that they will protect him in the exercise of those rights. Just as soon as the South gets over the old feeling that it is being forced by "foreigners," or "aliens," to do something which it does not want to do, I believe that the change in the direction that I have indicated is going to begin. In fact, there are indications that it is already beginning in a slight degree.

Let me illustrate my meaning. Suppose that some months before the opening of the Atlanta Exposition there had been a general demand from the press and public platform outside the South that a Negro be given a place on the opening programme, and that a Negro be placed upon the board of jurors of award. Would any such recognition of the race have taken place? I do not think so. The Atlanta officials went as far as they did because they felt it to be a pleasure, as well as a duty, to reward what they considered merit in the Negro race. Say what we will, there is something in human nature which we cannot blot out, which makes one man, in the end, recognize and reward merit in another, regardless of colour or race.

I believe it is the duty of the Negro — as the greater part of the race is already doing — to deport himself modestly in regard to political claims, depending upon the slow but sure influences that proceed from the possession of property, intelligence, and high character for the full recognition of his political rights. I think that the according of the full exercise of political rights is going to be a matter of natural, slow growth, not an over-night, gourd-vine affair. I do not believe that the Negro should cease voting, for a man cannot learn the exercise of self-government by ceasing to vote, any more than a boy can learn to swim by keeping out of the water, but I do believe that in his voting he should more and more be influenced by those of intelligence and character who are his next-door neighbours.

I know coloured men who, through the encouragement, help, and advice of Southern white people, have accumulated thousands of dollars' worth of property, but who, at the same time, would never think of going to those same persons for advice concerning the casting of their ballots. This, it seems to me, is unwise and unreasonable, and should cease. In saying this I do not mean that the Negro should truckle, or not vote from principle, for the instant he ceases to vote from principle he loses the confidence and respect of the Southern white man even.

I do not believe that any state should make a law that permits an ignorant and poverty-stricken white man to vote, and prevents a black man in the same condition from voting. Such a law is not only unjust, but it will react, as all unjust laws do, in time; for the effect of such a law is to encourage the Negro to secure education and property, and at the same time it encourages the white man to remain in ignorance and poverty. I believe that in time, through the operation of intelligence and friendly race relations, all cheating at the ballot-box in the South will cease. It will become apparent that the white man who begins by cheating a Negro out of his ballot soon learns to cheat a white man out of his, and that the man who does this ends his career of dishonesty by the theft of property or by some equally serious crime. In my opinion, the time will come when the South will encourage all of its citizens to vote. It will see that it pays better, from every standpoint, to have healthy, vigorous life than to have that political stagnation which always results when one-half of the population has no share and no interest in the Government.

As a rule, I believe in universal, free suffrage, but I believe that in the South we are confronted with peculiar conditions that justify the protection of the ballot in many of the states, for a while at least, either by an educational test, a property test, or by both combined; but whatever tests are required, they should be made to apply with equal and exact justice to both races.

1901

📝 选文评析：

1895 年 9 月 18 日，在佐治亚州亚特兰大市举行的棉花州和国际博览会上，布克·T. 华盛顿发表了这个著名演讲。他自称作为"黑人事业和黑人文明的代表"发言，演讲主题是改善南方种族关系，"最想说的是那些能巩固种族间友谊并带来他们之间真诚合作的话"。这次演说现场听众以白人为主，被认为是美国历史上最重要和最有影响力的演讲之一，为后来所谓的"亚特兰大妥协"(Atlanta compromise)奠定了基础，即美国非裔领导人和南方白人领导者达成协议，南方黑人将温和地工作，服从白人政治统治，而南方白人则保证黑人获得基本教育和正当法律权益保障。"亚特兰大妥协"这个说法是由 W. E. B. 杜波依斯最早给出的，他认为华盛顿的这次演讲对于黑人追求社会和政治平等的事业来说，并未作出足够承诺，反倒对白人作出太多妥协让步。

华盛顿在演讲中首先呼吁占南方人口三分之一的黑人放下仇恨、认真工作。他以海上航行迷失方向的船只来比喻蓄奴制被废除以后，美国黑人社会陷入的困顿状况。他说："对于那些想要改善他们在异国他乡的生活条件，或者低估了与他们隔壁南方白人邻居建立友好关系的重要性的人，我也想说：'就地放下你的桶'——放下它，拿出男子汉的大度气概，与我们身边的人交朋友。"在船上被困的人员口渴难耐，被动绝望地等待获得救援，但实际上水就在当前眼下，只要放下水桶就可以打水自救。也就是说，黑人不应一味抱怨自己所处的困难境地，而应该认真想办法逐步实现自我改善。他呼吁种族和解，黑人应当放下仇恨，耐心地工作，逐步提高自身生活状况和社会地位。"在农业、机械、商业、家政服务和专业领域都要'抛下水桶'"。在华盛顿看来，无论奴隶制给南方制造了多么大的罪恶，但现在一切都已经成为过去，黑人已经获得解放。他们和白人一样，"在纯粹而干净的(pure and simple)商业领域，黑人在南方都有机会获得一个男人的机会"。但在当时，很多黑人却更关心在议会政治选举等领域抗争平等权利，却忽视了在经济生活早已存在的平等创业机会。这在华盛顿看来，完全是本末倒置。"由于无知和缺乏经验，在我们的新生活刚开始的最初几年,我们试图从顶部而不是底部开始建造新生活,这并不奇怪;在国会或州立法机关获得席位比房地产或工业技能更受欢迎;政治会议或演讲比开办奶牛场或卡车花园更有吸引力。"他倡导的路线则恰好相反,黑人在政治领域的斗争——当时主要是黑人在议会的选举权和被选举权——可以先放缓,但在经济和文化领域的建设才是迫在眉睫。只有把黑人民族的经济和文化基础夯实,获得实实在在的社会提升,才有可能在政治领域取得进步。他说:"在从奴役到自由的大跳跃中,我们可能忽略了这样一个事实:我们大多数人都是靠我们的双手来生活的。……没有一个民族能够兴旺发达,除非它知道耕田和写诗一样有尊严。我们必须从底层开始建设生活,而不是从上层开始。我们也不应该让我们的不满掩盖我们的机会。"

华盛顿认为南方黑人的进步与社会待遇提升与保护白人自身利益也是密切相关的。他对白人听众说,他们应该雇佣全国 800 万黑人中的一部分,而不是依赖移民人口每年达到 100 万人的速度。他赞扬黑人对白人的忠诚、忠诚和热爱,但警告说,如果压迫继续下去,黑人可能成为社会的一个巨大负担,他劝告白人:

> 帮助和鼓励他们……并且教育他们的头脑、手和心,你会发现他们会买你多余的土地,在你的田地里开花结果,经营你的工厂。在这样做的同时,你可以像过去一样,确信在未来,你和你的家人身边将会充满世界所见过的最有耐心、最忠诚、最守法、最无怨言的人。正如我们过去证明对你们忠诚一样,在照顾你的孩子,在你父母病榻旁看着他们,常常带着泪眼朦胧地跟着他们走向坟墓,所以在未来,我们仍将以谦卑的方式,以一种任何外国人都无法接近的忠诚,如果需要的话,为了保护你们,也随时准备牺牲我们的生命,把我们的工业、商业、公民和宗教生活和你们的生活交织在一起,使两个种族的利益成为一体。在所有纯粹社会的事物中,我们可以像手指一样分开,但在所有对共同进步至关重要的事物中,我们可以像手一样合一。

他试图用数字打动那些精于算计的白人,让他们明白,帮助黑人也是一门对自己有好处的"生意","在这个方向每多投入一分努力,将会有十倍回报。……我们要么将构成南方三分之一以上的无知和犯罪,要么构成三分之一的智慧和进步;我们将为南方的工商业作出三分之一的贡献……"

华盛顿的演说赢得白人社会的巨大欢迎,美国各地的报纸都全文发表了这篇讲话,几个月后,还有媒体对其进行了赞美性评论。华盛顿成为家喻户晓的名人。演讲结束后,他立即被誉为弗雷德里克·道格拉斯的继任者,而巧合的是,道格拉斯也恰好在那年早些时候去世。但在黑人群体内,华盛顿的演说却招来很多批评。很多人认为他的演说对白人社会过于软弱退让,没有对黑人种族的"权利"发表足够强烈的意见。

应当说,在当时的社会语境下,华盛顿的演讲具有积极意义,他确实看清了黑人民族在获得解放后陷入的困境,太急于政治领域的胜利而忽略了经济基础建设,导致黑人整体处境与蓄奴制被废除之前并没有多少改善,甚至还有更加恶化的趋势。他提出的以实业促进民族提升的路线也并非全无道理。当然华盛顿的演说也存在很多不足,其中最根本性的一点就是,他只把种族主义理解为政治、经济和法律领域看得见的剥削,却没有看到它的本质是一种不正义的、制度性的社会剥削结构。在他看来，自蓄奴制被废除以后，种族主义已经不存在。虽然黑人在政治法律领域仍旧受到一些不公正对待，但至少在经济领域，他们完全可以和白人一样享有发展和奋斗的机会，可以用自己的勤劳和智慧改善自己的生活。而对于白人来说，种族分子也只是极少数，他们的种族偏见也完全只是因为对黑人真实状况的无知，"只有那些狭隘小人才会完全囿于自己的生活，他们从不读好书，不旅行，从不敞开自己的灵魂去接触其他灵魂——接触伟大的外部世界"。只要白人都能够像克利夫兰先生一样，拥有"朴实、伟大和粗犷的诚实"，没有任何肤色偏见，愿意友善对待哪怕最贫贱的穷苦黑人，那么真正的种族和解就能够实现。

总体来看，华盛顿对于种族主义的认识还不够深刻，对于彻底消灭种族主义、改善种族关系也过于乐观。虽然我们不能以 21 世纪的知识立场来要求华盛顿，但还是要看到他思想中的不足。实际上，自 20 世纪 90 年代以来兴起的"白人性研究"(whiteness studies)恰恰要批判华盛顿所代表的这种误解。白人性研究者认为，"白人特权"(white privilege)要比"种族歧视"更能揭示种族主义的深层秘密，而且这种特权并非是指在法律和道德上明确规定的各种特殊待遇，而是指所有白人——不管他是否在表面上支持种族主义——仅凭自己的白人身份便可确保的利益和优势。对没有特权的黑人来说，生活中处处遭遇种族主义的壁垒，它们就像透明玻璃一样，看不见却摸得着，阻碍黑人在精神和物质上实现法律允诺他们的各种经济和文化权益。白人性研究强调，这种制度性的种族主义远比暴力性的种族主义更隐蔽，也更难根除。它实际上在后民权运动时代完成了被法律明令禁止的种族主义行径。白人霸权之于种族主义社会就像男性霸权之于父权社会，它由白人主导，服务于白人利益，并不断在重复性的日常实践中得到再生和巩固。正是由于它的存在，才会衍生出形形色色的白人特权。反过来说，只要它的存在和再生机制未受挑战，那么即便清除日常生活中看得见的白人特权，依然无法改变结构性的种族差异，也就不可能从根本上铲除种族主义。

💬 推荐阅读文献：

Bailey, Budd. *Booker T. Washington and the Tuskegee Institute*. Cavendish Square Publishing, 2016.

Boston, Michael B. *The Business Strategy of Booker T. Washington: Its Development and Implementation*. UP of Florida, 2010.

Buckley, James, Jr. *Who Was Booker T. Washington*? Penguin Young Readers Group, 2018.

Flynn, John P. Booker T. Washington: Uncle Tom or Wooden Horse. *The Journal of Negro History*, 1969, 54(3): 262-274.

Gardner, Booker T. The Educational Contributions of Booker T. Washington. *The Journal of Negro Education*, 1975, 44(4): 502-518.

Hamilton, Kenneth M. *Booker T. Washington in American Memory*. U of Illinois P, 2017.

Shaw, Francis H. Booker T. Washington and the Future of Black Americans. *The Georgia Historical Quarterly*, 1972, 56(2): 193-209.

Smock, Raymond W. *Booker T. Washington*：*Black Leadership in the Age of Jim Crow*. Ivan R. Dee, 2009.

West, Michael. *The Education of Booker T. Washington*：*American Democracy and the Idea of Race Relations*. Columbia UP, 2006.

Washington, Booker T. *The Booker T. Washington Reader*. Start Publishing, 2013.

第六章　杜波依斯
（W. E. B. Du Bois，1868—1963）

W. E. B. 杜波依斯，全名威廉·爱德华·伯格哈特·杜波依斯（William Edward Burghardt du Bois）是美国著名的社会学家、历史学家、民权活动家、泛非主义者、作家和编辑。他于1868年出生于马萨诸塞州的大巴林顿，在一个以白人为主、种族关系相对宽容的社区长大。他的父亲是一个流浪汉，在他出生后一年内就抛弃了家庭。年轻的杜波依斯虽然从小失去父亲，但母亲的周到照顾让他并未因父爱缺失而造成很大创伤。他从小便是一个快乐的孩子，青年时期杜波依斯就读于家乡一所以白人为主的中学。在柏林大学和哈佛大学完成研究生学业后，成为第一个获得博士学位的非裔美国人，并成为亚特兰大大学历史、社会学和经济

学教授。杜波依斯还是1909年全美有色人种协进会（National Association for the Advancement of Colored People，简称NAACP）的创始人之一。在此之前，杜波依斯就曾作为尼亚加拉运动（Niagara Movement）的领导人在全国范围内崭露头角。尼亚加拉运动是一个致力于为黑人争取平等地位的美国非裔行动组织。

在20世纪初，杜波依斯是仅次于布克·T. 华盛顿的美国黑人领袖和代言人。种族主义是他一生论战的主要目标，他强烈抗议私刑、吉姆·克劳隔离法案以及在教育和就业方面的种族歧视。他与华盛顿在路线和观点上长期存在根本分歧。尽管杜波依斯最初赞同华盛顿的演讲内容，但后来很快和黑人中的其他少数精英群体一样，对华盛顿的路线持反对立场，尤其反对后者做出的亚特兰大妥协（具体参见上一章）。杜波依斯认为，美国黑人应该争取平等的政治权利和更高的社会上升机会，而不是被动地屈从于亚特兰大妥协所默许的种族隔离和歧视。与华盛顿相反，杜波依斯始终坚持政治斗争的重要性，认为充分的公民权利和政治代表性才是提高美国黑人社会地位的关键，而美国非裔知识精英的领导对于实现这个目标非常关键。不同于华盛顿所坚持的实业技能教育路线，杜波依斯认为非裔美国人要想真正实现民族提升，就必须发展高等教育。

1901年，杜波依斯还专门写了一篇评论，批评华盛顿的自传《超越奴役》，后来他把这篇文章加以扩展，并以《关于布克·T. 华盛顿及其他》("Of Mr. Booker T. Washington and Others")为题收入他的文集《黑人的灵魂》。两位黑人领袖的一个主要分歧是他们对待教育的态度：华盛顿认为，非裔美国人的学校应主要侧重于工商业和技能教育主题，包括农业和机械技能，因为南方黑人大多数生活在农村地区。但杜波依斯却认为，黑人学校也应该更多地关注实用性不是那么强的文科和学术性课程，比如古典文学、艺术和人文学科等，因为这些知识是培养领导精英所必需的。奴隶解放后，虽然黑人有了免受奴役的自由，但他们并没有获得享有自由的人的所有权利。为了成功，他们不仅需要身体自由，而且需要有选举权和接受教育。两者同为影响巨大的黑人精神领袖，却提出完全不同的民族发展路径。华盛顿号召黑人向前看，从苦难的奴隶经历中汲取前进力量，用努力的付出赢得民族进步和尊严，但由于其偏于幼稚的乐观主义精神而遭人批评；杜波依斯则用"双重意识"精确剖析了奴隶制给黑人留下的看不见的心理创伤，同时又号召黑人积极肯定自我价值，在文化和教育方面积极进取，敢于追求高尚的奋斗目标。然而，正如有些研究者指出的那样，华盛顿和杜波依斯在教育问题上的分歧实际上并非完全对立；两人都没有完全否定另一方所强调的教育形式的重要性。晚年的杜波依斯也曾后悔在那些文章中批评华盛顿。

杜波依斯是一位十分多产的作家。他在1903年出版散文集《黑人的灵魂》(The Souls of Black Folk)时，已经成为美国最有影响的非裔美国人知识分子之一，这部著作也早已被公认为美国非裔文学中的经典之作。他在1935年出版的另一部代表作《美国的黑人重建》(Black Reconstruction in America)中也挑战了当时的主流观念，即认为黑人应对重建时代的失败负责。他还从弗雷德里克·道格拉斯那里借用"种族分界线"(color line)这个词来代表美国社会和政治生活中普遍存在的各种不公正现象。他提出的中心论题之一"20世纪的问题是种族分界线的问题"，对后人思考整个20世纪乃至21世纪的很多种族和社会问题都深有启发。在担任全美有色人种协进会杂志《危机》(The Crisis)编辑期间，他刊发了许多有影响力的文章。杜波依斯秉持马克思主义的立场，认为资本主义才是种族主义的主要原因。他一生都非常同情和支持社会主义事业，是一位热心的世界和平活动家。在杜波依斯去世一年后颁布的《美国民权法案》(Civil Rights Act)体现了杜波依斯一生为之奋斗的许多成果。

由于杜波依斯拥有深厚的社会学知识背景和杰出的文学写作技能，他的《黑人的灵魂》既是一部开创性的社会学著作，在社会科学中占有重要地位，同时也被视为美国黑人文学的一块重要基石。作家詹姆斯·韦尔登·约翰逊(James Weldon Johnson)曾认为这本书对非裔美国人的影响堪比《汤姆叔叔的小屋》。全书共由14篇散文组成，每一章都以两段引言开始，一段取自白人诗人，另一段则取自黑人灵歌，以此来展示黑人和白人在文化和智力上的对等。整部书的一个重要主题就是非裔美国人面临的双重意识，或者说黑人必须始终同时拥有两个视野：既是美国人又是黑人；他们必须意识到他们如何看待自己，也必须意识到世界如何看待他们。下文选自《黑人的灵魂》第一章。

📖 作品选读:

The Souls of Black Folk

Chapter One
Of Our Spiritual Strivings

O water, voice of my heart, crying in the sand,

All night long crying with a mournful cry,

As I lie and listen, and cannot understand

The voice of my heart in my side or the voice of the sea,

O water, crying for rest, is it I, is it I?

All night long the water is crying to me.

Unresting water, there shall never be rest

Till the last moon droop and the last tide fail,

And the fire of the end begin to burn in the west;

And the heart shall be weary and wonder and cry like the sea,

All life long crying without avail,

As the water all night long is crying to me.

Arthur Symons①

Between me and the other world there is ever an unasked question: unasked by some through feelings of delicacy; by others through the difficulty of rightly framing it. All, nevertheless, flutter round it. They approach me in a half — hesitant sort of way, eye me curiously or compassionately, and then, instead of saying directly, How does it feel to be a problem? they say, I know an excellent colored man in my town; or, I fought at Mechanicsville; or, Do not these Southern outrages make your blood boil? At these I smile, or am interested, or reduce the boiling to a simmer, as the occasion may require. To the real question, How does it feel to be a problem? I answer seldom a word.

---

① 阿瑟·威廉·西蒙斯(Arthur William Symons, 1865—1945)是英国诗人、批评家和杂志编辑。此处杜波依斯引用的诗歌出自西蒙斯的作品《水的哭泣》(*The Crying of Water*)。另, 此处删去了杜波依斯原文中引用的一段黑人灵歌曲谱。

And yet, being a problem is a strange experience, — peculiar even for one who has never been anything else, save perhaps in babyhood and in Europe. It is in the early days of rollicking boyhood that the revelation first bursts upon one, all in a day, as it were. I remember well when the shadow swept across me. I was a little thing, away up in the hills of New England, where the dark Housatonic winds between Hoosac and Taghkanic to the sea. In a wee wooden schoolhouse, something put it into the boys' and girls' heads to buy gorgeous visiting — cards — ten cents a package — and exchange. The exchange was merry, till one girl, a tall newcomer, refused my card, — refused it peremptorily, with a glance. Then it dawned upon me with a certain suddenness that I was different from the others; or like, mayhap, in heart and life and longing, but shut out from their world by a vast veil. I had thereafter no desire to tear down that veil, to creep through; I held all beyond it in common contempt, and lived above it in a region of blue sky and great wandering shadows. That sky was bluest when I could beat my mates at examination time, or beat them at a foot race, or even beat their stringy heads. Alas, with the years all this fine contempt began to fade; for the words I longed for, and all their dazzling opportunities, were theirs, not mine. But they should not keep these prizes, I said; some, all, I would wrest from them. Just how I would do it I could never decide: by reading law, by healing the sick, by telling the wonderful tales that swam in my head, — some way. With other black boys the strife was not so fiercely sunny: their youth shrunk into tasteless sycophancy, or into silent hatred of the pale world about them and mocking distrust of everything white; or wasted itself in a bitter cry, Why did God make me an outcast and a stranger in mine own house? The shades of the prison — house closed round about us all: walls strait and stubborn to the whitest, but relentlessly narrow, tall, and unscalable to sons of night who must plod darkly on in resignation, or beat unavailing palms against the stone, or steadily, half hopelessly, watch the streak of blue above.

After the Egyptian and Indian, the Greek and Roman, the Teuton[①] and Mongolian, the Negro is a sort of seventh son[②], born with a veil, and gifted with second — sight in this American world, — a world which yields him no true self — consciousness, but only lets him see himself through the revelation of the other world. It is a peculiar sensation, this double — consciousness, this sense of always looking at one's self through the eyes of others, of measuring one's soul by the tape of a world that looks on in amused contempt and pity. One ever feels his twoness, — an American, a Negro; two souls, two thoughts, two unreconciled strivings; two warring ideals in one dark body, whose dogged strength alone keeps it from being torn asunder.

The history of the American Negro is the history of this strife, — this longing to attain self — conscious manhood, to merge his double self into a better and truer self. In this merging he wishes neither of the older selves to be lost. He would not Africanize America, for America has too much

---

① 条顿人(Teutones)是古代日耳曼人的一个分支，后世常用来泛指日耳曼人及其后裔。

② 杜波依斯前面所说的这六大民族(埃及人、印度人、希腊人、罗马人、日耳曼人和蒙古人)都曾在历史上创造过辉煌，故他在此说黑人是上帝的"第七个儿子"，暗示黑人同样有开创历史的机会。

to teach the world and Africa. He would not bleach his Negro soul in a flood of white Americanism, for he knows that Negro blood has a message for the world. He simply wishes to make it possible for a man to be both a Negro and an American, without being cursed and spit upon by his fellows, without having the doors of Opportunity closed roughly in his face.

This, then, is the end of his striving: to be a co — worker in the kingdom of culture, to escape both death and isolation, to husband and use his best powers and his latent genius. These powers of body and mind have in the past been strangely wasted, dispersed, or forgotten. The shadow of a mighty Negro past flits through the tale of Ethiopia the Shadowy and of Egypt the Sphinx. Through history, the powers of single black men flash here and there like falling stars, and die sometimes before the world has rightly gauged their brightness. Here in America, in the few days since Emancipation, the black man's turning hither and thither in hesitant and doubtful striving has often made his very strength to lose effectiveness, to seem like absence of power, like weakness. And yet it is not weakness, — it is the contradiction of double aims. The double — aimed struggle of the black artisan — on the one hand to escape white contempt for a nation of mere hewers of wood and drawers of water, and on the other hand to plough and nail and dig for a poverty — stricken horde — could only result in making him a poor craftsman, for he had but half a heart in either cause. By the poverty and ignorance of his people, the Negro minister or doctor was tempted toward quackery and demagogy; and by the criticism of the other world, toward ideals that made him ashamed of his lowly tasks. The would — be black savant was confronted by the paradox that the knowledge his people needed was a twice — told tale to his white neighbors, while the knowledge which would teach the white world was Greek to his own flesh and blood. The innate love of harmony and beauty that set the ruder souls of his people a dancing and a singing raised but confusion and doubt in the soul of the black artist; for the beauty revealed to him was the soul beauty of a race which his larger audience despised, and he could not articulate the message of another people. This waste of double aims, this seeking to satisfy two unreconciled ideals, has wrought sad havoc with the courage and faith and deeds of ten thousand thousand people, — has sent them often wooing false gods and invoking false means of salvation, and at times has even seemed about to make them ashamed of themselves.

Away back in the days of bondage they thought to see in one divine event the end of all doubt and disappointment; few men ever worshipped Freedom with half such unquestioning faith as did the American Negro for two centuries. To him, so far as he thought and dreamed, slavery was indeed the sum of all villainies, the cause of all sorrow, the root of all prejudice; Emancipation was the key to a promised land of sweeter beauty than ever stretched before the eyes of wearied Israelites. In song and exhortation swelled one refrain — Liberty; in his tears and curses the God he implored had Freedom in his right hand. At last it came, — suddenly, fearfully, like a dream. With one wild carnival of blood and passion came the message in his own plaintive cadences:

Shout, O children!

> Shout, you're free!
> For God has bought your liberty! ①

Years have passed away since then, — ten, twenty, forty; forty years of national life, forty years of renewal and development, and yet the swarthy spectre sits in its accustomed seat at the Nation's feast. In vain do we cry to this our vastest social problem: —

> Take any shape but that, and my firm nerves
> Shall never tremble! ②

The Nation has not yet found peace from its sins; the freedman has not yet found in freedom his promised land. Whatever of good may have come in these years of change, the shadow of a deep disappointment rests upon the Negro people, — a disappointment all the more bitter because the unattained ideal was unbounded save by the simple ignorance of a lowly people.

The first decade was merely a prolongation of the vain search for freedom, the boon that seemed ever barely to elude their grasp, — like a tantalizing will — o' — the — wisp, maddening and misleading the headless host. The holocaust of war, the terrors of the Ku — Klux Klan, the lies of carpet — baggers, the disorganization of industry, and the contradictory advice of friends and foes, left the bewildered serf with no new watchword beyond the old cry for freedom. As the time flew, however, he began to grasp a new idea. The ideal of liberty demanded for its attainment powerful means, and these the Fifteenth Amendment gave him. The ballot, which before he had looked upon as a visible sign of freedom, he now regarded as the chief means of gaining and perfecting the liberty with which war had partially endowed him. And why not? Had not votes made war and emancipated millions? Had not votes enfranchised the freedmen? Was anything impossible to a power that had done all this? A million black men started with renewed zeal to vote themselves into the kingdom. So the decade flew away, the revolution of 1876 came, and left the half — free serf weary, wondering, but still inspired. Slowly but steadily, in the following years, a new vision began gradually to replace the dream of political power, — a powerful movement, the rise of another ideal to guide the unguided, another pillar of fire by night after a clouded day. It was the ideal of "book — learning"; the curiosity, born of compulsory ignorance, to know and test the power of the cabalistic letters of the white man, the longing to know. Here at last seemed to have been discovered the mountain path to Canaan; longer than the highway of Emancipation and law, steep and rugged, but straight, leading to heights high enough to overlook life.

Up the new path the advance guard toiled, slowly, heavily, doggedly; only those who have

---

① 这几行诗取自一首题为《呼喊吧，孩子们!》(*Shout, O Children*) 的南方黑人教会灵歌。
② 引文出自莎士比亚经典剧目《麦克白》第三幕第四场。

watched and guided the faltering feet, the misty minds, the dull understandings, of the dark pupils of these schools know how faithfully, how piteously, this people strove to learn. It was weary work. The cold statistician wrote down the inches of progress here and there, noted also where here and there a foot had slipped or someone had fallen. To the tired climbers, the horizon was ever dark, the mists were often cold, the Canaan was always dim and far away. If, however, the vistas disclosed as yet no goal, no resting — place, little but flattery and criticism, the journey at least gave leisure for reflection and self — examination; it changed the child of Emancipation to the youth with dawning self — consciousness, self — realization, self — respect. In those sombre forests of his striving his own soul rose before him, and he saw himself, — darkly as through a veil; and yet he saw in himself some faint revelation of his power, of his mission. He began to have a dim feeling that, to attain his place in the world, he must be himself, and not another. For the first time he sought to analyze the burden he bore upon his back, that dead — weight of social degradation partially masked behind a half — named Negro problem. He felt his poverty; without a cent, without a home, without land, tools, or savings, he had entered into competition with rich, landed, skilled neighbors. To be a poor man is hard, but to be a poor race in a land of dollars is the very bottom of hardships. He felt the weight of his ignorance, — not simply of letters, but of life, of business, of the humanities; the accumulated sloth and shirking and awkwardness of decades and centuries shackled his hands and feet. Nor was his burden all poverty and ignorance. The red stain of bastardy, which two centuries of systematic legal defilement of Negro women had stamped upon his race, meant not only the loss of ancient African chastity, but also the hereditary weight of a mass of corruption from white adulterers, threatening almost the obliteration of the Negro home.

A people thus handicapped ought not to be asked to race with the world, but rather allowed to give all its time and thought to its own social problems. But alas! while sociologists gleefully count his bastards and his prostitutes, the very soul of the toiling, sweating black man is darkened by the shadow of a vast despair. Men call the shadow prejudice, and learnedly explain it as the natural defence of culture against barbarism, learning against ignorance, purity against crime, the "higher" against the "lower" races. To which the Negro cries Amen! and swears that to so much of this strange prejudice as is founded on just homage to civilization, culture, righteousness, and progress, he humbly bows and meekly does obeisance. But before that nameless prejudice that leaps beyond all this he stands helpless, dismayed, and well — nigh speechless; before that personal disrespect and mockery, the ridicule and systematic humiliation, the distortion of fact and wanton license of fancy, the cynical ignoring of the better and the boisterous welcoming of the worse, the all — pervading desire to inculcate disdain for everything black, from Toussaint to the devil, — before this there rises a sickening despair that would disarm and discourage any nation save that black host to whom "discouragement" is an unwritten word.

But the facing of so vast a prejudice could not but bring the inevitable self — questioning, self — disparagement, and lowering of ideals which ever accompany repression and breed in an atmosphere of contempt and hate. Whisperings and portents came home upon the four winds: Lo! we are diseased and dying, cried the dark hosts; we cannot write, our voting is vain; what need of education, since we must always cook and serve? And the Nation echoed and enforced this self — criticism, saying: Be content to be servants, and nothing more; what need of higher culture for half — men? Away with the black man's ballot, by force or fraud, — and behold the suicide of a race! Nevertheless, out of the evil came something of good, — the more careful adjustment of education to real life, the clearer perception of the Negroes' social responsibilities, and the sobering realization of the meaning of progress.

So dawned the time of Sturm und Drang[①]: storm and stress today rocks our little boat on the mad waters of the world — sea; there is within and without the sound of conflict, the burning of body and rending of soul; inspiration strives with doubt, and faith with vain questionings. The bright ideals of the past, — physical freedom, political power, the training of brains and the training of hands, — all these in turn have waxed and waned, until even the last grows dim and overcast. Are they all wrong, — all false? No, not that, but each alone was oversimple and incomplete, — the dreams of a credulous race childhood, or the fond imaginings of the other world which does not know and does not want to know our power. To be really true, all these ideals must be melted and welded into one. The training of the schools we need today more than ever, — the training of deft hands, quick eyes and ears, and above all the broader, deeper, higher culture of gifted minds and pure hearts. The power of the ballot we need in sheer self-defence, — else what shall save us from a second slavery? Freedom, too, the long — sought, we still seek, — the freedom of life and limb, the freedom to work and think, the freedom to love and aspire. Work, culture, liberty, — all these we need, not singly but together, not successively but together, each growing and aiding each, and all striving toward that vaster ideal that swims before the Negro people, the ideal of human brotherhood, gained through the unifying ideal of Race; the ideal of fostering and developing the traits and talents of the Negro, not in opposition to or contempt for other races, but rather in large conformity to the greater ideals of the American Republic, in order that someday on American soil two world-races may give each to each those characteristics both so sadly lack. We the darker ones come even now not altogether empty-handed: there are today no truer exponents of the pure human spirit of the Declaration of Independence than the American Negroes; there is no true American music but the wild sweet melodies of the Negro slave; the American fairy tales and folklore are Indian and African; and, all in all, we black men seem the sole oasis of simple faith and reverence in a dusty desert of dollars and smartness. Will America be poorer if she replaces her brutal dyspeptic blundering with light — hearted but determined Negro humility? or her coarse and cruel wit with loving jovial good — humor? or her vulgar music with the soul of the Sorrow Songs?

---

① "Sturm und Drang",指 18 世纪 60—80 年代德国文学艺术领域的狂飙突进运动,是文艺形式从古典主义向浪漫主义的过渡阶段。

Merely a concrete test of the underlying principles of the great republic is the Negro Problem, and the spiritual striving of the freedmen's sons is the travail of souls whose burden is almost beyond the measure of their strength, but who bear it in the name of an historic race, in the name of this the land of their fathers' fathers, and in the name of human opportunity.

And now what I have briefly sketched in large outline let me on coming pages tell again in many ways, with loving emphasis and deeper detail, that men may listen to the striving in the souls of black folk.

选文评析：

《我们的精神斗争》("Of Our Spiritual Strivings")是《黑人的灵魂》整本书中的第一篇导读性文章。在这篇文章的开头，杜波依斯设想了一个大多数白人都想问他的问题："成为一个问题是什么感觉"，或者更直白地说，"作为白人眼中有问题的一类人中的一员，你是什么感觉?"虽然白人从来没有直接提出过这个问题，却总是能够以旁敲侧击的方式让黑人知道这是他们想问的。这在当时是一种很普遍的看法，即多数白人认为黑人大多是坏人，或者至少是"有问题的人"，只有少数例外。生活在种族隔离时代，杜波依斯最初并未意识到自己在社会中的地位很低。虽然他了解别人对他的看法和感受，但由于他受过良好教育，他并不认为自己是一个"问题"。而且根据经常提出这个问题的白人的判断标准，他算得上是黑人群体中一个典型的好人。

他接着讲述了在学校遇到的一件小事：一个白人女孩拒绝与他交换卡片，这个小小的"创伤经历"成为年轻的杜波依斯人格成长的催化剂，逐渐让杜波依斯从一个无知的年轻人转变成一个有见地的学者。在此之前，杜波依斯并未因自己的黑人身份而受到困扰。由于从小生活在一个种族关系比较融洽的社区，还曾得到周边白人的很多帮助，所以即便杜波依斯从小被父亲抛弃，他的童年也并未陷入悲惨境遇，甚至可以说相当乐观向上。但在他的卡片被女孩"只看了一眼就断然拒绝"的一瞬间，杜波依斯第一次意识到自己是个"问题"。"一切在一天之内发生，一个人第一次突然得到启示。"他意识到自己在这个以白人为主的学校里是个与众不同的另类：

> 我突然意识到，我和其他人不一样，或者说，也许在内心、生活和渴望上都是一样的，但却被一层巨大的帷幕隔绝在他们的世界之外。从此以后，我再也不想戳穿那层帷幕，不想悄悄钻过它；我把一切都轻蔑地放在它的外面，生活在它上面的一片蓝天和茫茫人影之中。当我能在考试中打败我的队友，或者在赛跑中超过他们，甚至能打败他们的尖头时，天空是最蓝的。

从那一刻开始，他决心在生活中的大多数事情上，他都要努力做得比白人更好、更优秀。他没有气馁，让自己屈服于"帷幕"的不公正，而是决定去追求能赋予他力量的教育。但更多的黑人却不能像杜波依斯那样拥有强大的内心，他们往往在让人压抑沮丧的现实面前感到绝望，"他们的青春萎缩成无味的谄媚，或是默默地憎恨周围苍白的世界，对一切白人的事物报以嘲笑和不信任；或是在痛苦的哭泣中消瘦，上帝为什么要让我在自己的家里成为一个被遗弃的陌生人？"

杜波依斯在此使用帷幕来隐喻种族分界线。他认为，所有非裔美国人面前都被遮挡着一层帷幕，导致他们对世界的看法及其潜在的经济、政治和社会机会与白人有着天壤之别。帷幕是种族分界线的视觉表现，它既是福也是祸，也是杜波依斯毕生努力解决的问题。"帷幕"是非裔美国人一生都要面对的体验。他们总是生活在一种认识中，即他们是另类，而且别人也视其为另类。不管他们多么努力，他们永远无法摆脱这个比喻或这种另类标签。杜波依斯用一种指责的语气来解释这个概念。通过他的写作，他很明显在批评美国政府将非裔美国人的生活限制在帷幕之内。不过他也暗示，只有那些像他一样通过接受教育摆脱了无知的人才能意识到这种心理负担的存在。而那些没有受过教育的黑人则不一定会为帷幕的存在而感到焦虑，因为他们可能根本不知道它的存在。

在这一章的第三段，杜波依斯还提出了他最著名的"双重意识"理论。他说：

> 在埃及和印度、希腊和罗马、条顿和蒙古之后，黑人是第七个儿子，生下来就戴着帷幕，在这个美国世界里，他们拥有视觉天赋，这个世界不会让他产生真正的自我意识，但只会让他通过另一个世界的启示来认识自己。这是一种奇特的感觉，一种双重意识，一种总是通过别人的眼睛看自己的感觉，一种用一盘世界的磁带来衡量自己的灵魂的感觉，这个世界是以一种有趣的轻蔑和怜悯的眼光看待的。一个人曾经感受到他的两种身份，一个是美国人，一个是黑人；两个灵魂，两种思想，两种不妥协的斗争；两个交战的理想，在一个黑暗的身体里，只有顽强的力量，才能使它不被撕裂。

他用这段文字深刻分析了"双重意识"的复杂性。① 双重意识在这里被认为是一种"感觉"，一种没有"真正的"自我意识的感觉，但仍然是一种自我意识。它也是一种更为复杂的"双重"感觉的一部分，即彼此不同和互相竞争的"思想""斗争"和"理想"。这不是一种偶然或偶发的感觉，而是一种固定和持续的意识形式。它是一种社会文化结构，而不是一种美国黑人特有的纯粹生物事实。杜波依斯还另外在《双重意识与帷幕》("Double Consciousness and the Veil")一文中进一步指出，双重意识是指同时拥有两种身份意识：一种是"黑人"身份及其所有的细微差别，另一种是美国社会强加给他们的"美国人"身份。黑人的任务是合并这两个相互冲突的身份，但他又永远不可能真正成为纯正的美国人或纯正的黑人，因为美国现有的社会条件不允许他这样做。"双重意识"这个短语定义了非裔美国人在美国的生活方式。他们的生活不只是黑人或美国人，而是这两种身份的交集，不能和平地融合在一起。黑人解放的历史进程加剧了这些相互矛盾的身份。"自由人还没有在自由中找到他的应许之地。无论这些年的变化带来了什么好处，黑人民众都会感到深深的失望。"解放并没有给黑人提供一个被美国社会同化的机会，反而只给一个曾经被奴役

---

① 此处参阅了《斯坦福哲学百科全书网站》有关"双重意识"的解释，https://plato.stanford.edu/entries/double-consciousness/.

的群体提供了很少的自由。

杜波依斯一直在追问，为什么上帝选择让黑人成为一个问题。他不明白为什么黑人是在所有其他种族的阴影下被创造出来的；他说黑人是上帝创造的"第七个儿子"，他天生具有双重意识，总是能够通过别人的眼睛看自己。但杜波依斯也认为，美国黑人不仅是一个问题，而且也是斗争的象征。他的双重独特身份在过去曾是一种障碍，但在未来却有可能是一种力量之源："从此以后，种族的命运可以被认为既不会导致同化，也不会导致分裂主义，而是带来让人骄傲的持久联结。这个群体不仅试图在多年的囚禁之后达到自我意识的成熟，而且还试图将两个相互冲突的身份融合成一个最终更好的身份"。对杜波依斯来说，这不仅是一种"感觉"，而且是美国黑人政治斗争的一个关键目标："美国黑人的历史就是这场斗争的历史，他们渴望获得自我意识的男子气概，把双重自我融合成一个更好、更真实的自我。在这种融合中，他不希望失去任何一个年长的自我。"

推荐阅读文献：

Bell, Bernard W. and Grosholz, Emily R. *W. E. B. Du Bois on Race and Culture*. Taylor & Francis Group, 1997.

Blum, Edward J. The Spiritual Scholar: W. E. B. Du Bois. *The Journal of Blacks in Higher Education*, 2007(57): 73-79.

Blum, Edward J. *W. E. B. Du Bois, American Prophet*. U of Pennsylvania P, 2009.

Bolden, Tonya. *W. E. B. Du Bois: A Twentieth-Century Life*. Penguin Young Readers Group, 2008.

Bromell, Nick and Kim, David Haekwon. *A Political Companion to W. E. B. Du Bois*. UP of Kentucky, 2018.

Bruce, Dickson D. Jr. W. E. B. Du Bois and the Dilemma of "Race". *American Literary History*, 1995, 7(2): 334-343.

Horne, Gerald and Burden-Stelly, Charisse. *W. E. B. Du Bois: a Life in American History*. ABC-CLIO, 2019.

Melamed, Jodi. W. E. B. Du Bois's UnAmerican End. *African American Review*, 2006, 40(3): 533-550.

Mostern, Kenneth. Three Theories of the Race of W. E. B. Du Bois. *Cultural Critique*, 1996(34): 27-63.

Rabaka, Reiland. W. E. B. Du Bois's Evolving Africana Philosophy of Education. *Journal of Black Studies*, 2003, 33(4): 399-449.

Young, Alford A., and Watts, Jerry Gafio. *Souls of W. E. B. Du Bois*. Taylor & Francis Group, 2006.

第七章　查尔斯·切斯纳特
（Charles Chesnutt，1858—1932）

查尔斯·切斯纳特是一位非裔美国作家、散文家、政治活动家和律师，是黑人文学的重要开拓者，被誉为美国"第一位真正的非裔作家"。他出生在俄亥俄州克利夫兰市，成长于北卡罗来纳州费耶特维尔（Fayetteville）。他的祖父是白人，父母都是自由的黑人，从外表上几乎看不出他是混血儿。当他8岁时，跟随父母回到费耶特维尔，一边在家庭杂货店兼职，一边就读于自由民局创办的黑人学校。1872年，经济上的需要迫使他在北卡罗来纳州的夏洛特市（Charlotte）开始教书生涯。1877年，他回到费耶特维尔，一年后结婚，1880年成为州立黑人师范学校的校长。此后，他继续学习英国古典文学、外语、音乐和速记等课程。1883年，他举家迁往克利夫兰。在那里，切斯纳特通过了州律师资格考试，还成立了自己的法庭速记公司，颇为成功。

切斯纳特从童年时期就梦想当作家。1880年，22岁的他在日记中写道："我觉得自己一定要写一本书。这一直是我怀有的梦想。我感觉到有一股无法抗拒的力量，呼唤着我去完成这项任务。"他明确表示，"我写作的目的与其说是为了提高有色人种，不如说是为了提高白人"。换言之，对切斯纳特来说，文学的功用就是要逐步地使公众接受这样一个观念，即黑人和白人应该是平等的，享有平等的机会。1887年，《大西洋月刊》（Atlantic Monthly）刊登了切斯纳特的短篇小说《毒葡萄》（"The Goophered Grapevine"），标志着黑人小说首次出现在那本著名的杂志上。

随着切斯纳特的短篇故事被其他杂志陆续接受，他将这些故事汇编成短篇小说集《巫婆》（The Conjure Woman，1899），一经出版，即被视为当时最优秀的作品。作者对黑人的生活观察入微，尤其善于刻画黑人的内部矛盾。他的第二部短篇小说集《他青年时代的妻子及关于种族界限的其他故事》（The Wife of His Youth and Other Stories of the Color Line，1899）以肤色界限为主题，作者认为，"混血问题更复杂，更难于处理"。切斯纳特比以往任何一位美国非裔作家都更广泛地涵盖了南方和北方种族的经历。同年，他还出版了一部传记作品《弗雷德里克·道格拉斯传》（Frederick Douglass）。接下来，在1900—1905年的五年间，切斯纳特出版了三部长篇小说：《雪松后的房子》(*The House Behind the Cedars*，1900)、《传统的精髓》(*The Marrow of Tradition*，1901)和《上校的梦想》(*The Colonel's Dream*，1905)，深入地探讨了 20 世纪末美国南部的种族关系。毫无疑问，他的作品在白人主导的美国文坛遭到冷落，评论也多指责他的种族观，对他的艺术成就闭口不谈。在极度气愤与失望之下，切斯纳特放弃了靠写作养家糊口的梦想，重操律师旧业。

1910 年开始，他积极参加全美有色人种协进会(NAACP)，为同年成立的全美有色人种协进会的官方杂志《危机》撰写了一些短篇小说和散文。此外，切斯纳特与杜波依斯、布克·T. 华盛顿等人一起工作，成为 20 世纪早期最著名的活动家和评论家之一。到了 20 世纪 20 年代，切斯纳特的作品重新获得关注。1922 年，《芝加哥保卫者》连载了《雪松后的房子》。1923 年，黑人电影工作者奥斯卡·米绍(Oscar Micheaux)把这部小说拍成电影。1928 年，因他"创造性地描绘美国黑人生活与斗争"，全美有色人种协进会授予切斯纳特斯平加恩奖章(Spingarn Medal)。切斯纳特于 1932 年去世，被安葬在克利夫兰湖景公墓，享年 74 岁。

📖 作品选读(一)：

The Marrow of Tradition

Chapter V
A Journey Southward

As the south-bound train was leaving the station at Philadelphia, a gentleman took his seat in the single sleeping-car attached to the train, and proceeded to make himself comfortable. He hung up his hat and opened his newspaper, in which he remained absorbed for a quarter of an hour. When the train had left the city behind, he threw the paper aside, and looked around at the other occupants of the car. One of these, who had been on the car since it had left New York, rose from his seat upon perceiving the other's glance, and came down the aisle.

"How do you do, Dr. Burns?" he said, stopping beside the seat of the Philadelphia passenger.

The gentleman looked up at the speaker with an air of surprise, which, after the first keen, incisive glance, gave place to an expression of cordial recognition.

"Why, it's Miller!" he exclaimed, rising and giving the other his hand, "William Miller — Dr. Miller, of course. Sit down, Miller, and tell me all about yourself, — what you're doing, where you've been, and where you're going. I'm delighted to meet you, and to see you looking so well — and so prosperous."

"I deserve no credit for either, sir," returned the other, as he took the proffered seat, "for I inherited both health and prosperity. It is a fortunate chance that permits me to meet you."

The two acquaintances, thus opportunely thrown together so that they might while away in conversation the tedium of their journey, represented very different and yet very similar types of manhood. A celebrated traveler, after many years spent in barbarous or savage lands, has said that among all varieties of mankind the similarities are vastly more important and fundamental than the differences. Looking at these two men with the American eye, the differences would perhaps be the more striking, or at least the more immediately apparent, for the first was white and the second black, or, more correctly speaking, brown; it was even a light brown, but both his swarthy complexion and his curly hair revealed what has been described in the laws of some of our states as a "visible admixture" of African blood.

Having disposed of this difference, and having observed that the white man was perhaps fifty years of age and the other not more than thirty, it may be said that they were both tall and sturdy, both well dressed, the white man with perhaps a little more distinction; both seemed from their faces and their manners to be men of culture and accustomed to the society of cultivated people. They were both handsome men, the elder representing a fine type of Anglo-Saxon, as the term is used in speaking of our composite white population; while the mulatto's erect form, broad shoulders, clear eyes, fine teeth, and pleasingly moulded features showed nowhere any sign of that degeneration which the pessimist so sadly maintains is the inevitable heritage of mixed races.

As to their personal relations, it has already appeared that they were members of the same profession. In past years they had been teacher and pupil. Dr. Alvin Burns was professor in the famous medical college where Miller had attended lectures. The professor had taken an interest in his only colored pupil, to whom he had been attracted by his earnestness of purpose, his evident talent, and his excellent manners and fine physique. It was in part due to Dr. Burns's friendship that Miller had won a scholarship which had enabled him, without drawing too heavily upon his father's resources, to spend in Europe, studying in the hospitals of Paris and Vienna, the two most delightful years of his life. The same influence had strengthened his natural inclination toward operative surgery, in which Dr. Burns was a distinguished specialist of national reputation.

Miller's father, Adam Miller, had been a thrifty colored man, the son of a slave who, in the olden time, had bought himself with money which he had earned and saved, over and above what he had paid his master for his time. Adam Miller had inherited his father's thrift, as well as his trade, which was that of a stevedore, or contractor for the loading and unloading of vessels at the port of Wellington. In the flush turpentine days following a few years after the civil war, he had made money. His savings, shrewdly invested, had by constant accessions become a competence. He had brought up his eldest son to the trade; the other he had given a professional education, in the proud hope that his children or his grandchildren might be gentlemen in the town where their ancestors had once been slaves.

Upon his father's death, shortly after Dr. Miller's return from Europe, and a year or two before the date at which this story opens, he had promptly spent part of his inheritance in founding a hospital, to which was to be added a training school for nurses, and in time perhaps a medical college and a school of pharmacy. He had been strongly tempted to leave the South, and seek a home for his family and a career for himself in the freer North, where race antagonism was less keen, or at least less oppressive, or in Europe, where he had never found his color work to his disadvantage. But his people had needed him, and he had wished to help them, and had sought by means of this institution to contribute to their uplifting.① As he now informed Dr. Burns, he was returning from New York, where he had been in order to purchase equipment for his new hospital, which would soon be ready for the reception of patients.

"How much I can accomplish I do not know," said Miller, "but I'll do what I can. There are eight or nine million of us, and it will take a great deal of learning of all kinds to leaven that lump."

"It is a great problem, Miller, the future of your race," returned the other, "a tremendously interesting problem. It is a serial story which we are all reading, and which grows in vital interest with each successive installment. It is not only your problem, but ours. Your race must come up or drag ours down."

"We shall come up," declared Miller; "slowly and painfully, perhaps, but we shall win our way. If our race had made as much progress everywhere as they have made in Wellington②, the problem would be well on the way toward solution."

"Wellington?" exclaimed Dr. Burns. "That's where I'm going. A Dr. Price, of Wellington, has sent for me to perform an operation on a child's throat. Do you know Dr. Price?"

"Quite well," replied Miller, "he is a friend of mine."

"So much the better. I shall want you to assist me. I read in the Medical Gazette, the other day, an account of a very interesting operation of yours. I felt proud to number you among my pupils. It was a remarkable case-a rare case. I must certainly have you with me in this one."

"I shall be delighted, sir," returned Miller, "if it is agreeable to all concerned."

Several hours were passed in pleasant conversation while the train sped rapidly southward. They were already far down in Virginia, and had stopped at a station beyond Richmond, when the conductor entered the car.

"All passengers," he announced, "will please transfer to the day coaches ahead. The sleeper has a hot box, and must be switched off here."

Dr. Burns and Miller obeyed the order, the former leading the way into the coach

---

① 此处意指"种族提升"（race uplift），即受过良好教育的黑人精英视自己为黑人种族进步的推动者，有责任帮助改善其他种族同胞的福祉。

② 暴乱发生前，威尔明顿的黑人中产阶级得到蓬勃发展，黑人占据总人口的大多数且享有选举权，地方政府由黑人议员、警察和治安法官组成。

immediately in front of the sleeping-car.

"Let's sit here, Miller," he said, having selected a seat near the rear of the car and deposited his suitcase in a rack. "It's on the shady side."

Miller stood a moment hesitatingly, but finally took the seat indicated, and a few minutes later the journey was again resumed.

When the train conductor made his round after leaving the station, he paused at the seat occupied by the two doctors, glanced interrogatively at Miller, and then spoke to Dr. Burns, who sat in the end of the seat nearest the aisle.

"This man is with you?" he asked, indicating Miller with a slight side movement of his head, and a keen glance in his direction.

"Certainly," replied Dr. Burns curtly, and with some surprise. "Don't you see that he is?"

The conductor passed on. Miller paid no apparent attention to this little interlude, though no syllable had escaped him. He resumed the conversation where it had been broken off, but nevertheless followed with his eyes the conductor, who stopped at a seat near the forward end of the car, and engaged in conversation with a man whom Miller had not hitherto noticed.

As this passenger turned his head and looked back toward Miller, the latter saw a broad-shouldered, burly white man, and recognized in his square-cut jaw, his coarse, firm mouth, and the single gray eye with which he swept Miller for an instant with a scornful glance, a well-known character of Wellington, with whom the reader has already made acquaintance in these pages. Captain McBane wore a frock coat and a slouch hat; several buttons of his vest were unbuttoned, and his solitaire diamond blazed in his soiled shirt-front like he headlight of a locomotive.

The conductor in his turn looked back at Miller, and retraced his steps. Miller braced himself for what he feared was coming, though he had hoped, on account of his friend's presence, that it might be avoided.

"Excuse me, sir," said the conductor, addressing Dr. Burns, "but did I understand you to say that this man was your servant?"

"No, indeed!" replied Dr. Burns indignantly. "The gentleman is not my servant, nor anybody's servant, but is my friend. But, by the way, since we are on the subject, may I ask what affair it is of yours?"

"It's very much my affair," returned the conductor, somewhat nettled at this questioning of his authority. "I'm sorry to part *friends*, but the law of Virginia does not permit colored passengers to ride in the white cars. You'll have to go forward to the next coach," he added, addressing Miller this time.

"I have paid my fare on the sleeping-car, where the separate-car law does not apply," remonstrated Miller.

[...]

"I can't help that. You can doubtless get your money back from the sleeping-car company. But this is a day coach, and is distinctly marked 'White,' as you must have seen before you sat down here. The sign is put there for that purpose."

He indicated a large card neatly framed and hung at the end of the car, containing the legend, "White," in letters about a foot long, painted in white upon a dark background, typical, one might suppose, of the distinction thereby indicated.

"You shall not stir a step, Miller," exclaimed Dr. Burns wrathfully. "This is an outrage upon a citizen of a free country. You shall stay right here."

"I'm sorry to discommode you," returned the conductor, "but there's no use kicking. It's the law of Virginia, and I am bound by it as well as you. I have already come near losing my place because of not enforcing it, and I can take no more such chances, since I have a family to support."

"And my friend has his rights to maintain," returned Dr. Burns with determination. "There is a vital principle at stake in the matter."

"Really, sir," argued the conductor, who was a man of peace and not fond of controversy, "there's no use talking — he absolutely cannot ride in this car."

"How can you prevent it?" asked Dr. Burns, lapsing into the argumentative stage.

"The law gives me the right to remove him by force. I can call on the train crew to assist me, or on the other passengers. If I should choose to put him off the train entirely, in the middle of a swamp, he would have no redress — the law so provides. If I did not wish to use force, I could simply switch this car off at the next siding, transfer the white passengers to another, and leave you and your friend in possession until you were arrested and fined or imprisoned."

"What he says is absolutely true, doctor," interposed Miller at this point. "It is the law, and we are powerless to resist it. If we made any trouble, it would merely delay your journey and imperil a life at the other end. I'll go into the other car."

"You shall not go alone," said Dr. Burns stoutly, rising in his turn. "A place that is too good for you is not good enough for me. I will sit wherever you do."

"I'm sorry again," said the conductor, who had quite recovered his equanimity, and calmly conscious of his power, could scarcely restrain an amused smile; "I dislike to interfere, but white passengers are not permitted to ride in the colored car."

"This is an outrage," declared Dr. Burns, "a d-d outrage! You are curtailing the rights, not only of colored people, but of white men as well. I shall sit where I please!"

"I warn you, sir," rejoined the conductor, hardening again, "that the law will be enforced. The beauty of the system lies in its strict impartiality — it applies to both races alike."

"And is equally infamous in both cases," declared Dr. Burns. "I shall immediately take steps."

"Never mind, doctor," interrupted Miller, soothingly, "it's only for a little while. I'll reach my destination just as surely in the other car, and we can't help it, anyway, I'll see you again at Wellington."

Dr. Burns, finding resistance futile, at length acquiesced and made way for Miller to pass him.

The colored doctor took up his valise and crossed the platform to the car ahead. It was an old car, with faded upholstery, from which the stuffing projected here and there through torn places. Apparently the floor had not been swept for several days. The dust lay thick upon the window sills, and the water — cooler, from which he essayed to get a drink, was filled with stale water which had made no recent acquaintance with ice. There was no other passenger in the car, and Miller occupied himself in making a rough calculation of what it would cost the Southern railroads to haul a whole car for every colored passenger. It was expensive, to say the least; it would be cheaper, and quite as considerate of their feelings, to make the negroes walk.

The car was conspicuously labeled at either end with large cards, similar to those in the other car, except that they bore the word "Colored" in black letters upon a white background. The author of this piece of legislation had contrived, with an ingenuity worthy of a better cause, that not merely should the passengers be separated by the color line, but that the reason for this division should be kept constantly in mind. Lest a white man should forget that he was white, — not a very likely contingency, — these cards would keep him constantly admonished of the fact; should a colored person endeavor, for a moment, to lose sight of his disability, these staring signs would remind him continually that between him and the rest of mankind not of his own color, there was by law a great gulf fixed.

Having composed himself, Miller had opened a newspaper, and was deep in an editorial which set forth in glowing language the inestimable advantages which would follow to certain recently acquired islands by the introduction of American liberty, when the rear door of the car opened to give entrance to Captain George McBane who took a seat near the door and lit a cigar. Miller knew him quite well by sight and by reputation, and detested him as heartily. He represented the aggressive, offensive element among the white people of the New South, who made it hard for a negro to maintain his self-respect or to enjoy even the rights conceded to colored men by Southern laws. McBane had undoubtedly identified him to the conductor in the other car. Miller had no desire to thrust himself upon the society of white people, which, indeed, to one who had traveled so much and so far, was no novelty; but he very naturally resented being at this late day — the law had been in operation only a few months — branded and tagged and set apart from the rest of mankind upon the public highways, like an unclean thing. Nevertheless, he preferred even this to the exclusive society of Captain George McBane.

"Porter," he demanded of the colored train attaché who passed through the car a moment later, "is this a smoking car for white men?"

"No, suh," replied the porter, "but they comes in here sometimes, when they ain' no cullud ladies on the kyar."

"Well, I have paid first-class fare, and I object to that man's smoking in here. You tell him to go out."

"I'll tell the conductor, suh," returned the porter in a low tone. "I'd jus' as soon talk ter the devil as ter that man."

The white man had spread himself over two seats, and was smoking vigorously, from time to time spitting carelessly in the aisle, when the conductor entered the compartment.

"Captain," said Miller, "this car is plainly marked 'Colored.' I have paid first-class fare, and I object to riding in a smoking car."

"All right," returned the conductor, frowning irritably. "I'll speak to him."

He walked over to the white passenger, with whom he was evidently acquainted, since he addressed him by name.

"Captain McBane," he said, "it's against the law for you to ride in the nigger car."

"Who are you talkin' to?" returned the other. "I'll ride where I damn please."

"Yes, sir, but the colored passenger objects. I'm afraid I'll have to ask you to go into the smoking-car."

"The hell you say!" rejoined McBane. "I'll leave this car when I get good and ready, and that won't be till I've finished this cigar. See?"

He was as good as his word. The conductor escaped from the car before Miller had time for further expostulation. Finally McBane, having thrown the stump of his cigar into the aisle and added to the floor a finishing touch in the way of expectoration, rose and went back into the white car.

Left alone in his questionable glory, Miller buried himself again in his newspaper, from which he did not look up until the engine stopped at a tank station to take water.

As the train came to a standstill, a huge negro, covered thickly with dust, crawled off one of the rear trucks unobserved, and ran round the rear end of the car to a watering-trough by a neighboring well. Moved either by extreme thirst or by the fear that his time might be too short to permit him to draw a bucket of water, he threw himself down by the trough, drank long and deep, and plunging his head into the water, shook himself like a wet dog, and crept furtively back to his dangerous perch.

Miller, who had seen this man from the car window, had noticed a very singular thing. As the dusty tramp passed the rear coach, he cast toward it a glance of intense ferocity. Up to that moment the man's face, which Miller had recognized under its grimy coating, had been that of an ordinarily good-natured, somewhat reckless, pleasure-loving negro, at present rather the worse for wear. The change that now came over it suggested a concentrated hatred almost uncanny in its murderousness. With awakened curiosity Miller followed the direction of the negro's glance, and saw that it rested upon a window where Captain McBane sat looking out. When Miller looked back, the negro had disappeared.

At the next station a Chinaman, of the ordinary laundry type, boarded the train, and took his seat in the white car without objection. At another point a colored nurse found a place with her mistress.

"White people," said Miller to himself, who had seen these passengers from the window, "do not object to the negro as a servant. As the traditional negro, — the servant, — he is welcomed; as an equal, he is repudiated."

Miller was something of a philosopher. He had long ago had the conclusion forced upon him that an educated man of his race, in order to live comfortably in the United States, must be either a philosopher or a fool; and since he wished to be happy, and was not exactly a fool, he had cultivated philosophy. By and by he saw a white man, with a dog, enter the rear coach. Miller wondered whether the dog would be allowed to ride with his master, and if not, what disposition would be made of him. He was a handsome dog, and Miller, who was fond of animals, would not have objected to the company of a dog, as a dog. He was nevertheless conscious of a queer sensation when he saw the porter take the dog by the collar and start in his own direction, and felt consciously relieved when the canine passenger was taken on past him into the baggage-car ahead. Miller's hand was hanging over the arm of his seat, and the dog, an intelligent shepherd, licked it as he passed. Miller was not entirely sure that he would not have liked the porter to leave the dog there; he was a friendly dog, and seemed inclined to be sociable.

📝 选文评析(一):

　　小说《传统的精髓》(*The Marrow of Tradition*, 1901)的主要故事基于 1898 年的威尔明顿大屠杀①,讲述了北卡罗来纳州一个叫威灵顿的小城里白人种族主义分子为了夺回政权而导演的流血事件。在这部小说里,切斯纳特运用现实主义手法详尽地描述了造成内战后南方的种族和社会状况的前因后果,并试图改善黑人的生存状况。因此,当时的许多评论家谴责这部小说公开的政治性。曾是切斯纳特早期作品忠实读者的一些中产阶级白人读者也认为这部小说的内容令人震惊,甚至令人反感。对于白人主导的文坛而言,切斯纳特创作的《传统的精髓》因过于真实地关注种族正义问题而遭到冷遇。本章节选自小说中的第 5章,讲述了混血主人公米勒乘坐火车所遭遇的种族隔离经历,说明了种族隔离制度下的白人特权以及切斯纳特对黑人解放的思考。

　　米勒是一名混血医生,他是新兴黑人中产阶级的一员。他的父亲曾是奴隶的儿子,却通过节俭勤奋为自己赎回自由之身,也使儿子接受教育成为绅士。米勒医生从欧洲留学归来并建立了一所医院,希望能够帮助自己的同胞。在他购买完设备乘坐火车归乡的途中,偶遇了来自北方的白人老师伯恩斯,便与其热切交谈。从外形上看,"他们又高又壮,穿着讲究;从他们的面容和举止来看,他们似乎都是有文化的人;他们都是英俊的男人"。

---

　　① 1898 年的威尔明顿暴动,又称 1898 年威尔明顿大屠杀,发生在 1898 年 11 月 10 日的北卡罗来纳州威尔明顿市。它被认为是重建后北卡罗来纳州政治的转折点。这一事件进一步加剧了南部地区的种族隔离状况。它最初被美国白人描述为由黑人引起的种族暴乱。然而,随着时间的推移,更多的事实被公开,这一事件又被视为政变。该州的白人民主党密谋并带领 2000 名白人群众推翻合法选举的地方联合主义政府之后,驱逐了反对党的黑人和白人政治领袖,摧毁了自内战以来建立起来的黑人公民的财产和商业,其中包括该市唯一的黑人报纸。该事件造成 60 人至 300 多人死亡。

但是，如果"用美国人的眼光看这两个人"，米勒和伯恩斯医生之间的差异就是云泥之别，"第一个是白皮肤，第二个是黑皮肤，或者更准确地说是棕色皮肤"。显然，"美国人的眼光"，或者更具体地说，"白人凝视"更加强调两人的不同肤色，并不关注他们内在的相似性。而作者通过提出种族之间的共同点高于不同点，试图颠覆传统的"白人凝视"，希望能够改变白人读者对于种族关系书写的集体期待。同时，作者也真实地描摹了新兴的黑人中产阶级儒雅、挺拔的形象，"黑白混血儿笔直的身材、宽阔的肩膀、清澈的眼睛、精致的牙齿和令人愉悦的造型，决不应该有任何退化的迹象"，回击了主流社会对黑人的模式化与丑化。

但当火车向南驶入弗吉尼亚州后，这种和谐的氛围就被打破了。由于种族隔离制度的存在，导致黑人只能以白人仆人的身份出现在白人车厢。因此，当列车员看到黑人米勒坐在白人车厢，在询问过伯恩斯并得到模棱两可的回复后，将其误当成白人医生的仆从而允许米勒继续坐在白人车厢。随后，当列车员从麦克班上尉处得知米勒的真实身份后，便开始驱逐米勒。他提出，"弗吉尼亚州的法律不允许有色人种乘客乘坐白人车厢"，"法律规定我有权强制执行"，以及"制度的美在于其严格的公正性，它同样适用于两个种族"。然而，种族隔离法却并没有得到公正的施行。白人乔治·麦克班上尉可以肆无忌惮地进入有色人种车厢，不受约束地坐下，"摊在两个座位上，不时地在过道里随意地吐痰，毫无顾忌地吸烟"，却并没有得到任何的惩戒。可见，种族隔离时期，不仅白人对黑人的经济剥削被视为合法，白人在道德上向黑人行不义之事，也被视为合理合法。这些名存实亡的法律及其背后隐藏着的白人享有的隐形特权，不仅剥夺了黑人应该享有的机遇、尊严与自由，而且实际上加剧了白人对黑人的歧视与迫害。

本节关于米勒观察车厢里的狗的片段也发人深省。当一个白人带着狗上车时，米勒对白人列车员如何处置狗产生了强烈的兴趣，"想知道这只狗是否可以和主人一起乘车"。狗最初是由狼驯化而来，但这只狗外表看起来英俊、温和，早已丧失了曾经的凶残与锐气。正如高大健壮、充满活力的黑人，从遥远的非洲部落来到美洲，失去了丛林的灵活，又被白人的文化所浸染，最终成为一个"被规训的文明人"，事事都遵循社会的规则法令。当售票员抓着狗的项圈将其带进储物车厢时，米勒"意识到一种奇怪的感觉"。对于米勒来说，种族隔离制度不正是狗的项圈吗？而米勒本人也正如这只被驯化的狗一样，虽然温顺有礼，却始终无法真正地融入白人社会。切斯纳特的小说中充满了类似的动物隐喻，它们成为考察切斯纳特利用文学话语为黑人发声的重要途径，体现了切斯纳特对于人与动物关系的深刻思考。

信奉白人至上的西方人类中心主义影响并导致美国白人社会对其他物种的漠视以及对种族他者的异化。人们通常认为，动物既不会像人一样具有灵魂，也缺乏高级情感，感知不到痛苦，它们存在的唯一目的就是为人类服务。因此，人们通过占有、控制、杀戮动物，彰显自身的道德主体性，从而边缘化动物，使其在这种二元对立的权力关系中始终处于无声、无名的状态。殖民时期以来，白人种族主义者为了宣扬白人至上的种族优越性，将黑人视为未完全进化之人，甚至将其降格为动物，从而强化社会内部的等级划分并合法化种族剥削制度。简单地说，一旦权力一方把被压迫群体与动物联系起来，他们的压迫与掠夺便被粉饰得合情合理了。因此，物种歧视才是潜隐于种族歧视背后的深层思想根源。

只有消除物种歧视，才有可能实现人类社会内部的平等共存，这也正是切斯纳特的作品试图传达给读者的要义。切斯纳特对于物种歧视的认识与动物解放者的观点不谋而合，成为西方动物权利运动的先声。

📖 作品选读(二)：

What Is a White Man?

The fiat① having gone forth from the wise men of the South that the "all-pervading, all-conquering Anglo-Saxon race" must continue forever to exercise exclusive control and direction of the government of this so-called Republic, it becomes important to every citizen who values his birthright to know who are included in this grandiloquent term. It is of course perfectly obvious that the writer or speaker who used this expression — perhaps Mr. Grady of Georgia② — did not say what he meant. It is not probable that he meant to exclude from full citizenship the Celts and Teutons and Gauls and Slavs③ who make up so large a proportion of our population; he hardly meant to exclude the Jews, for even the most ardent fire-eater would hardly venture to advocate the disfranchisement of the thrifty race whose mortgages cover so large a portion of Southern soil. What the eloquent gentleman really meant by this high-sounding phrase was simply the white race; and the substance of the argument of that school of Southern writers to which he belongs, is simply that for the good of the country the Negro should have no voice in directing the government or public policy of the Southern States or of the nation.

But it is evident that where the intermingling of the races has made such progress as it has in this country, the line which separates the races must in many instances have been practically obliterated. And there has arisen in the United States a very large class of the population who are certainly not Negroes in an ethnological sense, and whose children will be no nearer Negroes than themselves. In view, therefore, of the very positive ground taken by the white leaders of the South, where most of these people reside, it becomes in the highest degree important to them to know what race they belong to. It ought to be also a matter of serious concern to the Southern white people; for if their zeal for good government is so great that they contemplate the practical overthrow of the Constitution and laws of the United States to secure it, they ought at least to be

---

① Fiat：法令。

② Mr. Grady of Georgia：即亨利·格兰迪(Henry Grady，1850—1889)，美国南方记者和演讲家。

③ Celts, Teutons, Gauls, Slavs：即凯尔特人(爱尔兰)、条顿人(德国)、高卢人(法国)和斯拉夫人(东欧)。

sure that no man entitled to it by their own argument, is robbed of a right so precious as that of free citizenship; the "all-pervading, all conquering Anglo-Saxon" ought to set as high a value on American citizenship as the all-conquering Roman placed upon the franchise of his State two thousand years ago. This discussion would of course be of little interest to the genuine Negro, who is entirely outside of the charmed circle, and must content himself with the acquisition of wealth, the pursuit of learning and such other privileges as his "best friends" may find it consistent with the welfare of the nation to allow him; but to every other good citizen the inquiry ought to be a momentous one: What is a white man?

In spite of the virulence and universality of race prejudice in the United States, the human intellect long ago revolted at the manifest absurdity of classifying men fifteensixteenths white as black men; and hence there grew up a number of laws in different states of the Union defining the limit which separated the white and colored races, which was, when these laws took their rise, and is now to a large extent, the line which separated freedom and opportunity from slavery or hopeless degradation. Some of these laws are of legislative origin; others are judge-made laws, brought out by the exigencies of special cases which came before the courts for determination. Someday they will, perhaps, become mere curiosities of jurisprudence; the "black laws" will be bracketed with the "blue laws,"① and will be at best but landmarks by which to measure the progress of the nation. But today these laws are in active operation, and they are, therefore, worthy of attention; for every good citizen ought to know the law, and, if possible, to respect it; and if not worthy of respect, it should be changed by the authority which enacted it. Whether any of the laws referred to here have been in any manner changed by very recent legislation the writer cannot say, but they are certainly embodied in the latest editions of the revised statutes of the states referred to.

The colored people were divided, in most of the Southern States, into two classes, designated by law as Negroes and mulattoes respectively. The term Negro was used in its ethnological sense, and needed no definition; but the term "mulatto" was held by legislative enactment to embrace all persons of color not Negroes. The words "quadroon"② and "mestizo"③ are employed in some of the law books, tho' not defined; but the term "octoroon," as indicating a person having one-eighth of Negro blood, is not used at all, so far as the writer has been able to observe.

The states vary slightly in regard to what constitutes a mulatto or person of color, and as to what proportion of white blood should be sufficient to remove the disability of color. As a general rule, less than one-fourth of Negro blood left the individual white — in theory; race questions

---

① "blue laws"：蓝法，指美国殖民地时期按照清教道德所定的法律，比如禁止在星期天跳舞、喝酒等。

② quadroon：拥有四分之一非裔血统的混血儿。

③ mestizo：西班牙语，指西班牙人和美洲印第安人的混血儿。

being, however, regulated very differently in practice. In Missouri, by the code of 1855, still in operation, so far as not inconsistent with the Federal Constitution and laws, "any person other than a Negro, any one of whose grandmothers or grandfathers is or shall have been a Negro, tho' all of his or her progenitors except those descended from the Negro may have been white persons, shall be deemed a mulatto." Thus the color-line is drawn at one-fourth of Negro blood, and persons with only one-eighth are white.

By the Mississippi code of 1880, the color-line is drawn at one-fourth of Negro blood, all persons having less being theoretically white.

Under the code noir of Louisiana, the descendant of a white and a quadroon is white, thus drawing the line at one-eighth of Negro blood. The code of 1876 abolished all distinctions of color; as to whether they have been re-enacted since the Republican Party went out of power in that state the writer is not informed.

Jumping to the extreme North, persons are white within the meaning of the Constitution of Michigan who have less than one-fourth of Negro blood.

In Ohio the rule, as established by numerous decisions of the Supreme Court, was that a preponderance① of white blood constituted a person a white man in the eye of the law, and entitled him to the exercise of all the civil rights of a white man. By a retrogressive step the color-line was extended in 1861 in the case of marriage, which by statute was forbidden between a person of pure white blood and one having a visible admixture of African blood. But by act of legislature, passed in the spring of 1887, all laws establishing or permitting distinctions of color were repealed. In many parts of the state these laws were always ignored, and they would doubtless have been repealed long ago but for the sentiment of the southern counties, separated only by the width of the Ohio River from a former slave-holding state. There was a bill introduced in the legislature during the last session to re-enact the "black laws," but it was hopelessly defeated; the member who introduced it evidently mistook his latitude; he ought to be a member of the Georgia legislature.

But the state which, for several reasons, one might expect to have the strictest laws in regard to the relations of the races, has really the loosest. Two extracts from decisions of the Supreme Court of South Carolina will make clear the law of that state in regard to the color-line.

> The definition of the term mulatto, as understood in this state, seems to be vague, signifying generally a person of mixed white or European and Negro parentage, in whatever proportions the blood of the two races may be mingled in the individual. But it is not invariably applicable to every admixture of African blood with the European, nor is one having all the features of a white to be ranked with the degraded class designated by the laws of this state as persons of color, because of some remote taint of the Negro race. The line of distinction, however, is not

---

① Preponderance: 大多数。

ascertained by any rule of law.... Juries would probably be justified in holding a person to be white in whom the admixture of African blood did not exceed the proportion of one-eighth. But it is in all cases a question for the jury, to be determined by them upon the evidence of features and complexion afforded by inspection, the evidence of reputation as to parentage, and the evidence of the rank and station in society occupied by the party. The only rule which can be laid down by the courts is that where there is a distinct and visible admixture of Negro blood, the individual is to be denominated a mulatto or person of color.

In a later case the court held:

The question whether persons are colored or white, where color or feature are doubtful, is for the jury to decide by reputation, by reception into society, and by their exercise of the privileges of the white man, as well as by admixture of blood.

It is an interesting question why such should have been, and should still be, for that matter, the law of South Carolina, and why there should exist in that state a condition of public opinion which would accept such a law. Perhaps it may be attributed to the fact that the colored population of South Carolina always outnumbered the white population, and the eagerness of the latter to recruit their ranks was sufficient to overcome in some measure their prejudice against the Negro blood. It is certainly true that the color-line is, in practice as in law, more loosely drawn in South Carolina than in any other Southern State, and that no inconsiderable element of the population of that state consists of these legal white persons, who were either born in the state; or, attracted thither by this feature of the laws, have come in from surrounding states, and, forsaking home and kindred, have taken their social position as white people. A reasonable degree of reticence in regard to one's antecedents is, however, usual in such cases.

Before the War the color-line, as fixed by law, regulated in theory the civil and political status of persons of color. What that status was, was expressed in the Dred Scott decision.[1] But since the War, or rather since the enfranchisement of the colored people, these laws have been mainly confined — in theory, be it always remembered — to the regulation of the intercourse of the races in schools and in the marriage relation.

The extension of the color-line to places of public entertainment and resort, to inns and public highways, is in most states entirely a matter of custom. A colored man can sue in the courts of any Southern State for the violation of his common-law rights, and recover damages of say fifty cents without costs. A colored minister who sued a Baltimore steamboat company a few weeks ago for refusing him first-class accommodation, he having paid first-class fare, did not even meet with

---

① Dred Scott decision:即《德雷德·斯科特诉桑福德案》(*Dred Scott v. Sandford*, 1857),简称《斯科特案》,是美国最高法院于1857年判决的一个关于奴隶制的案件,裁定自由黑人不是美国公民。该案的判决被视为南北战争的关键起因之一。

that measure of success; the learned judge, a Federal judge by the way, held that the plaintiff's rights had been invaded, and that he had suffered humiliation at the hands of the defendant company, but that "the humiliation was not sufficient to entitle him to damages." And the learned judge dismissed the action without costs to either party.

Having thus ascertained what constitutes a white man, the good citizen may be curious to know what steps have been taken to preserve the purity of the white race, Nature, by some unaccountable oversight having to some extent neglected a matter so important to the future prosperity and progress of mankind. The marriage laws referred to here are in active operation, and cases under them are by no means infrequent. Indeed, instead of being behind the age, the marriage laws in the Southern States are in advance of public opinion; for very rarely will a Southern community stop to figure on the pedigree of the contracting parties to a marriage where one is white and the other is known to have any strain of Negro blood.

In Virginia, under the title "Offenses against Morality," the law provides that "any white person who shall intermarry with a Negro shall be confined in jail not more than one year and fined not exceeding one hundred dollars." In a marginal note on the statute-book, attention is called to the fact that "a similar penalty is not imposed on the Negro" — a stretch of magnanimity to which the laws of other states are strangers. A person who performs the ceremony of marriage in such a case is fined two hundred dollars, one-half of which goes to the informer.

In Maryland, a minister who performs the ceremony of marriage between a Negro and a white person is liable to a fine of one hundred dollars.

In Mississippi, code of 1880, it is provided that "the marriage of a white person to a Negro or mulatto or person who shall have one-fourth or more of Negro blood, shall be unlawful"; and as this prohibition does not seem sufficiently emphatic, it is further declared to be "incestuous and void," and is punished by the same penalty prescribed for marriage within the forbidden degrees of consanguinity.

But it is Georgia, the alma genetrix① of the chain-gang, which merits the questionable distinction of having the harshest set of color laws. By the law of Georgia the term "person of color" is defined to mean "all such as have an admixture of Negro blood, and the term 'Negro,' includes mulattoes." This definition is perhaps restricted somewhat by another provision, by which "all Negroes, mestizoes, and their descendants, having one-eighth of Negro or mulatto blood in their veins, shall be known in this State as persons of color." A colored minister is permitted to perform the ceremony of marriage between colored persons only; the white ministers are not forbidden to join persons of color in wedlock. It is further provided that "the marriage relation between white persons and persons of African descent is forever prohibited, and such marriages shall be null and void." This is a very sweeping provision; it will be noticed that the term "persons of color," previously defined, is not employed, the expression "persons of African

---

① alma genetrix: 此处意为蓄奴制的源头、滥觞之地。

descent" being used instead. A court which was so inclined would find no difficulty in extending this provision of the law to the remotest strain of African blood. The marriage relation is forever prohibited. Forever is a long time. There is a colored woman in Georgia said to be worth $300,000 — an immense fortune in the poverty stricken South. With a few hundred such women in that state, possessing a fair degree of good looks, the color-line would shrivel up like a scroll in the heat of competition for their hands in marriage. The penalty for the violation of the law against intermarriage is the same sought to be imposed by the defunct Glenn Bill① for violation of its provisions; i. e., a fine not to exceed one thousand dollars, and imprisonment not to exceed six months, or twelve months in the chain-gang.

Whatever the wisdom or justice of these laws, there is one objection to them which is not given sufficient prominence in the consideration of the subject, even where it is discussed at all; they make mixed blood a prima-facie② proof of illegitimacy. It is a fact that at present, in the United States, a colored man or woman whose complexion is white or nearly white is presumed in the absence of any knowledge of his or her antecedents, to be the offspring of a union not sanctified by law. And by a curious but not uncommon process, such persons are not held in the same low estimation as white people in the same position. The sins of their fathers are not visited upon the children, in that regard at least, and their mothers' lapses from virtue are regarded at least as misfortunes or as faults excusable under the circumstances. But in spite of all this, illegitimacy is not a desirable distinction, and is likely to become less so as these people of mixed blood advance in wealth and social standing. This presumption of illegitimacy was once, perhaps, true of the majority of such persons; but the times have changed. More than half of the colored people of the United States are of mixed blood; they marry and are given in marriage, and they beget children of complexions similar to their own. Whether or not, therefore, laws which stamp these children as illegitimate, and which by indirection establish a lower standard of morality for a large part of the population than the remaining part is judged by, are wise laws; and whether or not the purity of the white race could not be as well preserved by the exercise of virtue, and the operation of those natural laws which are so often quoted by Southern writers as the justification of all sorts of Southern "policies" — are questions which the good citizen may at least turn over in his mind occasionally, pending the settlement of other complications which have grown out of the presence of the Negro on this continent.

📝 选文评析(二)：

　　在乔治·华盛顿·卡贝尔(George Washington Cable)的鼓励下，切斯纳特开始写有关政治、种族问题的严肃文章。他的第一篇文章《黑人问题的内部观点》("An Inside View of

---

①　Glenn Bill：美国佐治亚州 1887 年出台法令，在学校强制推行种族隔离制。

②　prima-facie：初步的。

the Negro Question", 1889)因"即时性""政治化""党派化"的特点而屡次遭拒。1889年，由于对家庭的责任，切斯纳特拒绝了卡贝尔希望其担任秘书的邀请之后，于 5 月 30 日在《独立报》发表他的第二篇文章《什么是白人?》，比较了南方各州关于种族规定的法律。

切斯纳特在这篇文章里主要讨论了混血儿群体的身份问题，开篇就提到了那些"占据总人口很大一部分、从人种学的角度上看并不是黑人的群体"。他们虽然外表看起来和白人没有任何区别，却因为一滴血的原则，无法享有普通白人所拥有的平等权利，甚至被种族主义者比喻为骡子，认为他们是杂交产生的非自然的结果，是南方失败的活生生的象征，最终将湮没在历史进程中。对此，切斯纳特认为，美国的国家特色就在于它的种族混合。正如乔尔·威廉姆森(Joel Williamson)所说，"混血儿的行走、说话、呼吸都是对白人所创造的这个世界的控诉"，切斯纳特希望通过考察混血儿问题，早日打破黑人与白人之间的二元对立，消弭严格的肤色界限。

切斯纳特进一步阐明各州法律对种族身份规定的不一致性。具体而言，"1880 年的《密西西比法典》规定，肤色的界限是四分之一的黑人血统"；路易斯安那州的黑色法典显示，八分之一的黑人血统为肤色界线；在战前的俄亥俄州，如果一个人有一半以上的白人血统，那么他在法律上就是白人；在南卡罗来纳州的法院，"当一个人的肤色或特征值得怀疑时，应该由陪审团根据他的名声、社会接受程度、他对白人特权的行使以及血统的混合来决定"；根据佐治亚州的法律，"有色人种"一词指"所有具有黑人混合血统的人"。毫无疑问，法律规定的差异彰显了立法机构和法官在界定什么是白人方面存在着很大的困难。由此，切斯纳特试图向读者证明，肤色界限并不像他们认为的那样被严格监控，尝试削弱他们对种族的本质主义观念。

在论述的过程中，切斯纳特采用了一种准科学的方法，将血统分解成一定的比例，但南卡罗来纳州的法院裁定却完全指向了另一个方向："由陪审团根据他的名声、社会接受程度、他对白人特权的行使以及血统的混合来决定。"在这里，切斯纳特强调了白人性是一个可渗透的范畴，但更激进的是，他试图颠覆一个在 19 世纪晚期被白人普遍接受的认为种族是基于科学的"常识"，而这个科学常识实则是白人为了维持种族制度一厢情愿的想法。

切斯纳特在接下来的文章中用讽刺性的语调指出，"尽管种族偏见在美国具有毒害性和普遍性，但智者们早就对把具有十六分之十五的白人血统划分为黑人的荒谬感到反感"，这与南希·本特利(Nancy Bentley)曾提到的"黑白混血儿的形象是个丑闻——不仅是性丑闻，也是智力丑闻"的说法不谋而合。当他转向研究禁止异族通婚的法律时，挖苦性地再现了制定这种法律的"必要性"，"在某种程度上，大自然忽略了一个对人类未来的繁荣和进步如此重要的问题"。同样，在文章结尾，切斯纳特用质疑的语气提示他的读者，"白人种族的纯洁性是否能通过美德的运用，以及南方作家经常引用的自然法则的运作而得到很好的保护"。这篇文章发表之后，切斯纳特收到一封来自卡贝尔的信件。他在信中表示"非常认真、愉快地"阅读了这篇文章，并肯定了切斯纳特的研究方向，再次坚定了他继续写作并介入种族问题争论的信心。

🗩 推荐阅读文献：

Ames, Russell. Social Realism in Charles W. Chesnutt. *Phylon* (1940-1956), 1953, 14 (2): 199-206.

Ferguson, SallyAnn H. Charles W. Chesnutt's 'Future American'. *MELUS*, 1988, 15 (3): 95-107.

Izzo, David G. and Orban, Maria. *Charles Chesnutt Reappraised: Essays on the First Major African American Fiction Writer*. McFarland & Company, 2009.

Mcelrath, Joseph R. Jr. Why Charles W. Chesnutt Is Not a Realist. *American Literary Realism*, 2000, 32(2): 91-108.

McWilliams, Dean. *Charles W. Chesnutt and the Fictions of Race*. U of Georgia P, 2002.

Ramsey, William M. Family Matters in the Fiction of Charles W. Chesnutt. *The Southern Literary Journal*, 2001, 33(2): 30-43.

Sussman, Mark. Charles W. Chesnutt's Stenographic Realism. *MELUS*, 2015, 40(4): 48-68.

Wilson, Matthew. *Whiteness in the Novels of Charles W. Chesnutt*. UP of Mississippi, 2004.

Wright, Susan P. and Glass, Ernestine P. *Passing in the Works of Charles W. Chesnutt*. UP of Mississippi, 2010.

第八章 安娜·茱莉亚·库珀
（Anna Julia Cooper，1858—1964）

安娜·茱莉亚·库珀是美国历史上最有影响力的非裔知识分子之一，是一名杰出的黑人自由运动活动者、女性主义者、教育家、社会活动家和作家。她在内战前夕出生于北卡罗来纳州的一个种植园，是白人奴隶主与女奴的女儿。内战结束后，年仅九岁的库珀获得了圣奥古斯汀师范学校的奖学金，得以接受教育并开启学术生涯。1877年，库珀与圣公会牧师候选人、教师乔治·库珀结婚，然而婚后两年丈夫不幸去世。由于已婚妇女在当时不被允许从教，库珀因其寡妇身份得以从事教师职业。1881年，库珀进入奥博林学院学习，并获得数学专业硕士学位，成为当时受教育程度最高的美国非裔女性之一。毕业后，库珀进入首座公立黑人预科学校 M 街高中（M Street High School）任教，教授数学和科学等科目。这所学校的建立是黑人教育史上的重要事件。19 世纪 90 年代，库珀参与了黑人女性俱乐部运动，组织成员是受过教育的中产阶级女性，她们以帮助不幸的黑人同胞为己任，库珀在此运动期间逐渐成为一名出色的演说家，在 1895 年举办的有色人种全国会议和 1900 年的首届泛非会议上均发表言说。

库珀始终把提高黑人教育水平和智识能力作为教育目标，主张黑人与白人接受同样的学术教育，这在当时与颇受白人欢迎的布克·华盛顿倡导的黑人职业教育理念不相一致。1902 年，库珀被聘为 M 街高中校长。在她的领导下，学校的学术声誉获得哈佛大学等常青藤大学的认可，多名毕业生进入耶鲁大学、哈佛大学以及奥博林学院等知名高校深造。然而，库珀与其上司及当地其他非裔领导人意见相左，其女性身份也成为工作的障碍，她于 1906 年被全员男性的教育委员会开除，失去校长职位。库珀之后在密苏里州的林肯大学任教，并在 1910 年获邀重返 M 街高中担任拉丁文教师。1914 年，库珀在哥伦比亚大学攻读博士学位，研究奴隶制度，并在历经各种波折之后于 1925 年以 67 岁高龄在巴黎索邦大学获得博士学位。库珀终生致力于教育事业，直到 1964 年在华盛顿特区去世，她的远见卓识让黑人在种族平等的斗争中更进一步。

《来自南方的声音》（*A Voice from the South*）出版于 1892 年，书中讨论了妇女权利、种族进步、种族隔离等问题。这本书是对美国黑人女性处境进行分析的最早的长篇著作之一，清晰地阐述了美国社会种族化的性别歧视和性别化的种族歧视，并兼论了阶级与劳动、教育与智识发展、民主与公民身份等概念的重要性。库珀在这本书中集中表达了自己的思想，她的学思植根于西方古典哲学，因此其思想贡献集中于女性主义、认识论、种族批判和美国黑人研究等方面。书的前半部分围绕非裔妇女展开，库珀认为必须要把非裔女性教育纳入现有的教育体系，女性对种族的再生和进步有着重要作用。在该书后半部分，库珀讨论了斯托夫人、乔治·华盛顿·凯布尔等一些知名作家作品中的非裔形象，她认为这些作品并没有准确描绘出黑人的形象，因此她呼吁"在我去世之前我希望能看到一个黑人作家能够塑造出真实的黑人形象，同时偶尔也能够站在黑人的立场上刻画出白人形象"。下文选自《来自南方的声音》的第一章《妇女：种族新生和进步的关键因素》。

📖 作品选读：

Womanhood: A Vital Element in the Regeneration and Progress of a Race

The two sources from which, perhaps, modern civilization has derived its noble and ennobling ideal of woman are Christianity and the Feudal System.

......

Mahomet makes no account of woman whatever in his polity. The Koran, which, unlike our *Bible*, was a product and not a growth, tried to address itself to the needs of Arabian civilization as Mahomet with his circumscribed powers saw them. The Arab was a nomad. Home to him meant his present camping place. That deity who, according to our western ideals, makes and sanctifies the home, was to him a transient bauble to be toyed with so long as it gave pleasure and then to be thrown aside for a new one. As a personality, an individual soul, capable of eternal growth and unlimited development, and destined to mould and shape the civilization of the future to an incalculable extent, Mahomet did not know woman. There was no hereafter, no paradise for her. The heaven of the Mussulman is peopled and made gladsome not by the departed wife, or sister, or mother, but by houri① — a figment of Mahomet's brain, partaking of the ethereal qualities of angels, yet imbued with all the vices and inanity of Oriental women. The harem here, and dust to dust" hereafter, this was the hope, the inspiration, the summum bonum② of the Eastern woman's life! With what result on the life of the nation, the "Unspeakable Turk," the "sick man" of modern Europe, can to-day exemplify?

①　天堂的女神。

②　最好的。

Says a certain writer: "The private life of the Turk is vilest of the vile, unprogressive, unambitious, and inconceivably low." And yet Turkey is not without her great men. She has produced most brilliant minds; men skilled in all the intricacies of diplomacy and statesmanship; men whose intellects could grapple with the deep problems of empire and manipulate the subtle agencies which check-mate kings. But these minds were not the normal outgrowth of a healthy trunk. They seemed rather ephemeral excrescencies which shoot far out with all the vigor and promise, apparently, of strong branches; but soon alas fall into decay and ugliness because there is no soundness in the root, no life-giving sap, permeating, strengthening, and perpetuating the whole. There is a worm at the core! The homelife is impure! and when we look for fruit, like apples of Sodom,① it crumbles within our grasp into dust and ashes.

It is pleasing to turn from this effete and immobile civilization to a society still fresh and vigorous, whose seed is in itself, and whose very name is synonymous with all that is progressive, elevating, and inspiring, viz., the European bud and the American flower of modern civilization.

And here let me say parenthetically that our satisfaction in American institutions rests not on the fruition we now enjoy, but springs rather from the possibilities and promise that are inherent in the system, though as yet, perhaps, far in the future.

"Happiness," says Madame de Stael, ② "consists not in perfections attained, but in a sense of progress, the result of our own endeavor under conspiring circumstances toward a goal which continually advances and broadens and deepens till it is swallowed up in the Infinite." Such conditions in embryo are all that we claim for the land of the West. We have not yet reached our ideal in American civilization. The pessimists even declare that we are not marching in that direction. But there can be no doubt that here in America is the arena in which the next triumph of civilization is to be won; and here too we find promise abundant and possibilities infinite.

Now let us see on what basis this hope for our country primarily and fundamentally rests. Can anyone doubt that it is chiefly on the homelife and on the influence of good women in those homes? Says Macaulay:③"You may judge a nation's rank in the scale of civilization from the way they treat their women." And Emerson, "I have thought that a sufficient measure of civilization is the influence of good women." Now this high regard for woman, this germ of a prolific idea which in our own day is bearing such rich and varied fruit, was ingrafted into European civilization, we have said, from two sources, the Christian Church and the Feudal System. For although the Feudal System can in no sense be said to have originated the idea, yet there can be no doubt that the habits of life and modes of thought to which Feudalism gave rise, materially fostered and developed it; for they gave us chivalry, than which no institution has more sensibly magnified and

---

① Sodom: 索多玛,《圣经》中的堕落之城,由于其罪恶而被上帝摧毁。

② 德斯蒂尔夫人(Madame de Stael, 本名 Anna Louise Germaine de Staël-Holstein, 1766—1817): 法国女作家。

③ 托马斯·巴宾顿·麦考利(Thomas Babington Macaulay, 1800—1859): 英国历史学家和政治家。

elevated woman's position in society.

Tacitus[1] dwells on the tender regard for woman entertained by these rugged barbarians before they left their northern homes to overrun Europe. Old Norse legends too, and primitive poems, all breathe the same spirit of love of home and veneration for the pure and noble influence there presiding — the wife, the sister, the mother.

And when later on we see the settled life of the Middle Ages "oozing out," as M. Guizot[2] expresses it, from the plundering and pillaging life of barbarism and crystallizing into the Feudal System, the tiger of the field is brought once more within the charmed circle of the goddesses of his castle, and his imagination weaves around them a halo whose reflection possibly has not yet altogether vanished.

It is true the spirit of Christianity had not yet put the seal of catholicity on this sentiment. Chivalry, according to Bascom, was but the toning down and softening of a rough and lawless period. It gave a roseate glow to a bitter winter's day. Those who looked out from castle windows revelled in its "amethyst tints." But God's poor, the weak, the unlovely, the commonplace were still freezing and starving none the less in unpitied, unrelieved loneliness.

Respect for woman, the much lauded chivalry of the Middle Ages, meant what I fear it still means to some men in our own day — respect for the elect few among whom they expect to consort.

The idea of the radical amelioration of womankind, reverence for woman as woman regardless of rank, wealth, or culture, was to come from that rich and bounteous fountain from which flow all our liberal and universal ideas — the Gospel of Jesus Christ.

And yet the Christian Church at the time of which we have been speaking would seem to have been doing even less to protect and elevate woman than the little done by secular society. The Church as an organization committed a double offense against woman in the Middle Ages. Making of marriage a sacrament and at the same time insisting on the celibacy of the clergy and other religious orders, she gave an inferior if not an impure character to the marriage relation, especially fitted to reflect discredit on woman. Would this were all or the worst! but the Church by the licentiousness of its chosen servants invaded the household and established too often as vicious connections those relations which it forbade to assume openly and in good faith. "Thus," to use the words of our authority, "the religious corps became as numerous, as searching, and as unclean as the frogs of Egypt,[3] which penetrated into all quarters, into the ovens and kneading troughs, leaving their filthy trail wherever they went." Says Chaucer with characteristic satire, speaking of the Friars:

---

① 塔西佗(Tacitus, 56—117)：古罗马历史学家和参议员。
② 弗朗索瓦·吉佐特(Francois Guizot, 1787—1874)：法国历史学家和政治家。
③ frogs of Egypt：《圣经》中的第二次大瘟疫，见《出埃及记》7：25-8：11。

> Women may now go safely up and doun,
> In every bush, and under every tree,
> There is non other incubus but he,
> And he ne will don hem no dishonour.①

Henry, Bishop of Liege, could unblushingly boast the birth of twenty-two children in fourteen years.

It may help us under some of the perplexities which beset our way in "the one Catholic and Apostolic Church" to-day, to recall some of the corruptions and incongruities against which the Bride of Christ has had to struggle in her past history and in spite of which she has kept, through many vicissitudes, the faith once delivered to the saints. Individuals, organizations, whole sections of the Church militant may outrage the Christ whom they profess, may ruthlessly trample under foot both the spirit and the letter of his precepts, yet not till we hear the voices audibly saying "Come let us depart hence," shall we cease to believe and cling to the promise, "I am with you to the end of the world."②

> Yet saints their watch are keeping,
> The cry goes up 'How long!'
> And soon the night of weeping
> Shall be the morn of song.③

However much then the facts of any particular period of history may seem to deny it, I for one do not doubt that the source of the vitalizing principle of woman's development and amelioration is the Christian Church, so far as that church is coincident with Christianity.

Christ gave ideals not formulae. The Gospel is a germ requiring millennia for its growth and ripening. It needs, and at the same time helps, to form around itself a soil enriched in civilization, and perfected in culture and insight without which the embryo can be neither unfolded nor comprehended. With all the strides our civilization has made from the first to the nineteenth century, we can boast not an idea, not a principle of action, not a progressive social force but was already mutely foreshadowed, or directly enjoined in that simple tale of a meek and lowly life. The quiet face of the Nazarene④ is ever seen a little way ahead, never too far to come down to and touch the life of the lowest in days the darkest, yet ever leading onward, still onward, the tottering childish feet of our strangely boastful civilization.

---

① "Women may now go… no dishonour": 节选自《坎特伯雷故事集》的《巴斯妇》一章。

② "I am with you to the end of the world": 参见《马太福音》28：20.

③ "Yet saints… morn of song" 节选自萨缪尔·约翰逊创作的赞美诗《教会的根基》("The Church's One Foundation")。

④ Nazarene：拿撒勒的耶稣。

By laying down for woman the same code of morality, the same standard of purity, as for man; by refusing to countenance the shameless and equally guilty monsters who were gloating over her fall — graciously stooping in all the majesty of his own spotless-ness to wipe away the filth and grime of her guilty past and bid her go in peace and sin no more; and again in the moments of his own careworn and footsore dejection, turning trustfully and lovingly, away from the heartless snubbing and sneers, away from the cruel malignity of mobs and prelates in the dusty marts of Jerusalem to the ready sympathy, loving appreciation, and unfaltering friendship of that quiet home at Bethany; and even at the last, by his dying bequest to the disciple whom he loved, signifying the protection and tender regard to be extended to that sorrowing mother and ever afterward to the sex she represented — throughout his life and in his death he has given to men a rule and guide for the estimation of woman as an equal, as a helper, as a friend, and as a sacred charge to be sheltered and cared for with a brother's love and sympathy, lessons which nineteen centuries' gigantic strides in knowledge, arts, and sciences, in social and ethical principles have not been able to probe to their depth or to exhaust in practice.

It seems not too much to say then of the vitalizing, regenerating, and progressive influence of womanhood on the civilization of today, that, while it was foreshadowed among Germanic nations in the far away dawn of their history as a narrow, sickly, and stunted growth, it yet owes its catholicity and power, the deepening of its roots and broadening of its branches to Christianity.

The union of these two forces, the Barbaric and the Christian, was not long delayed after the Fall of the Empire. The Church, which fell with Rome, finding herself in danger of being swallowed up by barbarism, with characteristic vigor and fertility of resources, addressed herself immediately to the task of conquering her conquerors. The means chosen does credit to her power of penetration and adaptability, as well as to her profound, unerring, all-compassing diplomacy; and makes us even now wonder if aught human can successfully and ultimately withstand her far-seeing designs and brilliant policy, or gainsay her well-earned claim to the word Catholic.

She saw the barbarian, little more developed than a wild beast. She forbore to antagonize and mystify his warlike nature by a full blaze of the heartsearching and humanizing tenets of her great Head. She said little of the rule "If thy brother smite thee on one cheek, turn to him the other also"; [①] but thought it sufficient for the needs of those times, to establish the so-called "Truce of God" under which men were bound to abstain from butchering one another for three days of each week and on Church festivals. In other words, she respected their individuality: non-resistance pure and simple being for them an utter impossibility, she contented herself with less radical measures calculated to lead up finally to the full measure of the benevolence of Christ.

Next she took advantage of the barbarian's sensuous love of gaudy display and put all her magnificent garments on. She could not capture him by physical force; she would dazzle him by gorgeous spectacles. It is said that Romanism gained more in pomp and ritual during this trying

---

① "If thy brother smite thee... the other also"：见《马太福音》5：39。

period of the Dark Ages than throughout all her former history.

The result was she carried her point. Once more Rome laid her ambitious hand on the temporal power, and allied with Charlemagne,① aspired to rule the world through a civilization dominated by Christianity and permeated by the traditions and instincts of those sturdy barbarians.

Here was the confluence of the two streams we have been tracing, which, united now, stretch before us as a broad majestic river.

In regard to woman it was the meeting of two noble and ennobling forces, two kindred ideas the resultant of which, we doubt not, is destined to be a potent force in the betterment of the world.

Now, after our appeal to history comparing nations destitute of this force and so destitute also of the principle of progress, with other nations among whom the influence of woman is prominent coupled with a brisk, progressive, satisfying civilization, if in addition we find this strong presumptive evidence corroborated by reason and experience, we may conclude that these two equally varying concomitants are linked as cause and effect; in other words, that the position of woman in society determines the vital elements of its regeneration and progress.

Now, that this is so on a priori grounds all must admit. And this not because woman is better or stronger or wiser than man, but from the nature of the case, because it is she who must first form the man by directing the earliest impulses of his character.

Byron and Wordsworth were both geniuses and would have stamped themselves on the thought of their age under any circumstances; and yet we find the one a savor of life unto life, the other of death unto death. "Byron, like a rocket, shot his way upward with scorn and repulsion, flamed out in wild, explosive, brilliant excesses and disappeared in darkness made all the more palpable."

Wordsworth lent of his gifts to reinforce that "power in the Universe which makes for righteousness" by taking the harp handed him from Heaven and using it to swell the strains of angelic choirs. Two locomotives equally mighty stand facing opposite tracks; the one to rush headlong to destruction with all its precious freight, the other to toil grandly and gloriously up the steep embattlements to Heaven and to God. Who — who can say what a world of consequences hung on the first placing and starting of these enormous forces!

Woman, Mother, your responsibility is one that might make angels tremble and fear to take hold! To trifle with it, to ignore or misuse it, is to treat lightly the most sacred and solemn trust ever confided by God to human kind. The training of children is a task on which an infinity of weal or woe depends. Who does not covet it? Yet who does not stand awe-struck before its momentous issues! It is a matter of small moment, it seems to me, whether that lovely girl in whose accomplishments you take such pride and delight, can enter the gay and crowded salon with the ease and elegance of this or that French or English gentlewoman, compared with the decision as to

---

① 查理曼大帝(Charlemagne, 742—814): 法兰克国王和神圣罗马帝国第一位皇帝。

whether her individuality is going to reinforce the good or the evil elements of the world. The lace and the diamonds, the dance and the theater, gain a new significance when scanned in their bearings on such issues. Their influence on the individual personality, and through her on the society and civilization which she vitalizes and inspires — all this and more must be weighed in the balance before the jury can return a just and intelligent verdict as to the innocence or banefulness of these apparently simple amusements.

Now the fact of woman's influence on society being granted, what are its practical bearings on the work which brought together this conference of colored clergy and laymen in Washington? "We come not here to talk." Life is too busy, too pregnant with meaning and far reaching consequences to allow you to come this far for mere intellectual entertainment.

The vital agency of womanhood in the regeneration and progress of a race, as a general question, is conceded almost before it is fairly stated. I confess one of the difficulties for me in the subject assigned lay in its obviousness. The plea is taken away by the opposite attorney's granting the whole question.

"Woman's influence on social progress" — who in Christendom doubts or questions it? One may as well be called on to prove that the sun is the source of light and heat and energy to this many-sided little world.

Nor, on the other hand, could it have been intended that I should apply the position when taken and proven, to the needs and responsibilities of the women of our race in the South. For is it not written, "Cursed is he that cometh after the king"? And has not the King already preceded me in "The Black Woman of the South"?

They have had both Moses and the Prophets in Dr. Crummell and if they hear not him, neither would they be persuaded though one came up from the South.[1]

I would beg, however, with the Doctor's permission, to add my plea for the Colored Girls of the South — that large, bright, promising, fatally beautiful class that stand shivering like a delicate plantlet before the fury of tempestuous elements, so full of promise and possibilities, yet so sure of destruction; often without a father to whom they dare apply the loving term, often without a stronger brother to espouse their cause and defend their honor with his life's blood; in the midst of pitfalls and snares, waylaid by the lower classes of white men, with no shelter, no protection nearer than the great blue vault above, which half conceals and half reveals the one Care-Taker they know so little of. Oh, save them, help them, shield, train, develop, teach, inspire them! Snatch them, in God's name, as brands from the burning! There is material in them well worth your while, the hope in germ of a staunch, helpful, regenerating womanhood on which, primarily, rests the foundation stones of our future as a race.

It is absurd to quote statistics showing the Negro's bank account and rent rolls, to point to the hundreds of newspapers edited by colored men and lists of lawyers, doctors, professors, D. D's,

---

[1]　"They have had both Moses and the Prophets... from the South" 见《路加福音》16：31。

LLD's, etc., etc., etc., while the source from which the life-blood of the race is to flow is subject to taint and corruption in the enemy's camp.

True progress is never made by spasms. Real progress is growth. It must begin in the seed. Then, "first the blade, then the ear, after that the full corn in the ear." There is something to encourage and inspire us in the advancement of individuals since their emancipation from slavery. It at least proves that there is nothing irretrievably wrong in the shape of the black man's skull, and that under given circum stances his development, downward or upward, will be similar to that of other average human beings.

But there is no time to be wasted in mere felicitation. That the Negro has his niche in the infinite purposes of the Eternal, no one who has studied the history of the last fifty years in America will deny. That much depends on his own right comprehension of his responsibility and rising to the demands of the hour, it will be good for him to see; and how best to use his present so that the structure of the future shall be stronger and higher and brighter and nobler and holier than that of the past, is a question to be decided each day by every one of us.

The race is just twenty-one years removed from the conception and experience of a chattel, just at the age of ruddy manhood. It is well enough to pause a moment for retrospection, introspection, and prospection. We look back, not to become inflated with conceit because of the depths from which we have arisen, but that we may learn wisdom from experience. We look within that we may gather together once more our forces, and, by improved and more practical methods, address ourselves to the tasks before us. We look forward with hope and trust that the same God whose guiding hand led our fathers through and out of the gall and bitterness of oppression, will still lead and direct their children, to the honor of His name, and for their ultimate salvation.

But this survey of the failures or achievements of the past, the difficulties and embarrassments of the present, and the mingled hopes and fears for the future, must not degenerate into mere dreaming nor consume the time which belongs to the practical and effective handling of the crucial questions of the hour; and there can be no issue more vital and momentous than this of the womanhood of the race.

Here is the vulnerable point, not in the heel, but at the heart of the young Achilles;① and here must the defenses be strengthened and the watch redoubled.

We are the heirs of a past which was not of our fathers' moulding. "Every man the arbiter of his own destiny" was not true for the American Negro of the past: and it is no fault of his that he finds himself to-day the inheritor of a manhood and woman-hood impoverished and debased by two centuries and more of compression and degradation.

But weaknesses and malformations, which to-day are attributable to a vicious schoolmaster and a pernicious system, will a century hence be rightly regarded as proofs of innate corruptness

---

① "not in the heel... of young Achilles": 古希腊神话中英雄阿喀琉斯唯一的弱点即脚踝, 最终因脚踝被射中而死。

and radical incurability.

Now the fundamental agency under God in the regeneration, the re-training of the race, as well as the groundwork and starting point of its progress upward, must be the black woman.

With all the wrongs and neglects of her past, with all the weakness, the debasement, the moral thralldom of her present, the black woman of to-day stands mute and wondering at the Herculean task devolving upon her. But the cycles wait for her. No other hand can move the lever. She must be loosed from her bands and set to work.

Our meager and superficial results from past efforts prove their futility; and every attempt to elevate the Negro, whether undertaken by himself or through the philanthropy of others, cannot but prove abortive unless so directed as to utilize the indispensable agency of an elevated and trained womanhood.

A race cannot be purified from without. Preachers and teachers are helps, and stimulants and conditions as necessary as the gracious rain and sunshine are to plant growth. But what are rain and dew and sunshine and cloud if there be no life in the plant germ? We must go to the root and see that that is sound and healthy and vigorous; and not deceive ourselves with waxen flowers and painted leaves of mock chlorophyll.①

We too often mistake individuals' honor for race development and so are ready to substitute pretty accomplishments for sound sense and earnest purpose.

A stream cannot rise higher than its source. The atmosphere of homes is no rarer and purer and sweeter than are the mothers in those homes. A race is but a total of families. The nation is the aggregate of its homes. As the whole is sum of all its parts, so the character of the parts will determine the characteristics of the whole. These are all axioms and so evident that it seems gratuitous to remark it; and yet, unless I am greatly mistaken, most of the unsatisfaction from our past results arises from just such a radical and palpable error, as much almost on our own part as on that of our benevolent white friends.

The Negro is constitutionally hopeful and proverbially irrepressible; and naturally stands in danger of being dazzled by the shimmer and tinsel of superficials. We often mistake foliage for fruit and overestimate or wrongly estimate brilliant results.

The late Martin R. Delany,② who was an unadulterated black man, used to say when honors of state fell upon him, that when he entered the council of kings the black race entered with him; meaning, I suppose, that there was no discounting his race identity and attributing his achievements to some admixture of Saxon blood. But our present record of eminent men, when placed beside the actual status of the race in America to-day, proves that no man can represent the race. Whatever the attainments of the individual may be, unless his home has moved on *pari*

---

① Chlorophyll: 叶绿素。
② 马丁·德拉尼（1812—1885）：美国非裔作家、医生和社会活动家、废奴主义者。

passu,① he can never be regarded as identical with or representative of the whole.

Not by pointing to sun-bathed mountain tops do we prove that Phoebus② warms the valleys. We must point to homes, average homes, homes of the rank and file of horny-handed toiling men and women of the South (where the masses are) lighted and cheered by the good, the beautiful, and the true — then and not till then will the whole plateau be lifted into the sunlight.

Only the Black Woman can say "when and where I enter, in the quiet, undisputed dignity of my womanhood, without violence and without suing or special patronage, then and there the whole Negro race enters with me." Is it not evident then that as individual workers for this race we must address ourselves with no half-hearted zeal to this feature of our mission? The need is felt and must be recognized by all. There is a call for workers, for missionaries, for men and women with the double consecration of a fundamental love of humanity and a desire for its melioration through the Gospel; but superadded to this we demand an intelligent and sympathetic comprehension of the interests and special needs of the Negro.

I see not why there should not be an organized effort for the protection and elevation of our girls such as the White Cross League in England.③ English women are strengthened and protected by more than twelve centuries of Christian influences, freedom and civilization; English girls are dispirited and crushed down by no such all-levelling prejudice as that supercilious caste spirit in America which cynically assumes "A Negro woman cannot be a lady." English womanhood is beset by no such snares and traps as betray the unprotected, untrained colored girl of the South, whose only crime and dire destruction often is her unconscious and marvelous beauty. Surely then if English indignation is aroused and English manhood thrilled under the leadership of a Bishop of the English church to build up bulwarks around their wronged sisters, Negro sentiment cannot remain callous and Negro effort nerveless in view of the imminent peril of the mothers of the next generation. "I am my Sister's keeper!"④ should be the hearty response of every man and woman of the race, and this conviction should purify and exalt the narrow, selfish, and petty personal aims of life into a noble and sacred purpose.

We need men who can let their interest and gallantry extend outside the circle of their aesthetic appreciation; men who can be a father, a brother, a friend to every weak, struggling, unshielded girl. We need women who are so sure of their own social footing that they need not fear leaning to lend a hand to a fallen or falling sister. We need men and women who do not exhaust their genius splitting hairs on aristocratic distinctions and thanking God they are not as others; but earnest, unselfish souls, who can go into the highways and byways, lifting up and leading, advising and encouraging with the truly catholic benevolence of the Gospel of Christ.

---

① *pari passu*: 拉丁文, 势均力敌。

② Phoebus: 菲比斯, 古希腊神话中的太阳神。

③ White Cross League in England: 19 世纪晚期英国教会的道德改革运动。

④ "I am my Sister's keeper!"见《创世纪》4: 9, 该隐在被问及被谋杀的兄弟亚伯时对上帝的反驳。

As Church workers we must confess our path of duty is less obvious; or rather our ability to adapt our machinery to our conception of the peculiar exigencies of this work, as taught by experience and our own consciousness of the needs of the Negro, is as yet not demonstrable. Flexibility and aggressiveness are not such strong characteristics of the Church to-day as in the Dark Ages.

As a Mission field for the Church, the Southern Negro is in some aspects most promising; in others, perplexing. Aliens neither in language and customs, nor in associations and sympathies, naturally of deeply rooted religious instincts and taking most readily and kindly to the worship and teachings of the Church, surely the task of proselytizing the American Negro is infinitely less formidable than that which confronted the Church in the Barbarians of Europe. Besides, this people already look to the Church as the hope of their race. Thinking colored men almost uniformly admit that the Protestant Episcopal Church with its quiet, chaste dignity and decorous solemnity, its instructive and elevating ritual, its bright chanting and joyous hymning, is eminently fitted to correct the peculiar faults of worship — the rank exuberance and often ludicrous demonstrativeness of their people. Yet, strange to say, the Church, claiming to be missionary and Catholic, urging that schism is sin and denominationalism inexcusable, has made in all these years almost no inroads upon this semi-civilized religionism.

Harvests from this over ripe field of home missions have been gathered in by Methodists, Baptists, and not least by Congregationalists, who were unknown to the Freedmen before their emancipation.

Our clergy numbers less than two dozen priests of Negro blood and we have hardly more than one self-supporting colored congregation in the entire Southland. While the organization known as the A. M. E. Church has 14,063 ministers, itinerant and local, 4,069 self-supporting churches, 4,275 Sunday-schools, with property valued at $7,772,284, raising yearly for church purposes $1,427,000.

Stranger and more significant than all, the leading men of this race (I do not mean demagogues and politicians, but men of intellect, heart, and race devotion, men to whom the elevation of their people means more than personal ambition and sordid gain — and the men of that stamp have not all died yet), the Christian workers for the race, of younger and more cultured growth, are noticeably drifting into sectarian churches, many of them declaring all the time that they acknowledge the historic claims of the Church, believe her apostolicity, and would experience greater personal comfort, spiritual and intellectual, in her revered communion. It is a fact which any one may verify for himself, that representative colored men, professing that in their heart of hearts they are Episcopalians, are actually working in Methodist and Baptist pulpits; while the ranks of the Episcopal clergy are left to be filled largely by men who certainly suggest the propriety of a "perpetual Diaconate"[①] if they cannot be said to have created the necessity

---

① Diaconate: 职事，牧师的下属。

for it.

Now where is the trouble? Something must be wrong. What is it?

A certain Southern Bishop of our Church reviewing the situation, whether in Godly anxiety or in "Gothic antipathy" I know not, deprecates the fact that the colored people do not seem drawn to the Episcopal Church, and comes to the sage conclusion that the Church is not adapted to the rude untutored minds of the Freedmen, and that they may be left to go to the Methodists and Baptists whither their racial proclivities undeniably tend. How the good Bishop can agree that all-foreseeing Wisdom, and Catholic Love would have framed his Church as typified in his seamless garment and unbroken body, and yet not leave it broad enough and deep enough and loving enough to seek and save and hold seven millions of God's poor, I cannot see.

But the doctors, while discussing their scientifically conclusive diagnosis of the disease, will perhaps not think it presumptuous in the patient if he dares to suggest where at least the pain is. If this be allowed a Black woman of the South would beg to point out two possible oversights in this southern work which may indicate in part both a cause and a remedy for some failure. The first is not calculating for the Black man's personality; not having respect, if I may so express it, to his manhood or deferring at all to his conceptions of the needs of his people. When colored persons have been employed it was too often as machines or as manikins. There has been no disposition, generally, to get the black man's ideal or to let his individuality work by its own gravity, as it were. A conference of earnest Christian men has met at regular intervals for some years past to discuss the best methods of promoting the welfare and development of colored people in this country. Yet, strange as it may seem, they have never invited a colored man or even intimated that one would be welcome to take part in their deliberations. Their remedial contrivances are purely theoretical or empirical, therefore, and the whole machinery devoid of soul.

The second important oversight in my judgment is closely allied to this and probably grows out of it, and that is not developing Negro womanhood as an essential fundamental for the elevation of the race, and utilizing this agency in extending the work of the Church.

Of the first I have possibly already presumed to say too much since it does not strictly come within the province of my subject. However, Macaulay somewhere criticises the Church of England as not knowing how to use fanatics, and declares that had Ignatius Loyola① been in the Anglican instead of the Roman communion, the Jesuits would have been schismatics instead of Catholics; and if the religious awakenings of the Wesleys② had been in Rome, she would have shaven their heads, tied ropes around their waists, and sent them out under her own banner and blessing.

---

① 伊格内修斯·洛约拉(Ignatius Loyola, 1491—1556):西班牙贵族,创建了天主教教士组织耶稣会。

② awakenings of the Wesleys:卫斯理们指的是约翰·卫斯理(John Wesley, 1703—1791)和查尔斯·卫斯理(Charles Wesley, 1707—1788),他们的觉醒是建立卫理公会和实现美国宗教复兴的核心,也被称为 18 世纪和 19 世纪的"伟大的觉醒"。

Whether this be true or not, there is certainly a vast amount of force potential for Negro evangelization rendered latent, or worse, antagonistic by the halting, uncertain, I had almost said, trimming policy of the Church in the South. This may sound both presumptuous and ungrateful. It is mortifying, I know, to benevolent wisdom, after having spent itself in the execution of well conned theories for the ideal development of a particular work, to hear perhaps the weakest and humblest element of that work asking "what doest thou?"

Yet so it will be in life. The "thus far and no farther" pattern cannot be fitted to any growth in God's kingdom. The universal law of development is "onward and upward." It is God-given and inviolable. From the unfolding of the germ in the acorn to reach the sturdy oak, to the growth of a human soul into the full knowledge and likeness of its Creator, the breadth and scope of the movement in each and all are too grand, too mysterious, too like God himself, to be encompassed and locked down in human moulds.

After all, the Southern slave owners were right: either the very alphabet of intellectual growth must be forbidden and the Negro dealt with absolutely as a chattel having neither rights nor sensibilities; or else the clamps and irons of mental and moral, as well as civil, compression must be riven asunder and the truly enfranchised soul led to the entrance of that boundless vista through which it is to toil upwards to its beckoning God as the buried seed germ to meet the sun.

A perpetual colored diaconate, carefully and kindly superintended by the white clergy; congregations of shiny faced peasants with their clean white aprons and sunbonnets catechised at regular intervals and taught to recite the creed, the Lord's prayer, and the ten commandments — duty towards God and duty towards neighbor — surely such well-tended sheep ought to be grateful to their shepherds and content in that station of life to which it pleased God to call them. True, like the old professor lecturing to his solitary student, we make no provision here for irregularities. "Questions must be kept till after class," or dispensed with altogether. That some do ask questions and insist on answers, in class too, must be both impertinent and annoying. Let not our spiritual pastors and masters however be grieved at such self-assertion as merely signifies we have a destiny to fulfill and as men and women we must be about our Father's business.[①]

It is a mistake to suppose that the Negro is prejudiced against a white ministry. Naturally there is not a more kindly and implicit follower of a white man's guidance than the average colored peasant. What would to others be an ordinary act of friendly or pastoral interest he would be more inclined to regard gratefully as a condescension. And he never forgets such kindness. Could the Negro be brought near to his white priest or bishop, he is not suspicious. He is not only willing but often longs to unburden his soul to this intelligent guide. There are no reservations when he is convinced that you are his friend. It is a saddening satire on American history and manners that it takes something to convince him.

That our people are not "drawn" to a church whose chief dignitaries they see only in the

---

① "we must be about our Father's business": 见《路加福音》2: 49。

chancel, and whom they reverence as they would a painting or an angel, whose life never comes down to and touches theirs with the inspiration of an objective reality, may be "perplexing" truly (American caste and American Christianity both being facts) but it need not be surprising. There must be something of human nature in it, the same as that which brought about that "the Word was made flesh and dwelt among us" that He might "draw" us towards God.

Men are not "drawn" by abstractions. Only sympathy and love can draw, and until our Church in America realizes this and provides a clergy that can come in touch with our life and have a fellow feeling for our woes, without being imbedded and frozen up in their "Gothic antipathies," the good bishops are likely to continue "perplexed" by the sparsity of colored Episcopalians.

A colored priest of my acquaintance recently related to me, with tears in his eyes, how his reverend Father in God, the Bishop who had ordained him, had met him on the cars on his way to the diocesan convention and warned him, not unkindly, not to take a seat in the body of the convention with the white clergy. To avoid disturbance of their godly placidity he would of course please sit back and somewhat apart. I do not imagine that that clergyman had very much heart for the Christly (!) deliberations of that convention.

To return, however, it is not on this broader view of Church work, which I mentioned as a primary cause of its halting progress with the colored people, that I am to speak. My proper theme is the second oversight of which, in my judgment, our Christian propagandists have been guilty: or, the necessity of church training, protecting, and uplifting our colored womanhood as indispensable to the evangelization of the race.

Apelles[1] did not disdain even that criticism of his lofty art which came from an uncouth cobbler; and may I not hope that the writer's oneness with her subject both in feeling and in being may palliate undue obtrusiveness of opinions here. That the race cannot be effectually lifted up till its women are truly elevated we take as proven. It is not for us to dwell on the needs, the neglects, and the ways of succor, pertaining to the black woman of the South. The ground has been ably discussed and an admirable and practical plan proposed by the oldest Negro priest in America, advising and urging that special organizations such as Church Sisterhoods and industrial schools be devised to meet her pressing needs in the Southland. That some such movements are vital to the life of this people, and the extension of the Church among them, is not hard to see. Yet the pamphlet fell still-born from the press. So far as I am informed the Church has made no motion towards carrying out Dr. Crummell's suggestion.

The denomination which comes next to our own in opposing the proverbial emotionalism of Negro worship in the South, and which in consequence, like ours, receives the cold shoulder from the old heads, resting as we do under the charge of not "having religion" and not believing in conversion — the Congregationalists — have quietly gone to work on the young, have established

---

① 科斯的阿佩利斯(Apelles of Kos，前 4 世纪)：古希腊著名画家。

industrial and training schools, and now almost every community in the South is yearly enriched by a fresh infusion of vigorous young hearts, cultivated heads, and helpful hands that have been trained at Fisk, at Hampton, in Atlanta University, and in Tuskegee, Alabama.①

These young people are missionaries actual or virtual both here and in Africa. They have learned to love the methods and doctrines of the Church which trained and educated them; and so Congregationalism surely and steadily progresses.

Need I compare these well-known facts with results shown by the Church in the same field and during the same or even a longer time?

The institution of the Church in the South to which she mainly looks for the training of her colored clergy and for the help of the "Black Woman" and "Colored Girl" of the South, has graduated since the year 1868, when the school was founded, five young women;② and while yearly numerous young men have been kept and trained for the ministry by the charities of the Church, the number of indigent females who have here been supported, sheltered, and trained, is phenomenally small. Indeed, to my mind, the attitude of the Church toward this feature of her work is as if the solution of the problem of Negro missions depended solely on sending a quota of deacons and priests into the field, girls being a sort of *tertium quid*③ whose development may be promoted if they can pay their way and fall in with the plans mapped out for the training of the other sex.

Now I would ask in all earnestness, does not this force potential deserve by education and stimulus to be made dynamic? Is it not a solemn duty incumbent on all colored churchmen to make it so? Will not the aid of the Church be given to prepare our girls in head, heart, and hand for the duties and responsibilities that await the intelligent wife, the Christian mother, the earnest, virtuous, helpful woman, at once both the lever and the fulcrum for uplifting the race?

As Negroes and churchmen we cannot be indifferent to these questions. They touch us most vitally on both sides. We believe in the Holy Catholic Church. We believe that however gigantic and apparently remote the consummation, the Church will go on conquering and to conquer till the kingdoms of this world, not excepting the black man and the black woman of the South, shall have become the kingdoms of the Lord and of his Christ.

That past work in this direction has been unsatisfactory we must admit. That without a change of policy results in the future will be as meagre, we greatly fear. Our life as a race is at stake. The dearest interests of our hearts are in the scales. We must either break away from dear old landmarks and plunge out in any line and every line that enables us to meet the pressing need of our people, or we must ask the Church to allow and help us, untrammelled by the prejudices and

---

① Fisk, at Hampton, in Atlanta University, and in Tuskegee, Alabama: 当时美国南部的几所黑人教育机构。

② 这里指 1886 年后有五位黑人女性毕业。

③ *tertium quid*: 拉丁文,意为第三件事。

theories of individuals, to work aggressively under her direction as we alone can, with God's help, for the salvation of our people.

The time is ripe for action. Self-seeking and ambition must be laid on the altar. The battle is one of sacrifice and hardship, but our duty is plain. We have been recipients of missionary bounty in some sort for twenty-one years. Not even the senseless vegetable is content to be a mere reservoir. Receiving without giving is an anomaly in nature. Nature's cells are all little workshops for manufacturing sunbeams, the product to be given out to earth's inhabitants in warmth, energy, thought, action. Inanimate creation always pays back an equivalent.

Now, How much owest thou my Lord? Will his account be overdrawn if he call for singleness of purpose and self-sacrificing labor for your brethren? Having passed through your drill school, will you refuse a general's commission even if it entails responsibility, risk and anxiety, with possibly some adverse criticism? Is it too much to ask you to step forward and direct the work for your race along those lines which you know to be of first and vital importance?

Will you allow these words of Ralph Waldo Emerson? "In ordinary," says he, "we have a snappish criticism which watches and contradicts the opposite party: We want the will which advances and dictates [acts]. Nature has made up her mind that what cannot defend itself, shall not be defended. Complaining never so loud and with never so much reason, is of no use. What cannot stand must fall; and the measure of our sincerity and therefore of the respect of men is the amount of health and wealth we will hazard in the defense of our right."①

选文评析:

《妇女：种族新生和进步的关键因素》收录在《来自南方的声音》的第一部分,库珀敏锐地指出了种族、性别和社会的交错问题——包括黑人群体内部的种族政治和性别政治以及美国公开宣称的社会理想,探讨内容涉及了早期美国非裔哲学和政治思想,例如弗雷德里克·道格拉斯的同化主义和马丁·德莱尼的分离主义等。

库珀深受西方经典的影响,她深入剖析美国现代文明,从宗教教义和文化传统中寻找女性重要性的历史渊源。在论述的开始,她通过对比美国与土耳其等东方国家的女性地位,抨击了摧残女性、无视家庭的东方文明的落后愚昧,把美国描述为清新活力、朝气蓬勃、鼓舞人心的国度。同时,她承认美国社会的种族政治十分严重,黑人过着与白人完全不一样的生活,并非每个人都能充分体验美国现代文明的花香。库珀指出美国公民对国家制度的完美体验根植于其固有的可能性,而制度完善则依赖于女性所享有的待遇和地位,她引用宗教和文学典籍论证这一观点,并通过比较指责黑人男性缺乏保护女性的责任感,因而缺乏保护和教育的南方黑人女孩常面临着性剥削等各种陷阱。她指责圣公会等黑人宗教组织对黑人妇女的忽视,她对黑人种族内部的纯血统论并不认同,同时认为黑人男性并

---

① "In ordinary… of our right": 见爱默生:《社会与孤独》(*Society and Solitude*, 1870) 的"勇气"("Courage")一章。

不能代表整个黑人种族。她抨击著名黑人社会活动家马丁·德拉尼(Martin Delany)，认为德拉尼那样纯粹黑人血统的人并不能代表整个黑人群体，更重要的是"男性不能代表整个种族"，并驳斥了亚历山大·克鲁梅尔(Alexander Crummell)把有色人种和黑人区分开，认为受教育水平更高、更为富裕的有色人种受惠于白人亲属的善意和慷慨的观点。库珀援引基督教对女性职能的定义强调黑人女性在家庭中的重要使命，她认为，"我们国家的希望就寄托在家庭和这些家庭的优秀女性所产生的影响力上"，女性的职责是培养孩子，"女性的职责决定了种族重生和进步的可能性，这并不是因为女性比男性更为聪明或强壮，而是因为她们需要在早年引导孩子从而塑造他们的人格"。

与其同一时期的美国非裔理论相比，库珀的观点具有性别平等的先进性。她的辩论明显受到西方神学和哲学的影响，从传统经典中去探寻女性接受教育、受到平等对待的可能性。她提出黑人女性对种族发展的重要性，并指出教会等机构对南方黑人女性的保护和教育的不足，这些观点超出了同时代的很多黑人教育观，对黑人争取种族平等、性别平等的斗争作出了重要贡献。但不可否认的是，库珀的思想存在明显的时代局限性，她把女性的位置局限在家庭中，忽略了她们的工作能力和社会贡献。有评论者认为库珀的女性观与美国社会的女性气质论调相似，有鼓吹同化主义的嫌疑，她对土耳其等国家的刻板印象具有东方主义的偏见，对美国制度和种族未来抱有不切实际的乐观态度。

推荐阅读文献：

Maguire, Roberta S. Kate Chopin and Anna Julia Cooper: Critiquing Kentucky and the South. *The Southern Literary Journal*, 2002, 35(1): 123-137.

May, Vivian M. *Anna Julia Cooper, Visionary Black Feminist: A Critical Introduction*. Taylor & Francis Group, 2007.

May, Vivian M. Writing the Self into Being: Anna Julia Cooper's Textual Politics. *African American Review*, 2009, 43(1): 17-34.

Cooper, Anna J. and Lemert, Charles C. *The Voice of Anna Julia Cooper: Including a Voice from the South and Other Important Essays, Papers, and Letters*. Rowman & Littlefield Publishers, 1997.

Giles, Mark S. Special Focus: Dr. Anna Julia Cooper, 1858-1964: Teacher, Scholar, and Timeless Womanist. *The Journal of Negro Education*, 2006, 75(4): 621-634.

Moody-Turner, Shirley and Cooper, Anna J. 'Dear Doctor Du Bois': Anna Julia Cooper, W. E. B. Du Bois, and the Gender Politics of Black Publishing. *MELUS*, 2015, 40(3): 47-68.

Moody-Turner, Shirley and Stewart, James. Gendering Africana Studies: Insights from Anna Julia Cooper. *African American Review*, 2009, 43(1): 35-44.

哈莱姆文艺复兴时期

（约 20 世纪 20 年代至 20 世纪 30 年代）

第九章　詹姆斯·韦尔登·约翰逊

（James Weldon Johnson，1871—1938）

　　詹姆斯·韦尔登·约翰逊是美国非裔作家、诗人、作曲家、律师和外交官，他对哈莱姆文艺复兴的影响可与阿兰·洛克和杜波依斯比肩。他成果丰硕，才华横溢，代表作《一个前有色人种的自传》（*The Autobiography of an Ex-Colored Man*，1912）被认为是从美国内战到哈莱姆文艺复兴期间对黑人影响最为深远的作品，他谱写的歌曲《歌唱每个声音》（"Lift Every Voice and Sing"）被全美有色人种协进会采用，被誉为"黑人民族之歌"。

　　约翰逊 1871 年出生在佛罗里达州的一个中产阶级家庭，父母是巴哈马群岛移民，父亲在一家豪华酒店做领班，母亲是佛罗里达州第一位非裔女性公立学校教师。年轻的约翰逊从家乡的文法学校斯坦顿学院毕业后进入亚特兰大大学学习，他成绩优秀，表现出色。1894 年，约翰逊回到斯坦顿学院担任校长，同时创办了一份报纸《美国日报》（*The Daily American*，1895—1896），并在 1898 年成为佛罗里达州杜瓦尔县第一个获得律师资格的非裔律师。他与老友加德森·道格拉斯·维特莫尔（Judson Douglas Wetmore）成为合伙人，维特莫尔以白人身份在密歇根大学法学院获得学位，还两次与一个白人女性结婚，很多研究者认为《一个前有色人种的自传》的创作灵感来源于维特莫尔的人生经历。1902 年到 1906 年，约翰逊和哥哥约翰·罗萨蒙德（John Rosamond）及朋友鲍勃·科尔（Bob Cole）共同创作了多首流传甚广的歌曲，包括《歌唱每一个声音》《竹子下》（"Under the Bamboo Tree"）等。同时，约翰逊在纽约大学学习文学，师从美国现实主义先驱布兰德·马修（Brander Matthews）。1906 年，约翰逊前往委内瑞拉担任美国领事，1909 年调任至厄瓜多尔，1912 年离开南美回到纽约与妻子团聚。

　　约翰逊在厄瓜多尔任职期间完成了《一个前有色人种的自传》的撰写，并在 1912 年匿名出版了这部作品。故事讲述了一位混血钢琴师跨越种族线、以白人身份度过的一生。这部作品获得巨大成功，并在 1927 年以约翰逊的实名再版，被誉为"美国现代黑人种族的综合自传"，是哈莱姆文艺复兴的代表作品。1913 年 1 月 1 日，纪念奴隶解放宣言五十周年的诗歌《五十年》（"Fifty Years"）刊登在《纽约时报》上，引起西奥多·罗斯福、查尔斯·切斯纳特和杜波依斯等公众人物的广泛赞誉。1914 年，约翰逊成为美国主要黑人报纸《纽约时代》(*The New York Age*)的编辑,逐渐在黑人社区乃至全国产生具有了一定的影响力。1916 年,在杜波依斯的举荐下,约翰逊成为全美有色人种协进会的区域领导人。他在杜波依斯主张的激进主义立场与布克·华盛顿鼓吹的社会包容立场之间打造了一个中间阵地。华盛顿去世后,约翰逊倾向于杜波依斯的政治主张,并设立了多个有色人种协会的分支机构。他活跃在黑人争取自由的各项社会活动中,组织了纽约"无声抗议游行"等抗议活动,并撰文抨击美国占领海地的殖民行为。1920 年,他当选为全美有色人种协进会的秘书。

活跃在政坛的约翰逊仍然有着丰富的文艺产出。作为哈莱姆文艺复兴时期最多产的作家之一,约翰逊出版了《五十年及其他诗歌》(*Fifty Years and Other Poems*,1917),《上帝的号角:七节布道诗》(*God's Trombones: Seven Sermons in Verse*,1927)以及《圣彼得讲述一件事》(*Saint Peter Relates an Incident*,1934)。他还编纂了《美国黑人诗歌集》(*The Book of American Negro Poetry*,1922)、《美国黑人灵歌集》(*The Book of American Negro Spirituals*,1926)、《第二部美国黑人灵歌集》(*The Second Book of Negro Spirituals*,1925)等三部诗集,历史文化著作《黑人曼哈顿》(*Black Manhattan*,1930)、自传《一路走来》(*Along this Way*,1933)、《美国黑人,现在怎么办》(*Negro Americans, What Now?*)以及多篇论文。约翰逊的作品体现出了很高的美学和艺术水准,并没有陷入政治说教的窠臼。1930 年,约翰逊卸任全美有色人种协进会的秘书一职,成为菲斯克大学的创意写作教授,并在 1934 年到 1937 年的秋季学期前往纽约大学举办美国非裔文学文化领域的讲座。1938 年,约翰逊不幸在车祸中丧生。

选文是《美国黑人诗歌集》的序言。《美国黑人诗歌集》并不只是一部介绍非裔诗人作品的诗歌选,约翰逊以非裔诗歌为脉络梳理了黑人文化的发展历程及其在美国文化中的影响力,以此表现黑人并不输于其他种族的智力和才华,以艺术和文学为度量展现黑人的成就。这部诗集囊括了 31 位重要黑人诗人的作品,其中大多数诗人是第一次出现在公共视野之中。

📖 作品选读:

Preface to *The Book of American Negro Poetry*

There is, perhaps, a better excuse for giving an Anthology of American Negro Poetry to the public than can be offered for many of the anthologies that have recently been issued. The public, generally speaking, does not know that there are American Negro poets — to supply this lack of information is, alone, a work worthy of somebody's effort.

Moreover, the matter of Negro poets and the production of literature by the colored people in this country involves more than supplying information that is lacking. It is a matter which has a direct bearing on the most vital of American problems.

A people may become great through many means, but there is only one measure by which its greatness is recognized and acknowledged. The final measure of the greatness of all peoples is the amount and standard of the literature and art they have produced. The world does not know that a people is great until that people produces great literature and art. No people that has produced great literature and art has ever been looked upon by the world as distinctly inferior.

The status of the Negro in the United States' is more a question of national mental attitude toward the race than of actual conditions. And nothing will do more to change that mental attitude and raise his status than a demonstration of intellectual parity by the Negro through the production of literature and art.

Is there likelihood that the American Negro will be able to do this? There is, for the good reason that he possesses the innate powers. He has the emotional endowment, the originality and artistic conception, and, what is more important, the power of creating that which has universal appeal and influence.

I make here what may appear to be a more startling statement by saying that the Negro has already proved the possession of these powers by being the creator of the only things artistic that have yet sprung from American soil and been universally acknowledged as distinctive American products.

These creations by the American Negro may be summed up under four heads. The first two are the Uncle Remus stories,① which were collected by Joel Chandler Harris, and the "spirituals"② or slave songs, to which the Fisk Jubilee Singers③ made the public and the musicians of both the United States and Europe listen. The Uncle Remus stories constitute the greatest body of folklore that America has produced, and the "spirituals" the greatest body of folk-song. I shall speak of the "spirituals" later because they are more than folk-songs, for in them the Negro sounded the depths, if he did not scale the heights, of music.

The other two creations are the Cakewalk and ragtime. We do not need to go very far back to remember when cakewalking was the rage in the United States, Europe and South America. Society in this country and royalty abroad spent time in practicing the intricate steps. Paris pronounced it the "poetry of motion." The popularity of the cakewalk passed away but its influence remained. The influence can be seen to-day on any American stage where there is dancing.

---

①　"The Uncle Remus tales"是乔尔·钱德勒·哈里斯用黑人方言创作的美国非裔骗子系列故事。

②　"Spirituals"一般译为黑人灵歌，是一种起源于美国南方由黑人创作的歌曲流派。内容上通常传达基督教价值观以及黑人的悲苦生活。

③　"The Fisk Jubilee Singers"指田纳西州纳什维尔菲斯克大学的一支乐团。该大学始建于1866年，是第一所为有色人种开设艺术课程的大学。五年后学校陷入了财务困境，于是音乐教授乔治·怀特组建了一支9人合唱团进行全球巡演以挣钱资助学校。

The influence which the Negro has exercised on the art of dancing in this country has been almost absolute. For generations the "buck and wing" and the "stop-time" dances, which are strictly Negro, have been familiar to American theatre audiences. A few years ago the public discovered the "turkey trot," the "eagle rock," "ballin' the jack,"① and several other varieties that started the modern dance craze. These dances were quickly followed by the "tango," a dance originated by the Negroes of Cuba and later transplanted to South America. (This fact is attested by no less authority than Vincente Blasco Ibañez② in his "Four Horsemen of the Apocalypse.") Half the floor space in the country was then turned over to dancing, and highly paid exponents sprang up everywhere. The most noted, Mr. Vernon Castle, and, by the way, an Englishman, never danced except to the music of a colored band, and he never failed to state to his audiences that most of his dances had long been done by "your colored people," as he put it.

Anyone who witnesses a musical production in which there is dancing cannot fail to notice the Negro stamp on all the movements; a stamp which even the great vogue of Russian dances that swept the country about the time of the popular dance craze could not affect. That peculiar swaying of the shoulders which you see done everywhere by the blond girls of the chorus is nothing more than a movement from the Negro dance referred to above, the "eagle rock." Occasionally the movement takes on a suggestion of the, now outlawed, "shimmy."

As for Ragtime,③ I go straight to the statement that it is the one artistic production by which America is known the world over. It has been all-conquering. Everywhere it is hailed as "American music."

For a dozen years or so there has been a steady tendency to divorce Ragtime from the Negro; in fact, to take from him the credit of having originated it. Probably the younger people of the present generation do not know that Ragtime is of Negro origin. The change wrought in Ragtime and the way in which it is accepted by the country have been brought about chiefly through the change which has gradually been made in the words and stories accompanying the music. Once the text of all Ragtime songs was written in Negro dialect, and was about Negroes in the cabin or in the cotton field or on the levee or at a jubilee or on Sixth Avenue or at a ball, and about their love affairs. Today, only a small proportion of Ragtime songs relate at all to the Negro. The truth is, Ragtime is now national rather than racial. But that does not abolish in any way the claim of the American Negro as its originator.

Ragtime music was originated by colored piano players in the questionable resorts of St.

---

① "buck and wing", the "stop-time", "turkey trot," the "eagle rock" and "ballin' the jack" 均是不同种类的舞蹈。

② 文森特·布拉斯科·伊巴涅斯(Vicente Blasco Ibáñez, 1867—1928)：西班牙现实主义小说家、编剧及电影导演。

③ Ragtime：雷格拉姆音乐，爵士乐的前身之一，流行于 1899 年至 1917 年，其切分音特色对爵士乐有影响深刻。

Louis, Memphis, and other Mississippi River towns. These men did not know any more about the theory of music than they did about the theory of the universe. They were guided by their natural musical instinct and talent, but above all by the Negro's extraordinary sense of rhythm. Anyone who is familiar with Ragtime may note that its chief charm is not in melody, but in rhythms. These players often improvised crude and, at times, vulgar words to fit the music. This was the beginning of the Ragtime song.

Ragtime music got its first popular hearing at Chicago during the world's fair in that city. From Chicago it made its way to New York, and then started on its universal triumph.

The earliest Ragtime songs, like Topsy, "jes' grew." Some of these earliest songs were taken down by white men, the words slightly altered or changed, and published under the names of the arrangers. They sprang into immediate popularity and earned small fortunes. The first to become widely known was "The Bully," a levee song which had been long used by roustabouts along the Mississippi. It was introduced in New York by Miss May Irwin, and gained instant popularity. Another one of these "jes' grew" songs was one which for a while disputed for place with Yankee Doodle; perhaps, disputes it even to-day. That song was "A Hot Time in the Old Town To-night"; introduced and made popular by the colored regimental bands during the Spanish-American War.

Later there came along a number of colored men who were able to transcribe the old songs and write original ones. I was, about that time, writing words to music for the music show stage in New York. I was collaborating with my brother, J. Rosamond Johnson, and the late Bob Cole. I remember that we appropriated about the last one of the old "jes' grew" songs. It was a song which had been sung for years all through the South. The words were unprintable, but the tune was irresistible, and belonged to nobody. We took it, re-wrote the verses, telling an entirely different story from the original, left the chorus as it was, and published the song, at first under the name of "Will Handy." It became very popular with college boys, especially at football games, and perhaps still is. The song was, "Oh, Didn't He Ramble!"

In the beginning, and for quite a while, almost all of the Ragtime songs that were deliberately composed were the work of colored writers. Now, the colored composers, even in this particular field, are greatly outnumbered by the white.

The reader might be curious to know if the "jes' grew" songs have ceased to grow. No, they have not; they are growing all the time. The country has lately been flooded with several varieties of "The Blues."① These "Blues," too, had their origin in Memphis, and the towns along the Mississippi. They are a sort of lament of a lover who is feeling "blue" over the loss of his sweetheart. The "Blues" of Memphis have been adulterated so much on Broadway that they have lost their pristine hue. But whenever you hear a piece of music which has a strain like this in it,

---

①　Blues：布鲁斯是一种起源于 19 世纪 60 年代的美国南方腹地、由黑人创作的音乐形式，由非洲音乐传统、黑奴劳动号子以及灵歌发展而来。

you will know you are listening to something which belonged originally to Beale Avenue, Memphis, Tennessee. The original "Memphis Blues," so far as it can be credited to a composer, must be credited to Mr. W. C. Handy, a colored musician of Memphis.

As illustrations of the genuine Ragtime song in the making, I quote the words of two that were popular with the Southern colored soldiers in France. Here is the first:

> Mah mammy's lyin' in her grave,
> Mah daddy done run away,
> Mah sister's married a gambling' man,
> An' I've done gone astray.
> Yes, I've done gone astray, po' boy,
> An' I've done gone astray,
> Mah sister's married a gambling' man,
> An' I've done gone astray, po' boy.

These lines are crude, but they contain something of real poetry, of that elusive thing which nobody can define and that you can only tell that it is there when you feel it. You cannot read these lines without becoming reflective and feeling sorry for "Po' Boy."

Now, take in this word picture of utter dejection:

> I'm jes' as misabul as I can be,
> I'm unhappy even if I am free,
> I'm feelin' down, I'm feelin' blue;
> I wander 'round, don't know what to do.
> I'm go'n lay mah haid on de railroad line,
> Let de B. & O. come and pacify mah min'.

These lines are, no doubt, one of the many versions of the famous "Blues." They are also crude, but they go straight to the mark. The last two lines move with the swiftness of all great tragedy.

In spite of the bans which musicians and music teachers have placed on it, the people still demand and enjoy Ragtime. In fact, there is not a corner of the civilized world in which it is not known and liked. And this proves its originality, for if it were an imitation, the people of Europe, at least, would not have found it a novelty. And it is proof of a more important thing, it is proof that Ragtime possesses the vital spark, the power to appeal universally, without which any artistic production, no matter how approved its form may be, is dead.

Of course, there are those who will deny that Ragtime is an artistic production. American musicians, especially, instead of investigating Ragtime, dismiss it with a contemptuous word. But this has been the course of scholasticism in every branch of art. Whatever new thing the people like is pooh-poohed; whatever is popular is regarded as not worthwhile. The fact is, nothing great or enduring in music has ever sprung full-fledged from the brain of any master; the best he gives the world he gathers from the hearts of the people, and runs it through the alembic of his genius.

Ragtime deserves serious attention. There is a lot of colorless and vicious imitation, but there is enough that is genuine. In one composition alone, "The Memphis Blues," the musician will find not only great melodic beauty, but a polyphonic structure that is amazing.

It is obvious that Ragtime has influenced, and in a large measure, become our popular music; but not many would know that it has influenced even our religious music. Those who are familiar with gospel hymns can at once see this influence if they will compare the songs of thirty years ago, such as "In the Sweet Bye and Bye," "The Ninety and Nine," etc., with the up-to-date, syncopated tunes that are sung in Sunday Schools, Christian Endeavor Societies, Y. M. C. A. 's and like gatherings to-day.

Ragtime has not only influenced American music, it has influenced American life; indeed, it has saturated American life. It has become the popular medium for our national expression musically. And who can say that it does not express the blare and jangle and the surge, too, of our national spirit?

Anyone who doubts that there is a peculiar heel-tickling, smile-provoking, joy-awakening, response-compelling charm in Ragtime needs only to hear a skillful performer play the genuine article, needs only to listen to its bizarre harmonies, its audacious resolutions often consisting of an abrupt jump from one key to another, its intricate rhythms in which the accents fall in the most unexpected places but in which the fundamental beat is never lost in order to be convinced. I believe it has its place as well as the music which draws from us sighs and tears.

Now, these dances which I have referred to and Ragtime music may be lower forms of art, but they are evidence of a power that will someday be applied to the higher forms. And even now we need not stop at the Negro's accomplishment through these lower forms. In the "spirituals," or slave songs, the Negro has given America not only its only folksongs, but a mass of noble music. I never think of this music but that I am struck by the wonder, the miracle of its production. How did the men who originated these songs manage to do it? The sentiments are easily accounted for; they are, for the most part, taken from the Bible. But the melodies, where did they come from? Some of them so weirdly sweet, and others so wonderfully strong. Take, for instance, "Go Down, Moses"; I doubt that there is a stronger theme in the whole musical literature of the world.

It is to be noted that whereas the chief characteristic of Ragtime is rhythm, the chief characteristic of the "spirituals" is melody. The melodies of "Steal Away to Jesus," "Swing Low Sweet Chariot," "Nobody Knows de Trouble I See," "I Couldn't Hear Nobody Pray," "Deep River," "O, Freedom Over Me," and many others of these songs possess a beauty that is — what shall I say? poignant. In the riotous rhythms of Ragtime the Negro expressed his irrepressible buoyancy, his keen response to the sheer joy of living; in the "spirituals" he voiced his sense of beauty and his deep religious feeling.

Naturally, not as much can be said for the words of these songs as for the music. Most of the songs are religious. Some of them are songs expressing faith and endurance and a longing for freedom. In the religious songs, the sentiments and often the entire lines are taken bodily from the Bible. However, there is no doubt that some of these religious songs have a meaning apart from the Biblical text. It is evident that the opening lines of "Go Down, Moses,"

> Go down, Moses,
> 'Way down in Egypt land;
> Tell old Pharoah,
> Let my people go.

Have a significance beyond the bondage of Israel in Egypt.

The bulk of the lines to these songs, as is the case in all communal music, is made up of choral iteration and incremental repetition of the leader's lines. If the words are read, this constant iteration and repetition are found to be tiresome; and it must be admitted that the lines themselves are often very trite. And, yet, there is frequently revealed a flash of real, primitive poetry. I give the following examples:

> Sometimes I feel like an eagle in de air.
> You may bury me in de East,
> You may bury me in de West,
> But I'll hear de trumpet sound
> In-a dat mornin'.

> I know de moonlight, I know de starlight;
> I lay dis body down.
> I walk in de moonlight, I walk in de starlight;
> I lay dis body down.
> I know de graveyard, I know de graveyard,
> When I lay dis body down.
> I walk in de graveyard, I walk troo de graveyard
> To lay dis body down.
> I lay in de grave an' stretch out my arms;
> I lay dis body down.
> I go to de judgment in de evenin' of de day
> When I lay dis body down.
> An' my soul an' yo' soul will meet in de day
> When I lay dis body down.

Regarding the line, "I lay in de grave an' stretch out my arms," Col. Thomas Wentworth

Higginson of Boston, one of the first to give these slave songs serious study, said: "Never it seems to me, since man first lived and suffered, was his infinite longing for peace uttered more plaintively than in that line."

These Negro folksongs constitute a vast mine of material that has been neglected almost absolutely. The only white writers who have in recent years given adequate attention and study to this music, that I know of, are Mr. H. E. Krehbiel and Mrs. Natalie Curtis Burlin. We have our native composers denying the worth and importance of this music, and trying to manufacture grand opera out of so-called Indian themes.

But there is a great hope for the development of this music, and that hope is the Negro himself. A worthy beginning has already been made by Burleigh, Cook, Johnson, and Dett. And there will yet come great Negro composers who will take this music and voice through it not only the soul of their race, but the soul of America.

And does it not seem odd that this greatest gift of the Negro has been the most neglected of all he possesses? Money and effort have been expended upon his development in every direction except this. This gift has been regarded as a kind of side show, something for occasional exhibition; wherein it is the touchstone, it is the magic thing, it is that by which the Negro can bridge all chasms. No persons, however hostile, can listen to Negroes singing this wonderful music without having their hostility melted down.

This power of the Negro to suck up the national spirit from the soil and create something artistic and original, which, at the same time, possesses the note of universal appeal, is due to a remarkable racial gift of adaptability; it is more than adaptability, it is a transfusive quality. And the Negro has exercised this transfusive quality not only here in America, where the race lives in large numbers, but in European countries, where the number has been almost infinitesimal.

Is it not curious to know that the greatest poet of Russia is Alexander Pushkin, a man of African descent; that the greatest romancer of France is Alexander Dumas, a man of African descent; and that one of the greatest musicians of England is Coleridge-Taylor, a man of African descent?

The fact is fairly well known that the father of Dumas was a Negro of the French West Indies, and that the father of Coleridge-Taylor was a native-born African; but the facts concerning Pushkin's African ancestry are not so familiar.

When Peter the Great was Czar of Russia, some potentate presented him with a full-blooded Negro of gigantic size. Peter, the most eccentric ruler of modern times, dressed this Negro up in soldier clothes, christened him Hannibal, and made him a special body-guard.

But Hannibal had more than size, he had brain and ability. He not only looked picturesque and imposing in soldier clothes, he showed that he had in him the making of a real soldier. Peter recognized this, and eventually made him a general. He afterwards ennobled him, and Hannibal, later, married one of the ladies of the Russian court. This same Hannibal was great-grandfather of Pushkin, the national poet of Russia, the man who bears the same relation to Russian literature that Shakespeare bears to English literature.

I know the question naturally arises: If out of the few Negroes who have lived in France there came a Dumas; and out of the few Negroes who have lived in England there came a Coleridge-Taylor; and if from the man who was at the time, probably, the only Negro in Russia there sprang that country's national poet, why have not the millions of Negroes in the United States with all the emotional and artistic endowment claimed for them produced a Dumas, or a Coleridge-Taylor, or a Pushkin?

The question seems difficult, but there is an answer. The Negro in the United States is consuming all of his intellectual energy in this gruelling race-struggle. And the same statement may be made in a general way about the white South. Why does not the white South produce literature and art? The white South, too, is consuming all of its intellectual energy in this lamentable conflict. Nearly all of the mental efforts of the white South run through one narrow channel. The life of every Southern white man and all of his activities are impassably limited by the ever present Negro problem. And that is why, as Mr. H. L. Mencken puts it, in all that vast region, with its thirty or forty million people and its territory as large as a half a dozen Frances or Germanys, there is not a single poet, not a serious historian, not a creditable composer, not a critic good or bad, not a dramatist dead or alive.

But, even so, the American Negro has accomplished something in pure literature. The list of those who have done so would be surprising both by its length and the excellence of the achievements. One of the great books written in this country since the Civil War is the work of a colored man, "The Souls of Black Folk," by W. E. B. Du Bois.

Such a list begins with Phillis Wheatley. In 1761 a slave ship landed a cargo of slaves in Boston. Among them was a little girl seven or eight years of age. She attracted the attention of John Wheatley, a wealthy gentleman of Boston, who purchased her as a servant for his wife. Mrs. Wheatley was a benevolent woman. She noticed the girl's quick mind and determined to give her opportunity for its development. Twelve years later Phillis published a volume of poems. The book was brought out in London, where Phillis was for several months an object of great curiosity and attention.

Phillis Wheatley has never been given her rightful place in American literature. By some sort of conspiracy she is kept out of most of the books, especially the text-books on literature used in the schools. Of course, she is not a great American poet — and in her day there were no great American poets — but she is an important American poet. Her importance, if for no other reason, rests on the fact that, save one, she is the first in order of time of all the women poets of America. And she is among the first of all American poets to issue a volume.

It seems strange that the books generally give space to a mention of Urian Oakes, President of Harvard College, and to quotations from the crude and lengthy elegy which he published in 1667; and print examples from the execrable versified version of the Psalms made by the New England divines, and yet deny a place to Phillis Wheatley.

Here are the opening lines from the elegy by Oakes, which is quoted from in most of the books on American literature:

> Reader, I am no poet, but I grieve.
> Behold here what that passion can do,
> That forced a verse without Apollo's leave,
> And whether the learned sisters would or no.

There was no need for Urian to admit what his handiwork declared. But this from the versified Psalms is still worse, yet it is found in the books:

"The Lord's song sing can we? being in stranger's land, then let lose her skill my right hand if I Jerusalem forget."

Anne Bradstreet preceded Phillis Wheatley by a little over twenty years. She published her volume of poems, "The Tenth Muse," in 1750. Let us strike a comparison between the two. Anne Bradstreet was a wealthy, cultivated Puritan girl, the daughter of Thomas Dudley, Governor of Bay Colony. Phillis, as we know, was a Negro slave girl born in Africa. Let us take them both at their best and in the same vein. The following stanza is from Anne's poem entitled "Contemplation":

> While musing thus with contemplation fed,
> And thousand fancies buzzing in my brain,
> The sweet tongued Philomel percht o'er my head,
> And chanted forth a most melodious strain,
> Which rapt me so with wonder and delight,
> I judged my hearing better than my sight,
> And wisht me wings with her awhile to take my flight.
> And the following is from Phillis' poem entitled "Imagination":

> Imagination! who can sing thy force?
> Or who describe the swiftness of thy course?
> Soaring through air to find the bright abode,
> The empyreal palace of the thundering God,
> We on thy pinions can surpass the wind,
> And leave the rolling universe behind,
> From star to star the mental optics rove,
> Measure the skies, and range the realms above,
> There in one view we grasp the mighty whole,
> Or with new worlds amaze the unbounded soul.

We do not think the black woman suffers much by comparison with the white. Thomas

Jefferson said of Phillis: "Religion has produced a Phillis Wheatley, but it could not produce a poet; her poems are beneath contempt." It is quite likely that Jefferson's criticism was directed more against religion than against Phillis' poetry. On the other hand, General George Washington wrote her with his own hand a letter in which he thanked her for a poem which she had dedicated to him. He, later, received her with marked courtesy at his camp at Cambridge.

It appears certain that Phillis was the first person to apply to George Washington the phrase, "First in peace." The phrase occurs in her poem addressed to "His Excellency, General George Washington," written in 1775. The encomium, "First in war, first in peace, first in the hearts of his countrymen" was originally used in the resolutions presented to Congress on the death of Washington, December, 1799.

Phillis Wheatley's poetry is the poetry of the Eighteenth Century. She wrote when Pope and Gray were supreme; it is easy to see that Pope was her model. Had she come under the influence of Wordsworth, Byron or Keats or Shelley, she would have done greater work. As it is, her work must not be judged by the work and standards of a later day, but by the work and standards of her own day and her own contemporaries. By this method of criticism, she stands out as one of the important characters in the making of American literature, without any allowances for her sex or her antecedents.

According to "A Bibliographical Checklist of American Negro Poetry," compiled by Mr. Arthur A. Schomburg, more than one hundred Negroes in the United States have published volumes of poetry ranging in size from pamphlets to books of from one hundred to three hundred pages. About thirty of these writers fill in the gap between Phillis Wheatley and Paul Laurence Dunbar. Just here it is of interest to note that a Negro wrote and published a poem before Phillis Wheatley arrived in this country from Africa. He was Jupiter Hammon, a slave belonging to a Mr. Lloyd of Queens-Village, Long Island. In 1760 Hammon published a poem, eighty-eight lines in length, entitled "An Evening Thought, Salvation by Christ, with Penettential Cries." In 1788 he published "An Address to Miss Phillis Wheatley, Ethiopian Poetess in Boston, who came from Africa at eight years of age, and soon became acquainted with the Gospel of Jesus Christ." These two poems do not include all that Hammon wrote.

The poets between Phillis Wheatley and Dunbar must be considered more in the light of what they attempted than of what they accomplished. Many of them showed marked talent, but barely a half dozen of them demonstrated even mediocre mastery of technique in the use of poetic material and forms. And yet there are several names that deserve mention. George M. Horton, Frances E. Harper, James M. Bell and Alberry A. Whitman, all merit consideration when due allowances are made for their limitations in education, training and general culture. The limitations of Horton were greater than those of either of the others; he was born a slave in North Carolina in 1797, and as a young man began to compose poetry without being able to write it down. Later he received some instruction from professors of the University of North Carolina, at which institution he was employed as a janitor. He published a volume of poems, "The Hope of Liberty," in 1829.

Mrs. Harper, Bell and Whitman would stand out if only for the reason that each of them attempted sustained work. Mrs. Harper published her first volume of poems in 1854, but later she published "Moses, a Story of the Nile," a poem which ran to 52 closely printed pages. Bell in 1864 published a poem of 28 pages in celebration of President Lincoln's Emancipation Proclamation. In 1870 he published a poem of 32 pages in celebration of the ratification of the Fifteenth Amendment to the Constitution. Whitman published his first volume of poems, a book of 253 pages, in 1877; but in 1884 he published "The Rape of Florida," an epic poem written in four cantos and done in the Spenserian stanza, and which ran to 97 closely printed pages. The poetry of both Mrs. Harper and of Whitman had a large degree of popularity; one of Mrs. Harper's books went through more than twenty editions.

Of these four poets, it is Whitman who reveals not only the greatest imagination but also the more skilful workmanship. His lyric power at its best may be judged from the following stanza from the "Rape of Florida":

> Come now, my love, the moon is on the lake;
> Upon the waters is my light canoe;
> Come with me, love, and gladsome oars shall make
> A music on the parting wave for you.
> Come o'er the waters deep and dark and blue;
> Come where the lilies in the marge have sprung,
> Come with me, love, for Oh, my love is true!
> This is the song that on the lake was sung,
> The boatman sang it when his heart was young.

Some idea of Whitman's capacity for dramatic narration may be gained from the following lines taken from "Not a Man, and Yet a Man," a poem of even greater length than "The Rape of Florida":

> A flash of steely lightning from his hand,
> Strikes down the groaning leader of the band;
> Divides his startled comrades, and again
> Descending, leaves fair Dora's captors slain.
> Her, seizing then within a strong embrace,
> Out in the dark he wheels his flying pace;
> He speaks not, but with stalwart tenderness
> Her swelling bosom firm to his doth press;
> Springs like a stag that flees the eager hound,
> And like a whirlwind rustles o'er the ground.
> Her locks swim in dishevelled wildness o'er

147

His shoulders, streaming to his waist and more;
While on and on, strong as a rolling flood,
His sweeping footsteps part the silent wood.

It is curious and interesting to trace the growth of individuality and race consciousness in this group of poets. Jupiter Hammon's verses were almost entirely religious exhortations. Only very seldom does Phillis Wheatley sound a native note. Four times in single lines she refers to herself as "Afric's muse." In a poem of admonition addressed to the students at the "University of Cambridge in New England" she refers to herself as follows:

Ye blooming plants of human race divine,
An Ethiop tells you 'tis your greatest foe.

But one looks in vain for some outburst or even complaint against the bondage of her people, for some agonizing cry about her native land. In two poems she refers definitely to Africa as her home, but in each instance there seems to be under the sentiment of the lines a feeling of almost smug contentment at her own escape therefrom. In the poem, "On Being Brought from Africa to America," she says:

Twas mercy brought me from my pagan land,
Taught my benighted soul to understand
That there's a God and there's a Saviour too;
Once I redemption neither sought or knew.
Some view our sable race with scornful eye,
'their color is a diabolic dye.'
Remember, Christians, Negroes black as Cain,
May be refined, and join th' angelic train.

In the poem addressed to the Earl of Dartmouth, she speaks of freedom and makes a reference to the parents from whom she was taken as a child, a reference which cannot but strike the reader as rather unimpassioned:

Should you, my lord, while you peruse my song,
Wonder from whence my love of Freedom sprung,
Whence flow these wishes for the common good,
By feeling hearts alone best understood;
I, young in life, by seeming cruel fate
Was snatch'd from Afric's fancy'd happy seat;
What pangs excruciating must molest,

What sorrows labor in my parents' breast?
Steel'd was that soul and by no misery mov'd
That from a father seiz'd his babe belov'd;
Such, such my case. And can I then but pray
Others may never feel tyrannic sway?"

The bulk of Phillis Wheatley's work consists of poems addressed to people of prominence. Her book was dedicated to the Countess of Huntington, at whose house she spent the greater part of her time while in England. On his repeal of the Stamp Act, she wrote a poem to King George III, whom she saw later; another poem she wrote to the Earl of Dartmouth, whom she knew. A number of her verses were addressed to other persons of distinction. Indeed, it is apparent that Phillis was far from being a democrat. She was far from being a democrat not only in her social ideas but also in her political ideas; unless a religious meaning is given to the closing lines of her ode to General Washington, she was a decided royalist:

A crown, a mansion, and a throne that shine
With gold unfading, Washington! be thine.

Nevertheless, she was an ardent patriot. Her ode to General Washington (1775), her spirited poem, "On Major General Lee" (1776) and her poem, "Liberty and Peace," written in celebration of the close of the war, reveal not only strong patriotic feeling but an understanding of the issues at stake. In her poem, "On Major General Lee," she makes her hero reply thus to the taunts of the British commander into whose hands he has been delivered through treachery:

O arrogance of tongue!
And wild ambition, ever prone to wrong!
Believ'st thou, chief, that armies such as thine
Can stretch in dust that heaven-defended line?
In vain allies may swarm from distant lands,
And demons aid in formidable bands,
Great as thou art, thou shun'st the field of fame,
Disgrace to Britain and the British name!
When offer'd combat by the noble foe,
(Foe to misrule) why did the sword forego
The easy conquest of the rebel-land?
Perhaps TOO easy for thy martial hand.
What various causes to the field invite!
For plunder YOU, and we for freedom fight,
Her cause divine with generous ardor fires,

And every bosom glows as she inspires!
Already thousands of your troops have fled
To the drear mansions of the silent dead:
Columbia, too, beholds with streaming eyes
Her heroes fall — 'tis freedom's sacrifice!
So wills the power who with convulsive storms
Shakes impious realms, and nature's face deforms;
Yet those brave troops, innum'rous as the sands,
One soul inspires, one General Chief commands;
Find in your train of boasted heroes, one
To match the praise of Godlike Washington.
Thrice happy Chief in whom the virtues join,
And heaven taught prudence speaks the man divine.

What Phillis Wheatley failed to achieve is due in no small degree to her education and environment. Her mind was steeped in the classics; her verses are filled with classical and mythological allusions. She knew Ovid thoroughly and was familiar with other Latin authors. She must have known Alexander Pope by heart. And, too, she was reared and sheltered in a wealthy and cultured family, — a wealthy and cultured Boston family; she never had the opportunity to learn life; she never found out her own true relation to life and to her surroundings. And it should not be forgotten that she was only about thirty years old when she died. The impulsion or the compulsion that might have driven her genius off the worn paths, out on a journey of exploration, Phillis Wheatley never received. But, whatever her limitations, she merits more than America has accorded her.

Horton, who was born three years after Phillis Wheatley's death, expressed in all of his poetry strong complaint at his condition of slavery and a deep longing for freedom. The following verses are typical of his style and his ability:

Alas! and am I born for this,
To wear this slavish chain?
Deprived of all created bliss,
Through hardship, toil, and pain?
* * * * *
Come, Liberty! thou cheerful sound,
Roll through my ravished ears;
Come, let my grief in joys be drowned,
And drive away my fears."

In Mrs. Harper we find something more than the complaint and the longing of Horton. We find an expression of a sense of wrong and injustice. The following stanzas are from a poem addressed to the white women of America:

> You can sigh o'er the sad-eyed Armenian
> Who weeps in her desolate home.
> You can mourn o'er the exile of Russia
> From kindred and friends doomed to roam.
> * * * * *
> But hark! from our Southland are floating
> Sobs of anguish, murmurs of pain,
> And women heart-stricken are weeping
> O'er their tortured and slain.
> * * * * *
> Have ye not, oh, my favored sisters,
> Just a plea, a prayer or a tear
> For mothers who dwell 'neath the shadows
> Of agony, hatred and fear?
> * * * * *
> Weep not, oh my well sheltered sisters,
> Weep not for the Negro alone,
> But weep for your sons who must gather
> The crops which their fathers have sown."

Whitman, in the midst of "The Rape of Florida," a poem in which he related the taking of the State of Florida from the Seminoles, stops and discusses the race question. He discusses it in many other poems; and he discusses it from many different angles. In Whitman we find not only an expression of a sense of wrong and injustice, but we hear a note of faith and a note also of defiance. For example, in the opening to Canto II of "The Rape of Florida":

> Greatness by nature cannot be entailed;
>   It is an office ending with the man, —
> Sage, hero, Saviour, tho' the Sire be hailed,
>   The son may reach obscurity in the van:
> Sublime achievements know no patent plan,
>   Man's immortality's a book with seals,
> And none but God shall open — none else can —
>   But opened, it the mystery reveals, —
> Manhood's conquest of man to heaven's respect appeals.
> Is manhood less because man's face is black?
> Let thunders of the loosened seals reply!

Who shall the rider's restive steed turn back,
Or who withstand the arrows he lets fly
Between the mountains of eternity?
Genius ride forth! Thou gift and torch of heav'n!
The mastery is kindled in thine eye;
To conquest ride! thy bow of strength is giv'n —
The trampled hordes of caste before thee shall be driv'n!

    *   *   *   *   *

'Tis hard to judge if hatred of one's race,
By those who deem themselves superior-born,
Be worse than that quiescence in disgrace,
Which only merits — and should only — scorn.
Oh, let me see the Negro night and morn,
Pressing and fighting in, for place and power!
All earth is place — all time th' auspicious hour,
While heaven leans forth to look, oh, will he quail or cower?
Ah! I abhor his protest and complaint!
His pious looks and patience I despise!
He can't evade the test, disguised as saint;
The manly voice of freedom bids him rise,
And shake himself before Philistine eyes!
And, like a lion roused, no sooner than
A foe dare come, play all his energies,
And court the fray with fury if he can;
For hell itself respects a fearless, manly man.

It may be said that none of these poets strike a deep native strain or sound a distinctively original note, either in matter or form. That is true; but the same thing may be said of all the American poets down to the writers of the present generation, with the exception of Poe and Walt Whitman. The thing in which these black poets are mostly excelled by their contemporaries is mere technique.

Paul Laurence Dunbar stands out as the first poet from the Negro race in the United States to show a combined mastery over poetic material and poetic technique, to reveal innate literary distinction in what he wrote, and to maintain a high level of performance. He was the first to rise to a height from which he could take a perspective view of his own race. He was the first to see objectively its humor, its superstitions, its shortcomings; the first to feel sympathetically its heart-wounds, its yearnings, its aspirations, and to voice them all in a purely literary form.

Dunbar's fame rests chiefly on his poems in Negro dialect. This appraisal of him is, no doubt, fair; for in these dialect poems he not only carried his art to the highest point of perfection, but he made a contribution to American literature unlike what anyone else had made, a contribution which, perhaps, no one else could have made. Of course, Negro dialect poetry was written before Dunbar wrote, most of it by white writers; but the fact stands out that Dunbar was the first to use it as a medium for the true interpretation of Negro character and psychology. And, yet, dialect poetry does not constitute the whole or even the bulk of Dunbar's work. In addition to a large number of poems of a very high order done in literary English, he was the author of four novels and several volumes of short stories.

Indeed, Dunbar did not begin his career as a writer of dialect. I may be pardoned for introducing here a bit of reminiscence. My personal friendship with Paul Dunbar began before he had achieved recognition, and continued to be close until his death. When I first met him he had published a thin volume, "Oak and Ivy," which was being sold chiefly through his own efforts. "Oak and Ivy" showed no distinctive Negro influence, but rather the influence of James Whitcomb Riley. At this time Paul and I were together every day for several months. He talked to me a great deal about his hopes and ambitions. In these talks he revealed that he had reached a realization of the possibilities of poetry in the dialect, together with a recognition of the fact that it offered the surest way by which he could get a hearing. Often he said to me: "I've got to write dialect poetry; it's the only way I can get them to listen to me." I was with Dunbar at the beginning of what proved to be his last illness. He said to me then: "I have not grown. I am writing the same things I wrote ten years ago, and am writing them no better." His self-accusation was not fully true; he had grown, and he had gained a surer control of his art, but he had not accomplished the greater things of which he was constantly dreaming; the public had held him to the things for which it had accorded him recognition. If Dunbar had lived he would have achieved some of those dreams, but even while he talked so dejectedly to me he seemed to feel that he was not to live. He died when he was only thirty-three.

It has a bearing on this entire subject to note that Dunbar was of unmixed Negro blood; so, as the greatest figure in literature which the colored race in the United States has produced, he stands as an example at once refuting and confounding those who wish to believe that whatever extraordinary ability an Aframerican shows is due to an admixture of white blood.

As a man, Dunbar was kind and tender. In conversation he was brilliant and polished. His voice was his chief charm, and was a great element in his success as a reader of his own works. In his actions he was impulsive as a child, sometimes even erratic; indeed, his intimate friends almost looked upon him as a spoiled boy. He was always delicate in health. Temperamentally, he belonged to that class of poets who Taine says are vessels too weak to contain the spirit of poetry, the poets whom poetry kills, the Byrons, the Burns's, the De Mussets, the Poes.

To whom may he be compared, this boy who scribbled his early verses while he ran an elevator, whose youth was a battle against poverty, and who, in spite of almost insurmountable obstacles, rose to success? A comparison between him and Burns is not unfitting. The similarity between many phases of their lives is remarkable, and their works are not incommensurable. Burns took the strong dialect of his people and made it classic; Dunbar took the humble speech of his people and in it wrought music.

Mention of Dunbar brings up for consideration the fact that, although he is the most outstanding figure in literature among the Aframericans of the United States, he does not stand alone among the Aframericans of the whole Western world. There are Plácido and Manzano in Cuba; Vieux and Durand in Haiti, Machado de Assis in Brazil; Leon Laviaux in Martinique, and others still that might be mentioned, who stand on a plane with or even above Dunbar. Plácido and Machado de Assis rank as great in the literatures of their respective countries without any qualifications whatever. They are world figures in the literature of the Latin languages. Machado de Assis is somewhat handicapped in this respect by having as his tongue and medium the lesser known Portuguese, but Plácido, writing in the language of Spain, Mexico, Cuba and of almost the whole of South America, is universally known. His works have been republished in the original in Spain, Mexico and in most of the Latin-American countries; several editions have been published in the United States; translations of his works have been made into French and German.

Plácido is in some respects the greatest of all the Cuban poets. In sheer genius and the fire of inspiration he surpasses even the more finished Heredia. Then, too, his birth, his life and his death ideally contained the tragic elements that go into the making of a halo about a poet's head. Plácido was born in Habana in 1809. The first months of his life were passed in a foundling asylum; indeed, his real name, Gabriel de la Concepcion Valdés, was in honor of its founder. His father took him out of the asylum, but shortly afterwards went to Mexico and died there. His early life was a struggle against poverty; his youth and manhood was a struggle for Cuban independence. His death placed him in the list of Cuban martyrs. On the 27th of June, 1844, he was lined up against a wall with ten others and shot by order of the Spanish authorities on a charge of conspiracy. In his short but eventful life he turned out work which bulks more than six hundred pages. During the few hours preceding his execution he wrote three of his best known poems, among them his famous sonnet, "Mother, Farewell!"

Plácido's sonnet to his mother has been translated into every important language; William Cullen Bryant did it in English; but in spite of its wide popularity, it is, perhaps, outside of Cuba the least understood of all Plácido's poems. It is curious to note how Bryant's translation totally misses the intimate sense of the delicate subtility of the poem. The American poet makes it a tender and loving farewell of a son who is about to die to a heart-broken mother; but that is not the kind of a farewell that Plácido intended to write or did write.

The key to the poem is in the first word, and the first word is the Spanish conjunction Si (if). The central idea, then, of the sonnet is, "If the sad fate which now overwhelms me should bring a pang to your heart, do not weep, for I die a glorious death and sound the last note of my lyre to you." Bryant either failed to understand or ignored the opening word, "If," because he was not familiar with the poet's history.

While Plácido's father was a Negro, his mother was a Spanish white woman, a dancer in one of the Habana theatres. At his birth she abandoned him to a foundling asylum, and perhaps never saw him again, although it is known that she outlived her son. When the poet came down to his last hours he remembered that somewhere there lived a woman who was his mother; that although she had heartlessly abandoned him; that although he owed her no filial duty, still she might, perhaps, on hearing of his sad end feel some pang of grief or sadness; so he tells her in his last words that he dies happy and bids her not to weep. This he does with nobility and dignity, but absolutely without affection. Taking into account these facts, and especially their humiliating and embittering effect upon a soul so sensitive as Plácido's, this sonnet, in spite of the obvious weakness of the sestet as compared with the octave, is a remarkable piece of work.

In considering the Aframerican poets of the Latin languages I am impelled to think that, as up to this time the colored poets of greater universality have come out of the Latin-American countries rather than out of the United States, they will continue to do so for a good many years. The reason for this I hinted at in the first part of this preface. The colored poet in the United States labors within limitations which he cannot easily pass over. He is always on the defensive or the offensive. The pressure upon him to be propagandic is well nigh irresistible. These conditions are suffocating to breadth and to real art in poetry. In addition he labors under the handicap of finding culture not entirely colorless in the United States. On the other hand, the colored poet of Latin-America can voice the national spirit without any reservations. And he will be rewarded without any reservations, whether it be to place him among the great or declare him the greatest.

So I think it probable that the first world-acknowledged Aframerican poet will come out of Latin-America. Over against this probability, of course, is the great advantage possessed by the colored poet in the United States of writing in the world-conquering English language.

This preface has gone far beyond what I had in mind when I started. It was my intention to gather together the best verses I could find by Negro poets and present them with a bare word of introduction. It was not my plan to make this collection inclusive nor to make the book in any sense a book of criticism. I planned to present only verses by contemporary writers; but, perhaps, because this is the first collection of its kind, I realized the absence of a starting-point and was led to provide one and to fill in with historical data what I felt to be a gap.

It may be surprising to many to see how little of the poetry being written by Negro poets to-day is being written in Negro dialect. The newer Negro poets show a tendency to discard dialect; much of the subject-matter which went into the making of traditional dialect poetry, ' possums, watermelons, etc., they have discarded altogether, at least, as poetic material. This tendency will, no doubt, be regretted by the majority of white readers; and, indeed, it would be a distinct loss if the American Negro poets threw away this quaint and musical folk-speech as a medium of expression. And yet, after all, these poets are working through a problem not realized by the reader, and, perhaps, by many of these poets themselves not realized consciously. They are trying to break away from, not Negro dialect itself, but the limitations on Negro dialect imposed by the fixing effects of long convention.

The Negro in the United States has achieved or been placed in a certain artistic niche. When he is thought of artistically, it is as a happy-go-lucky, singing, shuffling, banjo-picking being or as a more or less pathetic figure. The picture of him is in a log cabin amid fields of cotton or along the levees. Negro dialect is naturally and by long association the exact instrument for voicing this phase of Negro life; and by that very exactness it is an instrument with but two full stops, humor and pathos. So even when he confines himself to purely racial themes, the Aframerican poet realizes that there are phases of Negro life in the United States which cannot be treated in the dialect either adequately or artistically. Take, for example, the phases rising out of life in Harlem, that most wonderful Negro city in the world. I do not deny that a Negro in a log cabin is more picturesque than a Negro in a Harlem flat, but the Negro in the Harlem flat is here, and he is but part of a group growing everywhere in the country, a group whose ideals are becoming increasingly more vital than those of the traditionally artistic group, even if its members are less picturesque.

What the colored poet in the United States needs to do is something like what Synge did for the Irish; he needs to find a form that will express the racial spirit by symbols from within rather than by symbols from without, such as the mere mutilation of English spelling and pronunciation. He needs a form that is freer and larger than dialect, but which will still hold the racial flavor; a form expressing the imagery, the idioms, the peculiar turns of thought, and the distinctive humor and pathos, too, of the Negro, but which will also be capable of voicing the deepest and highest emotions and aspirations, and allow of the widest range of subjects and the widest scope of treatment.

Negro dialect is at present a medium that is not capable of giving expression to the varied conditions of Negro life in America, and much less is it capable of giving the fullest interpretation of Negro character and psychology. This is no indictment against the dialect as dialect, but against the mould of convention in which Negro dialect in the United States has been set. In time these conventions may become lost, and the colored poet in the United States may sit down to write in dialect without feeling that his first line will put the general reader in a frame of mind which demands that the poem be humorous or pathetic. In the meantime, there is no reason why these poets should not continue to do the beautiful things that can be done, and done best, in the dialect.

In stating the need for Aframerican poets in the United States to work out a new and distinctive form of expression I do not wish to be understood to hold any theory that they should limit themselves to Negro poetry, to racial themes; the sooner they are able to write American poetry spontaneously, the better. Nevertheless, I believe that the richest contribution the Negro poet can make to the American literature of the future will be the fusion into it of his own individual artistic gifts.

Not many of the writers here included, except Dunbar, are known at all to the general reading public; and there is only one of these who has a widely recognized position in the American literary world, he is William Stanley Braithwaite. Mr. Braithwaite is not only unique in this respect, but he stands unique among all the Aframerican writers the United States has yet produced. He has gained his place, taking as the standard and measure for his work the identical standard and measure applied to American writers and American literature. He has asked for no allowances or rewards, either directly or indirectly, on account of his race.

Mr. Braithwaite is the author of two volumes of verses, lyrics of delicate and tenuous beauty. In his more recent and uncollected poems he shows himself more and more decidedly the mystic. But his place in American literature is due more to his work as a critic and anthologist than to his work as a poet. There is still another role he has played, that of friend of poetry and poets. It is a recognized fact that in the work which preceded the present revival of poetry in the United States, no one rendered more unremitting and valuable service than Mr. Braithwaite. And it can be said that no future study of American poetry of this age can be made without reference to Braithwaite.

Two authors included in the book are better known for their work in prose than in poetry: W. E. B. Du Bois whose well-known prose at its best is, however, impassioned and rhythmical; and Benjamin Brawley who is the author, among other works, of one of the best handbooks on the English drama that has yet appeared in America.

But the group of the new Negro poets, whose work makes up the bulk of this anthology, contains names destined to be known. Claude McKay, although still quite a young man, has already demonstrated his power, breadth and skill as a poet. Mr. McKay's breadth is as essential a part of his equipment as his power and skill. He demonstrates mastery of the three when as a Negro poet he pours out the bitterness and rebellion in his heart in those two sonnet-tragedies, "If We Must Die" and "To the White Fiends," in a manner that strikes terror; and when as a cosmic poet he creates the atmosphere and mood of poetic beauty in the absolute, as he does in "Spring in New Hampshire" and "The Harlem Dancer." Mr. McKay gives evidence that he has passed beyond the danger which threatens many of the new Negro poets — the danger of allowing the purely polemical phases of the race problem to choke their sense of artistry.

Mr. McKay's earliest work is unknown in this country. It consists of poems written and published in his native Jamaica. I was fortunate enough to run across this first volume, and I could not refrain from reproducing here one of the poems written in the West Indian Negro dialect. I have done this not only to illustrate the widest range of the poet's talent and to offer a comparison between the American and the West Indian dialects, but on account of the intrinsic worth of the poem itself. I was much tempted to introduce several more, in spite of the fact that they might require a glossary, because however greater work Mr. McKay may do he can never do anything more touching and charming than these poems in the Jamaica dialect.

Fenton Johnson is a young poet of the ultra-modern school who gives promise of greater work than he has yet done. Jessie Fauset shows that she possesses the lyric gift, and she works with care and finish. Miss Fauset is especially adept in her translations from the French. Georgia Douglas Johnson is a poet neither afraid nor ashamed of her emotions. She limits herself to the purely conventional forms, rhythms and rhymes, but through them she achieves striking effects.

The principal theme of Mrs. Johnson's poems is the secret dread down in every woman's heart, the dread of the passing of youth and beauty, and with them love. An old theme, one which poets themselves have often wearied of, but which, like death, remains one of the imperishable themes on which is made the poetry that has moved men's hearts through all ages. In her ingenuously wrought verses, through sheer simplicity and spontaneousness, Mrs. Johnson often sounds a note of pathos or passion that will not fail to waken a response, except in those too sophisticated or cynical to respond to natural impulses. Of the half dozen or so of colored women writing creditable verse, Anne Spencer is the most modern and least obvious in her methods. Her lines are at times involved and turgid and almost cryptic, but she shows an originality which does not depend upon eccentricities. In her "Before the Feast of Shushan" she displays an opulence, the love of which has long been charged against the Negro as one of his naïve and childish traits, but which in art may infuse a much needed color, warmth and spirit of abandon into American poetry.

John W. Holloway, more than any Negro poet writing in the dialect to-day, summons to his work the lilt, the spontaneity and charm of which Dunbar was the supreme master whenever he employed that medium. It is well to say a word here about the dialect poems of James Edwin Campbell. In dialect, Campbell was a precursor of Dunbar. A comparison of his idioms and phonetics with those of Dunbar reveals great differences. Dunbar is a shade or two more sophisticated and his phonetics approach nearer to a mean standard of the dialects spoken in the different sections. Campbell is more primitive and his phonetics are those of the dialect as spoken by the Negroes of the sea islands off the coasts of South Carolina and Georgia, which to this day remains comparatively close to its African roots, and is strikingly similar to the speech of the uneducated Negroes of the West Indies. An error that confuses many persons in reading or understanding Negro dialect is the idea that it is uniform. An ignorant Negro of the uplands of Georgia would have almost as much difficulty in understanding an ignorant sea island Negro as an Englishman would have. Not even in the dialect of any particular section is a given word always pronounced in precisely the same way. Its pronunciation depends upon the preceding and following sounds. Sometimes the combination permits of a liaison so close that to the uninitiated the sound of the word is almost completely lost.

The constant effort in Negro dialect is to elide all troublesome consonants and sounds. This negative effort may be after all only positive laziness of the vocal organs, but the result is a softening and smoothing which makes Negro dialect so delightfully easy for singers.

Daniel Webster Davis wrote dialect poetry at the time when Dunbar was writing. He gained great popularity, but it did not spread beyond his own race. Davis had unctuous humor, but he was crude. For illustration, note the vast stretch between his "Hog Meat" and Dunbar's "When de Co'n Pone's Hot," both of them poems on the traditional ecstasy of the Negro in contemplation of "good things" to eat.

It is regrettable that two of the most gifted writers included were cut off so early in life. R. C. Jamison and Joseph S. Cotter, Jr., died several years ago, both of them in their youth. Jamison was barely thirty at the time of his death, but among his poems there is one, at least, which stamps him as a poet of superior talent and lofty inspiration. "The Negro Soldiers" is a poem with the race problem as its theme, yet it transcends the limits of race and rises to a spiritual height that makes it one of the noblest poems of the Great War. Cotter died a mere boy of twenty, and the latter part of that brief period he passed in an invalid state. Some months before his death he published a thin volume of verses which were for the most part written on a sick bed. In this little volume Cotter showed fine poetic sense and a free and bold mastery over his material. A reading of Cotter's poems is certain to induce that mood in which one will regretfully speculate on what the young poet might have accomplished had he not been cut off so soon.

As intimated above, my original idea for this book underwent a change in the writing of the introduction. I first planned to select twenty-five to thirty poems which I judged to be up to a certain standard, and offer them with a few words of introduction and without comment. In the collection, as it grew to be, that "certain standard" has been broadened if not lowered; but I believe that this is offset by the advantage of the wider range given the reader and the student of the subject.

I offer this collection without making apology or asking allowance. I feel confident that the reader will find not only an earnest for the future, but actual achievement. The reader cannot but be impressed by the distance already covered. It is a long way from the plaints of George Horton to the invectives of Claude McKay, from the obviousness of Frances Harper to the complexness of Anne Spencer. Much ground has been covered, but more will yet be covered. It is this side of prophecy to declare that the undeniable creative genius of the Negro is destined to make a distinctive and valuable contribution to American poetry.

I wish to extend my thanks to Mr. Arthur A. Schomburg, who placed his valuable collection of books by Negro authors at my disposal. I wish also to acknowledge with thanks the kindness of Dodd, Mead & Co. for permitting the reprint of poems by Paul Laurence Dunbar; of the Cornhill Publishing Company for permission to reprint poems of Georgia Douglas Johnson, Joseph S. Cotter, Jr., Bertram Johnson and Waverley Carmichael; and of Neale & Co. for permission to reprint poems of John W. Holloway. I wish to thank Mr. Braithwaite for permission to use the included poems from his forthcoming volume, "Sandy Star and Willie Gee." And to acknowledge the courtesy of the following magazines: The Crisis, The Century Magazine, The Liberator, The Freeman, The Independent, Others, and Poetry: A Magazine of Verse.

James Weldon Johnson.

New York City, 1921.

📝 选文评析：

《序言》长达 47 页，占据全书近四分之一的篇幅，详细介绍了《美国黑人诗歌集》的出版背景和意义，将其置于"新黑人"的时代精神之下凸显了该诗集出版的必要性，并简要梳理了美国黑人诗歌的发展史，对选集中的诗人及其作品进行了富有卓见的评论。在约翰逊本人撰写的书评中，他特别提到序言的历史再书写对非裔民众重新认识民族历史的意义，指出黑人的民族自豪感和自信力对其身份建构的重要性。

约翰逊认为非裔被歧视的根源并不在于社会刻板印象中非裔天生低下的智力水平，而是来自社会的种族偏见。要想扭转社会的刻板印象，黑人必须展示出自己的过人天赋。没有什么能比文学和艺术的辉煌成就更能改变人们对黑人的偏见并提高黑人的社会地位了。约翰逊以"莱莫斯叔叔"系列民间故事、黑人灵歌、步态舞和雷格泰姆音乐为例，总结了黑人在美国文学和艺术领域的影响力，指出黑人在弘扬种族文化上的重任和方向。他追溯了普希金、柯勒律治等欧洲著名作家的黑人血统，以此反驳黑人智商低下的荒谬论断，将美国文坛缺乏黑人血液的原因归咎于黑人常年面对的不平等困境。

《序言》以菲利斯·惠特利为开端梳理了美国黑人诗歌的发展史，从 18 世纪深受西方经典韵律诗影响的惠特利到用黑人方言写作的邓巴，以及其他"并非被大众熟知"的作家如克洛德·麦凯等"新黑人"诗人以及詹姆逊、科特等英年早逝的天才诗人。他重点列举了惠特利和邓巴两位诗人，以其为中心对其他诗人的写作风格一一展开评论。国族意识形态和方言写作是约翰逊在诗歌史的讨论过程中关注的两个问题，他将黑人诗歌的美学价值与诗歌的意识形态表达及其方式挂钩。他认为评价诗人必须把诗人及其作品置于当时的背景中以获得对其艺术性的价值判断，饱受争议的惠特利在约翰逊看来是 19 世纪的天才诗人，针对她作品的评价标准应当区别于其他白人和黑人创作。约翰逊还把美国黑人诗人的方言写作置于泛非语境下，引入古巴、巴西等地黑人诗歌的方言写作传统。

《序言》确立了黑人文学的标准，指出把种族意识形态与美学价值结合的评价方向，是美国黑人文学史的里程碑。约翰逊在评价这些诗歌的时候具有知识考古学的视野，将诗歌产生的语境纳入诗歌文本本身。他在美国黑人诗歌评价标准的设立上与杜波依斯相似，都把黑人的国家与种族认同置于评价体系中，确立了艺术与政治结合的黑人文学创作传统，把黑人文学创作推向美国大众视野。《序言》秉承了新黑人运动的精神，明确指出黑人要想改变自身处境必须改变社会对黑人"愚昧顺从、智力低下"的刻板印象，用文艺创作来展示黑人的才智，与阿兰·洛克的《新黑人》形成互文，并推动了新黑人运动的发展。在《序言》的最后，约翰逊自信地写道，"我相信读者不仅可以从中找到对未来的信念，也可以获取现实的收获"。

💬 推荐阅读文献：

Adelman, Lynn. A Study of James Weldon Johnson. *The Journal of Negro History*, 1967, 52(2): 128-145.

Biers, Katherine. Syncope Fever: James Weldon Johnson and the Black Phonographic Voice. *Representations*, 2006, 96(1): 99-125.

Byrd, Rudolph, ed. *The Essential Writings of James Weldon Johnson*. Random House Publishing Group, 2011.

Collier, Eugenia W. James Weldon Johnson: Mirror of Change. *Phylon*, 1960, 21(4):

351-359.

Kostelanetz, Richard. The Politics of Passing: The Fiction of James Weldon Johnson. *Negro American Literature Forum*, 1969, 3(1): 22-24, 29.

Larkin, Lesley. *Race and the Literary Encounter: Black Literature from James Weldon Johnson to Percival Everett*. Indiana UP, 2012.

Long, Richard A. A Weapon of My Song: The Poetry of James Weldon Johnson. *Phylon*, 1971, 32(4): 374-382.

Payne, Ladell. Themes and Cadences: James Weldon Johnson's Novel. *The Southern Literary Journal*, 1979, 11(2): 43-55.

第十章　阿兰·洛克
（Alain Locke，1886—1954）

阿兰·洛克是 20 世纪初期的杰出非裔知识分子、酷儿哲学家、作家和教育家，是新黑人运动的领军人物，被誉为哈莱姆文艺复兴之父。1886 年 9 月 13 日，洛克出生于费城的一个中产阶级家庭，父母均是教师。他家境优渥，天资聪颖，从小接受了良好的教育，在非裔学习和工作普遍受限的时代里先后在哈佛大学、牛津大学、柏林大学求学。他在三年内完成了哈佛大学的四年制课程，获鲍德因奖，并于 1918 年在哈佛大学获得哲学博士学位，还是第一位获得罗德学者称号的美国非裔学者。他在华盛顿特区的霍华德大学担任哲学教授，直到 1953 年退休。1954 年 6 月 9 日，洛克在纽约去世。

洛克是 20 世纪初新黑人运动和哈莱姆文艺复兴的领导者，也是美国非裔民权意识和种族意识觉醒的重要启蒙者。"新黑人运动"是美国非裔历史上一次重要的文化运动，对非裔的种族意识觉醒有着重要的启蒙意义，一定程度上为 60 年代的现代民权运动高潮奠定了基础。他在 1925 年编辑的文选《新黑人》（The New Negro）提出了著名的"新黑人"（New Negro）哲学思想，批判并否定了非裔愚昧落后、驯顺奴性的刻板印象，即"旧黑人"形象，倡导树立人格独立、自尊自爱的新黑人形象，粉碎种族歧视的锁链，实现美国种族的自由和平等。这部文选收录了年轻一代美国非裔作家的小说、诗歌和戏剧等作品，意图通过文学和艺术挑战种族主义成规旧俗，提高种族素质，促进种族融合。他写道："黑人世界的脉搏已经在哈莱姆跳动。"哈莱姆文艺复兴以"新黑人"的哲学思想为内核，反对种族歧视，批判并否定汤姆叔叔型驯顺的旧黑人形象，鼓励黑人作家在艺术创作中歌颂新黑人精神，树立新黑人形象。洛克的思想指导了兰斯顿·休斯、简·图默、佐拉·尼尔·赫斯顿等一大批作家，与他们以及杜波依斯、布克·华盛顿等人一起促进了新黑人运动的发展。

洛克提出文化多元主义理论，强调个体人格的独特性，文化的多样性以及和睦的种族关系。他呼吁非裔艺术家认可和弘扬自己的种族文化遗产，坚持种族文化的独特性，同时努力融入美国社会并欣赏其他种族的文化习俗，从而摆脱社会对非裔的刻板印象，塑造健康文明的新黑人形象。他鼓励非裔艺术家去非洲文化中寻找素材，建立非裔的身份意识，鼓励作家在非裔社区中寻找写作灵感和主题，确立较高的艺术标准。

洛克为美国非裔历史文化的学术研究发展作出了卓越贡献。他编辑了黑人文化研究青铜手册系列丛书，在 20 多年间为刊物《机遇》(*Opportunity*)审阅黑人作家作品或与黑人相关的文学作品。从 1940 年起，洛克每年为大不列颠年鉴撰写黑人部分相关内容。他的作品包括《四位黑人诗人》(*Four Negro Poets*, 1927)，《弗莱德里克·道格拉斯：反奴隶制传记》(*Frederick Douglass, a Biography of Anti-Slavery*, 1935)，《黑人艺术：过去与现在》(*Negro Art: Past and Present*, 1936)以及《黑人与音乐》(*The Negro and His Music*, 1936)等作品，发掘和梳理了非裔传统文化以及非裔文学艺术的发展过程和未来走向，是美国非裔研究领域的奠基者和先驱。

以下选文摘自《新黑人》，该文被认为是哈莱姆文艺复兴宣言。这篇文章最早刊登在杂志《调查图表》(*Survey Graphic*)的哈莱姆生活特辑《哈莱姆：新黑人的麦加》(*Harlem: Mecca of the New Negro*, 1925 年 3 月)上，之后洛克将其收录于文选《新黑人》中，该文选还同时收录了兰斯顿·休斯、康迪·卡伦、佐拉·尼尔·赫斯顿、简·图默等年轻非裔作家的作品，阐释了洛克的"新黑人"哲学观。

📖 作品选读：

The New Negro

In the last decade something beyond the watch and guard of statistics has happened in the life of the American Negro and the three Norns① who have tradition-ally presided over the Negro problem have a changeling in their laps. The Sociologist, the Philanthropist, the Race-leader are not unaware of the New Negro, but they are at a loss to account for him. He simply cannot be swathed in their formula. For the younger generation is vibrant with a new psychology; the new spirit is awake in the masses, and under the very eyes of the professional observers is transforming what has been a perennial problem into the progressive phases of contemporary Negro life.

Could such a metamorphosis have taken place as suddenly as it has appeared to? The answer is no; not because the New Negro is not here, but because the Old Negro had long become more of a myth than a man. The Old Negro, we must remember, was a creature of moral debate and historical controversy. His has been a stock figure perpetuated as an historical fiction partly in innocent sentimentalism, partly in deliberate reactionism. The Negro himself has contributed his share to this through a sort of protective social mimicry forced upon him by the adverse

---

① Norns：诺恩三女神，主宰着神和人类的命运。

circumstances of dependence. So for generations in the mind of America, the Negro has been more of a formula than a human being — a something to be argued about, condemned or defended, to be "kept down," or "in his place," or "helped up," to be worried with or worried over, harassed or patronized, a social bogey or a social burden. The thinking Negro even has been induced to share this same general attitude, to focus his attention on controversial issues, to see himself in the distorted perspective of a social problem. His shadow, so to speak, has been more real to him than his personality. Through having had to appeal from the unjust stereotypes of his oppressors and traducers to those of his liberators, friends, and benefactors he has had to subscribe to the traditional positions from which his case has been viewed. Little true social or self-understanding has or could come from such a situation.

But while the minds of most of us, black and white, have thus burrowed in the trenches of the Civil War and Reconstruction, the actual march of development has simply flanked these positions, necessitating a sudden reorientation of view. We have not been watching in the right direction; set North and South on a sectional axis, we have not noticed the East till the sun has us blinking.

Recall how suddenly the Negro spirituals revealed themselves; suppressed for generations under the stereotypes of Wesleyan hymn harmony, secretive, half-ashamed, until the courage of being natural brought them out — and behold, there was folk-music. Similarly, the mind of the Negro seems suddenly to have slipped from under the tyranny of social intimidation and to be shaking off the psychology of imitation and implied inferiority. By shedding the old chrysalis of the Negro problem we are achieving something like a spiritual emancipation. Until recently, lacking self-understanding, we have been almost as much of a problem to ourselves as we still are to others. But the decade that found us with a problem has left us with only a task. The multitude perhaps feels as yet only a strange relief and a new vague urge, but the thinking few know that in the reaction the vital inner grip of prejudice has been broken.

With this renewed self-respect and self-dependence, the life of the Negro community is bound to enter a new dynamic phase, the buoyancy from within compensating for whatever pressure there may be of conditions from without. The migrant masses, shifting from countryside to city, hurdle several generations of experience at a leap, but more important, the same thing happens spiritually in the life-attitudes and self-expression of the Young Negro, in his poetry, his art, his education, and his new outlook, with the additional advantage, of course, of the poise and greater certainty of knowing what it is all about. From this comes the promise and warrant of a new leadership. As one of them has discerningly put it:

> We have tomorrow
> Bright before us
> Like a flame.

Yesterday, a night-gone thing
A sun-down name.

And dawn today
Broad arch above the road we came.
We march! ①

This is what, even more than any "most creditable record of fifty years of freedom," requires that the Negro of to-day be seen through other than the dusty spectacles of past controversy. The day of "aunties," "uncles," and "mammies" is equally gone. Uncle Tom and Sambo have passed on, and even the "Colonel" and "George" play barnstorm rôles from which they escape with relief when the public spotlight is off. The popular melodrama has about played itself out, and it is time to scrap the fictions, garret the bogeys, and settle down to a realistic facing of facts.

First we must observe some of the changes which since the traditional lines of opinion were drawn have rendered these quite obsolete. A main change has been, of course, that shifting of the Negro population which has made the Negro problem no longer exclusively or even predominantly Southern. Why should our minds remain sectionalized, when the problem itself no longer is? Then the trend of migration has not only been toward the North and the Central Midwest, but city-ward and to the great centers of industry — the problems of adjustment are new, practical, local, and not peculiarly racial. Rather they are an integral part of the large industrial and social problems of our present-day democracy. And finally, with the Negro rapidly in process of class differentiation, if it ever was warrantable to regard and treat the Negro en masse it is becoming with every day less possible, more unjust, and more ridiculous.

In the very process of being transplanted, the Negro is becoming transformed.

The tide of Negro migration, northward and city-ward, is not to be fully explained as a blind flood started by the demands of war industry coupled with the shutting off of foreign migration, or by the pressure of poor crops coupled with increased social terrorism in certain sections of the South and Southwest. Neither labor demand, the boll-weevil, ② nor the Ku Klux Klan is a basic factor, however contributory any or all of them may have been. The wash and rush of this human tide on the beach line of the northern city centers is to be explained primarily in terms of a new vision of opportunity, of social and economic freedom, of a spirit to seize, even in the face of an extortionate and heavy toll, a chance for the improvement of conditions. With each successive wave of it, the movement of the Negro becomes more and more a mass movement toward the larger and the more democratic chance — in the Negro's case a deliberate flight not only from

---

①　节选自兰斯顿·休斯(Langston Hughes, 1902—1967)的诗歌《青年》，该诗于 1924 年发表在全美有色人种协进会官方杂志《危机》上。

②　boll-weevil：棉铃象甲，一种害虫，在 1910 年到 1920 年摧毁了美国南方的棉花田。

countryside to city, but from medieval America to modern.

Take Harlem as an instance of this. Here in Manhattan is not merely the largest Negro community in the world, but the first concentration in history of so many diverse elements of Negro life. It has attracted the African, the West Indian, the Negro American; has brought together the Negro of the North and the Negro of the South; the man from the city and the man from the town and village; the peasant, the student, the businessman, the professional man, artist, poet, musician, adventurer and worker, preacher and criminal, exploiter and social outcast. Each group has come with its own separate motives and for its own special ends, but their greatest experience has been the finding of one another. Proscription and prejudice have thrown these dissimilar elements into a common area of contact and interaction. Within this area, race sympathy and unity have determined a further fusing of sentiment and experience. So what began in terms of segregation becomes more and more, as its elements mix and react, the laboratory of a great race-welding. Hitherto, it must be admitted that American Negroes have been a race more in name than in fact, or to be exact, more in sentiment than in experience. The chief bond between them has been that of a com-mon condition rather than a common consciousness; a problem in common rather than a life in common. In Harlem, Negro life is seizing upon its first chances for group expression and self-determination. It is — or promises at least to be — a race capital. That is why our comparison is taken with those nascent centers of folk-expression and self-determination which are playing a creative part in the world to-day. Without pretense to their political significance, Harlem has the same rôle to play for the New Negro as Dublin has had for the New Ireland or Prague for the New Czechoslovakia.

Harlem, I grant you, isn't typical — but it is significant, it is prophetic. No sane observer, however sympathetic to the new trend, would contend that the great masses are articulate as yet, but they stir, they move, they are more than physically restless. The challenge of the new intellectuals among them is clear enough — the "race radicals" and realists who have broken with the old epoch of philanthropic guidance, sentimental appeal, and protest. But are we after all only reading into the stirrings of a sleeping giant the dreams of an agitator? The answer is in the migrating peasant. It is the "man farthest down" who is most active in getting up. One of the most characteristic symptoms of this is the professional man himself migrating to recapture his constituency after a vain effort to maintain in some Southern corner what for years back seemed an established living and clientele. The clergyman following his errant flock, the physician or lawyer trailing his clients, supply the true clues. In a real sense it is the rank and file who are leading, and the leaders who are following. A transformed and transforming psychology permeates the masses.

When the racial leaders of twenty years ago spoke of developing race-pride and stimulating race-consciousness, and of the desirability of race solidarity, they could not in any accurate degree have anticipated the abrupt feeling that has surged up and now pervades the awakened centers. Some of the recognized Negro leaders and a powerful section of white opinion identified with "race work" of the older order have indeed attempted to discount this feeling as a "passing phase," an attack of "race nerves" so to speak, an "aftermath of the war," and the like. It has not abated, however, if we are to gauge by the present tone and temper of the Negro press, or by the shift in popular support from the officially recognized and orthodox spokesmen to those of the independent, popular, and often radical type who are unmistakable symptoms of a new order. It is a social disservice to blunt the fact that the Negro of the Northern centers has reached a stage where tutelage, even of the most interested and well-intentioned sort, must give place to new relationships, where positive self-direction must be reckoned with in ever increasing measure. The American mind must reckon with a fundamentally changed Negro.

The Negro too, for his part, has idols of the tribe to smash. If on the one hand the white man has erred in making the Negro appear to be that which would excuse or extenuate his treatment of him, the Negro, in turn, has too often unnecessarily excused himself because of the way he has been treated. The intelligent Negro of to-day is resolved not to make discrimination an extenuation for his shortcomings in performance, individual or collective; he is trying to hold himself at par, neither inflated by sentimental allowances nor depreciated by current social discounts. For this he must know himself and be known for precisely what he is, and for that reason he welcomes the new scientific rather than the old sentimental interest. Sentimental interest in the Negro has ebbed. We used to lament this as the falling off of our friends; now we rejoice and pray to be delivered both from self-pity and condescension. The mind of each racial group has had a bitter weaning, apathy or hatred on one side matching disillusionment or resentment on the other; but they face each other to-day with the possibility at least of entirely new mutual attitudes.

It does not follow that if the Negro were better known, he would be better liked or better treated. But mutual understanding is basic for any subsequent cooperation and adjustment. The effort toward this will at least have the effect of remedying in large part what has been the most unsatisfactory feature of our present stage of race relationships in America, namely the fact that the more intelligent and representative elements of the two race groups have at so many points got quite out of vital touch with one another.

The fiction is that the life of the races is separate, and increasingly so. The fact is that they have touched too closely at the unfavorable and too lightly at the favor-able levels.

While inter-racial councils have sprung up in the South, drawing on forward elements of both races, in the Northern cities manual laborers may brush elbows in their everyday work, but the community and business leaders have experienced no such interplay or far too little of it. These segments must achieve contact or the race situation in America becomes desperate. Fortunately, this is happening. There is a growing realization that in social effort the cooperative basis must supplant long-distance philanthropy, and that the only safeguard for mass relations in the future must be pro-vided in the carefully maintained contacts of the enlightened minorities of both race groups. In the intellectual realm a renewed and keen curiosity is replacing the recent apathy; the Negro is being carefully studied, not just talked about and discussed. In art and letters, instead of being wholly caricatured, he is being seriously portrayed and painted.

To all of this the New Negro is keenly responsive as an augury of a new democracy in American culture. He is contributing his share to the new social understanding. But the desire to be understood would never in itself have been sufficient to have opened so completely the protectively closed portals of the thinking Negro's mind. There is still too much possibility of being snubbed or patronized for that. It was rather the necessity for fuller, truer self-expression, the realization of the unwisdom of allowing social discrimination to segregate him mentally, and a counter-attitude to cramp and fetter his own living — and so the "spite-wall" that the intellectuals built over the "color-line" has happily been taken down. Much of this reopening of intellectual contacts has centered in New York and has been richly fruitful not merely in the enlarging of personal experience, but in the definite enrichment of American art and letters and in the clarifying of our common vision of the social tasks ahead.

The particular significance in the reestablishment of contact between the more advanced and representative classes is that it promises to offset some of the unfavorable reactions of the past, or at least to re-surface race contacts somewhat for the future. Subtly the conditions that are molding a New Negro are molding a new American attitude.

However, this new phase of things is delicate; it will call for less charity but more justice; less help, but infinitely closer understanding. This is indeed a critical stage of race relationships because of the likelihood, if the new temper is not understood, of engendering sharp group antagonism and a second crop of more calculated prejudice. In some quarters, it has already done so. Having weaned the Negro, public opinion cannot continue to paternalize. The Negro to-day is inevitably moving forward under the control largely of his own objectives. What are these objectives? Those of his outer life are happily already well and finally formulated, for they are none other than the ideals of American institutions and democracy. Those of his inner life are yet in process of formation, for the new psychology at present is more of a consensus of feeling than of opinion, of attitude rather than of program. Still some points seem to have crystallized.

Up to the present one may adequately describe the Negro's "inner objectives" as an attempt to repair a damaged group psychology and reshape a warped social perspective. Their realization has required a new mentality for the American Negro. And as it matures we begin to see its effects; at first, negative, iconoclastic, and then positive and constructive. In this new group psychology we note the lapse of sentimental appeal, then the development of a more positive self-respect and self-reliance; the repudiation of social dependence, and then the gradual recovery from hyper-sensitiveness and "touchy" nerves, the repudiation of the double standard of judgment with its special philanthropic allowances and then the sturdier desire for objective and scientific appraisal; and finally the rise from social disillusionment to race pride, from the sense of social debt to the responsibilities of social contribution, and offsetting the necessary working and commonsense acceptance of restricted conditions, the belief in ultimate esteem and recognition. Therefore, the Negro to-day wishes to be known for what he is, even in his faults and shortcomings, and scorns a craven and precarious survival at the price of seeming to be what he is not. He resents being spoken of as a social ward or minor, even by his own, and to being regarded a chronic patient for the sociological clinic, the sick man of American Democracy. For the same reasons, he himself is through with those social nostrums and panaceas, the so-called solutions of his "problem," with which he and the country have been so liberally dosed in the past. Religion, freedom, education, money — in turn, he has ardently hoped for and peculiarly trusted these things; he still believes in them, but not in blind trust that they alone will solve his life-problem.

Each generation, however, will have its creed, and that of the present is the belief in the efficacy of collective effort, in race cooperation. This deep feeling of race is at present the mainspring of Negro life. It seems to be the outcome of the reaction to proscription and prejudice; an attempt, fairly successful on the whole, to convert a defensive into an offensive position, a handicap into an incentive. It is radical in tone, but not in purpose and only the most stupid forms of opposition, misunderstanding or persecution could make it otherwise. Of course, the thinking Negro has shifted a little toward the Left with the world-trend, and there is an increasing group who affiliate with radical and liberal movements. But fundamentally for the present the Negro is radical on race matters, conservative on others, in other words, a "forced radical," a social protestant rather than a genuine radical. Yet under further pressure and injustice iconoclastic thought and motives will inevitably increase. Harlem's quixotic radical-isms call for their ounce of democracy today lest to-morrow they be beyond cure.

The Negro mind reaches out as yet to nothing but American wants, American ideas. But this forced attempt to build his Americanism on race values is a unique social experiment, and its ultimate success is impossible except through the fullest sharing of American culture and institutions. There should be no delusion about this. American nerves in sections unstrung with race hysteria are often fed the opiate that the trend of Negro advance is wholly separatist, and that the effect of its operation will be to encyst the Negro as a benign foreign body in the body politic. This cannot be — even if it were desirable. The racialism of the Negro is no limitation or reservation with respect to American life; it is only a constructive effort to build the obstructions in the stream of his progress into an efficient dam of social energy and power. Democracy itself is obstructed and stagnated to the extent that any of its channels are closed. Indeed, they cannot be selectively closed. So the choice is not between one way for the Negro and another way for the rest, but between American institutions frustrated, on the one hand, and American ideals progressively fulfilled and realized, on the other.

There is, of course, a warrantably comfortable feeling in being on the right side of the country's professed ideals. We realize that we cannot be undone without America's undoing. It is within the gamut of this attitude that the thinking Negro faces America, but with variations of mood that are if anything more significant than the attitude itself. Sometimes we have it taken with the defiant ironic challenge of McKay:

Mine is the future grinding down to-day
Like a great landslip moving to the sea,
Bearing its freight of debris far away
Where the green hungry waters restlessly
Heave mammoth pyramids, and break and roar
Their eerie challenge to the crumbling shore.①

Sometimes, perhaps more frequently as yet, it is taken in the fervent and almost filial appeal and counsel of Weldon Johnson's：

O Southland, dear Southland!
Then why do you still cling
To an idle age and a musty page,
To a dead and useless thing?②

But between defiance and appeal, midway almost between cynicism and hope, the prevailing mind stands in the mood of the same author's *To America*,③ an attitude of sober query and stoical challenge：

How would you have us, as we are?
Or sinking 'neath the load we bear,
Our eyes fixed forward on a star,
Or gazing empty at despair?

Rising or falling? Men or things?
With dragging pace or footsteps fleet?
Strong, willing sinews in your wings,
Or tightening chains about your feet?

More and more, however, an intelligent realization of the great discrepancy between the American social creed and the American social practice forces upon the Negro the taking of the moral advantage that is his. Only the steadying and sobering effect of a truly characteristic

---

① Mine is the future… the crumbling shore：节选自美国非裔诗人克劳德·麦凯(Claude McKay, 1889—1948)的诗歌《至根深蒂固的阶级》("To Entrenched Classes")，最早发表于1922年5月的废奴报纸《解放者》上。

② O Southland… useless thing? 节选自美国非裔作家詹姆斯·韦尔登·约翰逊的诗歌《啊南方》("Oh Southland!")，最早发表于《美国黑人诗歌集》(*The Book of American Negro Poetry*, 1922)。

③ 节选自詹姆斯·韦尔登·约翰逊的诗歌《致美国》("To America")，最早发表于他的诗集《五十年及其他诗歌》(1917)。

gentleness of spirit prevents the rapid rise of a definite cynicism and counter-hate and a defiant superiority feeling. Human as this reaction would be, the majority still deprecate its advent, and would gladly see it forestalled by the speedy amelioration of its causes. We wish our race pride to be a healthier, more positive achievement than a feeling based upon a realization of the shortcomings of others. But all paths toward the attainment of a sound social attitude have been difficult; only a relatively few enlightened minds have been able as the phrase puts it "to rise above" prejudice. The ordinary man has had until recently only a hard choice between the alternatives of supine and humiliating submission and stimulating but hurtful counter-prejudice. Fortunately, from some inner, desperate resourcefulness has recently sprung up the simple expedient of fighting prejudice by mental passive resistance, in other words by trying to ignore it. For the few, this manna may perhaps be effective, but the masses cannot thrive upon it.

Fortunately, there are constructive channels opening out into which the balked social feelings of the American Negro can flow freely.

Without them there would be much more pressure and danger than there is. These compensating interests are racial but in a new and enlarged way. One is the consciousness of acting as the advance-guard of the African peoples in their contact with twentieth-century civilization; the other, the sense of a mission of rehabilitating the race in world esteem from that loss of prestige for which the fate and conditions of slavery have so largely been responsible. Harlem, as we shall see, is the center of both these movements; she is the home of the Negro's "Zionism." The pulse of the Negro world has begun to beat in Harlem. A Negro newspaper carrying news material in English, French, and Spanish, gathered from all quarters of America, the West Indies, and Africa has maintained itself in Harlem for over five years. Two important magazines, both edited from New York, maintain their news and circulation consistently on a cosmopolitan scale. Under American auspices and backing, three pan-African congresses have been held abroad for the discussion of common interests, colonial questions, and the future cooperative development of Africa. In terms of the race question as a world problem, the Negro mind has leapt, so to speak, upon the parapets of prejudice and extended its cramped horizons. In so doing it has linked up with the growing group consciousness of the dark-peoples and is gradually learning their common interests. As one of our writers has recently put it: "It is imperative that we understand the white world in its relations to the non-white world." As with the Jew, persecution is making the Negro international.

As a world phenomenon this wider race consciousness is a different thing from the much asserted rising tide of color. Its inevitable causes are not of our making. The consequences are not necessarily damaging to the best interests of civilization. Whether it actually brings into being new armadas of conflict or argosies of cultural exchange and enlightenment can only be decided by the attitude of the dominant races in an era of critical change. With the American Negro, his new internationalism is primarily an effort to recapture contact with the scattered peoples of African derivation. Garveyism① may be a transient, if spectacular, phenomenon, but the possible rôle of the American Negro in the future development of Africa is one of the most constructive and universally helpful missions that any modern people can lay claim to.

Constructive participation in such causes cannot help giving the Negro valuable group incentives, as well as increased prestige at home and abroad. Our greatest rehabilitation may possibly come through such channels, but for the present, more immediate hope rests in the revaluation by white and black alike of the Negro in terms of his artistic endowments and cultural contributions, past and prospective. It must be increasingly recognized that the Negro has already made very substantial contributions, not only in his folk-art, music especially, which has always found appreciation, but in larger, though humbler and less acknowledged ways. For generations the Negro has been the peasant matrix of that section of America which has most undervalued him, and here he has contributed not only materially in labor and in social patience, but spiritually as well. The South has unconsciously absorbed the gift of his folk-temperament. In less than half a generation it will be easier to recognize this, but the fact remains that a leaven of humor, sentiment, imagination, and tropic nonchalance has gone into the making of the South from a humble, unacknowledged source. A second crop of the Negro's gifts promises still more largely. He now becomes a conscious contributor and lays aside the status of a beneficiary and ward for that of a collaborator and participant in American civilization. The great social gain in this is the releasing of our talented group from the arid fields of controversy and debate to the productive fields of creative expression. The especially cultural recognition they win should in turn prove the key to that revaluation of the Negro which must precede or accompany any consider-able further betterment of race relationships. But whatever the general effect, the pre-sent generation will have added the motives of self-expression and spiritual development to the old and still unfinished task of making material headway and progress. No one who understandingly faces the situation with its substantial accomplishment or views the new scene with its still more abundant promise can be entirely without hope. And certainly, if in our lifetime the Negro should not be able to celebrate his full initiation into American democracy, he can at least, on the warrant of these things, celebrate the attainment of a significant and satisfying new phase of group development, and with it a spiritual Coming of Age.

1925

✍ 选文评析:

阿兰·洛克的"新黑人"思想是其价值哲学观在种族问题上的体现。"新黑人"的提出是洛克针对当时美国社会种族关系和非裔社区发展的新状况的思索,是他的多元文化主义

---

① Garveyism:加维主义,美国黑人解放运动中的重要政治主张之一,由牙买加企业家马库斯·加维(1887—1940)推广,他宣扬黑人民族主义、泛非主义,支持把美国非裔送回非洲的政治举措。

和相对主义论的种族美学表达。选文围绕当代黑人展开了几个方面的讨论。首先，洛克分析了当代黑人与"旧黑人"的不同之处及其原因。"旧黑人"更像是残留在历史中的神话，是道德辩论和历史争议的产物，是感伤主义和反动主义虚构的结果。在美国主流话语中，黑人是被争议、被蔑视、被维护、被同情的他者，黑人总是以"嬷嬷""保姆"和黑奴的形象出现。非裔接受了这种教化的内部殖民，又进一步加强了这一刻板印象在美国社会的影响。

20 世纪 20 年代，大迁徙使黑人得以参与美国社会现代化进程。黑人涌入北方使种族矛盾不再局限于依然实施黑白隔离制度的南方。随着城市化、工业化的发展，黑人融入美国现代社会，并迅速实现了阶级分化。美国黑人这一"种族"更趋向于一个名称而非事实，近乎于一种情感而非体验。黑人共同体的联系在于共同的条件和同样的困难，而非共同意识和同样的生活。种族关系绝非美国社会和黑人社区的唯一和主导矛盾，种族之间并没有如想象中彼此隔离，而是有着密切的接触和联系。

为了改变美国社会对旧黑人的刻板印象，黑人作家和艺术家应当尽力把黑人描述成文明的、有能力为美国社会作贡献的种族，他们只需从奴隶制度和种族隔离制度中解放出来就可以发挥真正的潜力。这种作品的艺术目的是把黑人塑造成可以被社会接受的理想类型，是一种政治宣传的手段，即杜波依斯的"艺术为了政治宣传"主张。但洛克并不认同这种艺术功能，他认为艺术的政治宣传功能并非最终目标，白人的"刻板印象"和黑人艺术家创作的"反刻板印象"都把黑人符号化了，把黑人作为静态可供解读研究的客体。黑人知识分子也常年被禁锢在这种思维中，研究的对象一直是黑人的影子而非真实的黑人。黑人想要完全打开接受世界的门户，仅仅去接受知识和被理解是远远不够的，他们需要理解自己，表达自我，推翻隔离黑人的肤色之墙。

洛克继而指出新黑人应有的品质和态度。黑人需要调整内在目标，修复受损的集体心理，重塑扭曲的社会认知，摒弃过去的感伤主义式的情感依赖，发展出积极的、自尊自爱的独立精神，摒弃社会正义的双重标准，不再依赖社会上对黑人过剩的同情怜悯以及慈善系统的施舍，不再去计较种族社会对黑人的亏欠，继而产生种族自豪感和社会责任感。这些需要以黑人的自我理解为基础，进而互相理解实现种族间的合作，这也是美国种族形势好转的唯一办法和希望。这一任务需要黑白种族中少数的开明分子来完成。洛克将当前黑人社区存在的问题置于历史和国族视野中，逐一分析了民族主义、泛非主义等黑人的身份问题。他指出黑人的集体主义价值取向是目前黑人生活的主要行为动力，但这种激进的行为和价值取向是社会偏见的产物，黑人在种族事务上是激进的，而在其他社会事务上则持保守态度。洛克并不认同当时黑人社区的种族分裂倾向，如加文主义等黑人建国运动的导向。黑人的身份建立在美国人和种族价值观两者的基础之上，这是美国非裔独有的社会体验。黑人唯有与美国文化和制度融于一体，才可能实现自己的身份认同。黑人应该化社会的阻碍力量为有效能量，种族分裂绝不是解决问题的根本办法，捍卫美国的民主制度才能解决黑人问题。洛克强调了非洲的重要性，"所幸的是黑人现在有新的方式实现这一建设性的解决方案，其一是意识到非洲人民在于 20 世纪文明接触中的先锋作用，其二是重建黑人种族世界尊严的使命感"。种族问题是国际问题，并不局限于美国国土之内。哈莱姆区正是泛非运动的核心地点，黑人世界的脉搏在哈莱姆跳动。黑人报纸使用英语、法语和西班牙语刊登新闻,西印度群岛和非洲国家的文明以其独特的方式在哈莱姆存在多年。泛非会议在这里召开,讨论共同利用、殖民问题和未来非洲的合作发展。种族问题是世界范围的问题,黑人只有超越阵营的偏见才能把黑人的集体意识联系在一起,为黑人的共同利益奋斗,全世界的黑人是一个共同体。美国黑人在非洲的未来非洲中可能会扮演重要的角色。

洛克由此谈到纽约哈莱姆区的影响及年轻黑人艺术家们的艺术创作,他主张多元文化主义,鼓励黑人艺术家从黑人民间文化中汲取营养,展望未来黑人发展的方向。他认为黑人的艺术天赋和文化贡献必须被重新评价。自奴隶制度以来,黑人的价值总是被低估,他们从物质和精神上都为美国社会作出了巨大贡献。尤其在南方,黑人的幽默、情感、想象力和冷漠以一种卑微的不易察觉的方式参与塑造了南方气质。黑人参与了美国的建构,是美国民主制度的重要贡献者和维护者。"年轻黑人"(young black)聚集于纽约哈莱姆区,他们的生活态度、文艺创作、教育状况和视野都与前辈不可同日而语,这是黑人的未来和希望。哈莱姆之与黑人,就像都柏林之于爱尔兰人,是黑人第一次得以表达自决意识和群体意识之地。这代年轻黑人极有天赋,他们放弃了受监护人和受益者的身份转而成为美国文明的合作者和参与者,把群体的智慧从喋喋不休的争论中释放出来,投入到富有创造性的生产领域,黑人以此赢得文化认同从而促进种族良好关系的发展,新黑人将在尚未实现的物质富裕之上增添精神和自我表达的动机。洛克对黑人的未来充满希望,"即使在我们的有生之年黑人无法完全参与美国的民主制度建设,我们至少可以进入一个精神成熟的新的阶段"。

推荐阅读文献:

Carter, Jacoby Adeshei. *African American Contributions to the Americas' Cultures*: *A Critical Edition of Lectures by Alain Locke*. Palgrave Macmillan, 2016.

Grant, Carl, and Brown, Keffrelyn, etc. *Black Intellectual Thought in Education*: *The Missing Traditions of Anna Julia Cooper*, *Carter G. Woodson*, *and Alain Leroy Locke*, Taylor & Francis Group, 2015.

Harris, Leonard. Identity: Alain Locke's Atavism. *Transactions of the Charles S. Peirce Society*, 1988, 24(1): 65-83.

Harris, Leonard. Alain Locke and Community. *The Journal of Ethics*, 1997, 1(3): 239-247.

Harris, Leonard and Harris, Leonard. *The Philosophy of Alain Locke*: *Harlem Renaissance and Beyond*. Temple UP, 1989.

Helbling, Mark. Alain Locke: Ambivalence and Hope. *Phylon*, 1979, 40(3): 291-300.

Molesworth, Charles and Louis Gates, Henry., Jr. *The Works of Alain Locke*. Oxford UP, 2012.

Stewart, Jeffrey C. *The New Negro*: *The Life of Alain Locke*. Oxford UP, 2018.

Wright, Louis E. Alain Locke on Race Relations: Some Political Implications of His Thought. *Journal of Black Studies*, 2011, 42(2): 665-689.

第十一章 基恩·图默
（Jean Toomer，1894—1967）

基恩·图默，原名内森·品奇巴克·图默（Nathan Pinchback Toomer），是美国著名非裔诗人和小说家，被视为哈莱姆文艺复兴以及美国现代主义的代表作家。作为一个有较多白人血统的混血儿，图默的出身背景对他后来的文学创作有非常重要影响。图默的父亲先后结婚三次。他的第二任妻子虽是一位混血，却从白人种植园主父亲那里继承巨额遗产，被称为"美国最富有的有色人种妇女"。在其病故后，54 岁的老图默又娶了年仅 28 岁却非常富有的混血女孩妮娜·平贝克（Nina Pinchback）为第三任妻子，后者的父亲曾短暂担任路易斯安那州州长，是首位担任州长的非裔美国人。图默是父亲第三次婚  后所生，他的中间名字也正是来自母亲。后来父母离婚，母亲独自带着图默生活。当母亲再婚后，他们搬到纽约州新罗谢尔郊区，图默入读一所全白人学校。1909 年，在图默 15 岁时，母亲去世，他便回到华盛顿，与他的外祖父母住在一起。1914 年至 1917 年，图默曾先后就读于威斯康星大学、芝加哥大学、纽约大学等多所大学，学习农业、健身、生物、社会学和历史等众多课程，但并未获得任何学位。

由于图默的白人血统更多一些，单从外貌上很难判断他的种族身份。事实上，他也从未声称自己是白人或黑人，而是更愿意说他只是一个美国人。据著名美国非裔批评家小亨利·路易斯·盖茨（Henry Louis Gates, Jr.）研究发现，在 1920 年和 1930 年的人口普查中，图默曾被归为白人。但在 1917 年和 1942 年的登记中又两次被归类为黑人。部分原因是在当时，人口普查员经常根据个人的外貌、经济状况和居住地区等综合信息判断种族身份。1931 年，图默在威斯康星州与白人作家玛格丽·拉蒂默（Margery Latimer）结婚，当时结婚证上也注明两人都是白人。由于违反了跨种族婚姻禁忌，他们的结合遭到舆论猛烈批评。但这段婚姻仅持续一年，次年拉蒂默便不幸在分娩中去世。1934 年，图默又娶家境优渥的白人摄影师马娇瑞·康腾特（Marjorie Content）为妻。这段婚姻再次引发公众关注。1940 年，图默一家搬到了宾夕法尼亚州的多伊尔斯顿。

1921 年，图默在佐治亚州斯巴达的一所新农村黑人农工学校曾短暂当了几个月的校长。这所学校位于汉考克县中心，离他父亲曾生活过的地方很近。在对南方黑人的艰难生活现实有了更多了解后，图默逐渐开始认同自己的非裔美国人身份，也越来越认同父亲的

175

过去。也就在这短短几个月期间，图默根据自己在那里的经历开始创作短篇故事、小品文和诗歌，这些作品构成他在 1923 年出版的现代主义作品集《甘蔗》(Cane) 的基础。《甘蔗》受到黑人和白人精英读者和评论界的一致好评。包括内拉·拉森(Nella Larsen)、理查德·赖特(Richard Wright)、兰斯顿·休斯(Langston Hughes)等人在内的许多著名美国非裔评论家和作家都对《甘蔗》大加赞誉，视其为美国黑人文学史上艺术成就最高的作品之一，图默也被视为黑人知识分子型的作家代表。

作为美国黑人文学史上的一部非凡的实验之作，《甘蔗》在体裁上来说并不好归类。它不像是一部小说，而更像是由短篇小说、散文、诗歌和小品素描共同组成的文集。有些诗歌独立成篇，有的则是融入散文的诗作。其中有六个女人的故事相互交织在一起，包含一个明显的自传体线索。这部作品之所以取得成功，部分是因为它对美国乡土特色传统的贡献：它揭示了美国特定地区和城市独特的风俗、节奏、景象和生活声音，特别是使用了大量方言和俚语。图默把《甘蔗》的成功归于他的非洲血统和他对佐治亚州农村黑人民间文化的熟悉。他欣赏南方乡村黑人文化，并想描绘这种佐治亚州生活的衰落。图默后来在谈到佐治亚州的乡村时曾写道："这里的环境在某种程度上很简陋……但却出奇地富饶美丽。我开始感觉到它的影响，尽管我的状态，或也许，仅仅是因为它。有一个山谷，叫做'甘蔗谷'，白天有烟圈，晚上有雾。"①他的作品与人们熟悉的那种黑人种植园小说类型完全不同，后者是过去非裔作家成功进入白人社会阅读圈的最常见作品，而图默则最先尝试将黑人民间文化与白人前卫精英文化相结合。他的作品人物更复杂，背景也更多样化，文化和社会主题也不局限于黑人生活。图默承认从舍伍德·安德森(Sherwood Anderson)的短篇小说集《小城畸人》(Winesburg, Ohio, 1919)那里受到很多影响。除此之外，著名现代派诗人 T. S. 艾略特对图默的影响也不小。不过和大部分现代主义作品一样，虽然《甘蔗》大受批评家称赞，但是在普通读者那里却不受欢迎。

《甘蔗》主要由三部分组成。第一部分以南方农村黑人生活为主题；第二部分更关注城市和北方生活；第三部分则是一篇名为"卡布尼斯"(Kabnis)的散文。图默把它设想为一个短篇小说循环，一个贯穿主题是探索女性、黑人男子气概和工业现代化在南方社会的悲剧性交汇。很多人通常认为图默的《甘蔗》属于南方心理现实主义一脉，甚至堪与威廉·福克纳的最佳作品相媲美。下文选自《甘蔗》中的两个最著名短篇小说，分别是《卡琳塔》(Karintha) 和《燃血月亮》(Blood-Burning Moon)。

📖 作品选读(一)：

Karintha

Her skin is like dusk on the eastern horizon,

---

① 参见 https://www.gradesaver.com/cane.

O can't you see it,
O can't you see it,
Her skin is like dusk on the eastern horizon
... When the sun goes down.

Men had always wanted her, this Karintha, even as a child, Karintha carrying beauty, perfect as dusk when the sun goes down. Old men rode her hobby-horse upon their knees. Young men danced with her at frolics when they should have been dancing with their grown-up girls. God grant us youth, secretly prayed the old men. The younger fellows counted the time to pass before she would be old enough to mate with them. This interest of the male, that wishes to ripen a growing thing too soon, could mean no good to her.

Karintha, at twelve, was a wild flash that told the other folks just what it was to live. At sunset, when there was no wind, and the pinesmoke from over by the saw-mill hugged the earth, and you couldn't see more than a few feet in front, her sudden darting past you was a bit of vivid color, like a black bird that flashes in the light. With the other children one could hear, some distance away, their feet flopping in the two inch dust. Karintha's running was a whir. It had the sound of the red dust that sometimes makes a spiral in the road. At dusk, during the hush just after the mill had closed down, and before any of the women had started their supper-getting-ready songs, her voice, high-pitched, shrill, would put one's ears to itching. But no one ever thought to make her stop because of it. She stoned the cows, and beat her dog, and fought the other children... Even the preacher, who caught her at mischief, told himself that she was as innocently lovely as a November cotton-flower.

Already, rumors were out about her. Homes in Georgia are most often built on the two-room plan. In one, you cook and eat, in the other is where you sit and sleep, and where love goes on. Karintha had seen or heard, perhaps she had felt her parents loving. One could but imitate one's parents, for to follow them was the way of God. She played "home" with a small boy who was not afraid to do her bidding. That started the whole thing. Old men could no longer ride her hobby-horse upon their knees. But young men counted faster.

Her skin is like dusk,
O can't you see it,
Her skin is like dusk
When the sun goes down.

Karintha is a woman. She who carries beauty, perfect as dusk when the sun goes down. She has been married many times. Old men remind her that a few years back they rode her hobby-horse upon their knees. Karintha smiles, and indulges them when she is in the mood for it. She has contempt for them. Karintha is a woman. Young men run stills to make her money. Young men gamble to make her money. Young men go to the large cities and run on the road. Young men go away to college. They all want to bring her money. These are the young men who thought that all they had to do was to count time. But Karintha is a woman, and she has had a child. A child fell out of her womb onto a bed of pine-needles in the forest. Pine-needles are smooth and sweet. They are elastic to the feet of rabbits... A saw-mill was nearby. Its pyramidal saw-dust pile smouldered. It is a year before one completely burns. Meanwhile, the smoke curls up and hangs in odd wraiths about the forest, curls up, and spreads itself out over the valley... Weeks after Karintha returned home, the smoke was so heavy you tasted it in water. Someone made a song:

> Smoke is on the hills. Rise up.
> Smoke is on the hills, O rise
> And take my soul away to Jesus

Karintha is a woman. Men do not know that the soul of her was a growing thing ripened too soon. They will bring their money; they will die not having found it out... Karintha at twenty, carrying beauty, perfect as dusk when the sun goes down. Karintha...

> Her skin is like dusk on the eastern horizon,
> O can't you see it, O can't you see it,
> Her skin is like dusk on the eastern horizon
> ... When the sun goes down.
> Goes down...

📖 作品选读(二):

Blood-Burning Moon

1.

Up from the skeleton stone walls, up from the rotting floor boards and the solid hand-hewn beams of oak of the pre-war cotton factory, dusk came. Up from the dusk the full moon came. Glowing like a fired pine-knot, it illumined the great door and soft showered the Negro shanties aligned along the single street of factory town. The full moon in the great door was an omen. Negro women improvised songs against its spell.

Louisa sang as she came over the crest of the hill from the white folks' kitchen. Her skin was the color of oak leaves on young trees in fall. Her breasts, firm and up-pointed like ripe acorns. And her singing had the low murmur of winds in fig trees. Bob Stone, younger son of the people she worked for, loved her. By the way the world reckons things, he had won her. By measure of that warm glow which came into her mind at thought of him, he had won her. Tom Burwell, whom the whole town called Big Boy, also loved her. But working in the fields all day, and far away from her gave him no chance to show it. Though often enough of evenings he had tried to. Somehow, he never got along. Strong as he was with hands upon the ax or plow, he found it difficult to hold her. Or so he thought. But the fact was that he held her to factory town more firmly than he thought for. His black balanced, and pulled against, the white of Stone, when she thought of them. And her mind was vaguely upon them as she came over the crest of the hill, coming from the white folks' kitchen. As she sang softly at the evil face of the full moon.

A strange stir was in her. Indolently, she tried to fix upon Bob or Tom as the cause of it. To meet Bob in the canebrake, as she was going to do an hour or so later, was nothing new. And Tom's proposal which she felt on its way to her could be indefinitely put off. Separately, there was no unusual significance to either one. But for some reason, they jumbled when her eyes gazed vacantly at the rising moon. And from the jumble came the stir that was strangely within her. Her lips trembled. The slow rhythm of her song grew agitant and restless. Rusty black and tan spotted hounds, lying in the dark corners of porches or prowling around back yards, put their noses in the air and caught its tremor. They began plaintively to yelp and howl. Chickens woke up and cackled. Intermittently, all over the countryside dogs barked and roosters crowed as if heralding a weird dawn or some ungodly awakening. The women sang lustily. Their songs were cotton-wads to stop their ears. Louisa came down into factory town and sank wearily upon the step before her home. The moon was rising towards a thick cloud-bank which soon would hide it.

> Red nigger moon. Sinner!
> Blood-burning moon. Sinner!
> Come out that fact'ry door. .

2

Up from the deep dusk of a cleared spot on the edge of the forest a mellow glow arose and spread fan-wise into the low-hanging heavens. And all around the air was heavy with the scent of boiling cane. A large pile of cane-stalks lay like ribboned shadows upon the ground. A mule, harnessed to a pole, trudged lazily round and round the pivot of the grinder. Beneath a swaying oil lamp, a Negro alternately whipped out at the mule, and fed cane-stalks to the grinder. A fat boy waddled pails of fresh ground juice between the grinder and the boiling stove. Steam came from the copper boiling pan. The scent of cane came from the copper pan and drenched the forest and the hill that sloped to factory town, beneath its fragrance. It drenched the men in circle seated around the stove. Some of them chewed at the white pulp of stalks, but there was no need for them to, if all they wanted was to taste the cane. One tasted it in factory town. And from factory town one could see the soft haze thrown by the glowing stove upon the low-hanging heavens.

Old David Georgia stirred the thickening syrup with a long ladle, and ever so often drew it off. Old David Georgia tended his stove and told tales about the white folks, about moonshining and cotton picking, and about sweet nigger gals, to the men who sat there about his stove to listen to him. Tom Burwell chewed cane-stalk and laughed with the others till someone mentioned Louisa. Till someone said something about Louisa and Bob Stone, about the silk stockings she must have gotten from him. Blood ran up Tom's neck hotter than the glow that flooded from the stove. He sprang up. Glared at the men and said, "She's my gal." Will Manning laughed. Tom strode over to him. Yanked him up and knocked him to the ground. Several of Manning's friends got up to fight for him. Tom whipped out a long knife and would have cut them to shreds if they hadn't ducked into the woods. Tom had had enough. He nodded to Old David Georgia and swung down the path to factory town. Just then, the dogs started barking and the roosters began to crow. Tom felt funny. Away from the fight, away from the stove, chill got to him. He shivered. He shuddered when he saw the full moon rising towards the cloud-bank. He who didn't give a godam for the fears of old women. He forced his mind to fasten on Louisa. Bob Stone. Better not be. He turned into the street and saw Louisa sitting before her home. He went towards her, ambling, touched the brim of a marvelously shaped, spotted, felt hat, said he wanted to say something to her, and then found that he didn't know what he had to say, or if he did, that he couldn't say it. He shoved his big fists in his overalls, grinned, and started to move off.

"You all want me, Tom?"

"Thats what us wants, sho, Louisa."

"Well, here I am — "

"An here I is, but that aint ahelpin none, all th same."

"You wanted to say something? ..."

"I did that, sho. But words is like th spots on dice: no matter how y fumbles em, there's times when they jes wont come. I dunno why. Seems like th love I feels fo yo done stole m tongue. I got it now. Whee! Louisa, honey, I oughtnt tell y, I feel I oughtnt cause yo is young an goes t church an I has had other gals, but Louisa I sho do love y. Lil gal, Ise watched y from them first days when youall sat right here befo yo door befo th well an sang sometimes in a way that like t broke m heart. Ise carried y with me into th fields, day after day, an after that, an I sho can plow when yo is there, an I can pick cotton. Yassur! Come near beatin Barlo yesterday. I sho did. Yassur! An next year if ole Stone0. ll trust me, I'll have a farm. My own. My bales will buy yo what y gets from white folks now. Silk stockings an purple dresses — course I dont believe what some folks been whisperin as t how y gets them things now. White folks always did do for niggers what they likes. An they jes cant help alikin yo, Louisa. Bob Stone likes y. Course he does. But not th way folks is awhisperin. Does he, hon?"

I dont know what you mean, Tom."

"Course y dont. Ise already cut two niggers. Had t hon, t tell em so. Niggers always tryin t make somethin out a nothin. An then besides, white folks aint up t them tricks so much nowadays.

Godam better not be. Leastawise not with yo. Cause I wouldnt stand f it. Nassur."

"What would you do, Tom?"

"Cut him jes like I cut a nigger."

"No, Tom — "

"I said I would an there aint no mo to it. But that aint th talk f now. Sing, honey Louisa, an while I'm listenin t y I'll be makin love."

Tom took her hand in his. Against the tough thickness of his own, hers felt soft and small. His huge body slipped down to the step beside her. The full moon sank upward into the deep purple of the cloud-bank. An old woman brought a lighted lamp and hung it on the common well whose bulky shadow squatted in the middle of the road, opposite Tom and Louisa. The old woman lifted the well-lid, took hold the chain, and began drawing up the heavy bucket. As she did so, she sang. Figures shifted, restless like, between lamp and window in the front rooms of the shanties. Shadows of the figures fought each other on the gray dust of the road. Figures raised the windows and joined the old woman in song. Louisa and Tom, the whole street, singing:

> Red nigger moon. Sinner!
> Blood-burning moon. Sinner!
> Come out that fact'ry door.

3

Bob Stone sauntered from his veranda out into the gloom of fir trees and magnolias. The clear white of his skin paled, and the flush of his cheeks turned purple. As if to balance this outer change, his mind became consciously a white man's. He passed the house with its huge open hearth which, in the days of slavery, was the plantation cookery. He saw Louisa bent over that hearth. He went in as a master should and took her. Direct, honest, bold. None of this sneaking that he had to go through now. The contrast was repulsive to him. His family had lost ground. Hell no, his family still owned the niggers, practically. Damned if they did, or he wouldn't have to duck around so. What would they think if they knew? His mother? His sister? He shouldn't mention them, shouldn't think of them in this connection. There in the dusk he blushed at doing so. Fellows about town were all right, but how about his friends up North? He could see them incredible, repulsed. They didn't know. The thought first made him laugh. Then, with their eyes still upon him, he began to feel embarrassed. He felt the need of explaining things to them. Explain hell. They wouldn't understand, and moreover, who ever heard of a Southerner getting on his knees to any Yankee, or anyone. No sir. He was going to see Louisa tonight, and love her. She was lovely — in her way. Nigger way. What way was that? Damned if he knew. Must know. He'd known her long enough to know. Was there something about niggers that you couldnt know? Listening to them at church didn't tell you anything. Looking at them didn't tell you anything. Talking to them didn't tell you anything — unless it was gossip, unless they wanted to talk. Of course, about farming, and licker, and craps — but those weren't nigger. Nigger was something more. How much more? Something to be afraid of, more? Hell no. Who ever heard of being afraid of a nigger? Tom Burwell. Cartwell had told him that Tom went with Louisa after she reached home. No sir. No nigger had ever been with his girl. He'd like to see one try. Some position for him to be in. Him, Bob Stone, of the old Stone family, in a scrap with a nigger over a nigger girl. In the good old days…Ha! Those were the days. His family had lost ground. Not so much, though. Enough for him to have to cut through old Lemon's canefield by way of the woods, that he might meet her. She was worth it. Beautiful nigger gal. Why nigger? Why not, just gal? No, it was because she was nigger that he went to her. Sweet…The scent of boiling cane came to him. Then he saw the rich glow of the stove. He heard the voices of the men circled around it. He was about to skirt the clearing when he heard his own name mentioned. He stopped. Quivering. Leaning against a tree, he listened.

"Bad nigger. Yassur, he sho is one bad nigger when he gets started."

"Tom Burwell's been on th gang three times fo cuttin men."

"What y think he's agwine t do t Bob Stone?"

"Dunno yet. He aint found out. When he does — Baby!"

"Aint no tellin."

"Young Stone aint no quitter an I ken tell y that. Blood of th old uns in his veins."

"Thats right. He'll scrap, sho."

"Be gettin too hot f niggers round this away."

"Shut up, nigger. Y dont know what y talkin bout."

Bob Stone's ears burned as though he had been holding them over the stove. Sizzling heat welled up within him. His feet felt as if they rested on red-hot coals. They stung him to quick movement. He circled the fringe of the glowing. Not a twig cracked beneath his feet. He reached the path that led to factory town. Plunged furiously down it. Halfway along, a blindness within him veered him aside. He crashed into the bordering canebrake. Cane leaves cut his face and lips. He tasted blood. He threw himself down and dug his fingers in the ground. The earth was cool. Cane-roots took the fever from his hands. After a long while, or so it seemed to him, the thought came to him that it must be time to see Louisa. He got to his feet and walked calmly to their meeting place. No Louisa. Tom Burwell had her. Veins in his forehead bulged and distended. Saliva moistened the dried blood on his lips. He bit down on his lips. He tasted blood. Not his own blood; Tom Burwell's blood. Bob drove through the cane and out again upon the road. A hound swung down the path before him towards factory town. Bob couldn't see it. The dog loped aside to let him pass. Bob's blind rushing made him stumble over it. He fell with a thud that dazed him. The hound yelped. Answering yelps came from all over the countryside. Chickens cackled. Roosters crowed, heralding the bloodshot eyes of southern awakening. Singers in the town were silenced. They shut their windows down. Palpitant between the rooster crows, a chill hush settled upon the huddled forms of Tom and Louisa. A figure rushed from the shadow and stood before them. Tom popped to his feet.

"Whats y want?"

"I'm Bob Stone."

"Yassur — an I'm Tom Burwell. Whats y want?"

Bob lunged at him. Tom side-stepped, caught him by the shoulder, and flung him to the ground. Straddled him.

"Let me up."

"Yassur — but watch yo doins, Bob Stone."

A few dark figures, drawn by the sound of scuffle, stood about them. Bob sprang to his feet.

"Fight like a man, Tom Burwell, an I'll lick y."

Again he lunged. Tom side-stepped and flung him to the ground. Straddled him.

"Get off me, you godam nigger you."

"Yo sho has started somethin now. Get up."

Tom yanked him up and began hammering at him. Each blow sounded as if it smashed into a precious, irreplaceable soft something. Beneath them, Bob staggered back. He reached in his pocket and whipped out a knife.

"Thats my game, sho."

Blue flash, a steel blade slashed across Bob Stone's throat. He had a sweetish sick feeling. Blood began to flow. Then he felt a sharp twitch of pain. He let his knife drop. He slapped one hand against his neck. He pressed the other on top of his head as if to hold it down. He groaned. He turned, and staggered towards the crest of the hill in the direction of white town. Negroes who had seen the fight slunk into their homes and blew the lamps out. Louisa, dazed, hysterical, refused to go indoors. She slipped, crumbled, her body loosely propped against the woodwork of the well. Tom Burwell leaned against it. He seemed rooted there.

Bob reached Broad Street. White men rushed up to him. He collapsed in their arms.

"Tom Burwell...."

White men like ants upon a forage rushed about. Except for the taut hum of their moving, all was silent. Shotguns, revolvers, rope, kerosene, torches. Two high-powered cars with glaring searchlights. They came together. The taut hum rose to a low roar. Then nothing could be heard but the flop of their feet in the thick dust of the road. The moving body of their silence preceded them over the crest of the hill into factory town. It flattened the Negroes beneath it. It rolled to the wall of the factory, where it stopped. Tom knew that they were coming. He couldn't move. And then he saw the search-lights of the two cars glaring down on him. A quick shock went through him. He stiffened. He started to run. A yell went up from the mob. Tom wheeled about and faced them. They poured down on him. They swarmed. A large man with dead-white face and flabby cheeks came to him and almost jabbed a gun-barrel through his guts.

"Hands behind y, nigger."

Tom's wrists were bound. The big man shoved him to the well. Burn him over it, and when the woodwork caved in, his body would drop to the bottom. Two deaths for a godam nigger. Louisa was driven back. The mob pushed in. Its pressure, its momentum was too great. Drag him to the factory. Wood and stakes already there. Tom moved in the direction indicated. But they had to drag him. They reached the great door. Too many to get in there. The mob divided and flowed around the walls to either side. The big man shoved him through the door. The mob pressed in from the sides. Taut humming. No words. A stake was sunk into the ground. Rotting floor boards piled around it. Kerosene poured on the rotting floor boards. Tom bound to the stake. His breast was bare. Nails' scratches let little lines of blood trickle down and mat into the hair. His face, his eyes were set and stony. Except for irregular breathing, one would have thought him already dead. Torches were flung onto the pile. A great flare muffled in black smoke shot upward. The mob yelled. The mob was silent. Now Tom could be seen within the flames. Only his head, erect, lean, like a blackened stone. Stench of burning flesh soaked the air. Tom's eyes popped. His head settled downward. The mob yelled. Its yell echoed against the skeleton stone walls and sounded like a hundred yells. Like a hundred mobs yelling. Its yell thudded against the thick front wall and fell back. Ghost of a yell slipped through the flames and out the great door of the factory. It fluttered like a dying thing down the single street of factory town. Louisa, upon the step before her home, did not hear it, but her eyes opened slowly. They saw the full moon glowing in the great door. The full moon, an evil thing, an omen, soft showering the homes of folks she knew. Where were they, these people? She'd sing, and perhaps they'd come out and join her. Perhaps Tom Burwell would come. At any rate, the full moon in the great door was an omen which she must sing to:

> Red nigger moon. Sinner!
> Blood-burning moon. Sinner!
> Come out that fact'ry door.

📝 选文评析:

《甘蔗》中的每一篇故事都很短小,看起来好像很简单,但实际并非如此。图默运用了大量的现代主义手法,包括象征主义和蒙太奇,还模仿奴隶灵乐,并使用深奥的语言和隐喻,从而在很短的篇幅内表达极为丰富的意蕴,熟读数遍也未必能把它的所有深度都探究出来。它的每一首诗和每一个故事都引发数十篇评论文章;每一篇作品都可以在无数的语境中讨论。虽然整部作品在很多方面像是各种场景和故事的拼贴和大杂烩,但是实际上在分裂的不统一中却又贯穿着统一的主题,如男女之爱、南方风景、奴隶制以及私刑暴力的阴影等。

尽管整部作品是以蓄奴制被废除以后的重建时代为背景的,但蓄奴制度遗留下来的问题仍然萦绕在全书每一部分。南方的风景中依然回荡着在烈日下劳作和死去的奴隶的歌声,关于痛苦的记忆也还在持续影响着奴隶后代。奴隶制使人沦为动物和商品,即使被废除以后，它仍在阻碍几十年后非裔美国人的机会。它曾经以最严重的过度压迫、性虐待、暴力和对权力和霸权的垄断为特色，但现在却转化为整个社会方方面面可见和不可见的种族隔离。《甘蔗》中的人物以各种方式感受到奴隶制的历史重荷。他们必须与种族暴力和带有种族偏见的立法周旋，克服种族主义的压迫，主动或被动地融入白人主导的社会。他们努力在一个生存都很艰难的世界中形成身份、创造艺术和意义。蓄奴制在身体上是留有痕迹的，奴隶的身体被鞭挞、强奸、肢解和杀害。在吉姆·克劳时代，黑人的身体在很大程度上也仍旧受到种族结构的控制；黑人只能在白人退却之前在一定程度上维护自己的身体。他们的身体仍有伤疤，他们的集体无意识也是如此。

在图默笔下的南方社会，黑人身体试图与白人社会同化和融合，但这证明是困难的，因为它们已被剥夺了身体自治和种族自豪感。黑人女性的身体受到来自黑人和白人男性的注视和掌握，成为他们欲望的对象。她们的身体和能量受到男性和白人的控制。内部和外部的冲突在身体上展开。虽然《甘蔗》中的许多女性由于她们的性感和美丽有一定程度的权力，但她们仍然最终被一个男权制度所征服，这一制度把男性的凝视和男性的叙述放在优先位置。叙述者常常误解或轻视他所讨论的妇女。他看不见她们的真面目，也不知道她们的内心。男人声称拥有女人的身体并为之而战，但实际上他们蔑视她们，更愿意沉湎于对智力及社会生存和进步的追求，而不是情感上的联系。

在本章所选的第一个故事《卡琳塔》中，从主人公还是个小女孩开始，就成为身边男性垂涎的猎物。"男人们都想得到她，这个卡琳塔，从她还是一个孩子时，就那么美丽可人，完美如日落时的黄昏。老人们跪下帮她摇晃木马。小伙子们原本该和那些成年大姑娘跳舞，却都跑来和她嬉闹。老人们偷偷祈祷上帝让他们返老还童。年轻的小伙子们则整天数日子，盼着等她长大那天就可以婚配。"在男人们的撩拨之下，她变得很早熟，性格也越来越狂野放荡，"就像一只在阳光下闪烁的黑鸟"，能把身边男性玩弄于股掌之间。就连牧师都抵御不住她的诱惑，夸她"天真可爱得像一朵11月盛开的棉花花苞"。实际上，就卡琳塔而言，她并不是一个独立个体，而是被身边男人以及故事叙述者观看和解读的对象。她是欲望的化身，被淹没在男人渴望的目光中。她的身体与过去联系在一起，她只是一个符号和一个被动的物体，她的意义是外部强加给她的。她又是欲望的对象，她的力量只源于她吸引男人的能力。青春年少时，她可以随意玩弄身边男人，却又蔑视他们，不是真心和他们相爱。她虽然看上去似乎是一个能够驾驭男人的主人，实际上不过是被他们争抢的猎物。她很快就已结过多次婚，青春年华即将离她而去，未来的命运让人担忧。

第二个故事《燃血月亮》同样发生在蓄奴制阴影下的南方，一个"战前的棉花厂"。图默在这个故事中运用的拼贴结构有增无减，尽管有重复的主题和图像：松树，锯木厂和锯末，黄昏，甘蔗，烟，棉花，脸，燃烧，沉默和眼睛，但他能将这些与一些含蓄的和直接的暗示交织在一起，用以描述它血腥、压迫的过去，将南方暴力历史的阴暗记忆再一次带到了前台。在《甘蔗》整部作品中，这是少数几个有白人角色的故事之一，其中讲述的对黑人汤姆的私刑是种族重建时代一个令人震惊的血腥暴力的例子。此时种植园虽已不在，但那些熟悉的南方景观随处可见：甘蔗林、田野、高大松林、迷人的黄昏、在寒冷的冬天盛开的花朵、明亮的太阳、充满了锯木屑和浓烟气味的远景等。除了这些景观，随时可能发生的私刑迫害才是让吉姆·克劳时代的黑人们挥之不去的阴霾。

在《燃血月亮》中，白人鲍勃和黑人汤姆都"操演"了他们的种族身份，尽管他们都试图表现出与种族意识无关的样子。鲍勃是前白人奴隶主的儿子，汤姆则是奴隶的后代。两个人同时爱上了在鲍勃家工作的黑人女孩路易莎。但两人之间从一开始就并非平等的情敌竞争关系。对鲍勃来说，凭借其白人种族优势早已占据先机，"按当时社会上的普遍看法，他早已赢得了她"。汤姆虽然身高体壮，是全村人公认的"大男孩"，却只能"整天在地里干活，离她很远，没有机会表现"。他空有一身蛮力，却没受过教育，即使有机会，"他也不知道自己想说什么，即使知道，他也说不出来"。鲍勃只需要送路易莎一件漂亮的丝袜就可以打动她的芳心，汤姆向她求爱却只能表达一起"勤劳致富"的梦想："我带你下地，日复一日，年复一年，你在那儿的时候，我可以犁地，可以摘棉花。……明年如果老斯通信任我，我就会有一个农场。我自己的农场。我的钱包可以帮你买到你现在从白人那里得到的东西。丝袜，紫裙子。"

虽然鲍勃早已不是奴隶主，但他从骨子里仍旧迷恋那种种族优越感，也愤恨自己的家族失去了奴隶主的权力。"他的家族已失去地盘。他妈的，不，他的家族实际上仍然拥有这帮黑鬼。该死的，否则他就不必躲在那里了。"实际上他只是被路易莎的肉体所吸引，而且他很生气不能像过去的奴隶主那样随心所欲地占有她的身体。他曾经尝试着看自己是否能把她想象成只是一个女人，而不是一个"黑鬼"，却做不到，因为他之所以迷恋路易莎，正是因为她的种族身份给他带来了被禁忌的跨种族性刺激。鲍勃不由自主地迷恋路易莎，同时还和他瞧不起的黑人汤姆成了情敌，这让他深感耻辱，也担心自己的行为会让白人亲友耻笑。"他为自己的行为感到脸红……他能看到他们难以置信，深恶痛绝。……他开始感到尴尬。……他妈的，他也说不清楚……鲍勃·斯通，老斯通家族的后人，和一个黑鬼争夺一个黑妞。要是在过去那些好日子里……哈！那是什么样的日子！他的家族已失去地盘。"与之相反，汤姆虽然在社会经济地位上无法与他抗衡，但是拒绝承认自己更低贱，而且在身体的原始力量上更远胜鲍勃。两人都对各自的种族身份持怀疑态度，但两人最终却又都做出了似乎控制不了的事。可以说，两个人都是在"操演"他们身上的白色或黑色。鲍勃最终被汤姆所杀，汤姆又被白人暴徒私刑处决，这样的结果并非两人蓄意为之，但在被蓄奴制阴霾重重包围的种族重建时期的南方社会，这样的种族暴力似乎又不可避免。

💬 推荐阅读文献：

Carlin, Gerry. *Reading Jean Toomer's "Cane"*. Humanities-Ebooks, 2014.

Foley, Barbara. Jean Toomer's Sparta. *American Literature*, 1995, 67(4): 747-775.

Foley, Barbara. *Jean Toomer: Race, Repression, and Revolution*. U of Illinois P, 2014.

Ford, Karen Jackson. *Split-Gut Song: Jean Toomer and the Poetics of Modernity*. U of Alabama P, 2005.

Ramsey, William M. Jean Toomer's Eternal South. *The Southern Literary Journal*, 2003, 36 (1): 74-89.

Vetter, L. *Modernist Writings and Religio-Scientific Discourse: H. D., Loy, and Toomer*.

Palgrave Macmillan, 2010.

Webb, Jeff and Toomer, Jean. Literature and Lynching: Identity in Jean Toomer's 'Cane'. *ELH*, 2000, 67(1): 205-228.

Williams, Jennifer D. Jean Toomer's 'Cane' and the Erotics of Mourning. *The Southern Literary Journal*, 2008, 40(2): 87-101.

Woodson, Jon. *To Make a New Race: Gurdjieff, Toomer, and the Harlem Renaissance.* UP of Mississippi, 1999.

Whalan, Mark. Jean Toomer, Technology, and Race. *Journal of American Studies*, 2002, 36(3): 459-472.

第十二章　兰斯顿·休斯
（Langston Hughes，1901—1967）

兰斯顿·休斯，全名詹姆斯·默瑟·兰斯顿·休斯（James Mercer Langston Hughes）是美国杰出的小说家、剧作家、专栏作家和社会活动家，更是美国黑人文坛堪称最久负盛名的诗人。作为爵士诗的首创者之一，他将爵士乐、蓝调乐的节奏和音调融入自由诗的创作，形成了以既似吟咏又似书写般深沉别致的诗风和开阔深远的意境为特点的新艺术形式。他通过文学实验不断探索黑人民间素材与种族情感之间的契合，奠定了他在哈莱姆文艺复兴运动中的领袖地位，也成为他终其一生都在为激发种族共鸣而发声的缩影。

休斯于 1901 年出生于密苏里州乔普林（Joplin），他父亲的祖母及外祖母都是黑奴，而父亲的祖父及外祖父都是肯塔基州的白人奴隶主。休斯从小父母离异，母亲四处奔波，寻找工作，他主要由外祖母抚养，在堪萨斯州的劳伦斯市（Lawrence）长大。1921 年，他进入哥伦比亚大学（Columbia University）学习，由于校内种族歧视严重，仅一年之后休斯便辍学离开。随后他曾在非洲西海岸的远洋货轮上充当水手，继而流落巴黎。1924 年，他辗转回到美国，干过旅馆侍者等各种临时工作。这段时期内，休斯写作勤奋并在《机会》（*Opportunity*）等黑人杂志上刊发了不少作品。同时代的佐拉·尼尔·赫斯顿（Zora Neale Hurston）、华莱士·瑟曼（Wallace Thurman）等非裔作家与休斯志趣相投，他们都试图聚焦黑人劳工的生存痛点，批判黑人内部基于肤色的分裂和偏见，并于 1926 年一起创办了昙花一现的杂志《火!! 献给年轻的黑人艺术家》（*Fire!! Devoted to Younger Negro Artists*）。同年，休斯在《国家》（*The Nation*）杂志上发表的《黑人艺术家与种族之山》（"The Negro Artist and Racial Mountain"）被誉为他和合作同仁的共同宣言，这篇文章在哈莱姆文艺复兴时代为支持独立的黑人艺术起到了提纲挈领的作用。1929 年至 1934 年，他与赞助人夏洛特·奥斯古德·梅森（Charlotte Osgood Mason）的友好关系在首部小说《不是没有笑声》（*Not Without Laughter*, 1930）的创作过程中破裂，这在很大程度上导致他作品的整体基调在此之后沉降至压抑甚至绝望的状态。例如，现实主义短篇小说集《白人的行径》（*The Ways of White Folks*, 1934）极具讽刺性，流露着关于良好的种族、阶级关系幻灭的悲情。

1935 年，休斯获得古根海姆奖学金，实现了成立剧团的野心，即使大部分剧作反响平平，他依然选择于 1941 年在芝加哥创建"天阁剧团"(The Skyloft Players)，力求培养黑人剧作家，提供从黑人角度出发的戏剧。"二战"期间，他应聘成为《芝加哥卫报》(Chicago Defender)的每周专栏作家。围绕角色杰西·B. 辛普尔(Jesse B. Semple)的系列小说被视为他最受喜爱的作品，可谓是专栏亮点。与辛普尔有关的主题贯穿了他的五本诗集，并且跨越了不同的媒体。

始于 1942 年，持续 20 年的专栏见证了休斯职业生涯与文学成就的巅峰时刻。诗集《哈莱姆的莎士比亚》(Shakespeare in Harlem，1942)和《吉姆·克罗的最后一站》(Jim Crow's Last Stand，1943)标志着他的文学风格重回热烈。不论是夹带着激进政治立场的诗句，抑或休斯许多鲜为人知的政治诗作，如被纳入密苏里大学出版社两卷册中的《新歌》(A New Song，1938)，都暗示了他曾被共产主义吸引。战争结束后，右翼势力公开指责休斯加入了共产党，在被参议员约瑟夫·雷蒙德·"乔"·麦卡锡(Joseph Raymond "Joe" McCarthy)领导的参议院常设调查小组委员会召见时，休斯拒绝承认自己有任何鲜明的政治倾向。此后，他决定收起诗集中政治性的锋芒，当为《诗选》(Selected Poems，1959)选诗时，他将自己 20 世纪 30 年代蕴含社会主义箴言的内容全部排除在外，只着眼于抒情诗歌。这样看似矛盾的态度归根结底是休斯作为黑人作家的两难境地，他不得不在意识形态斗争中为求自保，同时却又渴望着将共产主义作为种族隔离的另一种替代性思维模式和情感宣泄的渠道。20 世纪 50 年代，休斯参与歌剧的填词，以及其中音乐和舞蹈的创作环节。商业舞台上取得的突破彻底扭转了他间歇式潦倒的生活窘境。休斯的作品同样以其广度和多样性著称，所写儿童读物多达十几本，另有《轻舞飞扬》(The Sweet Fly Flypaper of Life，1955)精准刻画哈莱姆区的百态图景。这部艺术摄影与文学诗作相辉映的作品兼具极高的史料、社会学层面的价值。

20 世纪 60 年代，休斯发现包括詹姆斯·鲍德温(James Baldwin)在内的新生代黑人作家对非裔美国人的身份及黑人民间文化缺乏自豪感，并指出作品中知识性过强则易落入俗套。多年的漂泊历程使休斯更深刻地理解和同情被忽视和受压迫的城市底层黑人。浸透着强烈种族意识的文学举措不仅是他选择抗议社会状况和争取权利的途径，也是他在黑人审美的理论与现实苦难生活的对话中对观众和艺术家进行再教育的一种尝试。1962 年，他的长篇诗歌《问你妈妈》(Ask Your Mama)问世，它强调从黑人音乐中汲取营养的非洲遗产蕴含着打破写作限定的潜能。休斯所支持的文化民族主义意在主张"通过照亮美国的黑人处境，以间接地照亮全人类的处境"，正如他鼓舞了世界范围内的黑人作家，尤其是那些引领了"黑人性"(Négritude)运动的法国非裔青年知识分子，他们与休斯一道为对抗殖民统治及其霸权主义余波提供了更多新的可能。休斯反对偏激式的过度愤怒或自我仇视，不免受到民权运动中的极端分子以及黑人媒体界崇尚种族融合者的排挤。前者将他温和的政治表态解释为对现状的妥协和逃避，后者认为他本质上属于"种族沙文主义者"。不过仍有部分年轻一代的黑人作家视休斯为偶像，如爱丽丝·沃克(Alice Walker)以致敬的姿态在作品中效仿他。

早在哥伦比亚求学期间，休斯已凭借成名作《黑人谈河》(The Negro Speaks of River)正式在非裔文学圈内崭露头角。这首诗篇最初发表在由 W. E. B. 杜波依斯(W. E. B. Du

Bois）担任编辑的全美有色人种协进会（NAACP）的官方杂志《危机》（*The Crisis*）上，后被收录在他的第一本诗集《疲惫的布鲁斯》（*The Weary Blues*, 1926）中。1967 年，休斯病逝于纽约，骨灰被安葬在哈莱姆区朔姆堡黑人文化研究中心门厅中央的地下。地板上的图案是题为"河流"的非洲宇宙图。在宇宙图的中心位置印刻的句子"我的灵魂像河流一样深邃"便取自《黑人谈河》。从刚果河到密西西比，这首诗沿河触碰美国黑人古老文明的遥远脉搏。与其说对非洲祖先留下的传统的眷恋是休斯笔下自我坚守的原则，不如说它是为庞大离散群体的后裔那无处安放的自尊供给着共有归属的不竭之源。

📖 作品选读：

The Negro Artist and the Racial Mountain

One of the most promising of the young Negro poets said to me once, "I want to be a poet — not a Negro poet," meaning, I believe, "I want to write like a white poet"; meaning subconsciously, "I would like to be a white poet"; meaning behind that, "I would like to be white." And I was sorry the young man said that, for no great poet has ever been afraid of being himself. And I doubted then that, with his desire to run away spiritually from his race, this boy would ever be a great poet. But this is the mountain standing in the way of any true Negro art in America — this urge within the race toward whiteness, the desire to pour racial individuality into the mold of American standardization, and to be as little Negro and as much American as possible.

But let us look at the immediate background of this young poet. His family is of what I suppose one would call the Negro middle class: people who are by no means rich yet never uncomfortable nor hungry — smug, contented, respectable folk, members of the Baptist church. The father goes to work every morning. He is a chief steward at a large white club. The mother sometimes does fancy sewing or supervises parties for the rich families of the town. The children go to a mixed school. In the home they read white papers and magazines. And the mother often says "Don't be like niggers" when the children are bad. A frequent phrase from the father is, "Look how well a white man does things." And so the word white comes to be unconsciously a symbol of all virtues. It holds for the children beauty, morality, and money. The whisper of "I want to be white" runs silently through their minds. This young poet's home is, I believe, a fairly typical home of the colored middle class. One sees immediately how difficult it would be for an artist born in such a home to interest himself in interpreting the beauty of his own people. He is never taught to see that beauty. He is taught rather not to see it, or if he does, to be ashamed of it when it is not according to Caucasian patterns. For racial culture the home of a self-styled "high-class"

Negro has nothing better to offer. Instead there will perhaps be more aping of things white than in a less cultured or less wealthy home. The father is perhaps a doctor, lawyer, landowner, or politician. The mother may be a social worker, or a teacher, or she may do nothing and have a maid. Father is often dark but he has usually married the lightest woman he could find. The family attend a fashionable church where few really colored faces are to be found. And they themselves draw a color line. In the North they go to white theatres and white movies. And in the South they have at least two cars and a house "like white folks." Nordic manners, Nordic faces, Nordic hair, Nordic art (if any), and an Episcopal heaven. A very high mountain indeed for the would-be racial artist to climb in order to discover himself and his people.

But then there are the low-down folks, the so-called common element, and they are the majority — may the Lord be praised! The people who have their hip of gin on Saturday nights and are not too important to themselves or the community, or too well fed, or too learned to watch the lazy world go round. They live on Seventh Street in Washington or State Street in Chicago and they do not particularly care whether they are like white folks or anybody else. Their joy runs, bang! into ecstasy. Their religion soars to a shout. Work maybe a little today, rest a little tomorrow. Play awhile. Sing awhile. O, let's dance! These common people are not afraid of spirituals, as for a long time their more intellectual brethren were, and jazz is their child. They furnish a wealth of colorful, distinctive material for any artist because they still hold their own individuality in the face of American standardizations. And perhaps these common people will give to the world its truly great Negro artist, the one who is not afraid to be himself. Whereas the better-class Negro would tell the artist what to do, the people at least let him alone when he does appear. And they are not ashamed of him — if they know he exists at all. And they accept what beauty is their own without question.

Certainly there is, for the American Negro artist who can escape the restrictions the more advanced among his own group would put upon him, a great field of unused material ready for his art. Without going outside his race, and even among the better classes with their "white" culture and conscious American manners, but still Negro enough to be different, there is sufficient matter to furnish a black artist with a lifetime of creative work. And when he chooses to touch on the relations between Negroes and whites in this country with their innumerable overtones and undertones surely, and especially for literature and the drama, there is an inexhaustible supply of themes at hand. To these the Negro artist can give his racial individuality, his heritage of rhythm and warmth, and his incongruous humor that so often, as in the Blues, becomes ironic laughter mixed with tears. But let us look again at the mountain.

A prominent Negro clubwoman in Philadelphia paid eleven dollars to hear Raquel Meller sing Andalusian popular songs. But she told me a few weeks before she would not think of going to hear "that woman," Clara Smith[①], a great black artist, sing Negro folksongs. And many an upper-

---

①　克拉拉·史密斯(Clara Smith，1894—1935)：美国蓝调歌手。

class Negro church, even now, would not dream of employing a spiritual in its services. The drab melodies in white folks' hymnbooks are much to be preferred. "We want to worship the Lord correctly and quietly. We don't believe in 'shouting.' Let's be dull like the Nordics," they say, in effect.

The road for the serious black artist, then, who would produce a racial art is most certainly rocky and the mountain is high. Until recently he received almost no encouragement for his work from either white or colored people. The fine novels of Chesnutt go out of print with neither race noticing their passing. The quaint charm and humor of Dunbar's dialect verse brought to him, in his day, largely the same kind of encouragement one would give a sideshow freak (A colored man writing poetry! How odd!) or a clown (How amusing!).

The present vogue in things Negro, although it may do as much harm as good for the budding colored artist, has at least done this: it has brought him forcibly to the attention of his own people among whom for so long, unless the other race had noticed him beforehand, he was a prophet with little honor. I understand that Charles Gilpin acted for years in Negro theatres without any special acclaim from his own, but when Broadway gave him eight curtain calls, Negroes, too, began to beat a tin pan in his honor. I know a young colored writer, a manual worker by day, who had been writing well for the colored magazines for some years, but it was not until he recently broke into the white publications and his first book was accepted by a prominent New York publisher that the "best" Negroes in his city took the trouble to discover that he lived there. Then almost immediately they decided to give a grand dinner for him. But the society ladies were careful to whisper to his mother that perhaps she'd better not come. They were not sure she would have an evening gown.

The Negro artist works against an undertow of sharp criticism and misunderstanding from his own group and unintentional bribes from the whites. "Oh, be respectable, write about nice people, show how good we are," say the Negroes. "Be stereotyped, don't go too far, don't shatter our illusions about you, don't amuse us too seriously. We will pay you," say the whites. Both would have told Jean Toomer not to write *Cane*. The colored people did not praise it. The white people did not buy it. Most of the colored people who did read *Cane* hate it. They are afraid of it. Although the critics gave it good reviews the public remained indifferent. Yet (excepting the work of Du Bois) *Cane* contains the finest prose written by a Negro in America. And like the singing of Robeson, it is truly racial.

But in spite of the Nordicized Negro intelligentsia and the desires of some white editors we have an honest American Negro literature already with us. Now I await the rise of the Negro theatre. Our folk music, having achieved world-wide fame, offers itself to the genius of the great individual American composer who is to come. And within the next decade I expect to see the work of a growing school of colored artists who paint and model the beauty of dark faces and create with new technique the expressions of their own soul-world. And the Negro dancers who will dance like flame and the singers who will continue to carry our songs to all who listen — they will be with us in even greater numbers tomorrow.

Most of my own poems are racial in theme and treatment, derived from the life I know. In many of them I try to grasp and hold some of the meanings and rhythms of jazz. I am as sincere as I know how to be in these poems and yet after every reading I answer questions like these from my own people: Do you think Negroes should always write about Negroes? I wish you wouldn't read some of your poems to white folks. How do you find anything interesting in a place like a cabaret? Why do you write about black people? You aren't black. What makes you do so many jazz poems?

But jazz to me is one of the inherent expressions of Negro life in America; the eternal tom-tom beating in the Negro soul — the tom-tom of revolt against weariness in a white world, a world of subway trains, and work, work, work; the tomtom of joy and laughter, and pain swallowed in a smile. Yet the Philadelphia club-woman is ashamed to say that her race created it and she does not like me to write about it. The old subconscious "white is best" runs through her mind. Years of study under white teachers, a lifetime of white books, pictures, and papers, and white manners, morals, and Puritan standards made her dislike the spirituals. And now she turns up her nose at jazz and all its manifestations — likewise almost everything else distinctly racial. She doesn't care for the Winold Reiss① portraits of Negroes because they are "too Negro." She does not want a true picture of herself from anybody. She wants the artist to flatter her, to make the white world believe that all Negroes are as smug and as near white in soul as she wants to be. But, to my mind, it is the duty of the younger Negro artist, if he accepts any duties at all from outsiders, to change through the force of his art that old whispering "I want to be white," hidden in the aspirations of his people, to "Why should I want to be white? I am a Negro — and beautiful!"

So I am ashamed for the black poet who says, "I want to be a poet, not a Negro poet," as though his own racial world were not as interesting as any other world. I am ashamed, too, for the colored artist who runs from the painting of Negro faces to the painting of sunsets after the manner of the academicians because he fears the strange un-whiteness of his own features. An artist must be free to choose what he does, certainly, but he must also never be afraid to do what he might choose. Let the blare of Negro jazz bands and the bellowing voice of Bessie Smith singing Blues penetrate the closed ears of the colored near-intellectual until they listen and perhaps understand. Let Paul Robeson singing "Water Boy," and Rudolph Fisher writing about the streets of Harlem, and Jean Toomer holding the heart of Georgia in his hands, and Aaron Douglas② drawing strange black fantasies cause the smug Negro middle class to turn from their white, respectable, ordinary books and papers to catch a glimmer of their own beauty. We younger Negro artists who create now intend to express our individual dark-skinned selves without fear or shame. If white people are pleased we are glad. If they are not, it doesn't matter. We know we are beautiful. And ugly too. The tom-tom cries and the tom-tom laughs. If colored people are pleased we are glad. If they are

---

① 温诺德·赖斯（Winold Reiss，1886—1953）：美国德裔艺术家、平面设计师和插画家。

② 亚伦·道格拉斯（Aaron Douglas，1898—1979）：美国非裔画家。

not, their displeasure doesn't matter either. We build our temples for tomorrow, strong as we know how, and we stand on top of the mountain, free within ourselves.

📝 选文评析：

作为 20 世纪 20 年代哈莱姆文艺复兴运动的领袖，休斯曾在哥伦比亚大学和林肯大学读书。当他还是林肯大学的学生时，于 1926 年 6 月 23 日在《国家》(The Nation)杂志上发表了这篇具有划时代意义的文章《黑人艺术家与种族山》，该文被许多人视为哈莱姆文艺复兴的奠基石和宣言书，不但在当时产生巨大影响，而且还在几十年后由理查德·赖特、拉尔夫·艾利森、詹姆斯·鲍德温、欧文·豪等人发起的围绕黑人文学的民族性和艺术个性问题产生的激烈争论中发挥了很大作用。就在本文发表一周前，乔治·斯凯勒(George S. Schuyler)刚刚在《国家》上发表了一篇颠覆传统的短文《黑人艺术杂谈》("The Negro Art Hokum")。休斯的这篇文章也正是对斯凯勒的回应。

休斯在文中谴责了当时很多非裔美国作家的不良倾向，他们"将种族个性注入美国标准化的模型中，尽量不做黑人、尽可能多做美国人"。休斯认为，黑人艺术家对自己种族世界的热情投入是必要的："我们这些年轻的黑人艺术家现在正在创作，他们打算表达我们自己的黑色皮肤，而不感到恐惧或羞耻……我们知道我们是美丽的。"休斯在文中表达了拥抱黑人文化的重要性，以及黑人艺术家拒绝服从标准化——即白人艺术理念——的必要性。他在文章开头引用了一位匿名诗人的名言，很多人根据细节推测他所指的就是同时代的康提·卡伦(Countee Cullen)。[①] 卡伦的主要意思是他想成为一个有价值的诗人，而不只是一个"黑人诗人"。休斯对卡伦否认自己的肤色和种族遗产的做法感到震惊，他在文章第一段中明确指出，黑人艺术家为"标准化"和白色而努力的这种情况就是一座巨大的种族之山，所有非裔美国人要想成为一名真正的艺术家，都需要奋力攀登并跨越过去。

休斯进而分析了他引用的这位年轻诗人的生活背景，他谈到了诗人是如何因为他的成长环境而努力追求白人价值观的。他可能来自一个舒适的黑人中产阶级家庭，父母都为富有的白人工作，他们经常去教堂做礼拜，他还就读于一所没有种族歧视的学校，这是他成长的地区为数不多的学校之一，这些可能是他拒绝继承种族遗产的原因之一。休斯写到，由于他的成长，这位诗人从来没有被教导过有关他自己的种族遗产的美丽和价值，而是相信只有白人的文化才更美丽和有价值。休斯指出，在另一方面，大多数普通黑人家庭过着与这位年轻诗人完全不同的生活。他描述了华盛顿和芝加哥充满爵士乐、饮酒和跳舞的黑人底层社区的欢乐和嬉戏。这些地方的黑人更活跃，也不那么保守，以自己的文化传统为荣。休斯明确表示，在这些社区，黑人并非拒绝白人的生活方式，而是过着自己选择的生活，一种让他们感到快乐的生活，并不在乎白人怎么看。休斯说得很清楚，他很庆幸有更多这样的非裔美国人家庭，那里有黑人传统和文化的骄傲。

然后休斯开始更明确地讨论他对白人文化主导的标准化的厌恶，他觉得白人价值标准

---

① 卡伦(1903—1946)擅长古典诗体创作，反对被人贴上"黑人诗人"的标签。他的作品在当时赢得不少赞誉和诗歌奖项。

阻碍了黑人艺术家的声音。20世纪20年代的美国正经历一个重视黑人艺术和黑人写作的文化时刻。休斯指出，在当代美国，欣赏黑人音乐、艺术和写作是时髦的，而不是让黑人艺术家在创作作品几周后就从聚光灯下消失。他认为，这也很危险。他对迎合白人兴趣的黑人艺术如何冲淡艺术家的独特性表示担忧，而正是这种独特性使他们一开始就很受欢迎。相反，那些生活在底层的普通黑人民众却能够更好地肯定自己的文化。他们并不厌恶自己的出身，也没有兴趣汇入白人主导的标准文化，仍然保持着自己的文化个性，"毫无疑问地接受什么是自己的美"。这样的黑人生活也就为黑人艺术家提供了丰富多彩、与众不同的素材，也有可能给这个世界带来真正伟大的黑人艺术家，"一个不怕做自己的人"。

休斯当然知道，对黑人艺术家来说，真正做自己是很难的。无论是在白人还是黑人那里，他们都常常得不到积极的鼓励。比如图默和切斯纳特，尽管他们的作品非常有创造力，却仍然长期被人们忽视。而且在得到白人文化界的肯定之前，黑人艺术家更难得到本民族的肯定，这是非常不公平的。来自黑人群体的声音经常要求他只展示本民族好的一面以便讨好白人，而来自白人群体的声音又要求他的创作必须保持白人对黑人艺术的一贯印象。这种两难处境使得黑人艺术家缺乏创作自由，也就很难成为真正伟大的艺术家。休斯呼吁黑人艺术家要勇敢地做自己，"一个艺术家必须有选择自己所做的事情的自由，当然，他也决不能害怕做他可能选择的事情。……如果白人高兴，我们就高兴。如果不是，那也没关系。我们知道我们很漂亮，也很难看。……如果有色人种高兴，我们就高兴。如果他们没有，他们的不满也不重要"。

推荐阅读文献：

Congdon, Brad. Langston Hughes, Esquire, and the Professional-Managerial Class. *The Journal of Modern Periodical Studies*, 2019, 10(1-2): 27-51.

Dunham, Montrew. *Langston Hughes: Young Black Poet*. Simon & Schuster Children's Publishing, 1995.

Gray, Stephen. Anthologizing Africa: Langston Hughes and His Correspondents. *Research in African Literatures*, 2011, 42(2): 1-7.

Hayes, Terrance. As for Langston Hughes. *BOMB*, 2018(143): 145-151.

Johnson, Durst. *Race in the Poetry of Langston Hughes*. Claudia Greenhaven Publishing, 2013.

Leach, Laurie. *Langston Hughes: A Biography*. ABC-CLIO, 2004.

Miller, R. Baxter. *The Art and Imagination of Langston Hughes*. UP of Kentucky, 1989.

Miller, W. Jason. *Langston Hughes and American Lynching Culture*. UP of Florida, 2011.

Nielson, Erik. A 'High Tension' in Langston Hughes's Musical Verse. *MELUS*, 2012, 37(4): 165-185.

Tracy, Steven C. *A Historical Guide to Langston Hughes*. Oxford UP, 2003.

Trotman, C. James and Trotman, C. James. *Langston Hughes: The Man, His Art, and His Continuing Influence*. Taylor & Francis Group, 1995.

第十三章　佐拉·尼尔·赫斯顿
（Zora Neale Hurston，1891—1960）

　　佐拉·尼尔·赫斯顿是哈莱姆文艺复兴时期著名的黑人女作家、民俗学家、人类学家，20世纪美国文学的重要人物之一，也是当代美国文学史上最有争议的人物之一。她1891年生于美国亚拉巴马州诺塔萨尔加（Notasulga），三岁随家人迁往美国首座黑人小城佛罗里达州的伊顿维尔市（Eatonville）。父亲是小城市长兼浸信会牧师，母亲是教师。1904年母亲不幸去世，赫斯顿被父亲和继母送到寄宿学校，后因父亲停止支付学费而被迫辍学，离开伊顿维尔，寄宿于亲戚家。她自力更生，干过女佣等工作。1917年起，赫斯顿重新开始接受教育。20世纪20年代在哈莱姆地区求学期间，赫斯顿结识了兰斯顿·休斯（Langston Hughes）等非裔作家，并很快成为哈莱姆文艺复兴的核心人物之一。1925年，她进入纽约市哥伦比亚大学巴纳德学院（Barnard College）就读，这期间追随著名人类学家弗朗茨·博厄斯（Franz Boas）进行人种学研究。1927年至1932年，在著名慈善家、文学赞助人夏洛特·奥斯古德·梅森（Charlotte Osgood Mason）的资助下，赫斯顿回到美国南部搜集有关黑人文化的材料。1937年，赫斯顿获得古根海姆奖学金，前往加勒比地区开展人种史研究，这期间完成了她最受欢迎的小说《他们眼望上苍》（*Their Eyes Were Watching God*）。她一生婚姻坎坷，先后几段婚姻均以失败告终，后独自移居佛罗里达州皮尔斯堡（Fort Pierce）。1950年起，随着获得的经济资助减少，她开始以家政服务等兼职作为额外收入来源，晚年生活穷困潦倒，被迫进入圣卢西县福利院，1960年病逝于此。

　　赫斯顿的作品关注美国南部的种族斗争，着力表现黑人文化语境下的黑人经验。她毕生为保持黑人文化传统而奋斗，收集出版了《骡与人》（*Mules and Men*，1935），这是第一部由美国黑人收集整理出版的美国黑人民间故事集。其小说的艺术特点之一是大量使用美国黑人独特的民间口语表达方式和形象化的语言。《他们眼望上苍》（*Their Eyes Were Watching God*，1937）一般被视为她的代表作。在这部作品里，她一改美国黑人文学的性别模式，塑造出一个寻找自我、表现自我、肯定自我的黑人女性，使被遮蔽的女性自信与自强重新成为社会的关注点。该小说是黑人文学中第一部充分展示黑人女子内心女性意识觉醒的作品，它不仅打破了传统美国文学禁区，也为后来黑人文学整体振兴铺平了道路，在黑人女性形象的创造上具有里程碑式的意义，被公认是黑人文学的经典作品之一。美国黑人文学著名评论家芭芭拉·克里斯琴（Barbara Christian）高度评价《他们眼望上苍》，指出它是"60 年代和 70 年代黑人文学的先行者"。《诺顿美国非裔文学选集》（*Norton Anthology of African American Literature*）将这部作品列为"哈莱姆文艺复兴时期最伟大的作品之一"。

赫斯顿对自己的非裔美国人的身份非常骄傲和自豪，否认自己有既是美国人又是黑人的"双重意识"困扰。她拒绝把黑人当成美国社会的"问题"，拒绝将黑人描写成种族歧视制度下产生的畸形儿。赫斯顿在作品中深刻地揭示了当时黑人社区内部存在的自我鄙视的黑人种族主义思想对黑人灵魂的腐蚀，力图唤醒黑人对自我身份的肯定和热爱。然而，哈莱姆文艺复兴的高潮退去以后，以理查德·赖特为代表的黑人"抗议文学"成为当时黑人文学的主流，赫斯顿及其作品被湮没在美国文学的尘埃里无人问津。直到 20 世纪 60 年代的黑人权力运动兴起，以及黑人民族主义意识的唤醒，加之黑人女作家艾丽丝·沃克（Alice Walker）1975 年在《女士杂志》（*Ms. Magazine*）上发表的名为《寻找佐拉·尼尔·赫斯顿》（"In Search of Zora Neale Hurston"）的文章的助力，赫斯顿才在一片荒冢中被重新发现。实际上，赖特式的"抗议"与赫斯顿式的"赞美"只是非裔美国人在美国社会求得生存的既矛盾又统一的两种策略。

📖 作品选读（一）：

Their Eyes Were Watching God

Chapter 2

[…]

Pheoby's hungry listening helped Janie to tell her story. So she went on thinking back to her young years and explaining them to her friend in soft, easy phrases while all around the house, the night time put on flesh and blackness. She thought awhile and decided that her conscious life had commenced at Nanny's gate.

On a late afternoon Nanny had called her to come inside the house because she had spied Janie letting Johnny Taylor kiss her over the gatepost. It was a spring afternoon in West Florida. Janie had spent most of the day under a blossoming pear tree in the back-yard. She had been spending every minute that she could steal from her chores under that tree for the last three days. That was to say, ever since the first tiny bloom had opened. It had called her to come and gaze on a mystery. From barren brown stems to glistening leaf-buds; from the leaf-buds to snowy virginity of bloom. It stirred her tremendously. How? Why? It was like a flute song forgotten in another existence and remembered again. What? How? Why? This singing she heard that had nothing to do with her ears. The rose of the world was breathing out smell. It followed her through all her waking moments and caressed her in her sleep. It connected itself with other vaguely felt matters that had struck her outside observation and buried themselves in her flesh. Now they emerged and quested about her consciousness.

She was stretched on her back beneath the pear tree soaking in the alto chant of the visiting bees, the gold of the sun and the panting breath of the breeze when the inaudible voice of it all came to her. She saw a dust-bearing bee sink into the sanctum of a bloom; the thousand sister-calyxes arch to meet the love embrace and the ecstatic shiver of the tree from root to tiniest branch creaming in every blossom and frothing with delight. So this was a marriage! She had been summoned to behold a revelation. Then Janie felt a pain remorseless sweet that left her limp and languid.

After a while she got up from where she was and went over the little garden field entire. She was seeking confirmation of the voice and vision, and everywhere she found and acknowledged answers. A personal answer for all other creations except herself. She felt an answer seeking her, but where? When? How? She found herself at the kitchen door and stumbled inside. In the air of the room were flies tumbling and singing, marrying and giving in marriage. When she reached the narrow hallway she was reminded that her grandmother was home with a sick headache. She was lying across the bed asleep so Janie tipped on out of the front door. Oh to be a pear tree — any tree in bloom! With kissing bees singing of the beginning of the world! She was sixteen. She had glossy leaves and bursting buds and she wanted to struggle with life but it seemed to elude her. Where were the singing bees for her? Nothing on the place nor in her grandma's house answered her. She searched as much of the world as she could from the top of the front steps and then went on down to the front gate and leaned over to gaze up and down the road. Looking, waiting, breathing short with impatience. Waiting for the world to be made.

Through pollinated air she saw a glorious being coming up the road. In her former blindness she had known him as shiftless Johnny Taylor, tall and lean. That was before the golden dust of pollen had beglamored his rags and her eyes.

In the last stages of Nanny's sleep, she dreamed of voices. Voices far-off but persistent, and gradually coming nearer. Janie's voice. Janie talking in whispery snatches with a male voice she couldn't quite place. That brought her wide awake. She bolted upright and peered out of the window and saw Johnny Taylor lacerating her Janie with a kiss.

"Janie!"

The old woman's voice was so lacking in command and reproof, so full of crumbling dissolution — that Janie half believed that Nanny had not seen her. So she extended herself outside of her dream and went inside of the house. That was the end of her childhood.

Nanny's head and face looked like the standing roots of some old tree that had been torn away by storm. Foundation of ancient power that no longer mattered. The cooling palma christi① leaves that Janie had bound about her grandma's head with a white rag had wilted down and become part and parcel of the woman. Her eyes didn't bore and pierce. They diffused and melted Janie, the room and the world into one comprehension.

"Janie, youse uh 'oman, now, so — "

"Naw, Nanny, naw Ah ain't no real 'oman yet."

The thought was too new and heavy for Janie. She fought it away.

Nanny closed her eyes and nodded a slow, weary affirmation many times before she gave it voice.

"Yeah, Janie, youse got yo' womanhood on yuh. So Ah mout ez well tell yuh whut Ah been savin' up for uh spell. Ah wants to see you married right away."

"Me, married? Naw, Nanny, no ma'am! Whut Ah know 'bout uh husband?"

"Whut Ah seen just now is plenty for me, honey, Ah don't want no trashy nigger, no breath-and-britches, lak Johnny Taylor usin' yo' body to wipe his foots on."

Nanny's words made Janie's kiss across the gatepost seem like a manure pile after a rain.

"Look at me, Janie. Don't set dere wid yo' head hung down. Look at yo' ole grandma!" Her voice began snagging on the prongs of her feelings. "Ah don't want to be talkin' to you lak dis. Fact is Ah done been on mah knees to mah Maker many's de time askin' please — for Him not to make de burden too heavy for me to bear."

"Nanny, Ah just — Ah didn't mean nothin' bad."

"Dat's what makes me skeered. You don't mean no harm. You don't even know where harm is at. Ah'm ole now. Ah can't be always guidin' yo' feet from harm and danger. Ah wants to see you married right away."

"Who Ah'm goin' tuh marry off-hand lak dat? Ah don't know nobody."

"De Lawd will provide. He know Ah done bore de burden in de heat uh de day. Somebody done spoke to me 'bout you long time ago. Ah ain't said nothin' 'cause dat wasn't de way Ah placed you. Ah wanted yuh to school out and pick from a higher bush and a sweeter berry. But dat ain't yo' idea, Ah see."

"Nanny, who — who dat been askin' you for me?"

"Brother Logan Killicks. He's a good man, too."

"Naw, Nanny, no ma'am! Is dat whut he been hangin' round here for? He look like some ole skullhead in de grave yard."

The older woman sat bolt upright and put her feet to the floor, and thrust back the leaves from her face.

---

① 此处指蓖麻(Ricinus communis)，由于蓖麻的叶子外形很像张开的手掌，故又被称为"palma christi"，直译即为"基督之掌"。在非洲巫医传统中，用蓖麻叶子覆盖人的身体既可以退热，也可以有其他神奇疗效。

"So you don't want to marry off decent like, do yuh? You just wants to hug and kiss and feel around with first one man and then another, huh? You wants to make me suck de same sorrow yo' mama did, eh? Mah ole head ain't gray enough. Mah back ain't bowed enough to suit yuh!"

The vision of Logan Killicks was desecrating the pear tree, but Janie didn't know how to tell Nanny that. She merely hunched over and pouted at the floor.

"Janie."

"Yes, ma'am."

"You answer me when Ah speak. Don't you set dere poutin' wid me after all Ah done went through for you!"

She slapped the girl's face violently, and forced her head back so that their eyes met in struggle. With her hand uplifted for the second blow she saw the huge tear that welled up from Janie's heart and stood in each eye. She saw the terrible agony and the lips tightened down to hold back the cry and desisted. Instead she brushed back the heavy hair from Janie's face and stood there suffering and loving and weeping internally for both of them.

"Come to yo' Grandma, honey. Set in her lap lak yo' use tuh. Yo' Nanny wouldn't harm a hair uh yo' head. She don't want nobody else to do it neither if she kin help it. Honey, de white man is de ruler of everything as fur as Ah been able tuh find out. Maybe it's some place way off in de ocean where de black man is in power, but we don't know nothin' but what we see. So de white man throw down de load and tell de nigger man tuh pick it up. He pick it up because he have to, but he don't tote it. He hand it to his womenfolks. De nigger woman is de mule uh de world so fur as Ah can see. Ah been prayin' fuh it tuh be different wid you. Lawd, Lawd, Lawd!"

For a long time she sat rocking with the girl held tightly to her sunken breast. Janie's long legs dangled over one arm of the chair and the long braids of her hair swung low on the other side. Nanny half sung, half sobbed a running chant-prayer over the head of the weeping girl.

"Lawd have mercy! It was a long time on de way but Ah reckon it had to come. Oh Jesus! Do, Jesus! Ah done de best Ah could."

Finally, they both grew calm.

"Janie, how long you been 'lowin' Johnny Taylor to kiss you?"

"Only dis one time, Nanny. Ah don't love him at all. Whut made me do it is — oh, Ah don't know."

"Thank yuh, Massa Jesus."

"Ah ain't gointuh do it no mo', Nanny. Please don't make me marry Mr. Killicks."

"'tain't Logan Killicks Ah wants you to have, baby, it's protection. Ah ain't gittin' ole, honey. Ah'm done ole. One mornin' soon, now, de angel wid de sword is gointuh stop by here. De day and de hour is hid from me, but it won't be long. Ah ast de Lawd when you was uh infant in mah arms to let me stay here till you got grown. He done spared me to see de day. Mah daily prayer now is tuh let dese golden moments rolls on a few days longer till Ah see you safe in life."

"Lemme wait, Nanny, please, jus' a lil bit mo'."

"Don't think Ah don't feel wid you, Janie, 'cause Ah do. Ah couldn't love yuh no more if Ah had uh felt yo' birth pains mahself. Fact uh de matter, Ah loves yuh a whole heap more'n Ah do yo' mama, de one Ah did birth. But you got to take in consideration you ain't no everyday chile like most of 'em. You ain't got no papa, you might jus' as well say no mama, for de good she do yuh. You ain't got nobody but me. And mah head is ole and tilted towards de grave. Neither can you stand alone by yo'self. De thought uh you bein' kicked around from pillar tuh post is uh hurtin' thing. Every tear you drop squeezes a cup uh blood outa mah heart. Ah got tuh try and do for you befo' mah head is cold."

A sobbing sigh burst out of Janie. The old woman answered her with little soothing pats of the hand.

"You know, honey, us colored folks is branches without roots and that makes things come round in queer ways. You in particular. Ah was born back due in slavery so it wasn't for me to fulfill my dreams of whut a woman oughta be and to do. Dat's one of de hold-backs of slavery. But nothing can't stop you from wishin'. You can't beat nobody down so low till you can rob 'em of they will. Ah didn't want to be used for a work-ox and a brood-sow and Ah didn't want mah daughter used dat way neither. It sho wasn't mah will for things to happen lak they did. Ah even hated de way you was born. But, all de same Ah said thank God, Ah got another chance. Ah wanted to preach a great sermon about colored women sittin' on high, but they wasn't no pulpit for me. Freedom found me wid a baby daughter in mah arms, so Ah said Ah'd take a broom and a cook-pot and throw up a highway through de wilderness for her. She would expound what Ah felt. But somehow she got lost offa de highway and next thing Ah knowed here you was in de world. So whilst Ah was tendin' you of nights Ah said Ah'd save de text for you. Ah been waitin' a long time, Janie, but nothin' Ah been through ain't too much if you just take a stand on high ground lak Ah dreamed."

Old Nanny sat there rocking Janie like an infant and thinking back and back. Mind-pictures brought feelings, and feelings dragged out dramas from the hollows of her heart.

Chapter 3

[...]

"Whut's de matter, sugar? You ain't none too spry dis mornin'."

"Oh, nothin' much, Ah reckon. Ah come to get a lil information from you."

The old woman looked amazed, then gave a big clatter of laughter. "Don't tell me you done got knocked up already, less see — dis Saturday it's two month and two weeks."

"No'm, Ah don't think so anyhow." Janie blushed a little.

"You ain't got nothin' to be shamed of, honey, youse uh married 'oman. You got yo' lawful husband same as Mis' Washburn or anybody else!"

"Ah'm all right dat way. Ah know 'tain't nothin' dere."

"You and Logan been fussin'? Lawd, Ah know dat grassgut, liver-lipted nigger ain't done took and beat mah baby already! Ah'll take a stick and salivate 'im!"

"No'm, he ain't even talked 'bout hittin' me. He says he never mean to lay de weight uh his hand on me in malice. He chops all de wood he think Ah wants and den he totes it inside de kitchen for me. Keeps both water buckets full."

"Humph! don't 'spect all dat tuh keep up. He ain't kissin' yo' mouf when he carry on over yuh lak dat. He's kissin' yo' foot and 'tain't in uh man tuh kiss foot long. Mouf kissin' is on uh equal and dat's natural but when dey got to bow down tuh love, dey soon straightens up."

"Yes'm."

"Well, if he do all dat whut you come in heah wid uh face long as mah arm for?"

" 'Cause you told me Ah mus gointer love him, and, and Ah don't. Maybe if somebody was to tell me how, Ah could do it."

"You come heah wid yo' mouf full uh foolishness on uh busy day. Heah you got uh prop tuh lean on all yo' bawn days, and big protection, and everybody got tuh tip dey hat tuh you and call you Mis' Killicks, and you come worryin' me 'bout love."

"But Nanny, Ah wants to want him sometimes. Ah don't want him to do all de wantin'."

Onliest organ in town, amongst colored folks, in yo' parlor. Got a house bought and paid for and sixty acres uh land right on de big road and... Lawd have mussy! Dat's de very prong all us black women gits hung on. Dis love! Dat's just whut's got us uh pullin' and uh haulin' and sweatin' and doin' from can't see in de mornin' till can't see at night. Dat's how come de ole folks say dat bein' uh fool don't kill nobody. It jus' makes you sweat. Ah betcha you wants some dressed up dude dat got to look at de sole of his shoe everytime he cross de street tuh see whether he got enough leather dere tuh make it across. You can buy and sell such as dem wid what you got. In fact you can buy 'em and give 'em away."

"Ah ain't studyin' 'bout none of 'em. At de same time Ah ain't takin' dat ole land tuh heart neither. Ah could throw ten acres of it over de fence every day and never look back to see where it fell. Ah feel de same way 'bout Mr. Killicks too. Some folks never was meant to be loved and he's one of 'em."

"How come?"

"'Cause Ah hates de way his head is so long one way and so flat on de sides and dat pone uh fat back uh his neck."

"He never made his own head. You talk so silly."

"Ah don't keer who made it, Ah don't like de job. His belly is too big too, now, and his toe-nails look lak mule foots. And 'tain't nothin' in de way of him washin' his feet every evenin' before he comes tuh bed. 'tain't nothin' tuh hinder him 'cause Ah places de water for him. Ah'd ruther be shot wid tacks than tuh turn over in de bed and stir up de air whilst he is in dere. He don't even never mention nothin' pretty."

She began to cry.

"Ah wants things sweet wid mah marriage lak when you sit under a pear tree and think. Ah..."

" 'tain't no use in you cryin', Janie. Grandma done been long uh few roads herself. But folks is meant to cry 'bout somethin' or other. Better leave things de way dey is. Youse young yet. No tellin' whut mout happen befo' you die. Wait awhile, baby. Yo' mind will change."

Nanny sent Janie along with a stern mien, but she dwindled all the rest of the day as she worked. And when she gained the privacy of her own little shack she stayed on her knees so long she forgot she was there herself. There is a basin in the mind where words float around on thought and thought on sound and sight. Then there is a depth of thought untouched by words, and deeper still a gulf of formless feelings untouched by thought. Nanny entered this infinity of conscious pain again on her old knees. Towards morning she muttered, "Lawd, you know mah heart. Ah done de best Ah could do. De rest is left to you." She scuffled up from her knees and fell heavily across the bed. A month later she was dead.

So Janie waited a bloom time, and a green time and an orange time. But when the pollen again gilded the sun and sifted down on the world she began to stand around the gate and expect things. What things? She didn't know exactly. Her breath was gusty and short. She knew things that nobody had ever told her. For instance, the words of the trees and the wind. She often spoke to falling seeds and said, "Ah hope you fall on soft ground," because she had heard seeds saying that to each other as they passed. She knew the world was a stallion rolling in the blue pasture of ether. She knew that God tore down the old world every evening and built a new one by sun-up. It was wonderful to see it take form with the sun and emerge from the gray dust of its making. The familiar people and things had failed her so she hung over the gate and looked up the road towards way off. She knew now that marriage did not make love. Janie's first dream was dead, so she became a woman.

Chapter 4

Long before the year was up, Janie noticed that her husband had stopped talking in rhymes to her. He had ceased to wonder at her long black hair and finger it. Six months back he had told her, "If Ah kin haul de wood heah and chop it fuh yuh, look lak you oughta be able tuh tote it inside. Mah fust wife never bothered me 'bout choppin' no wood nohow. She'd grab dat ax and sling chips lak uh man. You done been spoilt rotten."

So Janie had told him, "Ah'm just as stiff as you is stout. If you can stand not to chop and tote wood Ah reckon you can stand not to git no dinner. 'scuse mah freezolity, Mist' Killicks, but Ah don't mean to chop de first chip."

"Aw you know Ah'm gwine chop de wood fuh yuh. Even if you is stingy as you can be wid me. Yo' Grandma and me myself done spoilt yuh now, and Ah reckon Ah have tuh keep on wid it."

One morning soon he called her out of the kitchen to the barn. He had the mule all saddled at the gate.

"Looka heah, LilBit, help me out some. Cut up dese seed taters fuh me. Ah got tuh go step off a piece."

"Where you goin'?"

"Over tuh Lake City tuh see uh man about uh mule."

"Whut you need two mules fuh? Lessen you aims to swap off dis one."

"Naw, Ah needs two mules dis yeah. Taters is goin' tuh be taters in de fall. Bringin' big prices. Ah aims tuh run two plows, and dis man Ah'm talkin' 'bout is got uh mule all gentled up so even uh woman kin handle 'im."

Logan held his wad of tobacco real still in his jaw like a thermometer of his feelings while he studied Janie's face and waited for her to say something.

"So Ah thought Ah mout as well go see." He tagged on and swallowed to kill time but Janie said nothing except, "Ah'll cut de p'taters fuh yuh. When yuh comin' back?"

"Don't know exactly. Round dust dark Ah reckon. It's uh sorta long trip — specially if Ah hafter lead one on de way back."

When Janie had finished indoors she sat down in the barn with the potatoes. But springtime reached her in there so she moved everything to a place in the yard where she could see the road. The noon sun filtered through the leaves of the fine oak tree where she sat and made lacy patterns on the ground. She had been there a long time when she heard whistling coming down the road.

It was a cityfied, stylish dressed man with his hat set at an angle that didn't belong in these parts. His coat was over his arm, but he didn't need it to represent his clothes. The shirt with the silk sleeveholders was dazzling enough for the world. He whistled, mopped his face and walked like he knew where he was going. He was a seal-brown color but he acted like Mr. Washburn or somebody like that to Janie. Where would such a man be coming from and where was he going? He didn't look her way nor no other way except straight ahead, so Janie ran to the pump and jerked the handle hard while she pumped. It made a loud noise and also made her heavy hair fall down. So he stopped and looked hard, and then he asked her for a cool drink of water.

Janie pumped it off until she got a good look at the man. He talked friendly while he drank.

Joe Starks was the name, yeah Joe Starks from in and through Georgy. Been workin' for white folks all his life. Saved up some money — round three hundred dollars, yes indeed, right here in his pocket. Kept hearin' 'bout them buildin' a new state down heah in Floridy and sort of wanted to come. But he was makin' money where he was. But when he heard all about 'em makin' a town all outa colored folks, he knowed dat was de place he wanted to be. He had always wanted to be a big voice, but de white folks had all de sayso where he come from and everywhere else, exceptin' dis place dat colored folks was buildin' theirselves. Dat was right too. De man dat built things oughta boss it. Let colored folks build things too if dey wants to crow over somethin'. He was glad he had his money all saved up. He meant to git dere whilst de town wuz yet a baby. He meant to buy in big. It had always been his wish and desire to be a big voice and he had to live nearly thirty years to find a chance. Where was Janie's papa and mama?

"Dey dead, Ah reckon. Ah wouldn't know 'bout 'em 'cause mah Grandma raised me. She dead too."

"She dead too! Well, who's lookin' after a lil girl-chile lak you?"

"Ah'm married."

"You married? You ain't hardly old enough to be weaned. Ah betcha you still craves sugartits, doncher?"

"Yeah, and Ah makes and sucks 'em when de notion strikes me. Drinks sweeten' water too."

"Ah loves dat mahself. Never specks to get too old to enjoy syrup sweeten' water when it's cools and nice."

"Us got plenty syrup in de barn. Ribbon-cane syrup. If you so desires — "

"Where yo' husband at, Mis' er-er."

"Mah name is Janie Mae Killicks since Ah got married. Useter be name Janie Mae Crawford. Mah husband is gone tuh buy a mule fuh me tuh plow. He left me cuttin' up seed p'taters."

"You behind a plow! You ain't got no mo' business wid uh plow than uh hog is got wid uh holiday! You ain't got no business cuttin' up no seed p'taters neither. A pretty doll-baby lak you is made to sit on de front porch and rock and fan yo'self and eat p'taters dat other folks plant just special for you."

Janie laughed and drew two quarts of syrup from the barrel and Joe Starks pumped the water bucket full of cool water. They sat under the tree and talked. He was going on down to the new part of Florida, but no harm to stop and chat. He later decided he needed a rest anyway. It would do him good to rest a week or two.

Every day after that they managed to meet in the scrub oaks across the road and talk about when he would be a big ruler of things with her reaping the benefits. Janie pulled back a long time because he did not represent sun-up and pollen and blooming trees, but he spoke for far horizon. He spoke for change and chance. Still she hung back. The memory of Nanny was still powerful and strong.

"Janie, if you think Ah aims to tole you off and make a dog outa you, youse wrong. Ah wants to make a wife outa you."

"You mean dat, Joe?"

"De day you puts yo' hand in mine, Ah wouldn't let de sun go down on us single. Ah'm uh man wid principles. You ain't never knowed what it was to be treated lak a lady and Ah wants to be de one tuh show yuh. Call me Jody lak you do sometime."

"Jody," she smiled up at him, "but s'posin' — "

"Leave de s'posin' and everything else to me. Ah'll be down dis road uh little after sunup tomorrow mornin' to wait for you. You come go wid me. Den all de rest of yo' natural life you kin live lak you oughta. Kiss me and shake yo' head. When you do dat, yo' plentiful hair breaks lak day."

Janie debated the matter that night in bed.

"Logan, you 'sleep?"

"If Ah wuz, you'd be done woke me up callin' me."

"Ah wuz thinkin' real hard about us; about you and me."

"It's about time. Youse powerful independent around here sometime considerin'."

"Considerin' whut for instance?"

"Considerin' youse born in a carriage 'thout no top to it, and yo' mama and you bein' born and raised in de white folks back-yard."

"You didn't say all dat when you wuz begging Nanny for me to marry you."

"Ah thought you would 'preciate good treatment. Thought Ah'd take and make somethin' outa yuh. You think youse white folks by de way you act."

"S'posin' Ah wuz to run off and leave yuh sometime."

There! Janie had put words in his held-in fears. She might run off sure enough. The thought put a terrible ache in Logan's body, but he thought it best to put on scorn.

"Ah'm gettin' sleepy, Janie. Let's don't talk no mo'. 'tain't too many mens would trust yuh, knowin' yo' folks lak dey do."

"Ah might take and find somebody dat did trust me and leave yuh."

"Shucks! 'tain't no mo' fools lak me. A whole lot of mens will grin in yo' face, but dey ain't gwine tuh work and feed yuh. You won't git far and you won't be long, when dat big gut reach over and grab dat little one, you'll be too glad to come back here."

"You don't take nothin' to count but sow-belly and cornbread."

"Ah'm sleepy. Ah don't aim to worry mah gut into a fiddle-string wid no s'posin'." He flopped over resentful in his agony and pretended sleep. He hoped that he had hurt her as she had hurt him.

Janie got up with him the next morning and had the breakfast halfway done when he bellowed from the barn.

"Janie!" Logan called harshly. "Come help me move dis manure pile befo' de sun gits hot. You don't take a bit of interest in dis place. 'tain't no use in foolin' round in dat kitchen all day long."

Janie walked to the door with the pan in her hand still stirring the cornmeal dough and looked towards the barn. The sun from ambush was threatening the world with red daggers, but the shadows were gray and solid-looking around the barn. Logan with his shovel looked like a black bear doing some clumsy dance on his hind legs.

"You don't need mah help out dere, Logan. Youse in yo' place and Ah'm in mine."

"You ain't got no particular place. It's wherever Ah need yuh. Git uh move on yuh, and dat quick."

"Mah mamma didn't tell me Ah wuz born in no hurry. So whut business Ah got rushin' now? Anyhow dat ain't whut youse mad about. Youse mad 'cause Ah don't fall down and wash-up dese sixty acres uh ground yuh got. You ain't done me no favor by marryin' me. And if dat's what you call yo'self doin', Ah don't thank yuh for it. Youse mad 'cause Ah'm tellin' yuh whut you already knowed."

Logan dropped his shovel and made two or three clumsy steps towards the house, then stopped abruptly.

"Don't you change too many words wid me dis mawnin', Janie, do Ah'll take and change ends wid yuh!

Heah, Ah just as good as take you out de white folks' kitchen and set you down on yo' royal diasticutis and you take and low-rate me! Ah'll take holt uh dat ax and come in dere and kill yuh! You better dry up in dere! Ah'm too honest and hard-workin' for anybody in yo' family, dat's de reason you don't want me!" The last sentence was half a sob and half a cry. "Ah guess some low-lifed nigger is grinnin' in yo' face and lyin' tuh yuh. God damn yo' hide!"

Janie turned from the door without answering, and stood still in the middle of the floor without knowing it. She turned wrongside out just standing there and feeling. When the throbbing calmed a little she gave Logan's speech a hard thought and placed it beside other things she had seen and heard. When she had finished with that she dumped the dough on the skillet and smoothed it over with her hand. She wasn't even angry. Logan was accusing her of her mamma, her grandmama and her feelings, and she couldn't do a thing about any of it. The sow-belly in the pan needed turning. She flipped it over and shoved it back. A little cold water in the coffee pot to settle it. Turned the hoe-cake with a plate and then made a little laugh. What was she losing so much time for? A feeling of sudden newness and change came over her. Janie hurried out of the front gate and turned south. Even if Joe was not there waiting for her, the change was bound to do her good.

The morning road air was like a new dress. That made her feel the apron tied around her waist. She untied it and flung it on a low bush beside the road and walked on, picking flowers and making a bouquet. After that she came to where Joe Starks was waiting for her with a hired rig. He was very solemn and helped her to the seat beside him. With him on it, it sat like some high, ruling chair. From now on until death she was going to have flower dust and springtime sprinkled over everything. A bee for her bloom. Her old thoughts were going to come in handy now, but new words would have to be made and said to fit them.

"Green Cove Springs," he told the driver. So they were married there before sundown, just like Joe had said. With new clothes of silk and wool.

They sat on the boarding house porch and saw the sun plunge into the same crack in the earth from which the night emerged.

选文评析(一):

《他们眼望上苍》是赫斯顿 1937 年发表的小说，被认为是 20 世纪 20 年代哈莱姆文艺复兴时期的经典之作，也是赫斯顿最著名的作品。小说讲述了女主人公珍妮·克劳福德如何从一个充满活力，但不能自由表达自我的少女成长为一个能够自主决定命运的女人的故事。小说以 20 世纪初佛罗里达州中部和南部为背景，采用了很多自传素材。赫斯顿最主要的灵感来自前情人珀西瓦尔·庞特(Percival Punter)，据她后来在自传中所透露，主人公珍妮和第三任丈夫"茶糕"之间的故事就是由此而来。就像小说中的珍妮一样，赫斯顿比她的情人年龄大很多，而且庞特也和她的前几任丈夫一样，控制欲很强且有暴力倾向。小说发表最初，读者和评论界反响平平。但自 20 世纪后半期以来，随着黑人女性主义和非裔文学批评热的兴起，尤其是在艾丽丝·沃克的大力推举之后，这部小说的重要价值才又迅速被评论界和读者重新认识。2005 年，《时代》杂志将这部小说列入自 1923 年以来 100 部最佳英语小说的名单。

小说主要是用方言和口语写成，由一个来自美国南部的黑人妇女珍妮的故事来表达。在整部小说中，珍妮既是主人公又是偶尔的叙述者，她详细描述了自己 40 年的生活经历，主要包括三次婚姻以及每一次婚姻的后果。整部小说共有两种截然不同的叙述风格，一种是以第三人称叙述的标准英语散文，另一种是在对话中使用南方黑人土语。贯穿小说始终的一个主题是女性寻找表达的自由。本文节选自《他们眼望上苍》的第 2 章至第 4 章，主要内容讲述的是主人公珍妮在祖母安排下被迫嫁给第一任丈夫洛根，以及后来与乔迪结识并计划私奔的故事。

她先从自己的性觉醒开始讲起。当地小男孩约翰尼吻了她一下，她如此描述那一刻的美妙感觉："一只带着花粉的蜜蜂进入了一朵花的圣堂，成千的姊妹花蕾躬身迎接这爱的拥抱，梨树从根到最细小的枝丫狂喜地战栗，凝聚在每一个花朵中，处处翻腾着喜悦。"这恰巧被祖母看在眼里。她非常担心珍妮会重蹈那些被男人玩弄之后抛弃的黑人女性的悲惨命运，"我不愿意让像约翰尼这样的穷光蛋黑人、只会卖弄嘴皮的放肆小子拿你的身子擦脚"，便强迫珍妮尽早嫁给憨厚可靠的单身老农民洛根为妻，可以过上安稳日子。祖母为她安排这段无爱婚姻的部分原因是，祖母出身于奴隶家庭，以往的阅历告诉她，黑人妇女对自己的命运根本没有自主选择权。"我是在农奴制度下出生的，因此我不可能实现自己关于女人应成为什么人、做什么事的梦想。"她只希望珍妮能嫁个可靠之人过上最稳妥的生活，比如无所事事地坐在门廊上，能有一定的经济保障和社会地位，无论付出什么样的情感代价都可以。祖母认为珍妮嫁给男人的目的不应该是为了爱情而是为了寻求保护，"你有了一个一辈子可以依靠的靠山，这么大的保护，人人都得向你脱帽打招呼，叫你基利克斯太太，可你却跑来和我翻扯什么爱情。"

饱经风霜的祖母还告诉珍妮："白人是一切的主宰……白人扔下担子叫黑人男人去接，他接了过来，因为不接不行，可他自己不挑，而是把担子交给家里的女人。就我所知，黑女人在世界上是头骡子。"祖母的话确实反映了在当时美国社会黑人妇女的普遍命运。在 20 世纪初后奴隶制时期的美国，黑人男子也普遍认同白人至上和男性至上的白人父权制度，在这种制度中，只有当女性具有性吸引力、已婚或通过婚姻获得经济保障时，她们才会受到尊重。特别是黑人妇女，她们常面临更大的压迫，因为她们自己争取独立的斗争会被认为是与争取整个黑人民族平等的斗争背道而驰的。她们是不公正的种族社会中最大的受害者，要遭受种族主义和男权主义的双重压迫。"黑女人是骡子"就是对她们命运的一个形象概括,也是整部小说中多次出现的一个比喻。骡子往往都是被农民买卖用做牲口,任劳任怨且不能表达自己,直到筋疲力尽耗完生命。随着时间推移,洛根开始强迫珍妮扮演她的性别应当承担的家庭妇女角色,还要给她买一头骡子,这样她就可以更好地担任他的农事帮手。除了体力劳动之外,她还要忍受丈夫的侮辱和殴打。这样的生活让珍妮彻底绝望,她开始了第二次觉醒:"婚姻并不能造成爱情。珍妮的第一个梦消亡了,她成了一个女人。"

为了寻找更多的自我价值,珍妮决定和乔迪私奔。乔迪是一个油嘴滑舌的男人,他的话对珍妮非常有诱惑力:"你根本不该和犁打交道,就跟猪不该度假一样!你也不该切土豆种。像你这么漂亮的小娃娃天生就该坐在前廊上的摇椅里,摇着扇子,吃特地给你种的土豆。"他带她来到佛罗里达州伊顿维尔黑人社区。乔迪买了一些土地,开了一个综合商店,并很快当选镇长。然而,珍妮很快意识到乔迪不过只是拿她当作一个花瓶,借以巩固他在镇上的地位,并协助经营商店,甚至禁止她参加镇上的社会生活。在他们二十年的婚姻中,他把她当作自己的财产,批评她,控制她,并对她进行身体虐待。虽然她与乔迪的第二次婚姻也没能给她带来真正幸福,但她至少能够体验到作为一个女人的部分独立。乔迪死后,她继承了他的商店和财产,得到了自由和经济稳定的生活。如果乔迪不死,或许珍妮也就这样度过一生了。但在乔迪病死之后,她又萌生了对新生活的渴望。在她与"茶糕"的最后一次婚姻中,珍妮经历了真爱,也终于学会了如何将自己视为一个女人。"茶糕"作为珍妮的最后一位丈夫,他对詹妮的态度比洛根和乔迪更平等,他和詹妮说话,陪她玩跳棋。虽然他们的关系不稳定,有时甚至伴随暴力,但珍妮终于有了她想要的爱情婚姻。总的来说,在她的三次婚姻中,珍妮经历了当时大多数黑人妇女所经历的苦难。

在整部小说中,女人都被男人看作需要通过各种手段,甚至是身体力量来追求、获得和控制的对象。珍妮发现自我身份和独立的旅程恰好是通过追求真爱来描绘的,她的梦想是通过与三个不同的男人结婚来实现的。她嫁的每个男人在某种程度上都符合当时的男性性别规范。女性的角色则和财产、骡子等相似。女性被认为是男性的战利品,她们只是看起来很漂亮,服从她们的丈夫。就像一只不能说话的牲口,在那里取乐和服务他人,牺牲自己的自由意志。

📖 作品选读(二):

How It Feels to Be Colored Me

I am colored but I offer nothing in the way of extenuating circumstances except the fact that I am the only Negro in the United States whose grandfather on the mother's side was not an Indian chief.

I remember the very day that I became colored. Up to my thirteenth year I lived in the little

Negro town of Eatonville, Florida. It is exclusively a colored town. The only white people I knew passed through the town going to or coming from Orlando. The native whites rode dusty horses, the Northern tourists chugged down the sandy village road in automobiles. The town knew the Southerners and never stopped cane chewing when they passed. But the Northerners were something else again. They were peered at cautiously from behind curtains by the timid. The more venturesome would come out on the porch to watch them go past and got just as much pleasure out of the tourists as the tourists got out of the village.

The front porch might seem a daring place for the rest of the town, but it was a gallery seat for me. My favorite place was atop the gate-post. Proscenium box for a born first-nighter. Not only did I enjoy the show, but I didn't mind the actors knowing that I liked it. I usually spoke to them in passing. I'd wave at them and when they returned my salute, I would say something like this: "Howdy-do-well-I-thank-you-where-yougoin'?" Usually automobile or the horse paused at this, and after a queer exchange of compliments, I would probably "go a piece of the way" with them, as we say in farthest

Florida. If one of my family happened to come to the front in time to see me, of course negotiations would be rudely broken off. But even so, it is clear that I was the first "welcome-to-our-state" Floridian, and I hope the Miami Chamber of Commerce will please take notice.

During this period, white people differed from colored to me only in that they rode through town and never lived there. They liked to hear me "speak pieces" and sing and wanted to see me dance the parse-me-la, and gave me generously of their small silver for doing these things, which seemed strange to me for I wanted to do them so much that I needed bribing to stop. Only they didn't know it. The colored people gave no dimes. They deplored any joyful tendencies in me, but I was their Zora nevertheless. I belonged to them, to the nearby hotels, to the county — everybody's Zora.

But changes came in the family when I was thirteen, and I was sent to school in Jacksonville. I left Eatonville, the town of the oleanders, as Zora. When I disembarked from the river-boat at Jacksonville, she was no more. It seemed that I had suffered a sea change. I was not Zora of Orange County any more, I was now a little colored girl. I found it out in certain ways. In my heart as well as in the mirror, I became a fast brown — warranted not to rub nor run.

But I am not tragically colored. There is no great sorrow dammed up in my soul, nor lurking behind my eyes. I do not mind at all. I do not belong to the sobbing school of Negrohood who hold that nature somehow has given them a lowdown dirty deal and whose feelings are all hurt about it. Even in the helter-skelter skirmish that is my life, I have seen that the world is to the strong regardless of a little pigmentation more or less. No, I do not weep at the world — I am too busy sharpening my oyster knife.

Someone is always at my elbow reminding me that I am the granddaughter of slaves. It fails to register depression with me. Slavery is sixty years in the past. The operation was successful and the patient is doing well, thank you. The terrible struggle that made me an American out of a potential slave said "On the line!" The Reconstruction said "Get set!"; and the generation before said "Go!" I am off to a flying start and I must not halt in the stretch to look behind and weep. Slavery is the price I paid for civilization, and the choice was not with me. It is a bully adventure and worth all that I have paid through my ancestors for it. No one on earth ever had a greater chance for glory. The world to be won and nothing to be lost. It is thrilling to think — to know — that for any act of mine, I shall get twice as much praise or twice as much blame. It is quite exciting to hold the center of the national stage, with the spectators not knowing whether to laugh or to weep.

The position of my white neighbor is much more difficult. No brown specter pulls up a chair beside me when I sit down to eat. No dark ghost thrusts its leg against mine in bed. The game of keeping what one has is never so exciting as the game of getting.

I do not always feel colored. Even now I often achieve the unconscious Zora of Eatonville before the Hegira.① I feel most colored when I am thrown against a sharp white background.

For instance, at Barnard. "Beside the waters of the Hudson" I feel my race. Among the thousand white persons, I am a dark rock surged upon, and overswept, but through it all, I remain myself. When covered by the waters, I am; and the ebb but reveals me again.

Sometimes it is the other way around. A white person is set down in our midst, but the contrast is just as sharp for me. For instance, when I sit in the drafty basement that is The New World Cabaret with a white person, my color comes. We enter chatting about any little nothing that we have in common and are seated by the jazz waiters. In the abrupt way that jazz orchestras have, this one plunges into a number. It loses no time in circumlocutions, but gets right down to business. It constricts the thorax and splits the heart with its tempo and narcotic harmonies. This orchestra grows rambunctious, rears on its hind legs and attacks the tonal veil with primitive fury, rending it, clawing it until it breaks through to the jungle beyond. I follow those heathen — follow them exultingly. I dance wildly inside myself; I yell within, I whoop; I shake my assegai② above my head, I hurl it true to the mark yeeeeooww! I am in the jungle and living in the jungle way. My face is painted red and yellow and my body is painted blue. My pulse is throbbing like a war drum. I want to slaughter something — give pain, give death to what, I do not know. But the piece ends. The men of the orchestra wipe their lips and rest their fingers. I creep back slowly to the veneer we call civilization with the last tone and find the white friend sitting motionless in his seat, smoking calmly.

"Good music they have here," he remarks, drumming the table with his fingertips. Music. The great blobs of purple and red emotion have not touched him. He has only heard what I felt. He is far away and I see him but dimly across the ocean and the continent that have fallen between

---

①　Hegira：也写作 Hijra，译为希吉拉，即迁徙的意思，指公元 622 年穆罕默德从麦加前往麦地那，也是伊斯兰教纪元的开始。

②　assegai：一种格斗长矛。

us. He is so pale with his whiteness then and I am so colored.

At certain times I have no race, I am me. When I set my hat at a certain angle and saunter down Seventh Avenue, Harlem City, feeling as snooty as the lions in front of the Forty-Second Street Library, for instance. So far as my feelings are concerned, Peggy Hopkins Joyce① on the Boule Mich with her gorgeous raiment, stately carriage, knees knocking together in a most aristocratic manner, has nothing on me. The cosmic Zora emerges. I belong to no race nor time. I am the eternal feminine with its string of beads.

I have no separate feeling about being an American citizen and colored. I am merely a fragment of the Great Soul that surges within the boundaries. My country, right or wrong. Sometimes, I feel discriminated against, but it does not make me angry. It merely astonishes me. How can any deny themselves the pleasure of my company? It's beyond me.

But in the main, I feel like a brown bag of miscellany propped against a wall. Against a wall in company with other bags, white, red and yellow. Pour out the contents, and there is discovered a jumble of small things priceless and worthless. A first-water diamond, an empty spool, bits of broken glass, lengths of string, a key to a door long since crumbled away, a rusty knife-blade, old shoes saved for a road that never was and never will be, a nail bent under the weight of things too heavy for any nail, a dried flower or two still a little fragrant. In your hand is the brown bag. On the ground before you is the jumble it held — so much like the jumble in the bags, could they be emptied, that all might be dumped in a single heap and the bags refilled without altering the content of any greatly. A bit of colored glass more or less would not matter. Perhaps that is how the Great Stuffer of Bags filled them in the first place — who knows?

📝 选文评析(二):

《给我上色是什么感觉?》是赫斯顿 1928 年写的一篇文章,最初发表于《明日世界》(*World Tomorrow*),目的是展示自己的身份意识的觉醒。它不仅面向黑人读者,也面向白人读者,让人们亲身体验一下黑人的感受和际遇。赫斯顿从小家境富裕,生活在一个全是黑人的社区。尽管她在经济、社会和情感上都做得很好,但在白人社会里却受到了不同的待遇。13 岁左右,母亲去世后,赫斯顿被迫和亲戚搬到了一个白人社区,这里的人与自己幼年成长的环境完全不同。因为自己所经历的文化冲击,她便萌生了写作《给我上色是什么感觉?》的想法。

文章的一个基本主题是为非裔美国人的传统而自豪。赫斯顿在开篇自豪地承认自己是 100% 的非裔美国人,这一点丝毫也不困扰她。她在这篇文章中详细阐述了种族主义错误地影响了她的身份意识。她不再是一个小女孩,而是被称为“有色人种的小女孩”。在那之前,她并不知道种族是人们关心的事情。后来,在杰克逊维尔的生活中,她开始明白了一个事实,那就是她对自己的传统感到羞耻,就好像她被自己的文化变成了种族主义者。

---

① 佩吉·霍普金斯·乔伊斯(Peggy Hopkins Joyce, 1893—1957):美国女演员。

这篇文章就是对这种羞耻感的一种自豪的蔑视，她转而充分地颂扬她的非洲传统。通过大胆而直接的文字，赫斯顿提醒她的读者，她实际上是在回应那些不言而喻的偏见。她不只是写一篇关于她的感受，或者她的生活是什么样的文章，她真正做的是提醒读者回顾他们的信仰，看看是否存在对黑人的偏见，是否不愿意承认黑人传统之美。

在赫斯顿的时代，非裔美国人面临来自方方面面的种族歧视。为了避免这种歧视，很多非裔美国人竭力掩饰或者排斥自己的种族身份。然而与他们不同，赫斯顿选择了正视和承认自己的非裔美国人身份。在当时，本质主义的种族观念依然很流行，即认为种族是一个人的本质或生物学特征。但赫斯顿却像波伏娃一样认识到了身份的建构性，即黑人并非生来就是黑人，而是逐渐"变成有色人种的"。她认为种族问题更多的是一个社会强化和改变观点的问题。简言之，在人们让她有这种感觉之前，她是没有肤色的。

赫斯顿描述了她在佛罗里达州伊顿维尔的童年生活，这是一个全黑人社区。她唯一见到白人的机会是他们在往返奥兰多的路上穿过小镇。镇上的人对骑着马的南方白人漠不关心，但开车经过的北方白人却让他们感到很好奇，许多人冒险走到门廊里呆呆地看着他们。赫斯顿将阶级和地理作为她童年时期对种族理解的关键因素。这说明种族的观念并不是完全稳定的，而是受到其他身份因素的影响。开车路过的北方白人显然要比骑马的南方白人更富有。赫斯顿不仅喜欢看他们，还会和他们打招呼、聊天，有时甚至和他们一起走一段路程，但她的家人却反对她和白人交往。起初，赫斯顿认为白人和黑人之间唯一的区别就是白人会经过城镇，但永远不会留下来。即便如此，她还是会为白人游客表演唱歌跳舞，他们有时会给她一些零钱做奖励。这让她很惊讶，因为她的表演只是出于热情，并非为了回报。

赫斯顿拒绝接受黑皮肤是一种卑贱之物的观念，她认为那是在培养一种对历史错误的委屈感或受害意识。相反，她会把更多的热情和精力投入工作和生活中去。当她忙着从生活中得到最大的好处时，不会总沉溺于对过去罪恶的回忆。她并没有否认奴隶制的恐怖和种族主义的盛行，而只是强调这个世界对她是开放的，一个有着非凡才能的非裔美国妇女仍然可以成功。

赫斯顿把她现在的经历描述为一次光荣冒险的大好机会。作为一个非裔美国人，她总是难以避免地被白人视为自己种族的代表，这就增加了她取得成就的难度。白人享有被视为个人的特权，他们的行为不影响他们更大的种族群体，然而一个非裔美国人的行为却必然代表着白人眼中所有非裔美国人的行为。虽然这通常被理解为有害的歧视，但赫斯顿认为这种关注也有一定的积极意义。考虑到她小时候在伊顿维尔与白人游客的交往经验，她觉得自己已经准备好迎接挑战。

赫斯顿把自己描述成一个棕色的袋子，混在白色、黄色和红色的袋子中。每个袋子里都装有一些杂乱无章的东西，其中既有很奇妙的也有很普通的物件，比如钻石或者干花。不同颜色的袋子是赫斯顿对不同种族的隐喻，不同的内容代表每个种族特有的思想、记忆、情感和经历。赫斯顿的意思是，人的思想内容要比平淡的肤色重要得多，也有趣得多。赫斯顿认为，所有的袋子都可以随意清空和更换，而不必改变每一个袋子的内容，使之适合袋子。她甚至猜测，这个"伟大的袋子填充者"可能最初是随机地装满袋子的。这也就是说，肤色差异并不等于思想、情感或才能方面的差异。如果允许个人自由，那么非白人也可以获得同样的经验和能力。"伟大的袋子填充者"或上帝，只是随机分布了这些品质，而不是划分了种族。

推荐阅读文献：

Boyd, Valerie. *Wrapped in Rainbows*：*The Life of Zora Neale Hurston*. Scribner, 2004.

Campbell, Josie P. Student Companion to Zora Neale Hurston. *ABC-CLIO*, 2001.

Jordan, Jennifer. Feminist Fantasies：Zora Neale Hurston's *Their Eyes Were Watching God*. *Tulsa Studies in Women's Literature*, 1988, 7(1)：105-117.

Kaplan, Carla. *Zora Neale Hurston*：*A Life in Letters*. Knopf, 2007.

Karanja, Ayana I. *Zora Neale Hurston*： *The Breath of Her Voice*. Peter Lang Publishing, 2000.

King, Lovalerie. *The Cambridge Introduction to Zora Neale Hurston*. Cambridge UP, 2008.

Lupton, Mary Jane. Zora Neale Hurston and the Survival of the Female. *The Southern Literary Journal*, 1982, 15(1)：45-54.

Meisenhelder, Susan E. *Hitting a Straight Lick with a Crooked Stick*：*Race and Gender in the Work of Zora Neale Hurston*. U of Alabama P, 1999.

Plant, Deborah G. and Plant, Deborah G. *The Inside Light*：*New Critical Essays on Zora Neale Hurston*. ABC-CLIO, 2010.

Thompson, Gordon E. Projecting Gender：Personification in the Works of Zora Neale Hurston. *American Literature*, 1994, 66(4)：737-763.

West, M. G. *Zora Neale Hurston and American Literary Culture*. UP of Florida, 2005.

第十四章　乔治·塞缪尔·斯凯勒
（George Samuel Schuyler，1895—1977）

乔治·塞缪尔·斯凯勒是饱受争议的美国非裔作家、记者、社会评论家，主要以其保守主义专栏作家的身份而闻名。他于 1895 年出生于罗得岛州的普罗维登斯（Providence），他的父亲在他三岁时便去世，斯凯勒随再婚的母亲搬到了纽约州的锡拉库扎（Syracuse）。1912 年，斯凯勒应征入伍，在尽数是黑人的美国第 25 步兵团服役，几年后取得了中尉的军衔，然而他的部队生涯因逃兵罪而中止，以关押 9 个月的形式告终。当时，一个奉命为斯凯勒擦鞋的希腊移民因为他的肤色而拒绝擦鞋。因此，擅离职守实际上是他针对军队中系统性的种族主义采取的回击策略。获释后，斯凯勒前往纽约市，靠打零工维持生计。在此期间，阅读激起了他对社会主义的

兴趣。但在参加了"全球黑人促进协会"（Universal Negro Improvement Association，简称 UNIA）举办的会议后，他对协会建立者，即黑人民族主义者马库斯·加维（Marcus Garvey）的哲学持很大异议。尽管他从此开始意识到自己无法全然适应社会主义思想，但依然尝试性地转而投身于加维协会的最大竞争对手——另一个黑人社会主义团体——黑人自由之友（Friends of Negro Freedom，简称 FNF）。该组织的创办者 A. 菲利普·伦道夫和钱德勒·欧文同时也是《信使》（The Messenger）杂志的创办者。斯凯勒很快获得他们的青睐并为《信使》撰写题为"轴与镖：一版的诽谤和讽刺"（"Shafts and Darts：A Page of Calumny and Satire"）的定期专栏。他精锐的文笔很快引起当时美国最大的两家黑人报纸之一《匹兹堡信使报》（Pittsburgh Courier）的经理艾拉·F. 刘易斯的关注。1924 年，他应邀成为《匹兹堡信使报》专栏作家。

20 世纪 20 年代中期，斯凯勒与著名社会评论家、记者、《美国水星报》（American Mercury）编辑亨利·路易斯·门肯（Henry Louis Mencken）保持着密切的联系。门肯高度评价斯凯勒，称他为"现在这个伟大的自由共和国中在实践方面最称职的社论作家"。由于他们有着兼容的政治观点，并且运用相似的手法进行犀利的讽刺，这一时期的斯凯勒常被贴上"黑人门肯"的标签。1926 年，斯凯勒以《匹兹堡信使报》首席社论撰稿人、编辑作家的身份在《国家》（The Nation）报刊上发表了备受争议的社论《黑人艺术杂谈》（"The Negro

Art Hokum"），对当时蓬勃发展的哈莱姆文艺复兴运动提出了严厉的批评。他坚持认为美国的黑人艺术家和白人艺术家一样具有多样性，并抗拒关于任何划一的风格或主题的期待。在他看来，对统一性的需求无非是刻板印象的另一种形态，是对艺术的限制和侮辱。不出意料，此言一出便卷起批判的浪潮，其中以将艺术根植于黑人感性的兰斯顿·休斯为典型。同年，他刊登在同一报刊《国家》上的《黑人艺术家与种族之山》（"The Negro Artist and Racial Mountain"）指出，当黑人艺术家对非裔的形象避而不谈时，他们刻画的任何东西其实都等同于想成为白人的佐证。种族与艺术的关系由此成为双方争辩的核心议题。反对用种族隔离艺术的斯凯勒声称"非洲人无非是蒙尘的盎格鲁-撒克逊人"，因为 300 年来，黑人已无法脱离欧美文化的影响。而颂扬专属黑人审美和艺术的休斯表示，既然白人种族的主导地位早已侵蚀了艺术领域，那么承认颠覆精致的现代主义作品是无意义的，也就是间接地承认了黑人与黑人文化的低劣性。虽然两派之间的分歧无法调和，但是他们都唯恐黑人作家失去了斗争的锋芒，成为体制附庸，且都企图用最有力的方式呈现与黑人最相关的问题。

　　20 世纪 50 年代，斯凯勒成为麦卡锡主义的忠实信徒。到了 60 年代，他在由大保守派约翰·伯奇协会（John Birch Society）主办的杂志《美国舆论》（American Opinion）上谴责 W. E. B. 杜波依斯，甚至马丁·路德·金等社会活动家，并反对 1964 年颁布的《民权法案》（Civil Rights Act）。他表明，白人对黑人的歧视"在道德上是错误的、无稽的、不公平的、非基督教的和残酷不公正的"，但他反对联邦采取行动来强制改变公众的态度。后来，大批读者无法接受他在政治上极端右翼的观点，并扬言要取消订阅《匹兹堡信使报》，以此抗议他的专栏，最终他失去了与之有关的一切工作。他的种族讽刺小说《黑人不再》（Black No More，1931）于 1999 年重新出版，就像自由派黑人作家伊什梅尔·斯科特·里德（Ishmael Scott Reed）在导言中所提到的，斯凯勒在晚年沦为黑人评论界避之若浼的对象，甚至连采访这位年迈的作家都被黑人圈子视为禁忌。但可以肯定的是，无论他的声音是怎样另类的存在，它彰显出的充满激情的思辨都是哈莱姆文艺复兴以及整个美国黑人文学界的重要组成部分。

作品选读：

The Negro Art Hokum

Negro art "made in America" is as non-existent as the widely advertised profundity of Cal Coolidge, the "seven years of progress" of Mayor Hylan,[1] or the reported sophistication of New Yorkers. Negro art there has been, is, and will be among the numerous black nations of Africa; but to suggest the possibility of any such development among the ten million colored people in this

---

① 约翰·弗朗西斯·海兰（John Francis Hylan, 1868—1936）：纽约市长（1918—1925）。

republic is self-evident foolishness. Eager apostles from Greenwich Village, Harlem, and environs proclaimed a great renaissance of Negro art just around the corner waiting to be ushered on the scene by those whose hobby is taking races, nations, peoples, and movements under their wing. New art forms expressing the "peculiar" psychology of the Negro were about to flood the market.

In short, the art of Homo Africanus was about to electrify the waiting world. Skeptics patiently waited. They still wait. True, from dark-skinned sources have come those slave songs based on Protestant hymns and Biblical texts known as the spirituals, work songs and secular songs of sorrow and tough luck known as the blues, that outgrowth of rag-time known as jazz (in the development of which whites have assisted), and the Charleston, an eccentric dance invented by the gamins around the public market-place in Charleston, S. C. No one can or does deny this. But these are contributions of a caste in a certain section of the country. They are foreign to Northern Negroes, West Indian Negroes, and African Negroes. They are no more expressive or characteristic of the Negro race than the music and dancing of the Appalachian highlanders or the Dalmatian peasantry are expressive or characteristic of the Caucasian race. If one wishes to speak of the musical contributions of the peasantry of the South, very well. Any group under similar circumstances would have produced something similar. It is merely a coincidence that this peasant class happens to be of a darker hue than the other inhabitants of the land. One recalls the remarkable likeness of the minor strains of the Russian mujiks[1] to those of the Southern Negro.

As for the literature, painting, and sculpture of Aframericans — such as there is — it is identical in kind with the literature, painting, and sculpture of white Americans: that is, it shows more or less evidence of European influence. In the field of drama little of any merit has been written by and about Negroes that could not have been written by whites. The dean of the Aframerican literati is W. E. B. Du Bois, a product of Harvard and German universities; the foremost Aframerican sculptor is Meta Warwick Fuller,[2] a graduate of leading American art schools and former student of Rodin; while the most noted Aframerican painter, Henry Ossawa Tanner, is dean of American painters in Paris and has been decorated by the French Government. Now the work of these artists is no more "expressive of the Negro soul" — as the gushers put it — than are the scribblings of Octavus Cohen[3] or Hugh Wiley.[4]

This, of course, is easily understood if one stops to realize that the Aframerican is merely a lampblacked Anglo-Saxon. If the European immigrant after two or three generations of exposure to our schools, politics, advertising, moral crusades, and restaurants becomes indistinguishable from

---

① mujik：农民。

② 梅塔·沃里克·富勒（Meta Warwick Fuller, 1877—1968）：美国非裔诗人和雕塑家。

③ 奥克塔武斯·罗伊·科恩（Octavus Roy Cohen, 1891—1959）：一位多产的美国小说家，对非裔美国人的生活有很多刻板描写。

④ 休·威利（Hugh Wiley, 1884—1969）：美国工程师、军官、小说家。写过一些关于非裔美国人生活的滑稽故事。

the mass of Americans of the older stock (despite the influence of the foreign-language press), how much truer must it be of the sons of Ham who have been subjected to what the uplifters call Americanism for the last three hundred years. Aside from his color, which ranges from very dark brown to pink, your American Negro is just plain American. Negroes and whites from the same localities in this country talk, think, and act about the same. Because a few writers with a paucity of themes have seized upon imbecilities of the Negro rustics and clowns and palmed them off as authentic and characteristic Aframerican behavior, the common notion that the black American is so "different" from his white neighbor has gained wide currency. The mere mention of the word "Negro" conjures up in the average white American's mind a composite stereotype of Bert Williams,① Aunt Jemima,② Uncle Tom, Jack Johnson,③ Florian Slappey,④ and the various monstrosities scrawled by the cartoonists. Your average Aframerican no more resembles this stereotype than the average American resembles a composite of Andy Gump,⑤ Jim Jeffries,⑥ and a cartoon by Rube Goldberg.

Again, the Africamerican is subject to the same economic and social forces that mold the actions and thoughts of the white Americans. He is not living in a different world as some whites and a few Negroes would have us believe. When the jangling of his Connecticut alarm clock gets him out of his Grand Rapids bed to a breakfast similar to that eaten by his white brother across the street; when he toils at the same or similar work in mills, mines, factories, and commerce alongside the descendants of Spartacus, Robin Hood, and Eric the Red;⑦ when he wears similar clothing and speaks the same language with the same degree of perfection; when he reads the same *Bible* and belongs to the Baptist, Methodist, Episcopal, or Catholic church; when his fraternal affiliations also include the Elks, Masons, and Knights of Pythias; when he gets the same or similar schooling, lives in the same kind of houses, owns the same makes of cars (or rides in them), and nightly sees the same Hollywood version of life on the screen; when he smokes the same brands of tobacco, and avidly peruses the same puerile periodicals; in short, when he responds to the same political, social, moral, and economic stimuli in precisely the same manner as his white neighbor, it is sheer nonsense to talk about "racial differences" as between the American black man and the American white man. Glance over a Negro newspaper (it is printed in good Americanese) and you will find the usual quota of crime news, scandal,

---

① 伯特·威廉姆斯(Bert Williams, 1874—1922):美国黑人喜剧演员。
② 杰米玛阿姨(Aunt Jemima):美国流行文化塑造的谄媚女黑奴的标志性形象。
③ 杰克·约翰逊(Jack Johnson, 1878—1946):20 世纪初美国黑人世界重量级拳王。
④ 弗洛里安·斯帕佩(Florian Slappey):美国漫画中描绘的一名黑人私家侦探。
⑤ 安迪·甘普(Andy Gump):20 世纪上半叶在美国流行的连环画《阿甘一家》(*The Gumps*)中的主要人物。
⑥ 吉姆·杰弗里斯(Jim Jeffries, 1875—1953):20 世纪初美国黑人世界重量级拳王。
⑦ "红胡子埃里克"(Eric the Red, 950—1003):也称"红毛埃里克",维京海盗和探险家,他发现了格陵兰岛,并在那里建立了一个斯堪的纳维亚人的定居点。

personals, and uplift to be found in the average white newspaper — which, by the way, is more widely read by the Negroes than is the Negro press. In order to satisfy the cravings of an inferiority complex engendered by the colorphobia of the mob, the readers of the Negro newspapers are given a slight dash of racialistic seasoning. In the homes of the black and white Americans of the same cultural and economic level one finds similar furniture, literature, and conversation. How, then, can the black American be expected to produce art and literature dissimilar to that of the white American?

Consider Coleridge-Taylor,① Edward Wilmot Blyden,② and Claude McKay, the Englishmen; Pushkin, the Russian③; Bridgetower,④ the Pole; Antar, the Arabian; Latino, the Spaniard; Dumas, père and fils,⑤ the Frenchmen; and Paul Laurence Dunbar, Charles W. Chesnutt, and James Weldon Johnson, the Americans. All Negroes; yet their work shows the impress of nationality rather than race. They all reveal the psychology and culture of their environment — their color is incidental. Why should Negro artists of America vary from the national artistic norm when Negro artists in other countries have not done so? If we can foresee what kind of white citizens will inhabit this neck of the woods in the next generation by studying the sort of education and environment the children are exposed to now, it should not be difficult to reason that the adults of today are what they are because of the education and environment they were exposed to a generation ago. And that education and environment were about the same for blacks and whites. One contemplates the popularity of the Negro-art hokum and murmurs, "How come?"

This nonsense is probably the last stand of the old myth palmed off by Negrophobists for all these many years, and recently rehashed by the sainted Harding,⑥ that there are "fundamental, eternal, and inescapable differences" between white and black Americans. That there are Negroes who will lend this myth a helping hand need occasion no surprise. It has been broadcast all over the world by the vociferous scions of slaveholders, "scientists" like Madison Grant⑦ and Lothrop Stoddard,⑧ and the patriots who flood the treasury of the Ku Klux Klan; and is believed, even today, by the majority of free, white citizens. On this baseless premise, so flattering to the white mob, that the blackamoor is inferior and fundamentally different, is erected the postulate that he

---

① 塞缪尔·柯勒律治-泰勒(Samuel Coleridge-Taylor, 1875—1912): 英国非裔古典作曲家。

② 爱德华·威尔莫特·布莱登(Edward Wilmot Blyden, 1832—1912), 利比里亚教育家和政治家。

③ 俄国诗人普希金(Pushkin, 799—1837): 普希金的外曾祖父是非洲喀麦隆传奇黑人将军汉尼拔(Abram Petrovich Gannibal, 1696—1781), 普希金的母亲是汉尼拔的孙女。

④ 乔治·布里奇托(George Bridgetower, 1778—1860), 波兰非裔小提琴家。

⑤ 法国作家大仲马(Alexandre Dumas père, 1802—1870) 和小仲马(Alexandre Dumas fils, 1824—1895): 大仲马是小仲马的父亲。大仲马拥有非裔血统, 他的父亲出生在海地, 是女黑奴与法国贵族所生。大小仲马在世时, 尽管名声显赫, 却也常因黑人血统而受到嘲讽。

⑥ 沃伦·哈丁(Warren G. Harding, 1865—1923): 美国第29任总统(1921—1923)。

⑦ 麦迪逊·格兰特(Madison Grant, 1865—1937): 美国律师和优生学倡导者。

⑧ 罗普·斯托达德(Lothrop Stoddard, 1883—1950): 美国历史学家和优生学倡导者。

must needs be peculiar; and when he attempts to portray life through the medium of art, it must of necessity be a peculiar art. While such reasoning may seem conclusive to the majority of Americans, it must be rejected with a loud guffaw by intelligent people.

选文评析:

1926 年 6 月 16 日,斯凯勒应邀在《国家》(*The Nation*)①杂志发表这篇题名为《黑人艺术杂谈》的文章,立即引起巨大争议。尤其是兰斯顿·休斯(Langston Hughes)仅在一周之后便发表著名文章《黑人艺术家与种族之山》批驳斯凯勒的立场。斯凯勒声称"非洲人无非是蒙尘的盎格鲁-撒克逊人",这一说法导致他被许多非裔美国同胞斥为保守的同化主义者,与美国种族隔离和制度化种族主义的现实脱节。但是,这些批评忽视了斯凯勒作为一个天才的讽刺作家和独立思想家刻意扮演的角色,他的小说和散文讽刺了美国的种族敏感性,揭露了其虚伪和欺诈的一面。与许多同时代的美国黑人艺术家不同,斯凯勒完全成长在黑人中产阶级家庭,他还拥有一半白人血统,其黑人祖先早在独立战争之前就已经获得自由。这种特殊的生活经历注定了他看待美国种族问题的视角与其他同时代的人有所不同。

斯凯勒开篇就说:"'美国制造'的黑人艺术是不存在的。"他指出,虽然非洲黑人艺术在过去、现在和将来都是众多非洲黑人民族艺术中的一员,但是在美国黑人中提出所谓的"黑人艺术的伟大复兴"是愚蠢的。他承认灵乐、蓝调和爵士乐的确都是黑人对美国文化的伟大贡献,但它们并非绝对的黑人独创,而是源自以新教圣歌和《圣经》文本为基础的奴隶歌曲,它们在发展过程中也受到来自白人文化的影响和帮助,而且这种黑人音乐也是黑人在美国土地上的生活经验的产物,它们对美国之外的黑人来说也完全是陌生的事物,因此并不能说它们表达了黑人的特异文化属性。"任何一个群体在类似的情况下都会产生类似的结果。"

斯凯勒进一步指出在文学、绘画和雕塑等领域,黑人艺术和白人艺术都没有绝对的区别,它们或多或少地受到欧洲影响,也没有哪种艺术是除了黑人之外别的种族的人不能创作出来的。绝大多数黑人艺术家都在欧洲或美国大学受过正规教育,系统接受过来自主流白人文化的影响。因此他们的作品必然含有白人文化基因。除了身体肤色不同,今天的美国黑人在文化基因上与白人并无多大差异,"美国黑人也只是普通的美国人"。今天的美国黑人和白人在言谈举止和行为方式上并没有太大差异,但由于"一些题材贫乏的作家抓住了黑人乡下人和小丑的愚蠢行为,把他们伪装成真实和典型的非裔行为",这才导致很多人鼓吹黑人文化的特异性,并让这种分离主义的艺术观念大行其道。斯凯勒认为,美国黑人和白人不是生活在一个不同的世界,他们受同样的经济和社会力量影响,也就会有相似的行为和思想。他们吃一样的早餐,在一起工作劳动,穿相似的衣服,说同样的语言,读同一部《圣经》,接受相同的学校教育,住同样的房子,使用同样品牌的汽车,在银幕

① 《国家》是美国历史最悠久的周刊之一,从 1865 年 7 月开始出版。它关注进步的政治文化观点,也是美国国内阅读量最大的进步杂志之一。

上看同样的好莱坞电影，阅读同样的期刊，因此在这样的背景下，"谈论美国黑人和美国白人之间的'种族差异'完全是无稽之谈"。在同样文化和经济水平的美国黑人和白人的家中，人们可以找到相似的家具、文学作品，听到同样的谈话。斯凯勒反问道，在这种情况下，"如何才能期望美国黑人创作出与白人不同的艺术和文学作品呢?"

斯凯勒还指出，相对于美国的黑人艺术家，其他国家的非裔艺术家似乎有更多的创作自由，他们并没有被要求去表现只属于自身种族的特质，而是自由地探索他们所处环境的心理和文化，肤色对他们来说似乎只是一个偶然因素。为什么美国的黑人艺术家要与整个国家通行的艺术规范有所不同呢? 在斯凯勒看来，"黑人和白人的教育和环境大体一样"，如果再去强调美国白人和黑人之间存在着"根本的、永恒的、不可避免的差异"，那么完全是"胡说八道"。他认为，追求黑人艺术的特异性反倒助长了种族主义的一贯论调，即强调黑人和白人之间具有本质差异，这种差异不但难以弥合，更重要的是它决定了黑人比白人更低等。反过来，不追求黑人艺术的特殊性，也就是真正地倡导种族平等。

斯凯勒认为美国黑人和白人在生活经验和文化传统上具有不可分割的共同性，这注定黑人艺术不可能有完全独立于主流标准之外的美学特异性。应当承认，斯凯勒的这种种族融合主义艺术观具有一定的积极意义，但也要看到其思想中的局限性，特别是当他认为"美国黑人也只是普通的美国人""黑人和白人的教育环境基本一样"的时候，他的视角中的肤色盲视也显而易见。这与其相对优渥的中产阶级生活背景应当是分不开的。

🗨 推荐阅读文献：

Bain, Alexander M. 'Shocks Americana!': George Schuyler Serializes Black Internationalism. *American Literary History*, 2007, 19(4): 937-963.

Favor, J. Martin. Authentic Blackness: The Folk in the New Negro Renaissance. *Duke UP*, 1999.

Goyal, Yogita. Black Nationalist Hokum: George Schuyler's Transnational Critique. *African American Review*, 2014, 47(1): 21-36.

Joo, Hee-Jung Serenity. Miscegenation, Assimilation, and Consumption: Racial Passing in George Schuyler's 'Black No More' and Eric Liu's 'The Accidental Asian'. *MELUS*, 2008, 33(3): 169-190.

Patterson, Martha H. Fascist Parody and Wish Fulfillment: George Schuyler's Periodical Fiction of the 1930s. *The Journal of Modern Periodical Studies*, 2013, 4(1): 76-99.

Rayson, Ann. George Schuyler: Paradox among 'Assimilationist' Writers. *Black American Literature Forum*, 1978, 12(3): 102-106.

Retman, Sonnet H. Black No More: George Schuyler and Racial Capitalism. *PMLA*, 2008, 123(5): 1448-1464.

Zamalin, Alex. *Black Utopia: The History of an Idea from Black Nationalism to Afrofuturism*. Columbia UP, 2019.

20 世纪中期

（约 20 世纪 40 年代至 20 世纪 50 年代）

第十五章　理查德·赖特
（Richard Wright，1908—1960）

理查德·赖特是美国著名的非裔作家、评论家，被誉为"现代美国黑人小说之父"。他生于密西西比州纳奇兹（Natchez）附近的一处种植园。祖父是黑奴，内战后获得自由。父亲是种植园工，母亲是乡村教师，家境贫苦。赖特从小生活在充满敌意的环境中，深感自己是受歧视的黑人，又是"弃儿"和"局外人"，对社会，尤其对周围的白人世界怀着又恨又怕的心理。他进过孤儿院，曾在亲戚家寄养，15 岁起独立谋生，同时勤奋自学，立志成为作家，深受西奥多·德莱塞（Theodore Dreiser）、辛克莱尔·刘易斯（Sinclair Lewis）、舍伍德·安德森（Sherwood Anderson）等美国现实主义作家的影响。1927 年，他同家人加入"黑人大迁移"（The Great Migration），离开实行《吉姆·克劳法案》（*Jim Crow Laws*）的南部，移居芝加哥。20 世纪 30 年代美国经济大萧条时期，赖特长期失业，对美国贫富悬殊、种族歧视的社会现状有了进一步的认识。1932 年，他加入美国共产党，开始学习以马克思主义的视角观察社会，这使得他后来的创作能够相当深刻地揭露美国黑人的生存困境，控诉和抗议不合理的社会制度，因而成为 30—40 年代美国左翼文学中"抗议小说"（Protest Novel）的创始人之一。1937 年，赖特开始担任美共机关报《工人日报》（*The Daily Worker*）的哈莱姆区编辑，并结识了拉尔夫·艾里森（Ralph Ellison），两人建立起一段长久的友谊。次年，他的中篇小说集《汤姆叔叔的孩子们》（*Uncle Tom's Children*）出版，广受好评，标志着赖特开始在文坛崭露头角。1940 年，他的长篇小说《土生子》（*Native Son*）问世，使其一跃成为享誉美国文坛的非裔作家。这部小说一经出版即畅销全国，被美国著名的"每月一书读书会"（the Book of the Month Club）选中，还被改编成戏剧在百老汇上演。小说出版后不久，赖特曾在哈莱姆区的纽约公共图书馆里作《别格是怎样出生的?》（"How 'Bigger' Was Born"）演讲，详细阐述了他创作这部小说和创造别格这一艺术形象的过程。赖特成名后，逐渐与美国共产党的观点和政策产生分歧，终于在 1944 年退出共产党，1946 年迁居巴黎，直至病逝。

赖特的代表作《土生子》以 20 世纪 30 年代为背景，主要讲述了居住在芝加哥南区（South Side）贫民窟的黑人青年别格·托马斯（Bigger Thomas）因误杀白人姑娘而被判处死刑的故事。小说中,一改汤姆叔叔的传统黑人形象,赖特成功塑造了别格这一具有反叛精神的新黑人形象。他有复仇的怒火,敢于挑战现存的社会秩序,甚至盲目行动,成为白人眼中的"坏黑鬼"。作者对别格满怀同情,于书中深入剖析别格的犯罪活动与社会制度之间的内在联系,指出黑人的野蛮凶暴既非天性也非民族特性,而是美国社会制度造成的,别格的性格乃是美国文明的产物。自出生之日起,别格的种族身份就已被白人社会所预设,他唯有在犯下十恶不赦的罪行后才最终获得自我认知。除《土生子》外,赖特的自传《黑孩子》也产生了很大影响。美国当代著名非裔作家勒洛伊·琼斯(LeRoi Jones) 曾说:"赖特的《黑孩子》和《土生子》,是描写南方与北方的黑人的城市生活和非城市生活的两部最有永久价值的社会小说和社会批评。"

《土生子》开创了美国抗议小说的先河,被誉为"黑人文学中的里程碑",对后来的黑人文学创作影响深远。西方评论界一般认为从赖特的《土生子》出版后,黑人文学才在美国文学中取得地位,开始受到评论界的重视并在人民群众中产生较大影响。不少非裔作家继承他的传统,被称为"赖特派"(Wright School)。《土生子》的出版不仅轰动了美国文坛,更震撼了美国社会,有文学批评家认为他的作品帮助改变了 20 世纪中期美国的种族关系。然而,《土生子》在获得巨大成功的同时,关于这部作品,亦不乏批评和质疑的声音,曾被美国图书馆协会(American Library Association) 列为 100 本最具争议性的图书之一(1990—2000)。社会舆论抱怨《土生子》中别格的暴力形象似乎确证了白人恐惧情绪的合理性,对种族问题的解决和种族平等的实现产生了恶劣的负面影响。该作品甚至还受到一些美国非裔作家同行的抨击。詹姆斯·鲍德温(James Baldwin) 在 1948 年的散文《每个人的抗议小说》("Everybody's Protest Novel") (后收录于《土生子札记》(*Notes of a Native Son*,1955) 中毫不留情地批判赖特所塑造的别格形象过于刻板化,认为他的这部作品在人性理解以及美学价值方面均有严重欠缺。尽管饱受争议,《土生子》仍是美国黑人文学宝库中的一部经典之作,曾被美国现代图书馆(Modern Library) 列为 20 世纪 100 本最佳小说类图书排行榜第 20 位,还被《时代》杂志(*Time Magazine*) 选入《时代》100 部最佳英文小说榜单(1923—2005)。

📖 作品选读(一):

Native Son

Part One

"I'd like to see a movie," Bigger said.

"*Trader Horn*'s running again at the Regal. They're bringing a lot of old pictures back."

"How much is it?"

"Twenty cents."

"O. K. Let's see it."

Bigger strode silently beside Jack for six blocks. It was noon when they reached Forty-seven Street and South Parkway. The Regal was just opening. Bigger lingered in the lobby and looked at the colored posters while Jack bought the tickets. Two features were advertised: one, *The Gay Woman*①, was pictured on the posters in images of white men and white women lolling on beaches, swimming, and dancing in night clubs; the other, *Trader Horn*, was shown on the posters in terms of black men and black women dancing against a wild background of barbaric jungle. Bigger looked up and saw Jack standing at his side.

"Come on. Let's go in," Jack said.

"O. K."

He followed Jack into the darkened movie. The shadows were soothing to his eyes after the glare of the sun. The picture had not started and he slouched far down in a seat and listened to a pipe organ shudder in waves of nostalgic tone, like a voice humming hauntingly within him. He moved restlessly, looking round as though expecting to see someone sneaking upon him. The organ sang forth full, then dropped almost to silence.

"You reckon we'll do all right at Blum's?" he asked in a drawling voice tinged with uneasiness.

"Aw, sure," Jack said; but his voice, too, was uneasy.

"You know, I'd just as soon go to jail as take that damn relief job," Bigger said.

"Don't say that. Everything'll be all right."

"You reckon it will?"

"Sure."

"I don't give a damn."

"Let's think about how we'll do it, not about how we'll get caught."

"Scared?"

"Naw, You?"

"Hell, naw!"

They were silent, listening to the organ. It sounded for a long moment on a trembling note, then died away.

Then it stole forth again in whispering tones that could scarcely be heard.

"We better take our guns along this time," Bigger said.

"O. K. But we gotta be careful. We don't wanna kill nobody."

"Yeah. But I'll feel safer with a gun this time."

---

① 《荡妇》(*The Gay Woman*)和《商人角》(*Trader Horn*)是电影院正在上映的两部电影名字。作者在此处安排主人公看这两部电影，并非偶然，而是有很多象征意义。

"Gee, I wished it was three o'clock now. I wished it was over."

"Me too."

The organ sighed into silence and the screen flashed with the rhythm of moving shadows. There was a short newsreel which Bigger watched without much interest. Then came *The Gat Woman* in which, amid scenes of cocktail drinking, dancing, golfing, swimming, and spinning roulette wheels, a rich young white woman kept clandestine appointments with her lover while her millionaire husband was busy in the offices of a vast paper mill. Several times Bigger nudged Jack in the ribs with his elbow as the giddy young woman duped her husband and kept from him the knowledge of what she was doing.

"She sure got her old man fooled," Bigger said.

"Looks like it. He's so busy making money he don't know what's going on," Jack said. "Them rich chicks'll① do anything."

"Yeah. And she's a hot looking number, all right," Bigger said. "Say, maybe I'll be working for folks like that if I take the relief job. Maybe I'll be driving 'em around..."

"Sure," Jack said. "Man, you ought to take that job. You don't know what you might run into. y ma used to work for rich white folks and you ought to hear the tales she used to tell..."

"What she say?" Bigger asked eagerly.

"Ah, man, them rich white women'll go to bed with anybody, from a poodle up. Shucks, they even have their chauffeurs. Say, if you run into anything on that new job that's too much for you to handle, let me know..."

They laughed. The play ran on and Bigger saw a night club floor thronged with whirling couples and heard a swing band playing music. The rich young woman was dancing and laughing with her lover.

"I'd like to be invited to a place like that just to find out what it feels like," Bigger mused.

"Man, if them folks saw you they'd run," Jack said. "They'd think a gorilla broke loose from the zoo and put on a tuxedo."

They bent over low in their seats and giggled without restraint. When Bigger sat up again he saw the picture flashing on. A tall waiter was serving two slender glasses of drinks to the rich young woman and her lover.

"I bet their mattresses is stuffed with paper dollars," Bigger said.

"Man, them folks don't even have to turn over in their sleep," Jack said. "A butler stands by their beds at night, and when he hears 'em sigh, he gently rolls 'em over..."

They laughed again, then fell silent abruptly. The music accompanying the picture dropped to a low, rumbling note and the rich young woman turned and looked toward the front door of the night club from which a chorus of shouts and screams was heard.

"I bet it's her husband," Jack said.

---

① "rich chick"是黑人俚语, 指有钱的少妇。

"Yeah," Bigger said.

Bigger saw a sweating, wild-eyed young man fight his way past a group of waiters and whirling dancers.

"He looks like a crazy man," Jack said.

"What you reckon he wants?" Bigger asked, as though he himself was outraged at the sight of the frenzied intruder.

"Damn if I know," Jack muttered preoccupiedly.

Bigger watched the wild young man elude the waiters and run in the direction of the rich woman's table. The music of the swing band stopped and men and women scurried frantically into corners and doorways. There were shouts: Stop 'im! Stop 'im! The wild man halted a few feet from the rich woman and reached inside of his coat and drew forth a black object. There were more screams: He's got a bomb! Stop 'im! Bigger saw the woman's lover leap to the center of the floor, flings his hands high into the air and catch the bomb just as the wild man threw it. As the rich woman fainted, her lover hurled the bomb out of a window, shattering a pane. Bigger saw a white flash light up the night outside as the bomb exploded deafeningly. Then he was looking at the wild man who was now pinned to the floor by a dozen hands. He heard a woman scream: He's a Communist!

[...]

The scenes showed the wild man weeping on his knees and cursing through his tears. I wanted to kill 'im, he sobbed. Bigger now understood that the wild bomb-thrower was a Communist who had mistaken the rich woman's lover for her husband and had tried to kill him.

"Reds must don't like rich folks," Jack said.

"They sure must don't," Bigger said. "Every time you hear about one, he's trying to kill somebody or tear things up."

The picture continued and showed the rich young woman in a fit of remorse, telling her lover that she thanked him for saving her life, but that what had happened had taught her that her husband needed her. Suppose it had been he? she whimpered.

"She is going back to her old man," Bigger said.

"Oh, yeah," Jack said. "They got to kiss at the end."

Bigger saw the rich young woman rush home to her millionaire husband. There were long embraces and kisses as the rich woman and the rich man vowed never to leave each other and to forgive each other.

"You reckon folks really act like that? Bigger asked, full of the sense of a life he had never seen.

"Sure, man. They rich," Jack said.

"I wonder if this guy I'm going to work for is a rich man like that? Bigger asked.

"Maybe so," Jack said.

"Shucks. I got a great mind to take that job," Bigger said.

"Sure. You don't know what you might see,"

They laughed. Bigger turned his eyes to the screen, but he did not look. He was filled with a sense of excitement about his new job. Was what he had heard about rich white people really true? Was he going to work for people like you saw in the movies? If he were, then he'd see a lot of things from the inside; he'd get the dope, the low-down. He looked at *Trader Horn* unfold and saw pictures of naked black men and women whirling in wild dances and heard drums beating and then gradually the African scene changed and was replaced by images in his own mind of white men and women dressed in black and white clothes, laughing, talking, drinking and dancing. Those were smart people: they knew how to get hold of money, millions of it. Maybe if he were working for them something would happen and he would get some of it. He would see just how they did it. Sure, it was all a game and white people knew how to play it. And rich white people were not so hard on Negroes: it was the poor whites who hated Negroes. They hated Negroes because they didn't have their share of the money. His mother had always told him that rich white people liked Negroes better than they did poor whites. He felt that if he were a poor white and did not get his share of the money, then he would deserve to be kicked. Poor white people were stupid. It was the rich white people who were smart and knew how to treat people. He remembered hearing somebody tell a story of a Negro chauffeur who had married a rich white girl and the girl's family had shipped the couple out of the country and had supplied them with money.

Yes, his going to work for the Daltons was something big. Maybe Mr. Dalton was a millionaire. Maybe he had a daughter who was a hot kind of girl; maybe she spent lots of money; maybe she'd like to come to the South Side and see the sights sometimes. Or maybe she had a secret sweetheart and only he would know about it because he would have to drive her around; maybe she would give him money not to tell.

He was a fool for wanting to rob Blum's just when he was about to get a good job. Why hadn't he thought of that before? Why take a fool's chance when other things, big things, could happen? If something slipped up this afternoon he would be out of a job and in jail, maybe. And he wasn't so hot about robbing Blum's, anyway. He frowned in the darkened movie, hearing the roll of tom-toms and the screams of black men and women dancing free and wild, men and women who were adjusted to their soil and at home in their world, secure from fear and hysteria.

[...]

Outside his window he saw the sun dying over the roof-tops in the western sky and watched the first shade of dusk fall. Now and then a street car past. The rusty radiator hissed at the far end of the room. All day long it had been springlike; but now dark clouds were slowly swallowing the sun. All at once the street lamps came on and the sky was black and close to the house-tops.

Inside his shirt he felt the cold metal of the gun resting against his naked skin; he ought to put it back between the mattresses. No! He would keep it. He would take it with him to the Dalton place. He felt that he would be safer if he took it. He was not planning to use it and there was nothing in particular that he was afraid of, but there was in him an uneasiness and distrust that made him feel that he ought to have it along. He was going among white people, so he would take his knife and his gun; it would make him feel that he was the equal of them, give him a sense of completeness. Then he thought of a good reason why he should take it; in order to get to the Dalton place, he had to go through a white neighborhood. He had not heard of any Negroes being molested recently, but he felt that it was always possible.

Far away a clock boomed five times. He sighed and got up and yawned and stretched his arms high above his head to loosen the muscles of his body. He got his overcoat, for it was growing cold outdoors; then got his cap.

He tiptoed to the door, wanting to slip out without his mother hearing him. Just as he was about to open it, she called,

"Bigger!"

He stopped and frowned.

"Yeah, Ma."

"You going to see about that job?"

"Yeah."

"Ain't you going to eat?"

"I ain't got time now."

She came to the door, wiping her soapy hands upon an apron.

"Here; take this quarter and buy you something."

"O. K."

"And be careful, son."

He went out and walked south to Forty-sixth Street, then eastward. Well, he would see in a few moments it the Daltons for whom he was to work were like the people he had seen and heard in the movie. But while walking through this quiet and spacious white neighborhood, he did not feel the pull and mystery of the thing as strongly as he had in the movie. The houses he passed were huge: lights glowed softly in windows. The streets were empty, save for an occasional car that zoomed past on swift rubber tires. This was a cold and distant world; a world of white secrets carefully guarded. He could feel a pride, a certainty, and a confidence in these streets and houses. He came to Drexel Boulevard and began to look for 4605. When he came to it, he stopped and stood before a high, black, iron picket fence, feeling constricted inside. All he had felt in the movie was gone; only fear and emptiness filled him now.

Would they expect him to come in the front way or back? It was queer that he had not thought of that. Goddamn! He walked the length of the picket fence in front of the house, seeking for a walk leading to the rear. But there was none. Other than the front gate, there was only a driveway, the entrance to which was securely locked. Suppose a policeman saw him wandering in a white neighborhood like this? It would be thought that he was trying to rob or rape somebody. He grew angry. Why had he come to take this goddamn job? He could have stayed among his own people and escaped feeling this fear and hate. This was not his world; he had been foolish in thinking that he would have liked it. He stood in the middle of the sidewalk with his jaws clamped tight; he wanted to strike something with his fist. Well...Goddamn! There was nothing to do but to go in the front way. If he were doing wrong, they could not kill him, at least; all they could do was to tell him that he could not get the job.

Timidly, he lifted the latch in the gate and walked to the steps. He paused, waiting for someone to challenge him. Nothing happened. Maybe nobody was home? He went to the door and saw a dim light burning in a shaded niche above a doorbell. He pushed it and was startled to hear a soft gong sound within. Maybe he had pushed it too hard? Aw, what the hell! He had to do better than this; he relaxed his taut muscles and stood at ease, waiting.

The doorknob turned. The door opened. He saw a white face. It was a woman.

"Hello!"

"Yessum," he said.

"You want to see somebody?"

"Er...Er...I want to see Mr. Dalton."

"Are you the Thomas boy?"

"Yessum."

"Come in."

He edged through the door slowly, then stopped halfway. The woman was so close to him that he could see a tiny mole at the corner of her mouth. He held his breath. It seem that there was no room enough for him to pass without actually touching her.

"Come on in," the woman said.

"Yessum," he whispered.

He squeezed through and stood uncertainly in a softly lighted hallway.

"Follow me," she said.

With cap in hand and shoulders sloped, he followed, walking over a rug so soft and deep that it seemed he was going to fall at each step he took. He went into a dimly lit room.

"Take a seat," she said. "I'll tell Mr. Dalton that you're here and he'll be out in a moment."

"Yessum."

He sat and looked up at the woman; she was staring at him and he looked away in confusion. He was glad when she left. That old bastard! What's so damn funny about me? I'm just like she is.... He felt that the position in which she was sitting was too awkward and found that he was on the very edge of the chair. He rose slightly to sit farther back; but when he sat he sank down so suddenly and deeply that he thought the chair had collapsed under him. He bounded halfway up, in fear; then, realizing what had happened, he sank distrustfully down again. He looked round the room; it was lit by dim lights glowing from a hidden source. He tried to find them by roving his eyes, but could not. He had not expected anything like this; he had not thought that this world would be so utterly different from his own that it would intimidate him. On the smooth walls were several paintings whose nature he tried to make out, but failed. He would have liked to examine them, but dared not. Then he listened; a faint sound of piano music floated to him from somewhere. He was sitting in a white home; dim lights burned around him; strange objects challenged him; and he was feeling angry and uncomfortable.

"All right. Come this way."

He started at the sound of a man's voice.

"Suh?"

"Come this way."

Misjudging how far back he was sitting in the chair, his first attempt to rise failed and he slipped back, resting on his side. Grabbing the arms of the chair, he pulled himself upright and found a tall, lean, white-haired man holding a piece of paper in his hand. The man was gazing at him with an amused smile that made him conscious of every square inch of skin on his black body.

"Thomas?" the man asked. "Bigger Thomas?"

"Yessuh."

He followed the man out of the room and down a hall. The man stopped abruptly. Bigger paused, bewildered; then he saw coming slowly toward him a tall, thin, white woman, walking silently, her hands lifted delicately in the air and touching the walls to either side of her. Bigger stepped back to let her pass. Her face and hair were completely white; she seemed to him like a ghost. The man took her arm gently and held her for a moment. Bigger saw that she was old and her gray eyes looked stony.

"Are you all right?" the man asked.

"Yes," she answered.

"Where's Peggy?"

"She's preparing dinner. I'm quite all right, Henry."

"You shouldn't be alone this way. When is Mrs. Patterson coming back? the man asked.

"She'll be back Monday. But Mary's here. I'm all right; don't worry about me Is somebody with you?"

"Oh, yes. This is the boy the relief sent."

"The relief people were very anxious for you to work for us," the woman said; she did not move her body or face as she talked, but she spoke in a tone of voice that indicated that she was speaking to Bigger. "I hope you'll like it here."

"Yessum," Bigger whispered faintly, wondering as he did so if he ought to say anything at all.

"How far did you go in school?"

"To the eighth grade, mam."

"Don't you think it would be a wise procedure to inject him into his new environment at once, so he could get the feel of things?" the woman asked, addressing herself by the tone of her voice to the man now.

"Well, tomorrow'll be time enough," the man said hesitantly.

"I think it's important emotionally that he feels free to trust his environment," the woman said. "Using the analysis contained in the case record the relief sent us, I think we should evoke an immediate feeling of confidence..."

"But that's too abrupt," the man said.

Bigger listened, blinking and bewildered. The long strange words they used made no sense to him; it was another language. He felt from the tone of their voices that they were having a difference of opinion about him, but he could not determine what it was about. It made him uneasy, tense, as though there were influences and presences about him which he could feel but not see. He felt strangely blind.

"Well, let's try it," the woman said.

"Oh, all right. We'll see. We'll see," the man said.

The man let go of the woman and she walked on slowly, the long white fingers of her hands just barely touching the walls. Behind the woman, following at the hem of her dress, was a big white cat, pacing about without sound. She's blind! Bigger thought in amazement.

"Come on; this way," the man said.

"Yessuh."

He wondered if the man had seen him staring at the woman. He would have to be careful here. There were so many strange things. He followed the man into a room.

"Sit down."

"Yessuh," he said, sitting.

"That was Mrs. Dalton," the man said. "She's blind."

"Yessuh."

"She has a very deep interest in colored people."

"Yessuh," Bigger whispered. He was conscious of the effort to breathe; he licked his lips and fumbled nervously with his cap.

"Well, I'm Mr. Dalton."

"Yessuh."

"Do you think you'd like driving a car?"

"Oh, yessuh."

"Did you bring the paper?"

"Suh?"

"Didn't the relief give you a note to me?"

"Oh, yessuh!"

He had completely forgotten about the paper. He stood to reach into his vest pocket and, in doing so, dropped his cap. For a moment his impulses were deadlocked; he did not know if he should pick up his cap and then find the paper, or find the paper and then pick up his cap. He decided to pick up his cap.

"Put your cap here," said Mr. Dalton, indicating a place on his desk.

"Yessuh."

Then he was stone-still; the white cat bounded past him and leaped upon the desk; it sat looking at him with large placid eyes and mewed plaintively.

"What's the matter, Kate?" Mr. Dalton asked, stroking the cat's fur and smiling. Mr. Dalton turned back to Bigger. "Did you find it?"

"Nawsuh. But I got it here, somewhere."

He hated himself at that moment. Why was he acting and feeling this way? He wanted to wave his hand and blot out the white man who was making him feel like this. If not that, he wanted to blot himself out. He had not raised his eyes to the level of Mr. Dalton's face once since he had been in the house. He stood with his knees slightly bent, his lips partly open, his shoulders stooped; and his eyes held a look that went only to the surface of things. There was an organic conviction in him that this was the way white folks wanted him to be when in their presence; none had ever told him that in so many words, but their manner had made him feel that they did. He laid the cap down, noticing that Mr. Dalton was watching him closely. Maybe he was not acting right? Goddamn! Clumsily, he searched for the paper. He could not find it at first and he felt called upon to say something for taking do long.

"I had it right here in my vest pocket," he mumbled.

"Take your time."

"Oh, here it is."

He drew the paper forth. It was crumpled and soiled. Nervously, he straightened it out and handed it to Mr. Dalton, holding it by its very tip end.

"All right, now," said Mr. Dalton. "Let's see what you've got here. You live at 3721 Indiana Avenue?"

"Yessuh."

Mr. Dalton paused, frowned, and looked up at the ceiling.

"What kind of a building is that over there?"

"You mean where I live, suh?"

"Yes."

"Oh, it's just an old building."

"Where do you pay rent?"

"Down on Thirty-first Street."

"To the South Side Real Estate Company?"

"Yessuh."

Bigger wonder what all these questions could mean; he had heard that Mr. Dalton owned the South Side Real Estate Company, but he was not sure.

"How much rent do you pay?"

"Eight dollars a week."

"For how many rooms?"

"We just got one, suh."

"I see.... Now Bigger, tell me, how old are you?"

"I'm twenty, suh."

"Married?"

"Nawsuh."

"Sit down. You needn't stand. And I won't be long."

"Yessuh."

He sat. The white cat still contemplated him with large, moist eyes.

"Now, you have a mother, a brother, and a sister?"

"Yessuh."

"There are four of you?"

"Yessuh, there's four of us," he stammered, trying to show that he was not as stupid as he might appear. He felt a need to speak more, for he felt that maybe Mr. Dalton expected it. And he suddenly remembered the many times his mother had told him not to look at the floor when taking with white folks or asking for a job. He lifted his eyes and saw Mr. Dalton watching him closely. He dropped his eyes again.

"They call you Bigger?"

"Yessuh."

"Now, Bigger, I'd like to talk with you a little..."

Yes, goddammit! He knew what was coming. He would be asked about that time he had been accused of stealing auto tires and had been sent to the reform school. He felt guilty, condemned. He should not have come here.

"The relief people said some funny things about you. I'd like to talk to you about them. Now, you needn't feel ashamed with me," said Mr. Dalton, smiling. "I was a boy myself once and I think I know how things are. So just be yourself..." Mr. Dalton pulled out a package of cigarettes. "Here; have one."

"Nawsuh; thank you, suh."

"You don't smoke?"

"Yessuh. But I just don't want one now."

"Now, Bigger, the relief people said you were a very good worker when you were interested in what you were doing. Is that true?"

"Well, I do my work, suh."

"But they said you were always in trouble. How do you explain that?"

"I don't know, suh."

"Why did they send you to the reform school?"

His eyes glared at the floor.

"They said I was stealing!" he blurted defensively. "But I wasn't."

"Are you sure?"

"Yessuh."

"Well, how did you get mixed up in it?"

"I was with some boys and the police picked us up."

Mr. Dalton said nothing. Bigger heard a clock ticking somewhere behind him and he had a foolish impulse to look at it. But he restrained himself.

"Well, Bigger, how do you feel about it now?"

"Suh? 'Bout what?"

"If you had a job, would you steal now?"

"Oh, nawsuh. I don't steal."

"Well," said Mr. Dalton, "they say you can drive a car and I'm going to give you a job."

He said nothing.

"You think you can handle it?"

"Oh, yessuh."

"The pay calls for ＄20 a week, but I'm going to give you ＄25. The extra ＄5 is for yourself, for you to spend as you like. You will get the clothes you need and your meals. You're to sleep in the back room, above the kitchen. You can give the ＄20 to your mother to keep your brother and sister in school. How does that sound?"

"It sounds all right. Yessuh."

"I think we'll get along."

"Yessuh."

"Now, Bigger," said Mr. Dalton, "since that's settled, let's see what you'll have to do every day. I leave every morning for my office at nine. It's a twenty-minute drive. You are to be back at ten and take Miss Dalton to school. At twelve, you call for Miss Dalton at the University. From then until night you are more or less free. If either Miss Dalton or I go out at night, of course, you do the driving. You work every day, but we don't get up till noon on Sundays. So you will have Sunday morning to yourself, unless something unexpected happens. You get one full day off every two weeks."

"Yessuh."

"You think you can handle that?"

"Oh, yessuh."

"And any time you're bothered about anything, come and see me. Let's talk it over."

"Yessuh."

📝 选文评析(一)：

本文节选的两部分皆出自《土生子》的第一部分《恐惧》，分别讲述了别格与朋友杰克在皇家影院的观影体验，以及别格受电影情节的影响，下定决心前往道尔顿家应征工作的经历。前半部分所描述的观影活动富有强烈的视觉规训意味：影院的黑暗场域决定了别格观看者与被观看者双重视觉身份的辩证统一。毋庸置疑，别格是将银幕画面客体化为凝视对象的观影者：杰克替他付费购得此次观影体验，因而别格享有观影权利。然而，别格并非拥有批判性眼光的主动观看者，而是白人管控的规训对象。影院上映的影视作品受到幕后白人权力中心的严格筛选与精心安排：其剧情内容和主题思想需同白人统治者的价值体系保持一致。《荡妇》和《商人角》这两部影片被排在同一场次，此举可谓别有用心。在用于广告宣传的彩色招贴画上，白人与黑人的娱乐消遣活动呈现出巨大差异：《荡妇》的"几张招贴画上画的是一些白人男男女女在海滩上憩息、游泳，在夜总会里跳舞"；而《商人角》的"招贴画上画的是黑人男男女女在蛮荒的莽林前跳舞"。白与黑两民族的休闲方式相较之下，正如其各异的肤色般反差强烈：前者现代、文明、高雅而又理性；后者则原始、野蛮、低俗且迷狂。在后续情节中，透过别格的第一人称观影视角，这种刻意放大的种族差异再次得到强调和凸显：白人拥有自由选择的特权，放松途径丰富多样：名为《荡妇》的影片中"有不少喝鸡尾酒、跳舞、打高尔夫、玩轮盘赌等场景"；而黑人娱乐活动形式单一，选择严重受限：别格"看见《商人角》上映，眼看着裸体的黑人男男女女疯狂地旋转着跳舞，耳听着鼓声咚咚"。而这些正是白人群体为固化种族差异和对立所采取的视觉规训策略。

除将两者并置所产生的反差效果外，《荡妇》和《商人角》又各有主题侧重。《荡妇》是一部浸润着阶级主义思想的电影。在其放映过程中，白人统治阶级的认知图式被投射到银幕上，呈现出经过美化润饰处理的上流社会白人生活图景，继而在观影者的视网膜上形成满载"富有白人高贵而优越"信息素的映像，不着痕迹地将白人主流社会的价值观念植入观影者的个人价值体系，于潜移默化中影响并塑造着观影者的思想意识。因此，别格是以内化的白人视角凝视银幕画面，从而参与同白人统治者的眼神共谋：当一名"疯狂的小伙子"打破夜总会的秩序以及别格的美梦，强烈的代入感使得别格竟同电影中的上流社会白人整体产生视角融叠、情感共鸣，"仿佛看到这个疯狂的不速之客后觉得他自己受到了冒犯"。别格自觉站在白人立场上审视这名闯入者，参与对社会等级秩序的维护，并与白人统治阶级进行价值认同和对接："穷白人都很傻。有钱的白人才机灵，懂得如何待人。"借助影视叙述话语的视觉规训和离间效应，白人统治者得以进一步深化同属社会底层的黑人群体与边缘白人群体之间的阶级裂隙，确保阶级联合的彻底失效。

黑暗规训场域的影视叙述话语成功说服别格，使其决心接受救济署介绍的工作，前往道尔顿家。在这个"冷漠、疏远的世界"里，别格深切体会到白人目光强效的异化作用。道尔顿先生饱含种族歧视意味的锐利目光，令别格原本的不适和窘迫愈发深重："那人正凝视着他，像是看到了什么好玩的东西似的，面带笑容，那笑容使别格意识到自己身体上每一平方英寸的黑皮肤。"这种穿透肌体、直击灵魂的种族主义凝视激发出深植别格内心的自我憎恨和自我否定的消极意识，使他在恐惧和耻辱交融的情感泥淖中彻底陷落。

白人不但占据着凝视主体的种族制高点，还殚精竭虑地企图剥夺黑人凝视的权利。本书节选的第二部分对别格在道尔顿先生面前的窘迫表现及其对白人心理的精准揣摩作了精彩描述：

> 自从他进了这个宅子以后，他一次也不曾把他的眼睛抬得跟道尔顿先生的脸一样

高。他站在那儿，稍稍弯着膝盖，微张着嘴，弯腰曲背；眼睛看东西也是浮光掠影的。他心里有数，在白人跟前，他们就喜欢你这样。倒不是有人谆谆教导过他，而是白人的态度使他感到他们喜欢你这样。

别格同道尔顿先生的目视高度差明确了两者在这次视觉交流活动中的角色分配，从中不难推导出黑白两种族之间严重失衡的视觉权力关系：白人占据"看"的主体位置，他们是主动观看者，可以有选择地看或不看。黑人则通常是被看的对象，既无看的权利，也无权决定自己如何被看。别格清楚：在白人面前卑躬屈膝、诚惶诚恐，对白人唯命是从的汤姆叔叔型传统黑人形象才符合白人凝视主体对黑人民族的视觉预期。道尔顿先生自别格对白人凝视的垂首回避及其局促不安的举止表现中获取积极的视觉反馈，足以确证眼前这个黑孩子对自己白人威权的敬畏和服从。这种规训技术得以生效的事实能使道尔顿先生体会到权力增殖所孕生的充盈感和安全感，而这正是他"仔细瞅着"别格，迫使后者"把目光垂下"的深层心理原因。

📖 作品选读（二）：

Blueprint for Negro Writing

The Role of Negro Writing: Two Definitions

Generally speaking, Negro writing in the past has been confined to humble novels, poems, and plays, prim and decorous ambassadors who went a-begging to white America. They entered the Court of American Public Opinion dressed in the kneepants of servility, curtsying to show that the Negro was not inferior, that he was human, and that he had a life comparable to that of other people. For the most part these artistic ambassadors were received as though they were French poodles who do clever tricks.

White America never offered these Negro writers any serious criticism. The mere fact that a Negro could write was astonishing. Nor was there any deep concern on the part of white America with the role Negro writing should play in American culture; and the role it did play grew out of accident rather than intent or design. Either it crept in through the kitchen in the form of jokes; or it was the fruits of that foul soil which was the result of a liaison between inferiority-complexed Negro "geniuses" and burntout white Bohemians with money.

On the other hand, these often technically brilliant performances by Negro writers were looked upon by the majority of literate Negroes as something to be proud of. At best, Negro writing has been something external to the lives of educated Negroes themselves. That the productions of their writers should have been something of a guide in their daily living is a matter which seems never to have been raised seriously.

Under these conditions Negro writing assumed two general aspects: (1) It became a sort of conspicuous ornamentation, the hallmark of "achievement." (2) It became the voice of the educated Negro pleading with white America for justice.

Rarely was the best of this writing addressed to the Negro himself, his needs, his sufferings, his aspirations. Through misdirection, Negro writers have been far better to others than they have been to themselves. And the mere recognition of this places the whole question of Negro writing in a new light and raises a doubt as to the validity of its present direction.

The Minority Outlook

Somewhere in his writings Lenin makes the observation that oppressed minorities often reflect the techniques of the bourgeoisie more brilliantly than some sections of the bourgeoisie themselves. The psychological importance of this becomes meaningful when it is recalled that oppressed minorities, and especially the petty bourgeois sections of oppressed minorities, strive to assimilate the virtues of the bourgeoisie in the assumption that by doing so they can lift themselves into a higher social sphere.

But not only among the oppressed petty bourgeoisie does this occur. The workers of a minority people, chafing under exploitation, forge organizational forms of struggle to better their lot. Lacking the handicaps of false ambition and property, they have access to a wide social vision and a deep social consciousness. They display a greater freedom and initiative in pushing their claims upon civilization than even do the petty bourgeoisie. Their organizations show greater strength, adaptability, and efficiency than any other group or class in society.

That Negro workers, propelled by the harsh conditions of their lives, have demonstrated this consciousness and mobility for economic and political action there can be no doubt. But has this consciousness been reflected in the work of Negro writers to the same degree as it has in the Negro workers' struggle to free Herndon and the Scottsboro Boys, in the drive toward unionism, in the fight against lynching? Have they as creative writers taken advantage of their unique minority position?

The answer decidedly is no. Negro writers have lagged sadly, and as time passes the gap widens between them and their people.

How can this hiatus be bridged? How can the enervating effects of this longstanding split be eliminated?

In presenting questions of this sort an attitude of self-consciousness and self-criticism is far more likely to be a fruitful point of departure than a mere recounting of past achievements. An emphasis upon tendency and experiment, a view of society as something becoming rather than as something fixed and admired is the one which points the way for Negro writers to stand shoulder to shoulder with Negro workers in mood and outlook.

A Whole Culture

There is, however, a culture of the Negro which is his and has been addressed to him; a culture which has, for good or ill, helped to clarify his consciousness and create emotional attitudes which are conducive to action. This culture has stemmed mainly from two sources: (1) the Negro church; and (2) the folklore of the Negro people. It was through the portals of the church that the American Negro first entered the shrine of western culture. Living under slave conditions of life, bereft of his African heritage, the Negroes' struggle for religion on the plantations between 1820 — 60 assumed the form of a struggle for human rights. It remained a relatively revolutionary struggle until religion began to serve as an antidote for suffering and denial. But even today there are millions of American Negroes whose only sense of a whole universe, whose only relation to society and man, and whose only guide to personal dignity comes through the archaic morphology of Christian salvation.

It was, however, in a folklore molded out of rigorous and inhuman conditions of life that the Negro achieved his most indigenous and complete expression. Blues, spirituals, and folk tales recounted from mouth to mouth; the whispered words of a black mother to her black daughter on the ways of men, to confidential wisdom of a black father to his black son; the swapping of sex experiences on street corners from boy to boy in the deepest vernacular; work songs sung under blazing suns — all these formed the channels through which the racial wisdom flowed.

One would have thought that Negro writers in the last century of striving at expression would have continued and deepened this folk tradition, would have tried to create a more intimate and yet a more profoundly social system of artistic communication between them and their people. But the illusion that they could escape through individual achievement the harsh lot of their race swung Negro writers away from any such path. Two separate cultures sprang up: one for the Negro masses, unwritten and unrecognized; and the other for the sons and daughters of a rising Negro bourgeoisie, parasitic and mannered.

Today the question is: Shall Negro writing be for the Negro masses, molding the lives and consciousness of those masses toward new goals, or shall it continue begging the question of the Negroes' humanity? The Problem of Nationalism in Negro Writing in stressing the difference between the role Negro writing failed to play in the lives of the Negro people, and the role it should play in the future if it is to serve its historic function; in pointing out the fact that Negro writing has been addressed in the main to a small white audience rather than to a Negro one, it should be stated that no attempt is being made here to propagate a specious and blatant nationalism. Yet the nationalist character of the Negro people is unmistakable. Psychologically this nationalism is reflected in the whole of Negro culture, and especially in folklore.

In the absence of fixed and nourishing forms of culture, the Negro has a folklore which embodies the memories and hopes of his struggle for freedom. Not yet caught in paint or stone, and as yet but feebly depicted in the poem and novel, the Negroes' most powerful images of hope and despair still remain in the fluid state of daily speech. How many John Henrys have lived and died on the lips of these black people?

How many mythical heroes in embryo have been allowed to perish for lack of husbanding by alert intelligence?

Negro folklore contains, in a measure that puts to shame more deliberate forms of Negro expression, the collective sense of Negro life in America. Let those who shy at the nationalist implications of Negro life look at this body of folklore, living and powerful, which rose out of a unified sense of a common life and a common fate.

Here are those vital beginnings of a recognition of value in life as it is lived, a recognition that marks the emergence of a new culture in the shell of the old. And at the moment this process starts, at the moment when a people begin to realize a meaning in their suffering, the civilization that engenders that suffering is doomed.

The nationalist aspects of Negro life are as sharply manifest in the social institutions of Negro people as in folklore. There is a Negro church, a Negro press, a Negro social world, a Negro sporting world, a Negro business world, a Negro school system, Negro professions; in short, a Negro way of life in America. The Negro people did not ask for this, and deep down, though they express themselves through their institutions and adhere to this special way of life, they do not want it now. This special existence was forced upon them from without by lynch rope, bayonet and mob rule. They accepted these negative conditions with the inevitability of a tree which must live or perish in whatever soil it finds itself.

The few crumbs of American civilization which the Negro has got from the tables of capitalism have been through these segregated channels. Many Negro institutions are cowardly and incompetent; but they are all that the Negro has. And, in the main, any move, whether for progress or reaction, must come through these institutions for the simple reason that all other channels are closed. Negro writers who seek to mold or influence the consciousness of the Negro people must address their messages to them through the ideologies and attitudes fostered in this warping way of life.

The Basis and Meaning of Nationalism in Negro Writing

The social institutions of the Negro are imprisoned in the Jim Crow political system of the South, and this Jim Crow political system is in turn built upon a plantation-feudal economy. Hence, it can be seen that the emotional expression of group-feeling which puzzles so many whites and leads them to deplore what they call "black chauvinism" is not a morbidly inherent trait of the Negro, but rather the reflex expression of a life whose roots are imbedded deeply in Southern soil.

Negro writers must accept the nationalist implications of their lives, not in order to encourage them, but in order to change and transcend them. They must accept the concept of nationalism because, in order to transcend it, they must possess and understand it. And a nationalist spirit in Negro writing means a nationalism carrying the highest possible pitch of social consciousness. It means a nationalism that knows its origins, its limitations; that is aware of the dangers of its position; that knows its ultimate aims are unrealizable within the framework of capitalist America; a nationalism whose reason for being lies in the simple fact of self-possession and in the consciousness of the interdependence of people in modern society.

For purposes of creative expression, it means that the Negro writer must realize within the area of his own personal experience those impulses which, when prefigured in terms of broad social movements, constitute the stuff of nationalism.

For Negro writers even more so than for Negro politicians, nationalism is a bewildering and vexing question, the full ramifications of which cannot be dealt with here. But among Negro workers and the Negro middle class the spirit of nationalism is rife in a hundred devious forms; and a simple literary realism which seeks to depict the lives of these people devoid of wider social connotations, devoid of the revolutionary significance of these nationalist tendencies, must of necessity do a rank injustice to the Negro people and alienate their possible allies in the struggle for freedom.

Social Consciousness and Responsibility

The Negro writer who seeks to function within his race as a purposeful agent has a serious responsibility. In order to do justice to his subject matter, in order to depict Negro life in all of its manifold and intricate relationships, a deep, informed, and complex consciousness is necessary; a consciousness which draws for its strength upon the fluid lore of a great people, and molds this lore with the concepts that move and direct the forces of history today.

With the gradual decline of the moral authority of the Negro church, and with the increasing irresolution which is paralyzing Negro middle-class leadership, a new role is devolving upon the Negro writer. He is being called upon to do no less than create values by which his race is to struggle, live and die.

By his ability to fuse and make articulate the experiences of men, because his writing possesses the potential cunning to steal into the inmost recesses of the human heart, because he can create the myths and symbols that inspire a faith in life, he may expect either to be consigned to oblivion, or to be recognized for the valued agent he is. This raises the question of the personality of the writer. It means that in the lives of Negro writers must be found those materials and experiences which will create a meaningful picture of the world today. Many young writers have grown to believe that a Marxist analysis of society presents such a picture. It creates a picture which, when placed before the eyes of the writer, should unify his personality, organize his emotions, buttress him with a tense and obdurate will to change the world.

And, in turn, this changed world will dialectically change the writer. Hence, it is through a Marxist conception of reality and society that the maximum degree of freedom in thought and feeling can be gained for the Negro writer. Further, this dramatic Marxist vision, when consciously grasped, endows the writer with a sense of dignity which no other vision can give. Ultimately, it restores to the writer his lost heritage, that is, his role as a creator of the world in which he lives, and as a creator of himself.

Yet, for the Negro writer, Marxism is but the starting point. No theory of life can take the place of life. After Marxism has laid bare the skeleton of society, there remains the task of the writer to plant flesh upon those bones out of his will to live. He may, with disgust and revulsion, say no and depict the horrors of capitalism encroaching upon the human being. Or he may, with hope and passion, say yes and depict the faint stirrings of a new and emerging life. But in whatever social voice he chooses to speak, whether positive or negative, there should always be heard or overheard his faith, his necessity, his judgement.

His vision need not be simple or rendered in primer-like terms; for the life of the Negro people is not simple. The presentation of their lives should be simple, yes; but all the complexity, the strangeness, the magic wonder of life that plays like a bright sheen over the most sordid existence, should be there. To borrow a phrase from the Russians, it should have a complex simplicity. Eliot, Stein, Joyce, Proust, Hemingway, and Anderson; Gorky, Barbusse, Nexo, and Jack London no less than the folklore of the Negro himself should form the heritage of the Negro writer. Every iota of gain in human thought and sensibility should be ready grist for his mill, no matter how farfetched they may seem in their immediate implications.

The Problem of Perspective

What vision must Negro writers have before their eyes in order to feel the impelling necessity for an about-face? What angle of vision can show them all the forces of modern society in process, all the lines of economic development converging toward a distant point of hope? Must they believe in some "ism"? They may feel that only dupes believe in "isms"; they feel with some measure of justification that another commitment means only another disillusionment. But anyone destitute of a theory about the meaning, structure and direction of modern society is a lost victim in a world he cannot understand or control.

But even if Negro writers found themselves through some "ism," how would that influence their writing? Are they being called upon to "preach"? To be "salesmen"? To "prostitute" their writing? Must they "sully" themselves? Must they write "propaganda"?

No; it is a question of awareness, of consciousness; it is, above all, a question of perspective. Perspective is that part of a poem, novel, or play which a writer never puts directly upon paper. It is that fixed point in intellectual space where a writer stands to view the struggles, hopes, and sufferings of his people. There are times when he may stand too close and the result is a blurred vision. Or he may stand too far away and the result is a neglect of important things.

Of all the problems faced by writers who as a whole have never allied themselves with world movements, perspective is the most difficult of achievements. At its best, perspective is a preconscious assumption, something which a writer takes for granted, something which he wins through his living.

A Spanish writer recently spoke of living in the heights of one's time. Surely, perspective means just that. It means that a Negro writer must learn to view the life of a Negro living in New York's Harlem or Chicago's South Side with the consciousness that one-sixth of the earth surface belongs to the working class. It means that a Negro writer must create in his readers' minds a relationship between a Negro woman hoeing cotton in the South and the men who loll in swivel chairs in Wall Street and take the fruits of her toil.

Perspective for Negro writers will come when they have looked and brooded so hard and long upon the harsh lot of their race and compared it with the hopes and struggles of minority peoples everywhere that the cold facts have begun to tell them something.

The Problem of Theme

This does not mean that a Negro writer's sole concern must be with rendering the social scene; but if his conception of the life of his people is broad and deep enough, if the sense of the whole life he is seeking is vivid and strong in him, then his writing will embrace all those social, political, and economic forms under which the life of his people is manifest.

In speaking of theme one must necessarily be general and abstract; the temperament of each writer molds and colors the world he sees. Negro life may be approached from a thousand angles, with no limit to technical and stylistic freedom.

Negro writers spring from a family, a clan, a class, and a nation; and the social units in which they are bound have a story, a record. Sense of theme will emerge in Negro writing when Negro writers try to fix this story about some pole of meaning, remembering as they do so that in the creative process meaning proceeds equally as much from the contemplation of the subject matter as from the hopes and apprehensions that rage in the heart of the writer.

Reduced to its simplest and most general terms, theme for Negro writers will rise from understanding the meaning of their being transplanted from a "savage" to a "civilized" culture in all of its social, political, economic, and emotional implications. It means that Negro writers must have in their consciousness the foreshortened picture of the whole, nourishing culture from which they were torn in Africa, and of the long, complex (and for the most part, unconscious) struggle to regain in some form and under alien conditions of life a whole culture again.

It is not only this picture they must have, but also a knowledge of the social and emotional milieu that gives it tone and solidity of detail. Theme for Negro writers will emerge when they have

245

begun to feel the meaning of the history of their race as though they in one lifetime had lived it themselves throughout all the long centuries.

Autonomy of Craft

For the Negro writer to depict this new reality requires a greater discipline and consciousness than was necessary for the so-called Harlem school of expression. Not only is the subject matter dealt with far more meaningful and complex, but the new role of the writer is qualitatively different. The Negro writers' new position demands a sharper definition of the status of his craft, and a sharper emphasis upon its functional autonomy.

Negro writers should seek through the medium of their craft to play as meaningful a role in the affairs of men as do other professionals. But if their writing is demanded to perform the social office of other professions, then the autonomy of craft is lost and writing detrimentally fused with other interests. The limitations of the craft constitute some of its greatest virtues. If the sensory vehicle of imaginative writing is required to carry too great a load of didactic material, the artistic sense is submerged.

The relationship between reality and the artistic image is not always direct and simple. The imaginative conception of a historical period will not be a carbon copy of reality. Image and emotion possess a logic of their own. A vulgarized simplicity constitutes the greatest danger in tracing the reciprocal interplay between the writer and his environment.

Writing has its professional autonomy; it should complement other professions, but it should not supplant them or be swamped by them.

The Necessity for Collective Work

It goes without saying that these things cannot be gained by Negro writers if their present mode of isolated writing and living continues. This isolation exists among Negro writers as well as between Negro and white writers. The Negro writers' lack of thorough integration with the American scene, their lack of a clear realization among themselves of their possible role, have bred generation after generation of embittered and defeated literati.

Barred for decades from the theater and publishing houses, Negro writers have been made to feel a sense of difference. So deep has this white-hot iron of exclusion been burnt into their hearts that thousands have all but lost the desire to become identified with American civilization. The Negro writers' acceptance of this enforced isolation and their attempt to justify it is but a defense-reflex of the whole special way of life which has been rammed down their throats.

This problem, by its very nature, is one which must be approached contemporaneously from two points of view. The ideological unity of Negro writers and the alliance of that unity with all the progressive ideas of our day is the primary prerequisite for collective work. On the shoulders of white writers and Negro writers alike rests the responsibility of ending this mistrust and isolation.

By placing cultural health above narrow sectional prejudices, liberal writers of all races can help to break the stony soil of aggrandizement out of which the stunted plants of Negro nationalism grow. And, simultaneously, Negro writers can help to weed out these choking growths of reactionary nationalism and replace them with hardier and sturdier types.

These tasks are imperative in light of the fact that we live in a time when the majority of the most basic assumptions of life can no longer be taken for granted. Tradition is no longer a guide. The world has grown huge and cold. Surely this is the moment to ask questions, to theorize, to speculate, to wonder out of what materials can a human world be built.

Each step along this unknown path should be taken with thought, care, self-consciousness, and deliberation. When Negro writers think they have arrived at Something which smacks of truth, humanity, they should want to test it with others, feel it with a degree of passion and strength that will enable them to communicate it to millions who are groping like themselves.

Writers faced with such tasks can have no possible time for malice or jealousy. The conditions for the growth of each writer depend too much upon the good work of other writers. Every first-rate novel, poem, or play lifts the level of consciousness higher. 1937.

选文评析(二):

赖特赋予黑人作家以极大的民族责任感,他在《黑人写作蓝图》中表达的主要信息之一就是,黑人作家要意识到自己所代表的黑人民族的苦难并从中找到意义,因为只有在找到痛苦的意义之后,一个人才能从痛苦中走出,并有一个清晰的视野和新的目标。在赖特看来,过去的黑人作家——尤其以哈莱姆文艺复兴时期的作家群体为代表——就像"到美国白人面前乞讨的彬彬有礼的文化大使,穿着服务生的短裤",可怜巴巴地渴求白人的认同和赏识。他还讥讽他们"受到的接待就好像他们是会耍聪明把戏的法国贵宾犬一样",但白人从未把这些黑人作家真正放在眼里,他们对黑人写作在美国文化中应扮演的角色也没有任何深切的关心。

显而易见,赖特对此前黑人文学的成就评价非常低,认为"它要么是以笑话的形式从厨房里溜进来,要么是从那肮脏的土壤里结出的果实,这是有自卑情结的黑人'天才'和有钱的白种波希米亚人之间媾和的产物"。赖特把此前的黑人写作特点归结为两点:第一,它是一种引人注目的"成就"的标志。第二,它是受过教育的黑人向美国白人恳求正义的声音。虽然这些黑人作家在艺术上的表现被大多数有文化的黑人视为值得骄傲的东西,但在赖特看来却不值得表扬,他们的作品只是为了讨好白人而作,并不是真实黑人生活经验的反映,"即便是最优秀的黑人文学也极少面向黑人本人、他的需要、他的痛苦和他的愿望"。它们表达的完全是黑人生活之外的东西,因此也不能成为黑人日常生活的向导。赖特批判黑人文学误入歧途,因此需要"怀疑其目前方向的正确性"。他写这篇文章的目的也正是为黑人文学的未来发展绘制蓝图。

赖特于1934年正式加入美国共产党。在此后大约十年间,他的文学创作观也开始越来越多地受到马克思主义思想的影响，这在本文中也有很多表现。他认为，马克思主义可以让黑人作家拥有一种新的工具和世界观，可以发展出一种复杂的社会意识。一个马克思主义的世界观能够给他最完整的社会图景和创造性地表达自己的最佳方式，也能够给他创作的信心以及对社会未来的希望。他从列宁思想中得到启发，认为被压迫的黑人群体中的工人阶级要比黑人小资产阶级更能反映黑人生活中的问题。"他们为了改善命运，形成了有组织的斗争。他们不受虚假目标误导，也不为财产所束缚，有着广阔的社会视野和深刻的社会意识。他们比小资产阶级表现出更大的自由和主动性，表达出自己的主张。他们的组织比社会上任何其他群体或阶级都显示出更大的力量、适应性和效率。"但这种意识却从未反映在黑人文学作品中，黑人作家一味讨好趋近白人，却和他们的人民之间的差距越来越大。赖特认为，为了弥合这个间隙，消除这种长期分裂的消极影响，黑人作家就必须改变原来的创作立场，在情感和世界观上都应该与黑人工人并肩站在一起。从现在开始，黑人写作应该为黑人大众服务，"塑造他们的生活和意识走向新目标"，而不是继续探讨所谓黑人的人性问题。

赖特非常看重黑人民间文化传统，它深深扎根于黑人民族的苦难历史，是对黑人生活经验的最真切表达。但遗憾的是，这种民间传统很少得到严肃对待，从未被黑人作家认真书写出来，只是通过黑人底层民众的口耳相传得以传承。"蓝调、灵歌和民间故事都是口耳相传的；黑人母亲对黑人女儿低声说的关于男人的话；黑人父亲对黑人儿子的秘密智慧；用最深奥的方言在街角从男孩到男孩交换的性经验；在烈日下演唱的劳动歌曲——所有这些构成了种族智慧流动的渠道。"他认为黑人作家偏离了民间文学的创造性表达方式，转而采用一种更有礼貌、更"白人"的写作方式。这就产生了两种不同的文化，一种是以尚未被书写出来的黑人民间传说为基础的劳动阶级的文化，它虽然朴素，却真切生动、丰富多彩。另一种是基于黑人小资产阶级的写作，它虽然优雅，却是虚假做作的。赖特呼吁，真正的黑人写作必须继续并深化这种民间传统，以便在黑人作家和他们的人民之间创造一个更亲密、更深刻的艺术交流体系，而不是幻想可以通过个人成就来逃避种族的残酷命运。

赖特在本文中最关心的核心问题是黑人文化民族主义及其与黑人民间文化的关系。他认为黑人文化具有明显的民族主义特征，它在黑人的社会文化和民间传说中一样明显，"它就是美国黑人的生活方式"。白人所说的"黑人沙文主义"并不是黑人社会病态的固有特征，而是一种生活的反映，这种生活的根源深深地植根于南方土壤中。这种特殊的民族主义文化是由美国蓄奴制历史从外面强加给他们的。黑人民间传说则体现了他们争取自由的记忆和希望，在某种程度上也包含了黑人生活的集体意识。随着黑人教会道德权威的逐渐衰落，以及黑人资产阶级在白人社会面前的暧昧不决，黑人作家就要承担起领导民众的责任，他们被要求去创造积极的价值观，引领黑人种族去奋斗、生存和死亡。但要想塑造或影响黑人民众的意识，黑人作家就绝不能背离黑人民族主义传统，必须在黑人的生活中找到合适的素材和经历，用以创出一幅对当今世界有意义的画面。赖特认为，黑人民族主义最重要的方面在于其文化表现形式，而非其政治含义。这种民族主义最有力地反映在南部黑人身上，或是在芝加哥和哈莱姆（纽约）等北部城市中心的南部移民中发现的移植文化残余中。这并非要求黑人作家成为黑人民族主义的传声筒和代言人，而是要求他们真正处理好与民族主义的关系。他说："黑人作家必须接受他们生活中的民族主义的影响，但不是为了支持它们，而是为了改变和超越它们。他们必须接受民族主义的概念，因为为了超越它，他们必须拥有并理解它。"

赖特认为，由于各种原因，"黑人作家一直缺乏与美国社会场景的彻底融合"。为了真正理解并在作品中反映黑人生活，黑人作家应当学会从马克思主义角度出发来理解社会现实，这样才能获得"一种深刻的、有见识的、复杂的意识"，从而能够公正地对待他的创作主题，正确地描述黑人生活中各种各样的复杂关系，进而在不断变化的"现代"资本主义时代，为国际社会和政治变革作出独特贡献。"只有通过马克思主义的社会现实观，黑人作家才能在思想和感情上获得最大程度的自由。……它可以赋予作家一种其他任何视觉都无法给予的尊严感。"很多人担心借用马克思主义会让作家失去创作自由，沦为意识形态的"推销员"，文学创作成为政治宣传。赖特并不这么看，他辩护说："他们可能觉得只有傻瓜才相信'主义'，但是，任何一个对现代社会的意义、结构和方向缺乏理论的人，都是这个他无法理解或控制的世界中迷失的牺牲品。"马克思主义非但不会阻挡黑人作家的创作视野，反倒能够让他们更清楚地认清黑人社会现实，因为"一个黑人作家必须学会以意识到地球表面六分之一属于工人阶级的意识来看待生活在纽约哈莱姆区或芝加哥南区的黑人的生活。这意味着，一个黑人作家必须在读者心目中创造一种关系：一个在南方锄棉花的黑人妇女，一个在华尔街懒洋洋地坐在转椅上吃她辛劳果实的男人之间的关系"。然而，赖特也指出，对于黑人作家来说，马克思主义只是一个起点。"任何关于生活的理论都不能取代生活本身。在马克思主义揭示了社会的骨架之后，作家的任务仍然是把自己的生存意志植根于这些骨架之上。"

推荐阅读文献：

Craven, A. and Dow, William. *Richard Wright: New Readings in the 21st Century*. Palgrave Macmillan, 2011.

Dow, William E. and Craven, Alice Mikal. *Richard Wright in a Post-Racial Imaginary*. Bloomsbury Academic & Professional, 2016.

Ellison, Ralph. Richard Wright's Blues. *The Antioch Review*, 1999, 57(3): 263-276.

Gordon, Jane Anna and Curry, Tommy J. *The Politics of Richard Wright: Perspectives on Resistance*. UP of Kentucky, 2019.

Kiuchi, Toru and Hakutani, Yoshinobu. *Richard Wright: A Documented Chronology, 1908-1960*. McFarland & Company, 2013.

Lambert, Matthew. 'That sonofabitch could cut your throat': Bigger and the Black Rat in Richard Wright's 'Native Son'. *The Journal of the Midwest Modern Language Association*, 2016, 49(1): 75-92.

Moskowitz, Milton. The Enduring Importance of Richard Wright. *The Journal of Blacks in Higher Education*, 2008(59): 58-62.

Ryan, Melissa. Dangerous Refuge: Richard Wright and the Swimming Hole. *African*

American Review, 2017, 50(1): 27-40.

Smith, Virginia Whatley. *Richard Wright Writing America at Home and from Abroad*. UP of Mississippi, 2016.

Tuhkanen, Mikko. *The American Optic: Psychoanalysis, Critical Race Theory, and Richard Wright*. State University of New York Press, 2009.

Ward, Jerry W., Jr. and Butler, Robert J. *The Richard Wright Encyclopedia*. ABC-CLIO, 2008.

Wells, Ira. 'What I Killed for, I Am': Domestic Terror in Richard Wright's America. *American Quarterly*, 2010, 62(4): 873-895.

主要参考文献

Andrews, William and Foster, Frances Smith, eds. *The Oxford Companion to African American Literature*. Oxford UP, 1997.

Crawford, Margo N. *What Is African American Literature?* John Wiley & Sons, 2021. Currie, Stephen. *African American Literature*. Greenhaven Publishing, 2011.

Dawson, Alma and Fleet, Connie Van. *African American Literature: A Guide to Reading Interests*. Libraries Unlimited, 2004.

Graham, Maryemma and Pineault-Burke, Sharon. *Teaching African American Literature: Theory and Practice*. Taylor & Francis Group, 1998.

Graham, Maryemma and Ward, Jerry. *The Cambridge History of African American Literature*, Cambridge UP, 2011.

Jarrett, Gene Andrew. *African American Literature Beyond Race: An Alternative Reader*. New York UP, 2006.

Jarrett, Gene Andrew. *The Wiley Blackwell Anthology of African American Literature*. Volume 1: 1746—1920. John Wiley & Sons, 2014.

Miller, D. Quentin. *The Routledge Introduction to African American Literature*. Routledge, 2016.

Miller, Frederic and etc., eds. *African American Literature*. Alphascript Publishing, 2009.

Ostrom, Hans A. and Macey, John David, Jr. *African American Literature: an Encyclopedia for Students*. ABC-CLIO, 2019.

Warren, Kenneth W. *What Was African American Literature?* Harvard UP, 2011.